Praise for The Fatal Series by Marie Force

"This book starts out strong and keeps getting better.
Marie Force is one of those authors that
will be on my must-read list in the future."
—Dee Dailey, reviewer, *The Romance Studio* on *Fatal Affair*

"This is a suspense that never stops.
Add it to your book list today."
—*NightOwlRomance.com* (Top pick)

"Marie Force's second novel in the Fatal series is an
outstanding romantic suspense in its own right; that it
follows the fantastic first installment only sweetens the read."
—*RT Book Reviews* (4.5 stars) on *Fatal Justice*

"The author makes the reader part of the action,
effortlessly weaving the world of politics and murder
in which the characters come alive on the pages.
The plot was addictive and scandalous with so many family
secrets.... Drama, passion, suspense—*Fatal Affair* has it all!"
—*Book Junkie*

"Force's skill is also evident in the way that she develops
the characters, from the murdered and mutilated senator
to the detective and chief of staff who are trying to
solve the case. The heroine, Sam, is especially complex
and her secrets add depth to this mystery."
—*RT Book Reviews* (4.5 stars) on *Fatal Affair*

MARIE FORCE

is the bestselling, award-winning author of *Fatal Affair* and *Fatal Justice,* books one and two in her Fatal Series from Harlequin's Carina Press. "This novel is *The O.C.* does D.C., and you just can't get enough" (*RT Book Reviews,* 4.5 stars for *Fatal Affair*). In its July 2010 issue, *RT Book Reviews* named Marie a "Future Star of Romantic Suspense." Book four, *Fatal Flaw,* is coming soon.

Marie is also the author of *Everyone Loves a Hero, Line of Scrimmage, Love at First Flight, True North, The Fall* and *The Wreck.*

Since 1996, Marie has been the communications director for a national organization similar to the RWA. She is a member of RWA's New England, From the Heart and Published Authors' Special Interest Chapters.

While her husband was in the navy, Marie lived in Spain, Maryland and Florida, and she is now settled in her home state of Rhode Island. She is the mother of two human kids and a feisty dog named Brandy.

MARIE FORCE

FATAL
CONSEQUENCES

CARINA
PRESS™

For my daughter, Emily: Happy Sweet Sixteen.
You had me at hello.

CARINA PRESS™

ISBN-13: 978-0-373-06270-6

FATAL CONSEQUENCES

Copyright © 2011 by Marie Force

Recycling programs
for this product may
not exist in your area.

This edition published by arrangement with Harlequin Books S.A.

® and TM are trademarks of the publisher. Trademarks indicated with ® are registered in the United States Patent and Trademark Office, the Canadian Trade Marks Office and in other countries.

www.CarinaPress.com

Printed in U.S.A.

FATAL
CONSEQUENCES

Acknowledgments

First and foremost to my family: Dan, Emily and Jake, who accommodate my writing and ignore my manic mumblings, and my dad, who follows all the ups and downs. My mates in the Lair: Kendra, Cindy, Cheryl and Linda, you keep me sane and laughing—thank you! Thanks to all my buddies on Facebook who cheered me on as I wrote this book— the first one I've written to deadline—your support and encouragement made a big difference.

To Mitchell Waldman, thank you for the help with child custody legalities. Christopher Burnette astutely answered questions on forensics and lab test timing. Newport, RI Police Lt. Russell Hayes is my go-to guy for all things police-related, and he's always there with an answer that gives me ideas for new directions. Thank you, Russ! I spent a memorable evening scouting wedding locations in Washington with my friends Christina Camara and Julie Cupp, as well as my cousin, Steven Lopes. Thanks guys, it was fun playing pretend, and I'm delighted with what we decided on for Sam and Nick.

I'm thrilled—and lucky—to have three beta readers who love Sam and Nick as much as I do: Alyson Hackett, Ronlyn Howe and Kara Conrad. You ladies are the best and I can't thank you enough for the astute comments and insight. My editor, Jessica Schulte, has been the guiding hand behind this series, and I appreciate all the TLC she has shown to Sam, Nick and me. To everyone at Carina Press and Harlequin, your support of the Fatal Series means the world to me. I can't thank you all enough.

ONE

"I'LL BET there was less red at the St. Valentine's Day Massacre," Lt. Sam Holland said as she stood in the doorway to the Fraternal Order of Police Hall and surveyed the scene before her.

"Wow." Senator Nick Cappuano took a long look around the big room. "*Wow.*"

Sam's sister Tracy joined them. "Oh. My. God. Celia and her friends went freaking *nuts* with the hearts and flowers."

Every square inch of the large room was decorated with red flowers, balloons and streamers.

"I've seen murders that were less bloody than this reception," Sam said.

"It is her first wedding," Nick reminded them. "She has the right to go all out."

Sam wondered if he'd expect his first wedding to be as elaborate. She'd been there, done that and had no desire to do it again. But for him… Well, for him she'd do just about anything. However, she was drawing the line at hearts and flowers. She had a reputation to uphold.

"Holy shit," Sam's sister Angela said when she joined them. "Check out the ice sculpture. Jesus."

"Cupid, not Jesus," Nick said, smiling at the horror

on the sisters' faces. "Be nice, you guys. Celia is so excited."

"I had no idea she had this in her." Sam battled her way through the streamers and balloon ribbons to get to the bar. She needed a drink, and she needed it now.

"You'd be well advised to keep her far, *far* away from your wedding," Tracy said.

"No kidding." Sam downed a glass of pinot grigio and gestured for another. "How much of this do you suppose Dad knew about?"

"None of it," Angela said, smirking.

"He's a smart man," Nick said, "so I'm sure he told her to do whatever she wanted."

"Is that what a smart man does?" Sam asked, raising an eyebrow.

"Not *this* smart man. If I did that, we'd end up with beer and peanuts at O'Leary's."

"And that would be bad how exactly?"

Nick bent to kiss her. "We can do better."

Before Sam could tell him she didn't want to do better than O'Leary's, they were interrupted by the arrival of the bride and groom. Sam couldn't deny that her father and his new wife radiated happiness. How could Sam begrudge the woman who had married her paralyzed father the reception of her dreams? Her own wedding, Sam vowed silently, would be as low-key as she could possibly make it. In fact, eloping was starting to look *really* good to her.

DRESSED IN RED satin bridesmaid gowns, Celia's new stepdaughters stood faithfully by her side while she cut the heart-shaped red velvet cake and fed a piece to her groom. They endured the speeches and the toasts and smiled for no fewer than a thousand photographs. The ultimate insult, however, still awaited them.

"She can't make us," Tracy said when the DJ asked the sisters, their husbands and fiancé to come to the dance floor.

"Dad can make us," Angela said. "He still has that *look*. You know the one I mean."

"I've never wanted to be called to a murder scene more than I do right now," Sam said through gritted teeth.

"Ladies," Nick said with that charming smile he'd been using all day to manage them, "it's one dance, and then you're done."

"I know I speak for my sisters when I tell you to shut up and stop defending Valentine's Day Bridezilla," Sam said.

Nick laughed at the dismay on their faces as the first notes of Bette Midler's "The Rose" filled the room.

"I'm going to puke in my shoes," Angela muttered. Three-and-a-half months pregnant with her second child, she'd been green for weeks.

"Those are *my* Jimmy Choos," Sam reminded her, "and if you puke on them, I'll kill you."

Angela scowled at her. "Would you rather I puked on those?" She nodded to the Manolos that Nick had bought Sam to wear the night they got engaged.

Sam glanced down at the precious shoes. "Don't even think about it."

"Mine are from Payless," Tracy said. "Puke away."

Nick took Sam's hand as Angela's husband Spencer and Tracy's husband Mike did the same with their reluctant wives. The guys made for a dashing trio in the tuxedos they'd worn as Skip's groomsmen.

Across the room, Sam's partner, Detective Freddie Cruz, Detective Tommy "Gonzo" Gonzales and some of her other detectives were sharing a laugh that was— no doubt—at her expense. She'd think of some way to punish them on their next shift. It didn't escape her notice that Freddie had brought his girlfriend Elin Svendsen or that Gonzo was there with Nick's chief of staff Christina Billings. Sam didn't approve of either relationship, but no one had bothered to ask her opinion.

When she realized Nick wasn't going to let her escape the mandatory dance, Sam gave up the fight. Besides, being pressed against his muscular chest was one of her favorite places to be, so she may as well enjoy this obligatory moment.

At six foot four, he was one of the few people in her life who towered over her. Those broad shoulders, the chocolate brown hair that curled at the ends, amazing hazel eyes, smooth olive-toned skin…Sam had never known a sexier guy. And that mouth, *whoa*. Speaking of sexy…

"There," Nick said, apparently sensing her capitulation. "Isn't that better?"

"I'm still mad at you."

"You can punish me later." Bringing his lips in close to her ear, he added, "All night long."

Sam smiled at his softly spoken words. She didn't

want to because he was making her dance to the cheesiest, most clichéd song her stepmother could've possibly chosen. But let's face it, she was slow dancing with Nick, and that definitely went a long way toward making things all better.

Nick's lovely chest ruined the moment by vibrating against her cheek.

"Ignore it," he said of the BlackBerry he'd stashed in his chest pocket. "No phones today."

"You won't hear me arguing." They still hadn't managed a full day off together in the nearly two months since they'd reconnected after U.S. Senator John O'Connor's murder just before Christmas. Six years after a memorable one-night stand, they'd picked up right where they'd left off. Nick had since been tapped to complete the last year of John's term in the Senate and was now in the midst of the campaign to win the seat on his own in November. They'd looked forward to this day off for weeks and had big plans for a romantic early Valentine's Day celebration after the wedding.

Nick's phone buzzed again. "Ignore," he said more forcefully this time.

"What if it's your dad or there's some sort of disaster in Virginia? You can't just ignore it."

"Yes, I can." With all the campaigning he'd been doing lately, she knew he needed the day off even more than she did but if there was one thing Sam couldn't stand, it was a ringing phone.

"*Nick.*"

"*Sam.*"

She worked her hand into his jacket to retrieve the buzzing phone. "Henry Lightfeather," she read off the screen. Even she recognized the name of the senior senator from Arizona.

"Work." Nick tightened his arms around her. "He can wait until Monday."

"He's called twice."

"He can *wait*."

"There's a voice mail message. Aren't you curious?"

"Okay, it's official—you're an even bigger workaholic than I am."

"Not possible. Hey, he sent a text—'Call me, Nick. 911.'"

Nick stopped dancing and took the phone from her. "Now you've gone and done it," he said with a scowl.

"Done what?"

"If you had ignored it, I never would've seen that text. Now I have no choice but to call him."

She grinned at him. "At least we can escape this nightmare dance before the seed becomes a rose."

Phone pressed to his ear, Nick stalked off the dance floor. Halfway across the room, he stopped, turned and signaled to Sam.

Curious, she walked over to join him.

"He's actually looking for you, Lieutenant." Nick handed the phone to Sam and went to have a word with Skip and Celia.

"Senator," Sam said. "This is Sam Holland. What can I do for you?"

"I need you to come here," Lightfeather said. He

sounded rattled and undone. "Right now. I think she might be dead. I need you. Just you. No other cops."

"Who's dead?"

"Regina." His voice broke. "Beautiful Regina."

"How can you tell she's dead?"

"There's so much blood, and she's cold."

"Where are you, Senator?"

He rattled off an address in Columbia Heights, a culturally diverse neighborhood located in the city's northwestern corner.

"I'm on my way. Don't touch her. Don't touch anything. Do you understand?"

"Yes," he said, his voice breaking. "Hurry."

AFTER A QUICK trip to Nick's house so Sam could exchange the red satin bridesmaid monstrosity for jeans, Nick drove her from Capitol Hill to Columbia Heights. As he dodged the black BMW through traffic, Sam wondered when he'd started driving like a cop and how she'd failed to notice.

"What do you know about him?" she asked.

"He's a friend—one of the first to welcome me to the Senate, the first to tell me what I really needed to know, the first to offer his help."

"And?"

"And what?"

"What else do you know that you're not sure you should tell me in light of current events?"

"There are times when it's terribly annoying that you know me so well."

"Likewise. Now start talking."

He glanced over at her. "I think he might be living in his office."

"Why do you say that?"

"I've seen him there at odd hours in sweats and T-shirts. He showers in the gym, but I've never seen him work out."

"If you're there at odd hours, why can't he be?"

"It doesn't seem like he's actually working, you know? I hadn't really given it all that much thought, to be honest, until right now."

"Why would he be living in his office?"

"A lot of people in Congress struggle to support two places—one in their home state and another here. As we both know, it's not cheap to live around here, and despite what people think, not everyone in politics is independently wealthy."

"Does he have a family?"

"A wife back in Sedona and five children, all adopted, a few of them special-needs."

"That could be why he doesn't have the money for an apartment in Washington."

"Wouldn't surprise me."

"He sounds like a nice guy."

"He is."

"So what's he doing with a dead woman in Columbia Heights?"

"I have no idea."

COVERED IN BLOOD, Henry waited for them on the landing outside Regina's third-floor apartment. Sam took a quick inventory of the senator: medium build, dark complexion, jet-black hair and eyes. He was younger than he appeared on television—late forties, early fifties at most.

"Hurry," he said when he saw them coming. "This way." Henry grabbed Sam's arm and all but dragged her into a shabby apartment. She let him lead her only because he was Nick's friend. Anyone else would have a broken hand by now. "In the bedroom."

Regina lay naked on the floor in two pools of blood, one by her head, and the other between her legs. Her throat had been slit from ear to ear. She had long dark hair, a slender build, small but firm breasts and smooth skin that was marred only by a few stretch marks on her belly, indication that she'd probably birthed at least one child or lost a tremendous amount of weight. Based on her slender body, Sam was betting on the baby. She judged the victim to be in her mid-thirties and was able to see past all the blood to determine she'd been quite beautiful.

When Nick saw the bloody scene, he gasped but at least he didn't seem faint as he had at previous crime scenes. The more time he spent with her, the more used to such things he seemed to become. Sam wasn't sure if that was a good or bad thing.

Next to Sam, Henry broke down as he stared at the dead woman.

"How do you know her, Senator?" Sam asked Henry.

He was crying so hard he couldn't reply.

"She works for the company that cleans the Capitol," Nick said, his tone flat with shock. Sam had heard that

tone far too often after the murders of Nick's friends
John O'Connor and Julian Sinclair.

"Did you know her?" Sam asked Nick.

"I've seen her around."

She sensed there was more to it than that, but she
decided to wait until they were alone to grill him
further. To Henry, she said, "Senator, I need to call
this in."

"I have to go," he said, panicked. "I can't be here
when the police come."

"I'm afraid you'll have to stay, sir. You're a material
witness at the very least." She glanced at his blood-
covered dress shirt and then up at his dark eyes.

"At the very least? What does that mean?"

Well aware of the power this man yielded on Capitol
Hill, Sam swallowed hard. "I have no way to know
whether or not you're responsible for this without
investigating further."

Outrage mixed with grief as Henry stared at her. "I
called you because I thought you could help me! We
have to find the person who did this to her!" He looked
imploringly at Nick. "Tell her. You know me, Nick.
You know I couldn't have done something like this!"

To his credit, Nick said nothing.

"I can't believe this! *You actually think I could've
done this to her?*" He swiped ferociously at the tears
cascading down his face.

She fixed her eyes on his bloodstained shirt. "I need
to rule you out as a suspect. You can either help or
hinder that process, but either way, you're not going
anywhere, Senator. Do you understand?"

"Yeah," he said bitterly. "I get it."

"I'd like you both to move to the hallway." After they stepped out of the room, Sam reached for her cell phone. "This is Lieutenant Holland. I need to report a homicide in Columbia Heights."

TWO

"I'D PLACE TIME of death at around five o'clock," said Dr. Lindsey McNamara, chief medical examiner. Due to the senator's possible involvement, Sam had requested Lindsey be called to the scene. Once again they had a powder keg of a case on their hands, and Sam was leaving nothing to chance.

She glanced at her watch. It was now nine o'clock, and a long night lay ahead of them—not at all the romantic evening she and Nick had planned. Sam experienced a pang of remorse. They had so little time together that she hated to sacrifice a minute of it. But when she glanced at Regina Argueta de Castro on the floor, she was reminded that some things were more important.

"Sexually assaulted," Lindsey said as she turned the body. Bruises marked her back and buttocks. "He was rough with her, the poor thing."

Lindsey's empathetic nature was another reason Sam wanted her on the case. Regina would get far more compassion from Lindsey than she would from some of the deputy medical examiners.

While Lindsey completed her initial investigation, Sam took more photos before turning things over to the crime scene detectives who would sift through every item in the sparsely furnished apartment. Sam instructed the responding patrol officers to knock on neighboring doors to see if anyone had heard a disturbance coming from apartment 3B earlier in the evening.

When she was done giving orders, she joined Nick and Henry in the hallway. Nick leaned against the wall while Henry sat on the floor, holding his head in his hands. His shoulders were stooped with exhaustion and grief. Sam glanced at Nick, taking comfort in his steady presence. Whatever needed to be done, he'd be right there with her. For a woman who'd been so fiercely independent most of her life, she was still amazed by how much she'd come to depend on him in such a short time together.

"Senator," she said to Henry. "I have some questions for you, and I'd like to conduct the interview downtown."

He glanced up at her, his face filled with despair. "Am I under arrest?"

"Not at this time. However, we need to clear up a few things and until we do, we'll need to retain you."

"Do I need a lawyer?"

"That's entirely up to you, but I'd recommend that you cooperate as much as possible at this point so we can figure out what happened to Regina. I have the authority to retain you for twenty-four hours without charging you. In that time, I'm required to produce enough evidence to charge you with a crime. If I fail to do that, I'll release you. Do you understand?"

Nodding, he ran a trembling hand through his silky dark hair. "I want to find the person who did this to her." He glanced up at Sam. "Will it be all over the media that you're retaining me?"

"We'll do our best to keep it quiet for now, but I can only do so much. It's a safe bet that the media will catch wind of your involvement. Even if we don't file charges, you found the woman who cleans your office dead in her apartment."

Sam looked at Nick. His handsome face was set in an unreadable expression, but she had no doubt he was reliving the worst day of his life—when he'd found his boss and best friend dead in his apartment.

Releasing a resigned sigh, Henry stood up. "Would it be possible to call my wife? I have to talk to her before this is all over the news."

"I'll need to take a statement from you first, but after that I'll see what I can do."

Out of deference to his position and friendship with Nick, Sam didn't cuff Lightfeather, even though she rarely transported anyone without handcuffs. Once they had Henry settled in the backseat of the car, Nick rested his hand on Sam's arm to stop her.

She looked up to find him looking troubled. "What is it?"

"It may be nothing."

"Or it may be everything. Just tell me, and I'll figure out which it is."

"I think they might've been involved."

"Why do you say that?"

"Remember I told you I'd seen him in his office, looking relaxed and very casual at odd hours?"

Sam nodded.

"One time, recently, she was there with him. I stopped by his office on my way out late one night. The two of them were having a glass of wine. She was wearing the cleaning crew uniform, but she was sitting on his sofa with her feet up. They seemed to be having a grand old time. When I came in, she got this really guilty look on her face and darted out of there like I'd caught them naked or something."

"What did he say?"

"He shrugged it off and said she looked like she needed a drink."

"Did he look like he'd been caught doing something he shouldn't be doing?"

Nick thought about that for a minute and then shook his head. "He was his usual cool, collected self."

"So why do you think they were involved?"

"I only saw them unguarded for a minute, but there was something going on—something more than a glass of wine. I'm sure of it."

"I might need you to make a formal statement about what you saw that night. Would you be willing?"

He winced. "Could we wait and see if you need it?"

Sam studied that handsome, earnest face she loved so much. He'd been through the wringer lately with two close friends murdered in the scope of weeks. She'd do anything she could to spare him more pain. "Yeah, we can do that. Want me to drop you off at home before I go to HQ? Could be a long night."

"I'll hang with you in case you need me."

Sam smiled. "I always need you."

"That's why I'm sticking with you." He stole a quick

kiss and laughed at her reaction. She hated his public displays of affection, especially when other cops were around, which of course was why he loved to do it.

"Give me a minute to report in to Malone." She drew her cell phone from her coat pocket. The frigid air stole the breath from her lungs as she paced the sidewalk and waited for her mentor, Detective Captain Malone, to pick up.

"Lieutenant," he said, sounding slightly buzzed. "What had you hightailing it out of your father's wedding so quickly?"

"A little thing called murder."

She could picture him sitting up straighter at that news. "What've you got?"

Sam relayed what she knew thus far and told him she had taken the senator into custody but had not arrested him.

"What's in the water lately? All these powerful people involved in murders."

"I wish I knew. It's gonna be another hot one."

"At least this one doesn't involve your personal life."

"Well," Sam said, grimacing. "It could. Lightfeather is a friend of Nick's."

"Of course he is," Malone said.

Sam laughed. "Who isn't, right?"

"No kidding. The guy's nothing if not well connected. Want me to send over some of the A-team?"

"Nah, I didn't call them because I knew they'd been partying all day. Let them have their night off. I'll do what I can tonight, and then we'll hit it hard in the morning."

"Sounds good. I'll let them know they have a curfew."

"I'm sure they'll appreciate that. How's the groom holding up?"

"His new wife took him home about an hour ago. He was starting to get a little tired, but it was a good day for him. Nice to see him so happy."

"Yeah." After all her father had been through with her mother leaving him for another man and then the shooting that had left him a quadriplegic, Sam couldn't agree more.

"You and Cruz are still working the angle on the stuff you found in Reese's house, right?"

"We're trying." Every time they had a lead in her father's two-year-old unsolved shooting, they hit a new roadblock. "We're having trouble tracking down the guy who rented the house before Reese. We can't find the landlord so we can't even get a name. The neighbors claim to not remember who lived there before Reese. We think they're stonewalling us for some reason."

"Don't give up," Malone said. "If you keep asking the questions, eventually you'll get an answer."

"I sure hope you're right." After Clarence Reese murdered his family, detectives had uncovered newspaper clippings and photographs related to Skip Holland's shooting. Reese had claimed the box of clippings belonged to the former tenant who had never come back to get some of the things he'd left behind. Now, if they could just figure out *who* the former tenant was. Sam couldn't bear the frustration of being unable to solve the most important case of her career. It didn't help that one high-profile murder case after another sucked up all the time she wanted to be spending on her father's case.

"Keep me posted on the senator and the dead woman."

"I'm going to retain him at least until the morning to confirm his alibi, so you might want to let the chief know that the senior senator from Arizona will be our guest in the city jail for the evening."

Malone snickered at her choice of words. "Will do."

DETECTIVE FREDDIE CRUZ helped his girlfriend Elin Svendsen into his dilapidated Mustang and caught a glimpse of long, muscular leg as she settled herself into the seat. Imagining that long leg wrapped around him had his cock surging with anticipation. But then he remembered his mother, sick at home with the flu, and decided to go by and check on her before he attended to more pressing concerns.

The instant he slid into the driver's seat Elin's tongue was in his mouth and her hand was cupping his balls. Freddie wrapped his arm around her and gave into the carnal kiss for several heated minutes. She had him on the verge of a fast and embarrassing release when he once again thought of his sick mother.

Moaning with frustration, he pulled himself free of Elin's embrace. "I have to go by my mother's before we go home."

"Why?" Her fingers trailed up and down his inner thigh, and he grabbed her hand before she could reach her destination. "We were just there before the wedding."

"That was hours ago, and she's really sick."

Elin's face twisted into a petulant pout. "Doesn't she have any friends who can check on her?"

"Sure she does, but she only has one son."

"Who is a total mama's boy."

"Guilty as charged. She did everything in the world for me all my life, and there's nothing I wouldn't do for her. You'd better get used to that." The animosity between his mother and Elin had escalated over the last few weeks, which was the only black spot on an otherwise satisfying time in Freddie's life. After holding true to a vow of celibacy for twenty-nine long years, he was enjoying the hell out of his first sexual relationship—except for the fact that his beloved mother hated his new girlfriend and did very little to hide her contempt.

When he'd picked up Elin earlier and gotten his first glimpse of a black dress cut low enough that the cupid tattoo on her left breast was visible, he knew he would be the envy of all his cop friends at Skip's wedding. Sure enough, he'd gotten lots of nudges and winks from the guys who'd barely tried to hide the fact that they were lusting after *his* girl. Freddie loved that she was his and his alone. If only he could convince his mother to give Elin a chance. That was the only thing standing between him and true happiness. Well, that and the fact that his partner Sam could barely tolerate Elin, either. Two of the most important women in his life didn't much care for the third one, and their disapproval was taking something away from his enjoyment of the relationship. How he wished he could be the type of guy who could tell his mother and Sam to piss off, but that was *so* not him. It mattered that they disapproved, and he hated himself for letting it get to him.

He pulled up in front of his mother's apartment building, located just a few miles from his own place.

"Leave it running," Elin said. "Since she was so pleasant earlier, I'll wait here this time."

Freddie leaned over to kiss her. "I'll be quick."

"You'd better be. I'm losing the mood."

Freddie laughed. "When have you ever lost the mood?"

"If you don't hurry up, you might find out."

"I'm going. Lock the doors." He waited until he heard the click of the doors locking before he jogged into his mother's building. Since it was quicker than waiting for the elevator, he ran up the four flights, taking the stairs two at a time. His still-recovering shoulder made a small protest at the rapid movement. Freddie ignored it but wondered just how long it took for a bullet wound to fully heal.

Using his key, he let himself into his mother's neat, cheerful apartment. He found her propped up in bed sipping a cup of tea.

"Hi there." Even though her voice was heavy with illness, she still managed to work up a smile for her only child. "I didn't expect to see you again tonight."

"I couldn't go home without making sure you're doing okay."

"You're such a good boy."

He sat next to her on the bed and leaned over to kiss her warm forehead. In her early fifties, Juliette Cruz was still a beautiful woman. "I'm told I'm a mama's boy."

Juliette's expression hardened. "By your *girlfriend*, no doubt."

Freddie shrugged. "It's not like it isn't true."

"It's never been an issue before."

"Still isn't."

His mother put down her tea and reached for his hand. "She's all wrong for you, Freddie."

"So you've said. A few times now, in fact."

"I just don't get what you see in her."

He laughed. "Really? You don't? The other guys at the wedding had no trouble getting what I see in her."

His mother frowned. "You've never been one to let your head be turned by a pretty face and a killer body. There's a hard edge to her that I don't care for."

"I know you don't, Mom. Believe me, I know."

"I hope you're being careful…about protecting yourself."

He stared at her, incredulous. "Are we *really* having this conversation? I'm twenty-nine years old!"

"Don't think you're fooling me, Frederico Cruz."

"I would never presume to fool you." He brought their joined hands to his lips and kissed the back of hers. "Don't worry about me. I'm a big boy, and I can take care of myself."

"You *think* you can. You have no experience whatsoever in dealing with people like her."

Okay, that hurt. Was she forgetting what he did for a living? He released her hand, stood up and fought for control of his temper. She had given him everything, had sacrificed everything for him and he had no doubt her concerns were coming from a place of unconditional love. But he was a grown man—a mama's boy all the way—but a grown man nonetheless.

"I'm glad you're feeling well enough to lecture me, Mom, but I like her, and I'm asking you to let me make my own decisions. This guilt trip you're laying on me is making me crazy. You haven't even given her a chance, and you've already decided you don't like her. That's not how you brought me up, and I have to say I'm kind of disappointed you're acting this way toward a friend of mine—a really nice girl who you haven't bothered to get to know before judging her."

Juliette's face flushed with uncharacteristic chagrin.

"Don't hate her just because you're pissed I broke the vow," he said softly. "That's what this is really about, and you know it."

She looked up at him, her expression pained. "That's part of it. I won't lie to you. I'm disappointed in that."

Raised a devout Christian, he had taken a vow of celibacy at fifteen and stuck to it for fourteen long years—until he met Elin during the O'Connor investigation.

"Okay so we're both disappointed. It would mean a lot to me if you would give her a chance. That's all I'm asking."

Juliette studied him. "I'll try."

"Thank you," Freddie said. At this point, he'd take

whatever she was willing to give toward keeping the peace. "Call me if you feel worse during the night."

"I'll be fine. Don't worry."

"I'll always worry." He bent to kiss her forehead one last time. "That's what makes me a good mama's boy."

"You're a very good boy, Freddie. Don't let anyone tell you otherwise."

"I won't. Sleep well."

"You, too."

From the doorway, Freddie flashed a rakish grin and winked. "I hope I don't sleep *too* well."

She threw a pillow at him and just missed his head.

He tossed it back and blew her one last kiss. Laughing at how he'd managed—for once—to get the last word with her, he locked her in and hurried back to Elin.

THREE

"I WISH YOU'D tell me what's been bothering you all day," Christina said.

From the driver's seat, Metro Detective Tommy "Gonzo" Gonzales glanced over at her and then returned his eyes to the road.

Christina sighed with dismay. Since they met at Sam and Nick's New Year's Eve promotion party, she'd never seen this closed off, unreachable side of Tommy. She'd heard rumors that he'd been quite the player in the past and couldn't help but wonder if he was growing tired of their monogamous relationship. That thought saddened her. Here, finally, was a guy she connected with not only in bed, but everywhere else, too. She didn't want it to be over between them. Not yet.

She took a deep breath and swallowed all her hard-won self-esteem. "Did I do something to upset you?"

He reached for her hand. The warmth of his skin against hers filled her with a sense of rightness she hadn't experienced before. "It's nothing to do with you. I promise."

Christina laced her fingers through his, enveloping his hand between both of hers. "Is something wrong at work?"

"No."

"Then what?"

Even though she could see he wanted to tell her, he maintained the stony silence that had marked their day.

Frustrated and confused, Christina turned to look out at the winter night passing by as he drove her home.

They pulled up outside her town house in the swanky Georgetown neighborhood a short time later. Tommy killed the engine and stared at the windshield.

Christina reluctantly released his hand. "I guess I'll see you when I see you." One thing she'd learned over the last six weeks was that dating a cop was nothing if not unpredictable.

"Wait," he said.

Something in the way he said the single word tugged at her heart. He sounded so tormented that she wanted nothing more than to ease his pain. "What is it, Tommy? You can talk to me. Whatever it is, we'll figure it out."

He released a pained chuckle. "I hope you mean that."

"You know I do." She took his hand again. "Come in with me. Tell me what's got you so upset."

He got out of the car and followed her into the house, keeping his hand on her elbow the whole way in case they encountered ice on the sidewalk. It was just that kind of gesture that had endeared him to her from the very beginning. Underneath his suave, sexy Cuban exterior was a true gentleman.

They hung their coats on the brass stand inside the door. "Can I get you anything? A drink maybe?"

"Yeah," he said, dropping onto the sofa. "That'd be good."

She fixed him a glass of the scotch she now kept on hand for him and brought it to him.

"Nothing for you?"

Christina shook her head. She was too wound up for a drink that would no doubt go straight to her head after all the champagne she'd consumed at the wedding.

He held out his arm to invite her to sit closer to him.

Christina scooted over and rested her head on his chest, breathing him in as his arm tightened around her.

His lips found her forehead, and she was filled with relief. Whatever had him so troubled seemed to have nothing to do with her.

"I'm sorry I've been such a jerk all day."

"You weren't a jerk. You were quiet, which isn't like you." She tilted her head so she could look up at him as he sipped the scotch.

"You know me so well."

"Sometimes I feel like I don't know you at all, but I want to. I want to know you."

He tilted her chin up and brushed his lips over hers, a teasing promise of the delights to come if he could find a way to tell her what had him so burdened.

"You're good for me, Christina. You make me want to be a better man than I've been in the past."

She reached up to caress the stubble on his jaw. He was so insanely sexy that sometimes she had to pinch herself to believe she was really with a guy like him.

All her years of unrequited love for the late Senator John O'Connor seemed like a bad dream since she met Tommy. "Tell me."

He put down the glass and ran his free hand through his dark hair. "Last night, I got a text from a woman I went out with a couple of times. It was a year or so ago. I haven't seen her since."

"Does she want you back?" *Who could blame her?*

"Not exactly. She wanted to tell me about my son."

Christina's breath caught in her lungs. She sat up so she could see him. "You have a son."

"That's what she says, although I'm not sure I believe her. Who knows if he's mine or not?"

"You slept with her?"

He seemed ashamed to nod in agreement. "A couple of times, but I used condoms. You know how I am about that."

"Condoms fail."

"She said the same thing. She swears to God he's mine. All day today I've been trying to figure out what I should do."

Christina slipped into chief of staff mode. "The first thing you do is confirm he's really yours. Demand a DNA test."

"What if she won't do it?"

"I assume she's interested in financial support for the child."

"She didn't come right out and say that, but the implication was clear."

"If she wants your money, you're perfectly within your rights to require proof the child is actually yours."

"You're right, and that's what I'll do tomorrow." He looked down at the floor and then back at her. "What does this mean for us?"

"What does what mean?"

"I'd understand if this was too much for you. We haven't been together that long—"

Christina placed her hands on his face and kissed the words right off his lips. "We've been together just long enough that your problem is my problem, and we'll figure it out together."

"Really?" His expression was so rife with relief that Christina would've laughed if the situation hadn't been so serious. And here she had worried all day that he'd had enough of her.

"Really." She ran her fingers through his hair and guided his mouth back to hers. Running her tongue gently over his bottom lip, she coaxed him into participating in the kiss.

A groan rumbled through him as his arms tightened around her. "I thought you'd be so pissed. I was afraid to tell you."

"It happened a year ago. It's got nothing to do with me or us."

"And if I do have a son?"

"Then I guess we'll have to get a couple of cribs—one for your place and one for mine."

He shifted her under him on the sofa and looked down at her, his eyes hot with desire and relief. Even though he was so much bigger than her, he never handled her with anything other than total gentleness.

"I hate that you tortured yourself this way all day."

She massaged the tension from his neck and shoulders. "Next time something is bothering you, will you just tell me so we can figure it out rather than stewing in silence?"

"I'm not used to having someone to work things out with."

"Well now you do, so you'd better get used to it."

He flashed the sexy, dimpled smile that got him anything he wanted from her. "I love it when you get all bossy with me."

"Is that so?" she asked with the coy grin that usually had the same effect on him.

"You know it is."

Bringing his head down close to her lips, she whispered a two-word order in his ear.

His eyes widened with shock and then heated with passion. His lips came down hard on hers, and as she wrapped her arms around him, Christina wanted to weep with relief and joy that he had confided in her. Then his lips found her neck at the same instant his fingers closed around her nipple, and she ceased to think at all.

LINDSEY MCNAMARA JOINED Sam outside the interrogation room.

"What've you got?" Sam asked the pretty, redheaded medical examiner.

"Nothing new quite yet. As soon as we're done here, I'll get started on the autopsy."

"I'm going to talk him into giving up a DNA sample. You've got the kit with you?"

Lindsey held up the long swab used to collect a buccal sample. "Ready."

Sam glanced at her watch. Ten-thirty. Nick was watching from observation, and she still hoped they could salvage a bit of their romantic evening. "Let's get this done."

Inside the room, Senator Lightfeather startled out of his daze when the two women entered. "Senator, this is Chief Medical Examiner Dr. Lindsey McNamara. May I have your permission to record this interview?"

He nodded and waved his hand in agreement.

"Before we begin, I need to advise you of your rights in this matter." Sam ran through the Miranda warning. "Do you understand your rights as I have explained them?"

"Yes," he said, sounding broken and despondent.

"I want to be clear. We can charge you at any time with failing to immediately report Regina's murder to proper authorities. Calling your colleague whose fiancée happens to be a cop smacks of you trying to cover your own ass. However, if you cooperate with our investigation, I'll speak to the assistant U.S. attorney about waiving those charges. Do you understand?"

Lightfeather granted her a small nod. "I get it."

Sam pushed a piece of paper she'd prepared earlier across the table. "We'd like your consent to obtain a sample of your DNA."

He looked up at her, shocked by the request. "For what purpose?"

"To determine what, if any, contact you had with the victim."

"Can't I just tell you what contact I had with her?"

"We'd like you to do both."

Glancing from Sam to Lindsey and then back to Sam, he reached for the pen in his shirt pocket and scrawled his signature on the form before pushing it back across the table to Sam.

She nodded to Lindsey who explained the procedure before she swabbed the inside of the senator's cheek.

"Thanks, Dr. McNamara," Sam said. "Please ask Detective McBride to step in." They'd decided before that three officers entering the room together would've been one too many. The last thing Sam wanted was for the senator to shut down and lawyer up before she could figure out what he knew about their victim and what had happened to her.

Detective Jeannie McBride entered the room, and Sam introduced her to the senator. "If you could, Senator, can you tell us how you know Regina Argueta de Castro?"

"As Senator Cappuano mentioned earlier, she works for the company that cleans the Hart Senate Office Building."

Sam noticed that he still spoke of Regina in the present tense, as if he had yet to accept her death. "And you met her how long ago?"

"Two years. Maybe a little more." He took a moment to gather his thoughts. "I work late a lot of nights, and she'd come in to clean. We'd get talking, and over time I guess you could say we became friends."

"What did a United States senator have in common with a cleaning lady?" Sam asked.

His lips curved into a smile that didn't reach his eyes. "More than you'd think. We were both living away from our families, missing our kids, working hard to provide a better life for them. We understood each other."

"Where are her children?"

"Guatemala. They live there with her mother. Roberto is seven and Isabella is five. She was hoping to bring them here someday. She talked all the time about how happy she'd be once they were together again." A tear traveled unchecked down his cheek. "I'd like to be the one to tell them she's gone."

"I'll see what I can arrange in the morning."

"I have the number in my office."

"I can't help but wonder why you'd have the number to the Guatemalan cleaning lady's family."

The senator's face hardened into a difficult-to-read expression. "She gave it to me. In case something ever happened to her."

"Was she concerned about her safety?"

"Not that she ever said, but something was troubling her. The last few weeks, she'd been different, as if the weight of the world rested on her fragile shoulders. Even more so than usual."

"Can you think of anyone who might've wanted to harm her?"

"She was briefly married when she first came to this country, but she never told me his name or anything about him. I got the sense their breakup was acrimonious."

"Did she mention feeling threatened by him or anything like that?"

"Not that she ever said to me."

Sam made a note to check into Regina's brief marriage. "Were you romantically involved with her, Senator?"

New tears tumbled down his face. He brushed them away with the back of his trembling hand. "I never meant for it to happen. I swear to you. I love my wife and my children, but sometimes it just gets so lonely being away from them for weeks on end. Regina understood what that was like. We were friends for a long time before anything ever happened."

"What exactly happened?"

His shoulders hunched with defeat, as if it was registering all at once that his entire life was about to unravel. "It was her daughter's birthday. She was sad to be missing it. I gave her my international cell phone so she could call home, and she was so happy and thankful after speaking with her kids. We had a glass of wine and sat together on the sofa. We were talking about Isabella, about all the little moments we were both missing with our children—moments that could never be recaptured. It was all very innocent. Until I kissed her." He broke down into wretched sobs that shook his entire body. "I never meant..."

Sam gave him a few minutes to compose himself.

"It was just supposed to be comfort between friends," he said.

"But it was more than that?"

He nodded. "We made love right there in my office

where anyone could've discovered us. I never even stopped to lock the door. Afterward, I couldn't believe I'd let that happen. The chances I had taken with my family, my office, with Regina, my dearest friend. I've never before been unfaithful to my wife. I was literally sick with guilt."

"So it didn't happen again?"

The senator released a long rattling breath. "We were both so shocked by how carried away we'd been that we steered clear of each other. Another woman cleaned my office, and I didn't see Regina for many weeks."

"And how long ago was this?"

"Three months."

"Did you eventually see her again?"

"Her immigration status was in question. She had applied for a green card when she was married, but apparently the marriage was deemed suspect and the application was denied. Her work visa was running out, and she came to me to ask if there was anything I could do to help her. She'd applied for permanent residency on her own, but her application had been denied. The only way she could properly support her family was to stay in the United States, and it was important to her that she be here legally. She was getting quite desperate as the expiration date approached."

"Were you able to help her?"

"I made a few phone calls, but I had to be careful since she wasn't one of my constituents. We were able to get her a three-month extension, and I put in a good word for her with the Immigration and Naturalization

Service. I asked them to reconsider her application. That was all I could do without arousing suspicion."

"And did she appreciate your help?"

"Very much so."

"Did you rekindle your romantic relationship?"

A look of sheer torture came over his face. "You have to understand…my family is everything to me, but when I was with Regina, it was like I became someone else. I couldn't resist her."

"How many times were you intimate with her?"

"Too many."

"Ten? Twenty? Thirty? More?"

"Thirty or more, I guess. We were together just about every day for the last month."

"Where did these liaisons occur?"

"Most of the time at her apartment, but a few more times in my office—with the door locked."

"Why not your apartment?"

"With a wife and five kids in Sedona, I can't exactly afford a place here too," he said, seeming embarrassed. "I sleep on the sofa in my office."

Nick's hunch had been spot-on. "Was she involved with anyone else?"

Lightfeather's eyes widened. "Of course not. She wasn't promiscuous."

"You're sure of that?"

"Yes, I'm sure!"

"When was the last time you were intimate with Regina?"

"Earlier today. I was over there for lunch and we made love afterward. I was there for a couple of hours before I left to do some work in my office. I tried to call her a little while later on the cell phone I'd given her. When she didn't answer, I became concerned and went back to her apartment. There was so much blood. At first I couldn't figure out what was wrong, and then, when I saw her on the floor...I started screaming for help but no one came. That's when I called Nick. I didn't know what else to do."

"You could've called 911."

He looked right at her. "I'm a married United States senator who just found his mistress murdered in her apartment. If you were me, would you call 911 or would you call your friend whose fiancée is a homicide detective?"

"So you weren't so upset about your dead lover that you didn't take a moment to think about your family and your career before calling for help for her?"

He slapped a hand on the table, startling her. "I was horrified that someone had harmed this beautiful, sweet woman, and I wanted the best cop in this city to find out who did this to her. She was, *and is*, my first thought."

Something about the way he said that triggered a new realization for Sam. "You were in love with her."

"Yes," he said, breaking down again. "God help me, but I was in love with her, and I have no idea how I'll ever live without her."

FOUR

"GET OVER TO the Capitol and get me a security guard, a junior staffer, *anyone* who can put Senator Lightfeather in that building late this afternoon," Sam said to Detective McBride. "That place is crawling with cameras, so get me video on his movements all day yesterday and fill in the timeline on the murder board. I also want Regina's cell phone dumped and while you're at it, dump Lightfeather's too."

"You got it, LT," Jeannie said, gesturing to her partner, Detective Will Tyrone.

After they left the pit, Sam returned to her office and ran her hand through hair still sticky from the product the stylist had loaded it with before the wedding. She glanced at her desk and did a double take at how neat and orderly it was.

Nick approached her from behind, resting his hands on her shoulders and massaging the tense spots. He knew exactly where her stress collected, and it was all Sam could do to remain standing as his talented fingers hit all the right places. "It's getting late, babe."

"Did you clean up my desk again?"

"Maybe."

"It's a sickness. You have a sickness."

"Guilty as charged." He laughed softly and planted

a kiss on her neck. Desire rippled through her. She was so easy where he was concerned, and he knew it. "What's up with Henry?"

The facts of the case ran through her mind like a silent movie. "Until I get Lindsey's report, I'm at a standstill."

"Then let's go home."

Back in the day, Sam would've waited all night—if necessary—for the autopsy report and lab results. Now, though, she had a good reason to go home. She looked up at him. "Sorry for letting work invade our day off. Maybe one of these days we'll succeed in actually scoring a full day off."

"We can dream."

She let him help her into her coat and lead her from the office. "I know you really needed the break."

"Not your fault, and besides, I did get a day off from campaigning, so it's all good."

"We missed out on our early Valentine's Day," she said once they were in the car.

He reached for her hand, laced his fingers through hers. "Every day with you is Valentine's Day."

Sam smiled at him. "Even if we end up on different sides on this case?"

"We may not always agree, Sam, but we're always on the same side."

She relaxed into the heated leather seat and enjoyed the companionable silence. That was one of her favorite things about her relationship with Nick. Even in the quiet spaces between words, she was always in tune with him. In the past, when she'd been unhappily married to a manipulative man who wanted to control her every thought, she'd often been lonely even when he was sitting next to her on the sofa or lying next to her in bed. She had never once felt that way with Nick.

"What're you thinking about over there?" he asked.

"I'm thinking about us."

"What about us?"

"Could I ask you something and will you tell me the truth?"

He glanced at her. "Of course you can and of course I will."

"When we're together, do you ever feel lonely?"

"Lonely?" He released a short laugh. "That is one thing I never feel when I'm with you."

"Good," Sam said, relieved. "That's good."

Nick parallel parked on Ninth Street, killed the engine and turned to face her, reaching out to caress her cheek. "What's that all about?"

"Sometimes, well…a lot of the time when I was with Peter, I remember being lonely even when he was right there with me. I was thinking that I've never felt that way with you, and I was hoping you hadn't either."

"I've never felt that way, and I'm glad you haven't." He reached for her, and she leaned into his embrace. "If you're ever lonely, will you tell me?"

She nodded. "Will you?"

"I promise."

"I doubt it'll ever be an issue between us. Everything about this is different."

"Yes," he said, kissing her. "It is. Come on, let's go in."

Inside, Nick hung their coats in the closet.

"Would've been quicker to toss them on the sofa," Sam said. She loved goading him about his anal-retentive neatness.

"That's not where they go." He followed her upstairs and took advantage of the opportunity to smack her on the ass.

Sam laughed and took off running, knowing he'd give chase. He caught up to her in the bedroom, and they tumbled onto the bed. "You can run," he said, attempting a menacing look, "but you cannot hide."

"Wanna bet?"

"Mmm," he said, capturing her mouth for a deep, sensual kiss.

Sam pressed against the tight hold he had on her hands. "Let me go. I want to touch you."

Nick released her hands and removed her sweater.

Sam shivered from the cool air hitting her warm skin.

"Are you cold?" he asked.

"No." She freed the onyx studs from his tuxedo shirt, dropped them into a pile on the bed and pushed the shirt off his broad shoulders. "Too many clothes," she said, tugging at his undershirt.

Nick laughed and pulled it over his head. "Better?"

Sam ran her hands over his muscular chest. "Much."

He gathered her into a tight embrace and rocked against her.

She caressed his back. "What?"

Releasing a long deep breath, Nick pressed his lips to her neck. "Marry me, Samantha."

"I believe I've already agreed to that. Remember the Rose Garden?"

He raised his head to meet her eyes. "Soon. I don't want to wait."

She reached up to run her fingers through his hair. "I thought you wanted a nice wedding."

"We can't have a nice wedding soon?"

"How soon are we talking?"

"I don't know. A month?"

Sam laughed. "Weren't you there earlier when I was plunged into another complicated case? How do you expect me to plan a wedding and contend with that at the same time?"

"I'll plan it. Leave everything to me."

As much as she'd love to turn the whole thing over to him, their wedding was too important for her to be totally removed from the planning. "I thought we'd plan it together."

"Is that what you want?"

"I figured that's what *you'd* want."

"I want to be married. That's all I care about."

"That's not what you said the other night when my sisters were grilling you about what kind of wedding you wanted. You said you want the bells and whistles. What changed?"

He framed her face with his hands and leaned in to kiss her.

"Nick? What is it? Why the sudden urgency?"

"It's just…listening to Henry talk about Regina. I could relate to how he felt about her. I can't imagine what he must be going through."

"You're awfully certain he's not responsible for her murder."

"You heard him, Sam." Nick kissed her nose, both cheeks and then her lips. "He was in love with her. He doesn't know how he'll live without her. I understand how he feels."

She curled her legs around his. "Nothing's going to happen to me. There's no need to rush our wedding. You're only going to do this once, right?"

"That's the plan."

"Then you ought to do it right. The way you want it."

"What about what you want?"

"I already had that. This time can be all about what you want."

"No, babe," he said, shaking his head. "This time has to be all about what *we* want."

The idea of planning another elaborate wedding made Sam feel slightly ill. She'd do it for him, but she'd much rather call in a justice of the peace and be done with it. "What I want right now," she said with a saucy grin, "has nothing to do with cakes or flowers." She reached between them to free his belt and unzip his pants.

Nick gasped when she curled her hand around his erection. He gripped her hand and held her still. "I'll make you a deal."

"Why do we need a deal? In case you haven't noticed, I'm a sure thing."

He laughed and then moaned when she stroked him. "Do you want to hear my deal or not?"

"All right." She released her hold on him. "Shoot."

Bending over her, he pressed his lips to her belly and then turned those potent eyes up to meet hers. "If I can make you come three times in the next half hour, you'll let me set a date—any date I want."

Sam raised an eyebrow. "And if you can't?"

"I'll wait for you to set the date."

"You won't mention it again?"

"Not until you do."

She *never* came three times. Ever. "Okay. You're on. Do your best work."

His smile was nothing short of predatory as he kissed his way down her body.

Twenty-eight minutes later, Sam hovered on the brink of a third orgasm as Nick pumped into her from behind. Determined to hold it off, she jolted when he reached around to coax her. Damn it, she was powerless against that combination, and he knew it. Lesson learned: Never make a deal with the guy who knows you better than anyone. His fingers moved urgently over her most sensitive place as he went deep again, sending her tripping over the edge into yet another climax.

This time, he joined her. They fell into a heaving pile on the bed. He kissed her back and then her shoulder. His lips brushed against her ear.

"March 26."

SAM'S FIRST THOUGHT the next morning wasn't of the murder she needed to investigate. No, her first thought was of the deal she'd made with the devil himself. How would she ever manage to plan a wedding while in the midst of another complex investigation? And during his campaign. She sighed. Then she remembered how he'd gotten his new house put together in just under a week, in time to entertain his Supreme Court nominee friend. If anyone could pull off a classy wedding in just over a month's time, her fiancé could.

She glanced over at him, asleep with one arm thrown over his head. The sprinkle of whiskers on his usually smooth jaw only made him more appealing to her. At the end of one crazy month and a half, he'd be her husband and they'd have the rest of their lives together. Surely she could get through whatever she had to in the next few weeks to have forever with him. Right?

He shifted onto his side and reached for her in his sleep.

Smiling, Sam snuggled into him. No, she never felt lonely anymore. Even when he was asleep, he was still right here with her and he truly loved her. Of that, she had no doubt at all.

He tightened his hold on her. "What're you thinking about?" he mumbled.

"Our wedding." She shifted onto her back so she could see him. "What do you want me to do?"

"Dresses for you and your sisters, flowers and the cake." He still hadn't opened his eyes. "I'll take care of everything else."

"I've finally figured out how you get so much done. You work while you're asleep. That's the only possible explanation."

He chuckled softly. "I wish." His knee bumped her leg. "You need to get going."

"I know." Before she got up, she turned into his embrace and breathed in his warm, clean scent. "After I close this one, we're taking a day off. I don't care what we have to do, but we're getting our day."

"March 26." He finally opened his eyes as he kissed her. "We'll take that day off for sure—and the whole week after. The Senate goes into recess until mid-April."

"Won't you need to campaign?"

"I'll let Christina know I'm unavailable that week. I'll be on my honeymoon."

"And where will that be?"

"I haven't decided yet. Where do you want to go?"

"Anywhere that isn't the District of Columbia." Sam looked up at him. "You know, March 26 is only three months since we got back together."

His eyebrow arched. "Do you need more time to be sure you're doing the right thing?"

Sam thought of the six years she'd spent missing him after one unforgettable night together. "No."

His fingers spooled through her hair. "Neither do I. So we're on? March 26?"

"Yes," she said, kissing him. "We're on."

"WELL, THAT'S A first." Sam closed her cell phone and put it in the back pocket of her jeans.

"What is?" Nick asked as he stood before the bedroom mirror to knot his tie.

"Gonzo called in sick the day after we caught a hot case."

Nick turned to her. "That's odd. Christina called, too. She was supposed to go to Richmond with me today, but she said something came up."

Sam scowled. "They're probably lolling about in bed while we're giving up yet another Sunday to work."

"Or maybe they're actually sick."

"Hungover is more like it. He was putting away the scotch yesterday."

Nick came over to her and kissed her forehead. "We were all drinking. Don't be too hard on him."

"It's just not like him."

"He'd probably say it's not like you to hang out at home longer than necessary so you could have breakfast with your fiancé when you've got a body chilling in the morgue."

Sam replied with another scowl.

Nick laughed and cuffed her chin. "I'm just saying. People change. Life happens. And no one, not even you and me, can work all the time."

"We have been lately."

"A week off, coming soon. Can you take the full week?"

"I have like eight weeks of vacation built up, so it shouldn't be a problem."

"Just make sure you remember to ask."

She rolled her eyes at him even as the thought of an entire week alone with him made her heart race with anticipation. "Yes, dear. So what's up in Richmond today?"

"A rally at VCU," he said, referring to Virginia Commonwealth University, "a visit to one of the state homes for kids and then a fundraising dinner. I won't be home until late."

She went up on tiptoes to kiss him. "Me, too, so I'll catch you when I catch you."

When she started to draw back from him, he brought her in for a better kiss. "Mmm," he said several minutes later. "That oughta hold me until you catch me."

Smiling, she patted his freshly-shaven face and kissed him again. "See ya."

"Hey."

Sam turned back to him.

"Be careful today."

"Always am."

FIVE

"ARE YOU SURE it's a good idea to just show up without calling first?" Gonzo asked Christina. He eyed the nondescript white town house that might—or might not—house his son.

"I'm sure. This way she doesn't have time to pull any crap. She's not expecting you, so you gain the upper hand."

He glanced over at her. Even after a nearly sleepless night, she looked fresh-faced and polished. Sometimes he still wondered what the heck a classy woman like her saw in a rough-around-the-edges guy like him. "This is why you're so good at your job."

"It's called strategy," she said, smiling at the compliment. "You gotta have one." She leaned over to kiss the dimple in his chin that she'd once told him was ridiculously sexy. "Remember, you're just going to tell her you want to see the baby and talk about what you can do to help out. Keep it all friendly. We'll let the lawyer get into the DNA business with her. It'll be better if that doesn't come from you."

"Okay." He took a deep, fortifying breath. "Here goes nothing."

Christina squeezed his arm. "It'll be fine. You

haven't done anything wrong, Tommy. Just remember that."

Grateful for her calming presence, he nodded and reached for the door handle. At the last second, he stopped and turned to her. "Come with me."

"I thought we decided it would be better if I waited here."

"I don't care what we decided. I want you with me when I see him for the first time. It wasn't like I had a long relationship with her. How can she be put out if I have someone else now?"

"Are you sure?"

"Yeah. I'll feel better if you're there with me," he said, startled to realize it was true. He always felt better when she was around.

"Then let's go."

On the front stoop, Gonzo rang the bell. Would he know right away that the child was his? Would he be able to love a child he hadn't even known about? What if he couldn't love the baby, even if he *was* his?

The door swung open, and Lori gasped when she saw him. Her brown hair looked like it hadn't been washed in days and her oversized red T-shirt was stained with what might've been breast milk. Gonzo tried to recall what he'd once seen in her, but she had changed so much he barely recognized her.

She pushed open the storm door. "Tommy? What're you doing here?"

He swallowed hard. "I've come to see my son."

Lori's gaze shifted from him to Christina and then back to him.

"This is my, um, girlfriend, Christina." He was surprised he didn't choke on a word he usually went out of his way to avoid. "Christina, this is Lori."

The two women sized each other up for a long, long moment. Finally, Christina said, "Nice to meet you."

The sound of a baby wailing from inside ended the awkward moment. "Come in." Lori gestured them into a space cluttered with baby paraphernalia and piles of dirty clothes.

Gonzo eyed the overflowing ashtray on the coffee table with dismay. The place reeked of smoke.

"I'll just, um, go get him," Lori said, darting from the room.

When they were alone, Christina reached for his hand.

"How does he breathe in here?" Gonzo whispered.

"I was wondering the same thing."

When they heard Lori's footsteps on the stairs, Gonzo released Christina's hand.

She came into the room carrying the baby. The first thing he noticed was the baby's dark hair. Not that he knew much about babies, but he seemed to have a lot of hair. Gonzo's nephew Joey had been born with a similar head of hair. His stomach dropped as Lori handed the baby to him.

Gonzo and Christina gasped at the prominent dimple in the baby's chin.

He stared down at the puckered little face and fell instantly in love. Big eyes stared up at him, open and trusting, and it was all Gonzo could do not to weep.

The immediate tidal wave of love that surged through him left him defenseless in its wake.

Christina's hand landed on his back, and he glanced over at her to find that she, too, was overwhelmed.

"What's his name?" Gonzo asked.

"I haven't named him yet."

Startled, Gonzo looked up at her. "But he's a couple of months old!"

"Believe me, I know how old he is."

"You have to give him a name."

"So that's how this is going to go? You come into *my* home and start telling me how to raise *my* kid?"

"You called me, Lori. I never would've known about him if you hadn't called. Did you expect me to just go on with my life and act like I'd never heard about him?"

"Don't try to pretend you have any interest in him."

"Of course I'm interested in him. He's my son."

"Look, it's really nice of you to come all the way over here to see him, but the only thing I need from you is some money for diapers and day care. I don't expect anything else."

"I want more than that."

The front door swung open, bringing a blast of cold air and startling the baby. He began to wail.

Even though he had next to no experience with babies, Gonzo patted his back.

"I'll take him," Lori said, reaching for him.

"I don't mind that he's crying," Gonzo said.

"The lady wants her baby back," a deep voice said from the foyer.

Gonzo glanced over to find a giant of a man glaring

at him. He had a red bandana tied around his long hair and tattoos on his neck and arms.

"Take it easy, Rex," Lori said. "He's a cop."

"Doesn't give him the right to hold on to your kid when you want him back."

"He's my kid too," Gonzo said, using his best cop glare on the guy.

Rex's eyes widened with surprise. "That so?"

Lori nodded.

Rex glowered at her.

"You really need to go now," she said to Gonzo. This time when she reached for the baby he let her take him.

"I'll go," Gonzo said. "But I'll be back. Soon." With one last look at his son, Gonzo ushered Christina out the front door. Once they were outside, he took a deep gulping breath of fresh air. The stench of cigarette smoke clung to their coats. "She hasn't even given him a name," he said, filled with despair.

Christina pulled her cell phone from her coat pocket.

"Who are you calling?" Gonzo asked.

"Nick's lawyer friend Andy. He specializes in family law."

"I should probably check with Sam. She might not appreciate me calling on a friend of Nick's without asking her first."

"I'm sure Sam would want you to do everything you could to take care of your son."

He hoped Christina was right. "How could she not even care enough about him to give him a name?"

Christina squeezed his arm. "Don't worry. We're going to take care of him, okay?"

Gonzo nodded. His entire world had been turned upside down by one tiny dimpled chin, and he was grateful for her cool competence.

"GIVE ME SOMETHING, give me anything," Sam said to Dr. McNamara. Regina Argueta de Castro lay on the table under the glare of fluorescent lights.

"Twelve weeks pregnant," Lindsey said.

"Well, that's interesting. How soon until you know if the fetus's DNA matches Senator Lightfeather's?"

"A couple of days. I'm running it now."

"Anything else?"

"I got a partial print off the bruises on her buttocks. I ran it through AFIS," she said, referring to the Automated Fingerprint Identification System. "But no hits. Also, I found semen from two different men in her vagina."

"Of course there were two," Sam said, frustrated that her slam-dunk case against Senator Lightfeather seemed to be falling apart. "Let me know what the DNA shows."

"Will do. So how're the wedding plans coming?"

"Fine. I guess." Her stomach clenched when she thought of the wedding she'd agreed to in six short weeks.

"A proposal in the White House Rose Garden." Lindsey sighed. "So romantic."

"He does have his moments," Sam conceded. "Get me some info, Doc."

"I'm on it."

Sam left the morgue and headed for the pit where she found Freddie popping pills. "Are you hungover too?"

He startled and looked up at her, a guilty expression marking his handsome face. "What? No. Are you?"

"Not me. Gonzo. Called in sick today."

"He wasn't drinking that much because he had to work today."

"So what's your excuse?"

"I have a headache, if you must know. And it's not from drinking. I didn't sleep very well."

"Spare me the gories." Sam was surprised when he didn't fire back with the usual retort. "What's the matter?"

"Nothing." He reached for some papers on his desk. "I've got McBride's report from last night. She spoke with several security people at the Capitol who reported seeing Senator Lightfeather there yesterday afternoon into the early evening. One of them reported seeing him leaving around six, and he seemed to be in a rush."

Just as he'd said, Sam thought. "We've got a DNA match to his semen, but there was a second guy. Lindsey's running it."

"McBride reported that they 'interrogated the lock' on his office door and his key card swipes matched up with his timeline."

"Let's get him back into interrogation to cross the Ts before we let him go."

"You got it, boss. One other thing. We've had

several calls from the media asking for confirmation that we're holding Lightfeather in connection with the murder of a member of the Capitol cleaning staff."

"No comment for now."

"That's what I figured you'd say."

Sam nodded. "Go get him."

"On my way."

Sam watched him go, noting the slight hunch to his shoulders. Yes, something was definitely troubling her partner. Before the day was over, she'd get it out of him.

A few minutes later, she joined Freddie and the senator in one of the interrogation rooms. Lightfeather's night in jail seemed to have diminished him.

"Were you aware that Regina was pregnant?" Sam asked.

Lightfeather's hands trembled. "Yes."

"Was it yours?"

He nodded.

"You're certain of that?"

"Of course I am."

"You're *sure* she wasn't seeing anyone else?"

"We were together most nights, so I can't imagine how she'd have time for anyone else."

"Didn't she work nights cleaning the Capitol?"

"Five nights a week, four to midnight."

"You said you were together 'most nights'. What did she do on the nights she didn't spend with you?"

"I'm not sure. She never said."

"Did you ask?"

He nodded. "It was a…a bone of contention between us."

"Did she have girlfriends? Anyone she would've confided in?"

"She was quite friendly with several women she worked with, but I'm not sure what she confided in them. I'm confident she told no one about our relationship. She knew what was at stake."

"For you or for her?"

"For both of us. She couldn't risk losing her job."

"What about what was at risk for you?"

"Obviously, she was well aware of that too."

"Was she pressuring you for more? She's carrying your child, facing possible deportment. I imagine she was quite desperate for some safety and security."

"She knew I'd take care of her and the baby, but she wasn't pressuring me. She was painfully aware of my marital status."

"How were you planning to take care of her and the baby when you didn't have enough money to get an apartment in Washington?"

Lightfeather's slumped in his chair. "I was going to do whatever I could for her."

"Which wouldn't have been much, am I right?"

He shrugged.

"She had to be feeling quite desperate. Another mouth to feed, day care, diapers. How would she swing all that when she was supporting her family back home?"

"We didn't talk a lot about that. We were going to

work something out. I told her not to worry. I'd find the money. Somehow."

Freddie gestured to Sam, and she nodded to him.

"Senator," he said. "Are you familiar with the term 'anchor baby'?"

Lightfeather sat up straighter in his chair. "I am."

"I'm not," Sam said. "Enlighten me."

"When babies are born to illegal immigrants, they 'anchor' their mothers to the United States because the 14th Amendment grants automatic citizenship to anyone born in this country," Lightfeather said.

"Ahhh," Sam said, seeing where Freddie was going with this. Proud of his initiative, she waved her hand to give him the floor.

"Seeing as Regina's immigration status was in question, I'm wondering if her pregnancy was planned or not."

"It was most definitely *not* planned."

"How does that happen? I have to assume you both knew how to prevent an unwanted pregnancy."

The senator's hands, Sam noted, were trembling.

"We think it happened that first time. In my office."

"You didn't use protection?" Freddie asked.

"She said she was on the pill and I believed her."

"But she wasn't?"

"She was. I saw them later in her purse."

"Did she take them?"

"She swore she did. When she first discovered she was pregnant, she was furious that the pills hadn't worked."

"Or," Sam said, "they'd worked exactly as she'd intended."

Lightfeather's dark eyes narrowed. "What're you insinuating?"

"That you might've been duped, Senator. Seduced by a woman who knew *exactly* what she was doing when she allowed a United States senator to impregnate her."

"How dare you say such a thing about her? We were in love! Once I assured her I'd do everything I could to care for her and the baby, she was overjoyed about her pregnancy."

"She was overjoyed to be having a baby in the U.S. of A.," Sam said. "That it was the child of a high-ranking official was a bonus."

"I can't believe you'd say such a thing about a lovely woman who was brutally murdered. You don't care about her at all. I never should've called you."

Sam smacked her hand on the table, which startled him. "Don't tell me who and what I care about. I'll find out who killed her, and I'll make sure her killer pays for what he did to her."

Lightfeather broke down. "I'm sorry. I know you will. I'm just...I still can't believe this has happened." He turned tear-filled eyes up at Sam. "May I please call my wife? I can't have her hearing about this through the media."

Sam glanced at Freddie. "She may have already heard it. We've received numerous calls today from reporters who know we have you in custody."

The senator moaned and dropped his head into his hands.

"Detective, please arrange for an outside line for Senator Lightfeather," Sam said to Freddie.

"Yes, Lieutenant."

Sam stood up. "We'll give you a minute to make your call. Please be aware that we will be monitoring the call."

Freddie brought in a phone and plugged it into a jack. Handing the receiver to the senator, he hit the button to get an outside line.

Sam and Freddie left him alone and stepped into the observation room where they found Captain Malone and Chief Farnsworth waiting for them.

"What've you got, Lieutenant?" Farnsworth asked.

"Not enough to charge him," she said, frustrated. "Let's listen in for a minute."

"Annette," Lightfeather said, his head resting on his free hand. "Something has happened." He began to weep as he told his wife about his involvement with Regina. "I need you to come. Can you come?" He listened for a moment. "I know, honey, but I really need you. I've made a terrible mistake."

Sam wondered if he meant that. From what she'd seen, he'd hardly considered his affair with Regina a mistake. Part of her wanted to call Annette Lightfeather and tell her to stay put in Arizona. Sam hated when political wives stood by their scumbag husbands after they'd embroiled their families in scandal.

As the conversation ended, Sam deduced that Annette would arrive in Washington before the end of the day. She turned to the chief. "I'm going to release him with orders to stay in the city until we close the case. Even though he's got motive galore, his alibi for the time of death is tight." To Freddie, she said, "Tell me more about this anchor baby thing."

"I remember reading about it in the paper last year. The numbers were quite startling—something like 8 or 9 percent of all babies born in the U.S. in 2008 were anchor babies. There's been a lot of talk about repealing the 14th Amendment to close the loophole in the immigration laws."

"Didn't they just pass a new immigration bill?" Sam asked, thinking of the O'Connor-Martin bill that Nick had worked so hard on as John O'Connor's chief of staff. Ensuring passage of his friend's bill had been Nick's first order of business as a senator.

"Yes," Freddie said, "but it didn't address this issue."

Sam made a mental note to read up on the amendment and to get Nick's thoughts on the anchor baby issue. "It's time to start digging into Regina's life," she said.

"Agreed," Malone said.

"Go ahead and spring the senator," Farnsworth said. "But dig into his life too. He certainly had motive."

"We're on it," Sam said. "Cruz, let's have him make the call to Regina's family before we release him."

"One thing, LT," Freddie said, "McBride let me know that she's getting stonewalled by the cell phone company. They're not willing to release records for Regina or especially Lightfeather without subpoenas."

"McBride told them she'd been murdered?"

Freddie nodded. "The direct quote was something like, 'We're not giving you the private cell records of a United States senator without a subpoena. We don't care what he's suspected of.' Don't forget—her cell was in his name. He got it for her and paid for it, so they're both listed as his."

"Well, then get them the subpoenas. I want that data ASAP."

"You got it," Freddie said on his way out.

"I don't get these powerful guys who risk everything and think they're never going to get caught," Malone said.

"I don't get the passive political wives who stand by their men," Sam said. "If my husband cheated on me, there's no way he'd get me to stand meekly by him while he tried to explain away his failings." She watched as the two men exchanged amused glances. "What?"

"Given this some significant thought, huh?" Farnsworth said.

"Hardly," Sam said with a snort. "My future husband knows if he ever cheats on me I'd shoot him before I'd *ever* stand by his side like the humiliated little wife."

The two men laughed.

"You think I'm kidding?" Sam asked.

"Oh, we know you mean it," Malone said, making a poor attempt at a serious expression. "Poor Nick. Someone really ought to warn him."

"No one needs to warn him," Farnsworth said. "He

knows he's got the best of the best at home. Why would he ever look elsewhere?"

Embarrassed by the compliment, Sam smiled at the man she'd called Uncle Joe as a child. "Thank you for that."

"I only speak the truth." He headed for the door with Malone following him. "Keep us in the loop."

"I will." When she was alone, Sam got to work on her murder board, beginning at the left side with photos from the crime scene. She made a column for information about Lightfeather.

Freddie returned to the room. "Um, boss, we have a small problem."

"What's that?"

"The building is surrounded by press. They know we've got Lightfeather here, and they're clamoring for the story."

Sam thought for a second. "Here's what we're going to do."

SIX

NICK SLID INTO the back of the sedan and quickly shut the door. "Jesus," he said to his driver, Tony. "That was insane."

Tony chuckled. "You're more popular than ever, Senator. Never seen anything like the numbers you're drawing on the stump."

"Senator O'Connor had similar turnouts."

"Not like this he didn't." He glanced into the rearview mirror. "Ready for your next stop?"

"Yes." Nick rested his head back against the seat. "Thanks." He watched the VCU campus roll past. "What do you suppose it is, Tony?"

"Sir?"

"That brings them out in such numbers."

Once again, Tony laughed. "You're young, handsome, full of hope, humble. People relate to you and your story."

"Senator O' Connor was all those things too."

"He didn't have the same...what's the word I'm looking for? Charisma."

"It's because I took his place after he died."

"You'd be selling yourself short if you think it's just that. There's something about you they've connected with."

"Yeah, my love life. They're all connected to that."

"Doesn't hurt," Tony said, smiling into the mirror. "It's a combination of all those things. You were the right guy at the right time."

"I guess." Nick pondered what Tony had said. He'd known the man a long time as he'd been John's driver for years. Living as close as he did to the state he represented, Nick—and John before him—relied on Tony to get him around to campaign stops that were within driving distance.

He usually made use of the time in the car to work. Today, he was using the time to think. More than one hundred thousand people had shown up for the VCU rally, which was four times the number they'd expected. Despite the cold, the numbers had forced the rally outdoors to Monroe Park.

"I hear they've got four thousand on the waiting list for tonight's fundraiser," Tony said. "The money is rolling in."

Millions had flooded into his campaign since he'd declared his candidacy. "It's an embarrassment of riches," Nick said.

"Enjoy it while it lasts. You'll do something to screw it up eventually."

Nick cracked up at the dryly spoken comment. "Gee, thanks."

"I'm just razzing ya. You've got the golden touch, Senator. You can ride the wave all the way to Pennsylvania Avenue at this rate."

The Democratic National Committee had already expressed an interest in running him in the primary in three years. President Nelson had started out strong, but his numbers had fallen off in recent months, and the party was considering its options should their incumbent choose not to seek a second term. Nick couldn't believe his name was even in the mix. He'd only been in the Senate for a month and a half and was in the midst of his first campaign. The notion of running for president was almost laughable—until he remembered the sea of people at the rally chanting his name and clamoring for a handshake or autograph. This whole thing was still unreal to him. His best friend and boss had been murdered by the twenty-year-old son John kept hidden from even his closest friend. Despite all the doors John's death had opened for Nick, he'd gladly give it all up to have his friend back.

Tony pulled up to the curb outside a nondescript red brick building in downtown Richmond. "Here ya are, Senator."

This stop had not been on his official schedule for the day, and Nick was relieved to note that his traveling band of reporters had not followed him here. "See you in a bit," he said to Tony on the way out of the car.

Inside, Irene Littlefield, director of the state home for children, greeted him. She'd appealed to his office for help in ensuring the continuation of a crucial federal grant that helped to fund the program. Nick figured her to be in her early sixties. "Senator," she said, shaking his hand, "it's such an honor to have you here. The children have been looking forward to your visit."

"It's great to be here. I've heard wonderful things about your program."

"That's nice of you to say. We do what we can with the resources made available to us. Let me introduce you to the children."

"That'd be great." He followed her through sterile-looking hallways in what used to be a VCU dormitory to a homey-looking common area filled with sofas, a big-screen TV, games and books. About thirty scrubbed and polished children waited patiently to say hello. Over the next half hour, Nick visited with each of them and marveled at their excellent manners and enthusiasm.

"We've asked Scotty to give you a tour of the facility," Mrs. Littlefield said after each of the children had had a chance to visit with Nick. She had her hands on the shoulders of a boy who was maybe eleven or twelve. His dark hair looked like it had been brushed into submission for the occasion. He wore a smart-looking navy sweater with khaki pants.

He flashed a mischievous grin. "I've been here the longest, so I got the short straw."

Nick laughed. "I'll try not to ask too many questions."

Scotty smiled at him. "Right this way, Senator."

As Nick followed him through the hallways, Scotty kept up a steady stream of chatter, pointing out the kitchen and dining room and discussing the food, which apparently ranged from fabulous to gross, depending on the chef's mood.

"What's your favorite meal?" Nick asked him.

"Spaghetti," Scotty said without hesitation.

"Ahhh, a man after my own heart."

"That's your favorite too?"

"Sure is. A good Italian boy like me has to get his pasta fix at least once a week."

"I don't know if I'm Italian, but I'd eat spaghetti every day if I could."

Nick felt a pull of compassion for the boy. "What are some of your other favorite things?"

"Baseball," Scotty said without hesitation.

"What team?"

"The Red Sox."

"Get out of here," Nick said, laughing. "You're just saying that to impress me."

"I am not! I've always loved the Sox."

"I grew up just north of Boston. I've been a Sox fan all my life."

Scotty's eyes got very big. "Have you been to Fenway Park?"

"Many times." He didn't add that he'd been twenty-four the first time he could afford to attend a game at the fabled ballpark.

"Oh, you're so lucky! I'd give anything to go there and sit in the Monster seats. I've read every book I could find on the Red Sox and Fenway Park. Did you see the movie *Fever Pitch*? It's my favorite."

Nick wished he could wave a magic wand and be sitting atop the Green Monster wall in Fenway Park with Scotty and a couple of Fenway Franks. "I loved that movie. I'm sure you'll get to Fenway someday."

"As soon as I have any money, that's the first place I'll go."

"How did you become a fan?"

"My grandfather was from Boston. He talked about the Red Sox all the time. Ted Williams was his favorite player. Did you ever see him play?"

Nick winced. "How old do you think I am, man?"

"Oh, sorry."

Nick mussed his hair. "Don't be sorry. I was just kidding. Is your grandfather still alive?"

Scotty shook his head. "He had a heart attack when I was six. A month later, my mom OD'ed. That's how I ended up here." He ushered Nick into his small room. "But it's not so bad."

Nick's heart broke when he imagined the horror of six-year-old Scotty losing his grandfather and then his mother. "You don't have any other family?"

"Nope. My mom had sisters but they were estringed."

"You mean estranged?"

"Yeah, that's it. They didn't talk to her because of her drug problems."

"What about your dad?"

"Never knew him." He rifled through some things on the desk. "Check this out—a Dustin Pedroia rookie card."

Nick examined the cellophane-sealed baseball card. "Wow. Look at that. You should take really good care of it. I bet it'll be worth big money someday."

"That's what Mr. Sanchez said. He was my math teacher last year. He's a Nats fan," Scotty said, referring to the Washington Nationals. "He took me to a game when the Nats played the Sox in interleague play. It was my first time to a real ballpark, and I got to see the Sox. Best day of my life."

"I went to one of those games."

"The one I went to, the Sox won three to two."

"That's the one I was at!"

"Hey, that's cool."

Nick sat on the bed and looked around at the sparse room. "You need some posters for your walls. Who's your favorite player? I'll send you one."

"That's really nice of you, but we aren't allowed to hang stuff on our walls. The custodian says the tape takes the paint off."

Nick's scowl made the boy laugh.

"Rules are rules," Scotty said with a shrug.

"If we were breaking the rules for a minute, who would you want on your wall?"

"That's easy—Big Papi. He's the *bomb*."

Nick smiled. "His *bat* is the bomb."

"That's why I love him." Scotty sat next to Nick on the bed. "So you're really a senator?"

Even though it was still hard to believe sometimes, Nick said, "I really am."

"Isn't that kind of a boring job?"

Nick hooted with laughter. "It can be. You have to do a *lot* of reading."

Scotty's face screwed up with distaste. "I wouldn't like that. I *hate* to read."

"I used to hate it too, but now it's easier. Do you play any sports?"

"Just baseball with some of the other kids here. There's no money for Little League or anything like that."

Nick ached listening to his easy acceptance of the hand life had dealt him. Talking with Scotty brought back memories of his own lonely childhood, spent with a grandmother who'd never missed the opportunity to remind him that there were other things she'd rather be doing than raising her son's child.

"Do you play any sports?" Scotty asked.

"Just some pickup basketball here and there at the gym. I used to play a lot of hockey. I was pretty good at that."

"I'd *love* to play hockey, but it's really expensive."

"Yeah, it can be." Nick recalled how grateful he'd been the year his father sent enough money for him to play. "So this seems like a nice place to live."

"It's okay. One of the kids in my class at school is in foster care, and he has to move a lot. I wouldn't like that."

"You probably have more of a chance of being adopted here."

"Nah, everyone wants babies. They go fast. The rest of us have each other. It's kind of like having thirty brothers and sisters to fight with."

He was so matter of fact that Nick realized the child had stopped hoping anything would ever change.

Mrs. Littlefield appeared at the door. "I guess you can see why we call Scotty 'The Mayor,' Senator," she said with a smile. "He's never met a stranger."

"He's an excellent tour guide," Nick said, earning

a grin from the boy. "The next time the Sox come to Baltimore or Washington, what'd you say I get us a couple of tickets to a game?"

Scotty's eyes widened. "For real?"

"Sure. I'd love to take in a game with another Sox fan."

"But how would I get there?"

"You let me worry about that. You just take care of doing really well in school, okay?"

"Okay! Thank you!"

Nick stood up and shook hands with the boy. "It was great to meet you, Scotty."

"You too, Senator. Thanks for coming to see us."

"It was my pleasure." It had been, Nick realized, the most pleasant half hour he'd spent at work since he took the oath of office. With one last smile for the boy, Nick followed Mrs. Littlefield from the room. "What a delightful kid."

"He's the heart and soul of this place. The other kids follow him around like the Pied Piper. I don't know what we'd ever do without him."

"There's really no chance of him being adopted?"

Mrs. Littlefield sighed. "Unfortunately, the older he gets the less likely it becomes. But not to worry, we'll take good care of him until he comes of age."

"And then what? Who'll take care of him then?"

"I'm afraid I don't understand, Senator. He'll be an adult."

"I apologize for my tone. It's just that I was thrust out on my own at eighteen and found the world to be a rather harsh place for an 'adult.'"

"I understand what you mean, and I can assure you that Scotty will have plenty of adults to call on should he encounter any difficulties. My staff and I are quite fond of him."

"I have something I'd like to send him. Would it be possible to get his last name and the address here?"

She wrote the information on the back of her business card and handed it to him. "Here you go."

"Thank you."

They reached the front door and Nick shook her hand. "I appreciate your time today, Mrs. Littlefield. I'll have a chat with the people overseeing your grant and see what we can do about getting it renewed."

"We'll appreciate anything you can do, Senator."

"I'll be in touch," Nick said on his way out.

Tony held the car door open for him. Once inside the car, Nick looked back at the building. From an upstairs window, Scotty watched him leave. Nick glanced down at the business card in his hand. Scotty Dunlap. He reached for his BlackBerry and got busy ordering a David "Big Papi" Ortiz jersey.

SEVEN

SAM HIT THE speaker button and punched in the phone number for Regina's mother in Guatemala. Calling victims' families was the thing she hated most about her job, so she was relieved to turn the task over to Senator Lightfeather. Freddie, who spoke Spanish, was prepared to take notes on the exchange.

A woman answered the phone with a cheerful, "*Hola.*"

Appearing frozen, Lightfeather stared at the phone. Sam had no doubt that this phone call was even harder for him than the one he'd made earlier to his wife. "Senator?" she said softly.

He startled, seeming to realize all at once that everyone was waiting for him.

"*Hola?*" the woman said again.

"Señora Argueta?" he said, his voice rough with emotion. "*Yo estoy Senator Lightfeather.*"

Sam's limited Spanish allowed her to deduce that Mrs. Argueta recognized the senator's name and knew he was a friend of her daughter's.

He spoke softly for another moment before the woman on the other end released a wail of despair.

Sam's stomach clenched. How anyone survived receiving the news that their child had been murdered she'd never know. These moments were the only time she was ever grateful to be childless.

Tears cascaded down the senator's tanned face. He brushed them away as he continued to speak softly to the woman on the phone.

Sam glanced at Freddie's notes. Promising to arrange to have the body sent home as soon as he can, Freddie had written. Promising to continue helping her and Regina's children. No mention of the baby she'd been expecting.

Lightfeather concluded the phone call and rested his head on his folded arms. His shoulders shook with sobs.

Sam signaled to Freddie that they should give him a moment. Freddie followed her from the room.

"Hard to watch," Freddie muttered.

"Yeah."

"No question he genuinely loved her."

"Or had himself convinced that he did," Sam said.

"True. How do you want to get him out of here?"

"Take him out through the morgue. Check him into a hotel so we can keep tabs on him. Put a couple of officers on the door and let them know his wife will be joining him later today."

"Got it. What about the media?"

"I'll handle them." Sam left him to deal with the senator and returned to her office to find her nemesis, Lt. Stahl, waiting for her. "What do you want?"

"Nice to see you too, Lieutenant," Stahl said with a smarmy smile.

"I'm busy."

"Ahhh, yes, another homicide involving your 'boyfriend.' Quite a track record he has lately."

"He has nothing to do with this, nor did he have anything to do with John O'Connor's murder or Julian Sinclair's, as you well know. And PS, he's my *fiancé.*"

"Your *fiancé* knew all the victims."

"And that proves what, exactly?"

"That being an acquaintance of his can be bad for your health," Stahl said, laughing at his own joke.

"You aren't threatening me—again—are you, Lieutenant?"

"So touchy. Such a woman that way."

As usual in his presence, Sam held back the urge to smash her fist into his fat face. "As delightful as this conversation has been, I have work to do. If the rat squad isn't keeping you busy enough, Lieutenant, I'm sure Captain Malone can find something for you to do with your copious free time."

His jowls jiggled as he scowled at her. "Heard an interesting rumor today."

"Good for you."

"About your ex."

That got Sam's attention. "What about him?"

"That the case against him isn't as airtight as you thought it was."

She pushed her hands into her pockets to keep from punching him. "That case is airtight. I saw to it myself."

"Not all of it you didn't." On his way out the door, he said, "Have a nice day, Lieutenant."

Hands trembling, Sam reached for the phone to call Malone. "What do you know about Peter?"

The question was greeted with silence, which sent her heart into a wild gallop. "Tell me. Right now."

Under normal circumstances, she'd never speak so forcefully to her superior officer. But anything having to do with Peter tossed all the usual rules out the window.

"His attorney has requested a suppression hearing to determine whether the evidence gathered from his apartment is fruit of the poisonous tree."

The term turned her blood to ice. If the bomb-making evidence Freddie, Gonzo and Arnold had found in Peter's apartment had been gathered improperly, their entire case against him would be in jeopardy.

"We have his print on one of the bombs," Sam reminded Malone. "The one he strapped to Nick's car. The one that didn't detonate."

"It's a partial print, Sam. Not enough to hang the case on. We need the stuff from his apartment."

The very idea of Peter being set free after he'd tried to murder her and Nick made her sick.

"Don't panic yet," Malone said. "His attorney still has to convince the judge."

"What's the lawyer basing the challenge on?"

"That they kicked in Peter's door without any evidence linking him to the bombing other than your suspicion."

"But he did it!"

"We all know he did it, Sam. It's just the timeline of how we confirmed it that's under examination. They should've waited for the warrant before they busted into the apartment."

"They had reason to believe that he had bomb-making materials in there! Were they supposed to wait until he blew up the entire building before they acted?"

"They were running on adrenaline and emotion after you were nearly killed."

Sam sank into her desk chair. "He can*not* be released. He just can't be."

"We'll fight it. Try not to worry."

"You're worried. I can hear it in your voice."

"The chain of events concerns me. It has all along."

Sam released a low moan. "Oh, *God*. Oh my God."

"We have media out front clamoring for information about Lightfeather. Do you want me to handle them?"

"No," Sam said, pulling herself together. "I'll do it."

"We're doing everything we can to keep him where he belongs, Sam."

"I'm counting on that. Keep me posted?"

"I will."

She hung up the phone and tried to breathe through the pain circulating in her gut. Since Nick's doctor friend Harry had ordered her to give up soda, her stomach troubles had been dramatically better. Hearing that Peter might be released from prison, however, brought the pain back in fierce waves. Sam forced herself to breathe—in through the nose, out through the mouth. Repeat.

A few minutes later, she stood up on shaking legs and reached for her coat. She had a job to do, and not even the threat of her malicious ex-husband being released from jail could keep her from doing what needed to be done on Regina's behalf. The dead woman's family was counting on Sam for answers, and she would get them what they needed no matter what might be happening in her own life.

Fueled by determination to do what needed to be done, Sam headed for the lobby.

Chief Farnsworth flagged her down before she could head outside. "Lieutenant." His warm gray eyes studied her with concern.

"Chief."

"You've heard the news about Gibson."

"Lieutenant Stahl took great pleasure in cueing me in."

"Sorry. I was on my way to talk to you about it when I got waylaid. Are you all right?"

She nodded. "I'm working the de Castro case. Doing what I do."

"We're making use of all available resources to keep Gibson where he belongs."

"I'm counting on that. Well, the press is looking to take a piece out of me, and you know how I hate to keep them waiting."

The chief laughed. "Allow me to have your back," he said, gesturing for the door.

As always, Sam was grateful for his unwavering support.

The instant they stepped through the double doors, the reporters pounced.

"Has Senator Lightfeather been arrested for murder?"

"How does he know the dead woman?"

"Were they having an affair?"

"Is he in custody?"

The chief held up his hands to stop the barrage of questions. "If you give Lieutenant Holland the chance to speak, she has a brief statement that should answer some of your questions."

Sam stepped forward, burrowing deeper into her coat. The February day had grown frigid and stormy. "Senator Lightfeather discovered Regina Argueta de Castro dead last night in her Columbia Heights apartment."

"How did he know her?"

"She worked for the company that cleans the Capitol and congressional offices. Throughout the night, the senator cooperated with our efforts to confirm his alibi, which we have now done. He has been released with instructions to remain in the District until we close the case. Ms. Argueta de Castro was from Guatemala and was in the country legally. Her mother and two children in Guatemala survive her, and they have been notified of her death. That is all I'm going to say at this point. We'll keep you informed as developments occur."

"Were they romantically involved?"

"No comment."

"How do you feel about your ex being sprung from prison?"

"Absolutely no comment."

As Chief Farnsworth ushered her back inside, Sam

realized if the press knew about Peter it was only a matter of time before Nick would hear about it too.

"I need to make a phone call," she said to the chief.

"Go right ahead."

Sam started to walk away but turned back when he called out to her.

"If he gets sprung," the chief said, "we'll be so far up his ass he won't be able to fart without us knowing about it."

"Thanks." Sam didn't trust herself to say anything more without losing her famous cool. She knew he was trying to comfort her, but the very thought of that monster on the loose again was enough to turn her legs to jelly. He'd tried to *blow her up*. All because she'd reconciled with Nick—six years after Peter had gone to extraordinary lengths to keep them apart.

Back in the detective's pit, she closed the door to her office, sank into her chair and called Nick.

"Hey, babe," he said. "How's it going?"

The smile she heard in his voice went a long way toward soothing her frayed nerves. "I've had better days. You?"

"What's wrong? And don't say it's nothing."

"This time it's not nothing." She told him about Peter's case possibly falling apart.

"You've got to be fucking kidding me."

That he was swearing told her a lot about how upset he was. Nick never swore. That was *her* claim to fame. "I wish I was."

"We've got to do something. What can we do?"

"There will be a hearing, and hopefully the judge has an ounce of sense."

"If they let him go, he'll come at you again."

"Maybe his stint in prison has scared some sense into him."

"You don't believe that any more than I do. He's totally obsessed with you, and now he's even more pissed off than he was before."

"Malone and Farnsworth assured me they're doing everything they can to keep him in jail."

"Does he have a leg to stand on with this hearing?"

"He might," Sam said, hating to admit it. She filled him in on the issue with the warrant. "If they suppress the evidence we found in his apartment, our entire case falls apart. A partial print isn't enough to prosecute."

"This is such *bullshit*! He was caught red-handed!"

"I hate to do this to you when you're so busy. Sorry."

"I'm never too busy for you, babe. And you have nothing to be sorry about. You're the victim in this case."

"We both are." He'd been more severely injured in the bombing, suffering a mild concussion and a cut over his eye that had required stitches and left a scar.

"I'll make a few phone calls," he said. "See what I can find out."

"Don't do anything politically risky, Nick. That'd be playing right into his hand."

"They're phone calls. That's all."

She had no doubt one of those calls would be to the U.S. Attorney himself. Her fiancé was nothing if not well connected in Washington.

"Are you okay?" he asked softly.

"I'll be better when you get home tonight."

"I'll be there as soon as I can break free of the fundraising thing."

"Good luck with that."

"Thanks. How's Henry?"

"Sprung for now. His wife is on her way here from Arizona."

"Yikes. I don't envy him that confrontation."

"If he'd kept his fly zipped, there'd be nothing to confront him about."

"True," Nick said, chuckling.

"You know I'd have to kill you, don't you?"

"Kill me for what? What've I done now?"

"If you ever cheated," she said in a small voice, instantly regretting going there. She tensed, awaiting his reply.

"Samantha," he said, his tone chastising. "Tell me you didn't just say that."

"I didn't just say that. I know I have nothing to worry about, even when all that senatorial power goes to your head."

"It may go to my head, but it'll never get to my zipper."

Sam laughed. He always knew just what to say to her. "I'll see you when you get home."

"Yes, you will, and we'll have a more in-depth discussion about who gets access to my zipper—and who does not."

"I'll look forward to that, Senator."

"As well you should. Love you, babe. Thanks for calling and giving me a heads-up about Peter."

She'd learned the hard way not to keep things from him and appreciated that he recognized she was making an effort in that area of their relationship. "Love you too. See you soon."

Sam put down the phone and gave herself a moment to decompress before she considered her next move in Regina's case. She was going over the less-than-fruitful reports from the crime scene detectives and the canvas of Regina's building when Freddie stepped into the office, a grim expression on his face.

"What's the matter?"

EIGHT

"NOTHING," FREDDIE said, startled by the question. "I just walked in the door. What makes you think something's the matter?"

"I know you, and I can tell just by looking at you that something is wrong. You've been off all morning."

"So on top of all your other formidable skills, now you're psychic too?"

"Sit," she said, pointing to the door and then the chair on the other side of her desk.

Frowning, Freddie pushed the door closed and sat. "What?"

"Tell me what's wrong."

"It's nothing to do with work or the case. Lightfeather is stashed at the Washington Hilton with two guards as directed. No one followed us, and I checked him in under the name of Jim Dalton. Can I get back to work now?"

"Not until you tell me why your shoulders are hunched and you haven't smiled all day."

"I'm tired, and we're working a rape and murder. Am I supposed to be whistling 'Dixie' at the same time? I wasn't aware of that job requirement."

"Despite your sarcasm, you're not walking out that door until you tell me what's bugging you."

"Just because we've talked about stuff in the past doesn't mean I have to share my every thought with you."

Wow, he was really in a mood. Sam raised a brow to let him know he wasn't going to escape her clutches.

"I'm sorry," he muttered, slumping into the chair. "I shouldn't talk to you that way."

"When it's just you and me and the door is closed, you should speak to me any way you see fit." It was as close as she'd ever come to letting him know she valued their friendship as much as their working relationship.

Seeming surprised, he said, "So it's okay to tell you you're being nosy and that you should butt out?"

"Sure, but it doesn't mean I will."

"God, you're a *pain*."

She smiled. Nick often said the same thing about her, and Sam always took it as a compliment. "I prefer *dogged*."

"That too," Freddie said. "Fine! If you must know, my mother is driving me crazy."

Sam hadn't seen that coming. "Over what?"

Freddie gave her a "you know" look.

"Ahhh, Mama Cruz doesn't approve of the girl-friend, huh?"

"No," he said miserably. "And she won't even give Elin a chance. We had a good talk last night and I thought things would be better, but when I went to check on her before work this morning, we got into it again. Not sure if it's the fever or what, but she's making me nuts!"

Sam stood up, clipped her portable radio to her hip

and grabbed her car keys. "Let's discuss this on the road."

He stood. "Where're we going?"

"First to talk to Regina's boss and then hopefully to some of her coworkers."

"I'm with you, boss."

Sam waited while he got the trench coat that he claimed made him feel like Colombo and then led the way to her car. After starting the car she gave some considerable thought to Freddie's predicament. "I can understand where Mama is coming from."

"Great," he said, his voice dripping with sarcasm. "Thanks for the support. I really appreciate it."

"Wait. Hear me out. It's just that when I think of you with a woman, I see someone…different…than Elin for you. Someone…softer, I guess."

"What about what *I* see? Doesn't anyone care about what *I* want?"

"Hmm," Sam said. "How to say this delicately?"

"Oh, for crying out loud. Just say it. What do you care about being delicate?"

"It seems…to those of us on the outside looking in…that you may be letting your, um, little brain do the thinking for your big brain."

Out of the corner of her eye, she caught the glare he directed her way. "That's not the case."

"Are you sure of that?"

"I *like* her! Why doesn't anyone believe that's possible?"

"Okay, I'll bite. What do you like about her?"

"She's…fun and nice and sweet."

"Uh huh. What else?"

"What do you mean what else? Isn't that enough?"

"No. Fun and sweet and nice is not enough to build a relationship on."

"It's more than Nick started with. There's nothing nice or sweet about you."

Sam snorted with laughter. "Good one."

"Thank you. I try."

"What do you talk to her about besides 'your place or mine'?"

"We talk about sports and our friends, our work. The usual stuff."

"If you're together three hours, how much of that time is spent talking?"

"I don't know. I hardly keep track of that."

"Guess."

She could see him squirming in the passenger seat. "An hour or so."

"So one hour talking, two hours screwing. Can you see why your mother might be concerned?"

"No! She doesn't know that!"

"Freddie, come on. Of course she knows. You practically pant and drool whenever Elin is around. It's obvious to everyone that you're hot for her."

"I ask again…so *what*? Why does everyone care so much that I'm hot for her?"

"Because it's not like you to be so…preoccupied."

"I waited a long time for this, Sam. I wish everyone would butt the heck out and let me live my own life."

"We're worried about you. That's all."

"Well, don't worry. I'm a big boy, and I can take care

of myself. I don't need you and my mother ganging up on me and screwing with my head. I'm happy with Elin. Can't that be enough for you?"

"I'm sure you're very happy when you're in bed with her. It's the rest of the time we're concerned about."

"You don't know what you're talking about, and to be honest, it's none of your business. Or my mother's."

"That's very true. So I will do as you ask and butt out."

"Good."

"Fine."

They rode the rest of the way to the Capitol Cleaning Services headquarters in uneasy—and unusual—silence. Inside, they were ushered into the offices of JoAnn Smithson, the owner of the company.

Mrs. Smithson looked to be in her late fifties or early sixties, and judging from her haggard appearance, Sam deduced she hadn't slept well the night before.

After giving them permission to record the interview, Mrs. Smithson folded her hands on top of her cluttered desk. "What can I do to help you find the person who did this to Regina?"

"How long had she been in your employ?" Sam asked.

"Just over two years." She retrieved a file from a stack on the desk and handed it to them. "Here's her personnel file. As you can see, she had all the proper paperwork."

Freddie reached for the folder and flipped through the contents.

"If we checked the rest of your files, we'd find that to be true of all your employees?" Sam asked.

Mrs. Smithson stiffened. "We do *not* hire undocumented workers. We work for *Congress*, Lieutenant. How long do you think we'd hold that contract if I had illegal workers traipsing through the Capitol?"

"Not long I'd imagine. How well did you know Regina?"

"Quite well. I make it a point to know all my employees." She sagged into the chair. "Her poor mother and children. Have they been told of her death?"

"Yes. Were you aware of her relationship with Senator Lightfeather?"

Mrs. Smithson sat up straighter. "Relationship? What relationship did she have with a senator? She cleaned his office."

"According to the senator, they were romantically involved."

The color drained from Mrs. Smithson's face. "That's not possible," she sputtered. "We have rules… strict rules about decorum and behavior. She wouldn't have…" She glanced up at Sam and Freddie. Their expressions must have confirmed the truth. Once again she sagged. "I can't believe this."

"How much was she paid?"

"Seventeen dollars an hour, plus benefits."

"We'd like to speak to some of her friends or coworkers, anyone who might've been aware of what was going on between Regina and the senator. We're also looking for some insight into her life outside of work."

"Maria Espanosa," Mrs. Smithson said. "They were close friends."

"Where can we find her?"

Mrs. Smithson wrote down an address, also in Columbia Heights, and handed it to Sam. "She didn't come into work last night, and no one has heard from her. I planned to check on her when I leave the office."

Sam churned with anxiety. "Is it like her to miss work?"

"She's never missed a shift."

Sam glanced at Freddie and sensed they were on the same wavelength.

Mrs. Smithson watched their silent communication. "You don't think…"

"We'll check on her and let you know what we find."

"Will it be all over the media that Regina was messing around with a senator?"

"We haven't confirmed that information to the press yet," Sam said. "But it's only a matter of time before it becomes public."

"Oh God," Mrs. Smithson said, massaging her temples as tears flooded her already-reddened eyes. "God. Everything I've worked for…all these years. We have rules…"

"You might want to look into hiring a firm that specializes in crisis communication," Freddie suggested. "So you can be prepared to deal with the media."

"Yes," Mrs. Smithson said, brightening. "That's a good idea. Thank you."

"We'll be in touch if we need any further information."

"I'd appreciate that," Mrs. Smithson said as she escorted them past the wary glances of several other employees on their way to the main door. "Please let me know when you find Maria."

"We will," Freddie assured her.

"While we're on the Hill," Sam said to Freddie once they were outside, "let's take a look at the senator's office."

He grunted in reply.

Sam stopped and turned to him. "I know you're pissed with me, and that's your prerogative, but try to keep in mind that I only said what I did because I don't want you to end up heartbroken at the end of this. Trust me when I tell you that's no fun at all."

"I heard everything you said. And I've heard everything my mother has had to say. Now I'd really appreciate it if you'd both leave me alone to live my own life."

"Sure thing," she said, even as she wondered how she'd ever stand idly by and watch a woman walk all over his tender heart with stiletto heels. "I don't know about you, but I want to see this famous sofa where the senator boffed the cleaning lady."

Freddie rolled his eyes at her crudeness, and Sam hoped they'd put things back on track.

GONZO SAT PERFECTLY still and tried to stay focused on what the lawyer, Andy, was saying in response to Christina's many questions. Words flew past him:

DNA tests, custody hearings, social workers. All he could think about was that dimpled chin. He didn't need a DNA test to tell him he'd met his son earlier that day—and the child's mother hadn't even given him a name.

"He can't breathe in that house," Gonzo said, interrupting them. He felt like he was coming out of his skin as he remembered the conditions in which his son was living. "We have to get him out of there."

"We'll move as quickly as we can to file for custody," Andy assured him. Blond and handsome, he looked every bit the Yale-educated attorney. "Of course, we can't do a thing until we've confirmed paternity."

"He looks like me," Gonzo said. "He has my dimple."

"I'm glad you were able to see a basic resemblance," Andy said, smiling. "That'll help you to feel confident you're doing the right thing pursuing custody."

"I'd want him out of there if he was mine or not. She didn't even give him a name." Gonzo simply couldn't get his head around that.

"I know, Detective," Andy said. "It's inexcusable. I have a baby of my own and can't imagine him living nameless in a smoke-infested environment. However, I have to caution you, custody cases can often be an uphill battle for fathers. Even when the father proves he can provide a better home than the mother, the courts often rule in favor of the mother."

Gonzo couldn't believe what he was hearing. "Even if she's filling his little lungs with smoke?"

"Unfortunately, it often has to be something more than that to get the court's attention—abuse, drugs, criminal activity occurring inside the home. Smoke, on its own, won't be enough."

"I'd bet my badge that smoking isn't the only thing going on there." Gonzo cast a wary glance at Christina. "She was quite the partier when I knew her."

"Any information you happen to 'stumble upon' that can be used against her in court would be information worth having, if you catch my drift."

Gonzo took in the pointed look Andy directed his way and nodded to show he understood what Andy was telling him.

"I'll do what I can for you, as long as you understand that the odds are stacked against you going in," Andy said. "And these things can get very, very costly."

"I hate to ask this because I'll pay whatever it takes, but, ah, how much are we talking?"

"Tens of thousands."

Gonzo winced. He had some money, but not that much. No matter. He'd find a way to get what he needed to protect his son, including an appeal to his parents if it came to that.

"Don't worry about the money," Christina said, casting an uncomfortable glance his way. Before Gonzo could ask what she meant, she stood and extended her hand to Andy. "Thank you so much for coming into the office on a Sunday."

"Any friend of the senator's is a friend of mine." He shook Gonzo's hand. "I'll call Social Services to get them over there to check on him, and I'll get the ball rolling with the request for DNA from the baby. If she's interested in your money, she's apt to give up the DNA without objection. Give me a day or two, and I'll be in touch."

"Thank you," Gonzo said. "I appreciate your help."

Feeling as if he was outside himself watching someone else navigate the elevator, Gonzo was aware of Christina silently guiding him back to the car. Once there, he turned to her. "What'd you mean in there? About the money?"

She looked up at him. "I have some. If it comes to that."

Shaking his head, he said, "No way. I'm not taking money from you."

"You heard what he said, Tommy," she said, her hands resting on his chest. He wondered if she could feel his heart racing. "This could get really expensive. What if you run out of money before you get custody?"

"I'll borrow it, but I'm not taking it from you."

"I don't just have some," she said haltingly. "I have a lot. My parents…my family is, um, well, we have money. It'd be nothing to me to help you out if you need it."

"I appreciate the offer, but I'm sure it won't come to that." He stepped out of her embrace and opened the car door for her. When she was settled he went around to the driver's side. On the way to her place, Gonzo tried to process everything that had happened.

"Is this going to change everything between us?" she asked after a long period of silence.

"Is what? The baby?"

"The money," she said in a small voice that told him it had changed things for her in the past.

"Why should it?"

"You'd be surprised how it can change things." Rubbing a hand over her jeans, she added, "For what it's worth, I live on what I make. I've never allowed money to be a big deal in my life."

"Easy to do when you've always had plenty of it." The instant the words were out of his mouth, he regretted them. Her shocked expression indicated a direct hit. He reached for her hand. "I'm sorry. I didn't mean that the way it sounded. I appreciate the offer. I really do, but I hope it doesn't come to that."

"I hope not either, but if it does, the offer is on the table."

Gonzo squeezed her hand even as he continued to buzz with apprehension. The thought of the baby—his son—in that smoke-filled house… And that there might be nothing he could do about it… That made him shudder.

"Come in, Tommy," Christina said when they reached her house. "You shouldn't be alone tonight."

"I'm not fit for company."

"Don't do this. Don't push me away."

"Christina—"

She reached for him and pressed her lips to his.

When he tried to pull back, she sank her fingers into his hair and held him close to her. "Don't go."

"I'm all churned up."

"Then be churned up with me. We'll figure this out. I promise."

He leaned his forehead against hers. "You're sure you want to take all this on? I wouldn't blame you—"

She rested a finger over his lips. "Let's go in."

As Gonzo stepped out of the car and followed her inside, he had to admit he was grateful not have to spend the night alone with his thoughts.

NINE

In Henry Lightfeather's office, Sam studied the array of family photos displayed on the credenza. Like Henry, his wife Annette seemed to have Native American origins. Their five adopted children were ethnically diverse. One was in a wheelchair. They seemed to be a happy, smiling family in the many photographs. In addition to the group shot, there were individual photos of each of the children as well as framed samples of their artwork.

"I would've felt like they were watching," Sam said.

"Watching what?" Freddie asked.

"While I was doing the cleaning lady on the sofa, I'd have felt like my family was watching with all these pictures right here."

Freddie snorted. "I'll bet they were the last thing he was concerned about when he was doing the cleaning lady on the sofa." He opened a door. "We've got a closet full of suits and personal items. Shaving kit, running shoes, sweats."

Sam opened the door to talk to the Capitol Police officer who'd escorted them into the office. "Were you aware that he was living in his office?"

"We know everything that goes on in these buildings."

"Are there rules about members living in their offices?"

"It's frowned upon, but not unheard of. The cost of living in this city is exorbitant. A lot of members have trouble swinging two places."

"So we've heard." Sam took another look around the spacious office. "We're through here for now, but we may be back. Do us a favor and keep people out of here until we give you the okay."

"Does that include the senator?"

"That includes everyone."

He nodded in agreement.

"Thanks for the courtesy," Sam said.

Lindsey McNamara called as they headed for Maria Espanosa's apartment in Columbia Heights. "What've you got, Doc?"

"No match on the second semen sample with anyone in the system," Lindsey said. "And no shock that Lightfeather is a match for the other."

"Well, we knew he would be." Sam smacked the palm of her hand on the steering wheel. "Why couldn't the other guy have been in the system?"

"Because if it was that easy, none of us would have jobs," Lindsey quipped.

"Yeah, yeah. You're running the fetus, right?"

"As we speak. Another point of interest is the skin we found under her nails was a match with the mystery semen. So we can confirm it was the second guy who roughed her up, not the senator."

"At least that's something. She put up a fight."

"Judging from the skin we found, she scratched him good."

"Thanks for the info, Lindsey. Keep me posted on the fetus."

"You got it."

Sam punched the speaker button on the phone to shut it off. "What're you thinking so far?" she asked Freddie.

"I'm trying to picture how a cleaning lady becomes a United States senator's lover."

"Well, if a cop can do it…"

Freddie laughed.

"Sorry, bad joke. Please proceed."

"While it doesn't seem that Lightfeather did the murder, how can her affair with him not be related somehow?"

"I agree. It would've been a huge bombshell for both of them if anyone found out."

"With him having the most to lose."

"Or so we assume. Maybe the stakes were higher for her."

"Her immigration status would be in jeopardy if she lost her job, and her family was counting on her support," Freddie said.

"The stakes were high for both of them."

"You gotta wonder what they were thinking that first time."

"Probably safe to assume not much thinking was involved."

"Imagine afterward though…when the reality sunk in."

"Total freak-out," Sam said. "On both parts."

"What if someone found out? Someone who would've been furious or jealous or threatened."

"Do you think she'd tell anyone?"

"No," Freddie said emphatically. "Absolutely not."

"Not even her closest friends?"

"I wonder if she had close friends here."

"Let's talk to Maria Espanosa and find out," Sam said.

Maria lived in a basement apartment about four blocks from Regina's place. They knocked on the door and waited.

"Something stinks," Freddie said.

"She ain't home," a young voice from the street called down to them.

They turned to face the boy, who Sam gauged to be ten or eleven.

"Any idea where she is?" Sam asked.

The kid shrugged. "Don't know. Haven't seen her in a coupla days."

Sam and Freddie exchanged glances.

"You cops?" the boy asked.

"That's right," Freddie said.

"Cool. Can I watch?"

"Not this time, buddy." Freddie went up the half set of stairs to speak to the boy while Sam called in their location to dispatch.

"Possible DOA," she told the dispatcher. To the kid, she called, "Any idea where we can find the super?"

"Sure. My grandpa. I'll get him for ya."

"Thanks, man," Freddie said. "Tell him to bring his keys."

The kid scampered off, and Freddie came back down to join Sam. "Smell plus gone a few days equals murder."

"Your thinking matches mine."

"Who would have a beef with two members of the Capitol Cleaning Services?"

"Not sure yet, but you can bet we're going to find out."

The super arrived a few minutes later with a fat wad of keys. His grandson trailed behind him.

"You might want to get the kid out of here," Sam said.

"Mario," the old man barked. "Scram!"

"Aw, Gramps, come on!"

"*Scram*, I said!"

"Nothing fun *ever* happens around here, and then when it does..." His mutterings faded as he clomped off.

The old man unlocked the door. "Holy hell, what's that reek?"

"Most likely a dead body," Sam said as she pushed past him.

He startled. "Hey, this ain't that kinda place! I run a clean building."

Sam ignored him as she followed the smell to the bedroom where she found Maria's naked, bloody body on the bed. "Call it in," she said to Freddie as she stepped in for a closer look at the open wound on Maria's neck. A pool of blood between her legs indicated a vicious sexual assault. "Same as Regina."

"Defensive injuries to her hands," Freddie said.

"Looks like she connected with the knife before it found her throat."

He shook his head with dismay. "Poor thing."

"Start a canvas of the neighborhood. See if you can figure out when she was last seen alive."

"Judging from the smell and the condition of the body, I'd guess thirty-six hours or more."

"Agreed. Which means he did her before Regina. That leads me to wonder if there are others waiting to be found."

"I'll get going on that canvas," Freddie said. "I assume you'll want her cell phone dumped?"

Sam nodded. "How much you want to bet it's the same company? Get a subpoena and let them know if they continue to stonewall us, they'll be hearing from the U.S. Attorney himself."

"Got it."

Left alone with the dead woman, Sam studied the framed photographs on the bedside table. Several young children and a shot of Maria with what must've been her parents. Sam wondered if, like Regina, Maria also had children living in another country. The one-room apartment where she'd been killed was spartanly furnished with just a bed and dresser. A small television sat on top of the dresser. Sam deduced that Maria did little more than sleep and bathe in this space. There wasn't much room for anything else.

While waiting for crime scene detectives to arrive,

Sam went through the papers she found in the bedside table drawer. Along with a passport from Belize, she found papers authorizing Maria to work in the United States as well as cards and letters from her family at home. Drawing a notebook from her back pocket, Sam wrote down the name and return address that appeared most frequently on the letters in anticipation of making another of those dreaded phone calls.

Lindsey McNamara came down the short flight of stairs into the apartment. "What've you got, Sam?"

"Same M.O. as Regina, right down to the rape."

"Someone's gunning for young immigrant women," Lindsey said as she snapped on latex gloves.

"Starting to seem that way. They had that in common along with their jobs, but what's the motive? Could it be that they stumbled upon something in the course of their jobs that someone didn't want them to know?"

"I can't imagine that members of Congress leave sensitive information laying around the offices for the cleaning staff to find."

"Unless they were sent in to look for something specific," Sam speculated.

"I suppose that's possible."

Crime scene detectives soon descended upon the apartment.

"Get me that report ASAP, Doc," Sam said on her way out.

"You got it," Lindsey said.

Sam took the stairs to the street level where a crowd had formed, no doubt hoping for a glimpse of the murdered woman's body. As she took deep gulping breaths to rid her senses of the death smell, Sam doubted they'd be so curious if they saw even a fraction of what she did on any given day.

Freddie jogged down the street to join her. "Last confirmed sighting was yesterday morning," he reported, consulting his notes. "The owner of the coffee shop on the corner said she bought her usual soy latte after her morning run. From what the neighbors said, she worked nights, ran five miles after her shift ended, got her latte and then went home to sleep. Never deviated from the routine. Seven days a week."

"So someone was either watching her or knew her routine and was waiting for her when she got back to her apartment. Maybe took her by surprise or pulled the knife to get her inside."

"No one I've talked to so far recalls a man hanging out in the area."

"Mrs. Smithson said they work five nights a week cleaning the Capitol, right?"

"Uh huh."

"And Lightfeather said Regina spent 'most nights' after work with him, but they argued about where she was the other nights."

"Right."

"I want to know where they were those other two nights too." Sam consulted her watch. Almost seven o'clock. "Let's turn the canvas over to second shift and pick this up in the morning. We'll meet at HQ at seven and bring everyone up to speed on what we have so far. I'll talk to Malone about putting out an alert to immigrant women in the city, just in case this isn't related to where they worked."

"You don't think it's unrelated, though, do you?"

Sam rested her hands on her hips. "I'm leaning toward related, but I've learned not to make assumptions until I know more."

"We'll hit it hard in the morning," Freddie said.

"You bet we will."

She handed him the slip of paper with Maria's family contact information. "Until then, I need you to make a phone call."

Freddie glanced at the paper. "Ugh. Do I have to?"

"Someone does, and just in case they don't speak English, you get the short straw. While you're at it, give JoAnn Smithson a call too. Let her know about Maria."

"Oh gee, lucky me." He snatched the paper from her. "I hate making these calls."

"Don't we all, Detective? Don't we all?"

SAM SPENT AN hour at HQ updating the murder board and making notes about what she knew about the two victims, which wasn't much. Regina was thirty, Maria twenty-eight. Both had been in the country for about two years. Both had applied for permanent citizenship. Sam knew Regina's application had been denied, but Maria's status was unclear. She wondered if Senator Lightfeather would know and decided to pay him a visit on the way home.

After consulting with Captain Malone, she issued an alert to the media to warn young immigrant women living in the city to be vigilant in and around their places of residence. She didn't mention the similarities between the two murders, lest she set off hysteria in the city. Hopefully, they could apprehend the perpetrator before that became necessary.

On her way to the Washington Hilton on Connecticut Avenue, she received a call from Darren Tabor.

"No comment," she said as she activated the speaker on her phone.

"I haven't asked the question yet."

"Just because Nick and I gave you one exclusive doesn't mean you can randomly call me any time you want." Sam had reluctantly agreed to sit for a joint interview with Nick after their engagement. They'd granted the interview to Tabor because he'd given them a heads-up that the *Reporter* tabloid planned to run a story about Sam's long-ago near-abortion and figured they owed him one. Now they were even—at least as far as Sam was concerned.

"I made you look really good in that article," Tabor said.

Sam snorted. "I don't need your help to look really good."

Laughing, Tabor said, "You might want to work on your self-esteem, Lieutenant. I hate to see you so down on yourself."

Sam choked back a chuckle. She wouldn't give him the satisfaction.

"Just saw your alert to immigrant women," Tabor said. "What else can you tell me?"

"Nothing yet."

"Do you have a second victim?"

"Maybe. Maybe not."

"You must if you saw fit to issue the alert."

"Don't you dare report that, Darren. I'm not confirming anything."

"That's okay. I can check the logs. They'll tell me what you're not."

"I'll leave you to make your own conclusions."

"What's Lightfeather's status?"

"I told you all earlier—he's been cleared on any involvement in the murder of Regina Argueta de Castro."

"You can't do your favorite reporter a favor and confirm they were involved?"

"Give it a rest, Darren. I'm outta here." She shut off the phone and pulled up to the Washington Hilton a few minutes later. Flashing her badge to the bellhop who met her, Sam said, "I'll be just a few minutes."

"The person you no doubt wish to see is on the seventh floor."

"Thank you." Now why couldn't everyone be that cooperative toward the police?

Sam took the elevator to the seventh floor and made her way to the room at the end of the hallway where two of her colleagues stood watch outside the door. "How goes it?" she asked them.

"Pretty quiet, Lieutenant."

"Is the wife here yet?"

"Arrived about thirty minutes ago."

"Any fireworks?"

The two young men smirked.

"That's one way to describe it. She is *not* happy with him."

"With good reason," Sam said as she knocked on the door.

Annette Lightfeather opened the door and blanched at the sight of Sam's badge. "Yes?"

"Mrs. Lightfeather, I'm Detective Lieutenant Sam Holland. I'd like to speak to your husband, please."

"I understood that he'd been cleared of any involvement in the…the—"

"Murder of Regina Argueta de Castro."

The attractive woman swallowed hard. "Yes." Her eyes were red and raw, as if she'd cried her way across the country. Sam couldn't blame her. In her place, Sam would probably never stop crying.

"I have some follow-up questions I'd like to ask him."

Annette gestured for her to come in.

Henry sat on the sofa, head in his hands.

"Senator," Sam said.

His head shot up, and his eyes widened when he saw her there. "Lieutenant. Have you found the person who killed Regina?"

Annette's lips tightened into an expression of supreme dismay. Her attractive face was totally transformed by rage.

"I'm afraid not," Sam said. "In fact, there's been a second murder. Were you acquainted with Regina's friend Maria Espanosa?"

Henry gasped and his mouth fell open in apparent shock. "Not Maria too!"

"Were you also sleeping with her?" Annette's voice was one note shy of a shriek.

"Of course not," Henry said haltingly. "She was a close friend of Regina's."

"What was Maria's immigration status?"

He glanced at his wife and then at Sam. "Like Regina, she'd applied for permanent residency but had been denied."

"Did you intervene on her behalf as well?" Sam asked.

As Annette watched the proceedings, her expression shifted from dismay to disbelief. "You went to INS for her?" she asked.

"I made some phone calls," Henry said. "That's all it was. Phone calls."

"For your *lover*," Annette spat back at him. "Did she make you feel like the big powerful man?"

"Mrs. Lightfeather." Sam wished the floor would open up and swallow her. She'd rather be anywhere else on earth than in the midst of their marital meltdown. "I understand you're upset—"

"*Upset*? You think I'm *upset*? While I'm at home raising our *five* children, he's here banging the cleaning lady *in his office*? I'm not upset, Lieutenant. I'm *livid*."

"Annette—"

"Shut up, Henry. Just shut up." She stormed from the suite's living room and slammed the bedroom door.

Sam let an uncomfortable minute pass before she ventured a glance at Henry. The guy looked awful. Under most circumstances, Sam had sympathy for someone who'd lost a loved one in a violent manner.

In this case, however, she was having trouble working up the usual level of sympathy.

"I, um, I know this is a difficult time for you, Senator, but I wondered if you might be willing to answer a few more questions."

Sighing, he gestured for her to go ahead.

Sam sat in a high-backed chair facing him. "How well did you know Maria?"

"I'd met her a few times. When Regina and I took a break from our relationship, Maria cleaned my office. I just don't understand why anyone would want to hurt them. They were hard-working women who only wanted to better themselves and their families. What could anyone have against them?"

"I don't know yet, but we're going to find out. What was Maria's immigration status?"

"It was similar to Regina's. She'd been denied permanent residency, and we'd appealed it."

"Did Regina ask you to do that?"

He nodded. "Once again, I had to be careful not to get too involved because neither of them was my constituent. However, I did make a few calls to see if there was anything that could be done. Last I heard, both applications were under review. We were hopeful for a positive outcome."

"I know you told your wife you weren't involved with Maria." She cleared her throat. "Too. Is that the truth?"

Henry gaped at her. "Yes! I swear to God, it was only Regina."

"Have you assisted any of Regina's other friends with their immigration status?"

He shook his head. "Just Maria."

"Did Maria have any friends, boyfriends, anyone in the city she was close to that you know of?"

"I think it was just Regina. They relied on each other, kept to themselves for the most part."

Having gotten what she came for, Sam stood. "I appreciate the additional information. I have to remind you to stay put until we close the case."

"The media's caught wind of the affair. Believe me, I'm not going anywhere." He walked Sam to the door. "I know what you must think of me, Lieutenant."

Sam turned to him. "What I think of you has no bearing on the fact that I'm going to do my job and get justice for two women who were killed in my city."

"I'm not a bad person. I just made a bad mistake."

"So you've decided that falling in love with Regina was a mistake?" For some reason, Sam took perverse pleasure in picking at the scab. "That's not what you said last night."

He glanced over his shoulder, as if to gauge whether his wife might be able to hear him. "I *loved* her," he said in a hoarse whisper. "And I don't regret that. I *do* regret the pain my mistake in judgment is causing my wife and family. I deeply regret that."

"I'm sure you do," Sam said. "I'll be in touch."

TEN

SAM ARRIVED AT home just as Nick's driver was dropping him off. From inside her car, she watched him emerge from the Town Car, still wearing the tuxedo from the fundraiser. He leaned into the car to say something to the driver, and as he closed the door, he glanced over to find her watching him. A smile lit up his face.

Sam got out of her car and met him on the sidewalk.

He was carrying his overcoat, a garment bag and briefcase but still managed to slide an arm around her and kiss her forehead.

Sam leaned into his embrace, breathing in the clean fresh scent of home.

"Long day, huh?" he asked.

"For both of us."

He guided her into the house and hung their coats in the closet. Tugging off the bow tie and releasing the top button on his shirt, he went into the kitchen. "How about a glass of wine?"

Sam sat on the sofa and put her feet up on the coffee table. "Yes, please."

"Coming right up." He returned a few minutes later with two glasses of pinot grigio and put them on the table. "First things first." Sitting next to her, he reached for her and kissed her gently. "There," he said against her lips. "That's what I've been needing for hours now."

Sam ran her fingers over the stubble on his jaw and urged him into another kiss. He stretched out on top of her as one kiss became two and then three. Sam's fingers were buried in his soft hair as his lips moved from her mouth to her face and then her neck.

"I missed you today," he whispered, sending sensation darting through her.

She raised her hips and pressed against his erection, drawing a gasp from him. "So I can tell."

"I didn't plan to jump you the minute we walked in the door."

"You didn't. You were just saying hello."

That smile of his was so potent. She wondered if he had any idea what it did to her.

"Exactly," he said. "Now how about that wine?" He helped her sit up and handed a glass to her.

Sam curled her legs under her and watched the play of muscles in his chest and arms as he removed the tuxedo jacket and reached for his own glass. "How'd the fundraiser go?"

"One-point-five million. Judson seemed happy," he said, referring to the chairman of the Virginia Democratic Party.

"*Whoa*. That's amazing!"

"You should've seen the people who turned out for the rally at VCU. They had to move it outside to Monroe Park. Even though it was freezing, we still filled the place up."

"You're on fire, Senator. I'm so proud."

He shrugged off the compliment. "How's the case?"

"Doubly complicated. We've got a second vic. Same M.O. Worked with Regina."

"Who was it?"

"Maria Espanosa."

"Oh, no! Not Maria." He sagged into the sofa. "She's so sweet. She cleans our office."

Sam winced at his reaction. "Did you know her well?"

"Just to say hello to. She was very quiet, kept to herself, but she did a great job. How anyone could harm her…it's just hard to believe."

And even though she was hardly a friend, it was another loss on top of so many others he'd sustained recently. Sam caressed his face. "I'm sorry to just drop it on you that way. I wasn't thinking that you might know her."

"It's really sad."

"Talk to me about anchor babies."

Startled, he said, "What about them?"

"Regina was pregnant."

His eyes went wide. "Was it Henry's?"

"He says it was."

"Damn. What a mess."

"Freddie introduced the anchor baby concept to me earlier. I hadn't heard about it before."

"It's a major issue. The numbers have exploded in the last few years. Lots of immigrant women have resorted to getting pregnant to stay in the country.

Babies born on U.S. soil are automatically citizens and 'anchor' their mothers to the U.S."

"I see."

"The law can't be changed without amending the Constitution. There was some talk about closing that loophole in the 14th Amendment when we were pushing O'Connor-Martin through, but nothing came of it."

"So Regina's baby would've kept her in the country?"

"Most likely. The INS isn't out to separate babies from their mothers. The country has no appetite for that kind of enforcement."

"I'll bet she got pregnant on purpose. She told Henry she was on the pill, and he said he saw them in her purse, but I wonder if she was taking them."

"So you think he was duped?"

"Hard to say. The emotion could've been real, but no doubt she got exactly what she wanted from him on that sofa."

"Jeez. What was he thinking?"

"Not much I suppose." She took a closer look at him and saw the fatigue and weariness he worked so hard to hide from her. "You need some sleep, Senator."

"Are we going to talk about it?"

"About what?"

He raised an eyebrow.

"Oh. Peter." For a while there, she'd almost forgotten about it. Almost. Sam wanted to reassure Nick. She wanted to tell him they had nothing to worry about. That's what she would've done a few weeks ago. But she'd been working on not keeping things from him, and that included her own worries.

"Talk to me, Sam. You have to be spun up about it."

"I'm trying not to think about it until I have to."

"How does he even have a case for dismissal? He tried to *kill* you."

"No one's questioning that. They're questioning the evidence gathering." Sam fiddled with her fingers. "If this comes to pass, it'll kill Cruz, Gonzo and Arnold. If they jumped the gun, it was only because he came at me."

He reached for her hand and laced his fingers through hers. "I don't want you to worry. If it happens, we'll deal with it together."

"And that makes it bearable." She leaned her head on his shoulder. "It does kind of freak me out to think of him on the streets again. Stalking me—and you."

"He won't get anywhere near you." A shudder rippled through his big frame. "God, just the thought of him on the loose makes me crazy. I'll do everything I can to make sure it doesn't happen."

"I said it before, but please don't do anything foolish on my behalf."

"Who else would I do foolish things for?"

"Don't make jokes."

"I'm not joking, Sam. I know you can more than take care of yourself, but you can't expect me to sit idly by and let that maniac come after you again."

Just the thought of it made Sam sick. "Let's talk about something else—anything else."

After taking a sip of his wine, he put the glass on

the table and turned to her. "I met a really neat kid today." He told her about Scotty and the instant bond he'd felt with him.

"Why does talking about him make you look so sad?"

"Does it?" he asked, seeming surprised.

She nodded.

Nick hesitated for a moment. "Meeting him brought back a lot of memories." He combed his fingers through the long hair he released from the clip she wore to work. "Not all of them good."

His difficult childhood was something he didn't often speak of.

Sam put down her wineglass and reached for him, cradling his head against her chest.

"Would you mind too terribly if I became friends with a twelve-year-old? I know our lives are so chaotic, and there's so much going on, but now that I've met him, there's no way I can just forget about him."

"Of course I wouldn't mind. He sounds like a terrific kid."

"He really is. I want you to meet him."

"I'd like that." She smoothed her hand over his hair and kissed his forehead. "What do you say we get some sleep?"

"Mmm."

"Upstairs."

"Mmm hmm."

"Nick…"

"Coupla minutes, babe. Just give me a coupla minutes right here."

Since he had so much trouble sleeping, she tightened her hold on him and gave him what he needed.

SAM WOKE UP as Nick carried her upstairs. "What time is it?"

"Three-thirty."

"Put me down. I'm too heavy."

"No, you're not."

She glanced up at him. "Did you sleep?"

"Like a rock."

"Will you be able to go back to sleep?"

In the bedroom, he set her down and turned on the bedside lamp. "Hope so." When she started to take off her sweater, he stopped her. "Let me."

Sam forced herself to stand still while he removed her clothes and pressed strategic kisses to each bit of skin as he uncovered it. "My turn?" she asked when he was finished.

"Sure," he said, reaching for her. "Since you're the *only* one with access to my zipper, have at it."

She swatted his hands away and quickly divested him of the remnants of the tuxedo. "I shouldn't have said that before. It's not something I worry about. It was just the case and this situation with Henry…"

With his fingers on her chin, he tilted her face up to meet his gaze. "It's not something you'll *ever* have to worry about. I promise you that."

She looped her arms around his neck and went up on tiptoes to kiss him. "I know."

"Come here," he said, leading her into bed.

Sam moved into his embrace.

"Mmm, perfect," he said when he had her arranged on top of him. His fingers kneaded the tension from her shoulders and back.

"You need to sleep," she reminded him as she sank into the massage.

"I am sleeping."

"One part of you is most definitely *not* sleeping."

"As long as he's awake…" He raised his hips and cupped her ass.

"He's always awake."

"Only when you're naked in bed with me. Or if you're in the same room. Or in the shower. Or in the car. Or—"

Laughing, she silenced him with a kiss. "Since I want you to sleep, I'd better deal with him."

"That's probably for the best," he said with a grave expression that made her laugh again.

Pushing herself up, she straddled him and slid her damp heat over his length.

Nick groaned and clutched her hips, encouraging her to take him in.

Sam continued to tease him, enjoying the fierce look on his face as she denied him what he wanted.

Suddenly, he turned them over and entered her in one deep thrust.

Sam cried out and arched into him as he withdrew and then slid into her again.

He gazed down at her and brushed his lips over hers.

"Nick…"

"What, babe?" He flexed his hips, and Sam exploded. Holding her tight against him, Nick went with her.

"God," she whispered. "Where'd that come from?"

He laughed and kissed her once more before he rolled off her, bringing her with him. "I love you, Samantha."

She reached over him to turn off the light. "Love you too."

"When are you going to officially move in with me?"

"I sleep here every night. Isn't that official enough?"

"Not as long as your stuff still lives down the street."

"You're sure you're ready for all that comes with me?"

"I'm very sure."

"Remember that when your anal-retentive freaka-zoidal self is tripping over my crap and you're swearing at me."

"I'll never swear at you."

She could feel him relaxing into sleep. "You say that now...have I mentioned the other fifty pairs of shoes I have in storage?"

"Doesn't scare me."

Kissing his chest, she smiled. He had no idea. No idea at all.

SAM STROLLED UP the ramp to her father's house, three doors down Ninth Street from Nick's place. Standing on the front stoop, she debated for a minute before she knocked on the door.

Celia opened the door, and her smile became perplexed when she saw Sam standing there. "Why are you knocking?" she asked as she waved her stepdaughter inside.

"You crazy kids are still on your honeymoon. I didn't want to intrude."

Celia's heart-shaped face turned bright red. "Don't be ridiculous. And don't ever knock on that door again. You hear me?"

"Yes, ma'am." Sam appreciated the warm welcome from her new stepmother. She'd suspected little would change between them now that Skip's longtime nurse had become his wife. Sam had been shocked to learn a few months ago that Celia and her dad had been secretly dating at the time of his shooting. Celia had immediately volunteered to oversee his home care and had quickly become indispensible to the family she was now a part of. "How's the groom?"

"Doing well. He was a little tired yesterday but seems better today. We're planning to have a quiet day. How are you?"

"Caught a murder during the wedding. Sorry we had to leave early."

"When duty calls, you have to go. We know that."

"Duty has been calling a little too often lately." She swallowed hard, hoping she could pull this off. "It was a, ah, nice wedding."

"Aww, thanks, honey. That's sweet of you to say." Celia's green eyes turned mischievous. "So tell me, was the senator involved with the cleaning lady?"

Sam followed Celia into the kitchen. "I can neither confirm nor deny…"

"*I knew it*! His poor wife at home in Arizona with all those kids."

"Don't breathe a word of that," Sam said. "We've yet to confirm the affair to the media."

"My lips are sealed," Celia said.

"Got yourself another hot one, Lieutenant," retired Metro Deputy Chief Skip Holland said. His wheelchair was positioned at the kitchen table where Celia had set him up to peruse the *Washington Post*. His brown and silver hair was still damp from an earlier washing, and his sharp blue eyes were focused on his youngest daughter.

Sam kissed his cheek, sat at the table and accepted the cup of coffee Celia handed her, even though she'd much prefer the diet cola her body still craved in the morning. Dr. Harry had recently broken the news to her that the carbonation in the soda was eating a hole in her stomach. The guy was a killjoy. "It's hot and getting hotter," Sam said of the case.

She told him about Regina being pregnant with Lightfeather's baby as well as the discovery of Maria Espanosa's dead body and the fear that a killer was targeting young immigrant women in the city. "They don't have anything in common, that we can find, other than their place of employment."

"You'll want to talk to some of their other coworkers," Skip said. "Maybe there was something else that tied them to each other."

"That's on the docket for today." She fiddled with her mug for a moment before she glanced over at him again. "I heard yesterday that it's possible Peter could get sprung."

Her father and Celia gasped.

"You can't be serious," Celia said.

Sam told them what she knew, even though she hated to upset them. It was all part of her new effort to be more forthright with the people she loved. "Nick's going to talk to Forrester," she said, referring to the U.S. Attorney. "But I told him not to stick his neck too far out. He needs to be thinking about his campaign."

"He needs to be making phone calls," Skip said emphatically. "Maybe he can do something to stop this insanity."

"Since when do you believe in taking advantage of friends in high places?" Sam asked in an attempt to lighten the mood.

"Since the monster who tried to murder my little girl might get sprung from jail."

"Let's try not to think about it until we have to," Sam said, touched by his fiercely spoken words. "That's what I'm trying to do."

Celia patted her shoulder. "Probably easier said than done, honey."

"I'm sure Farnsworth and Malone are doing all they can from their end," Skip said.

"They are." Anxious to end the discussion about one of her least favorite subjects, Sam stood up and bent to kiss her dad's forehead. "I gotta hit it."

"Let me know if I can help."

"I'll probably be back later to run through it with you. Don't know enough yet."

"I'll be here."

Sam smiled. "Counting on that." She glanced around at the homey kitchen and was swamped with relief at knowing her gravely injured father had someone who genuinely loved him overseeing his care. It freed Sam to dare to have a life of her own. For the first time in the two years since he was shot by an unknown assailant during a routine traffic stop gone bad, Sam was able to stop worrying constantly about him. "So Nick's making noise about me officially moving down the street."

"Probably time," Skip said.

"I guess so. Especially since we've set a wedding date." Sam still couldn't believe she'd agreed to this.

"Is that so?" Celia said, clapping her hands together with glee. "When?"

"Um, March 26."

"*This year*?" Skip and Celia said in stereo.

"It's all his idea. He's convinced it's no big deal."

"Oh my goodness!" Celia said. "We have to get going right away!"

"Nick said something about hiring someone to deal with all the details." Sam hoped her bald-faced lie wouldn't be obvious to them. As much as Sam loved her new stepmother, no way was Celia getting her hands on this wedding. *No way.* "We'll probably go that route." No doubt he knew someone who could make it all go away for them. She wondered why they hadn't thought of it sooner. "Well, I'm off. See you later."

"Let us know how we can help with the wedding," Celia called after her.

"You'll be the first to know," Sam said, scooting out the front door and taking her guilty conscience with her.

ELEVEN

SAM SCANNED THE faces of the detectives gathered in the conference room to go over the facts of the de Castro and Espanosa cases. Some of them looked like they had Monday morning-itis, especially Cruz, who was yawning his head off, and Gonzales, who seemed totally preoccupied. She hated that she was going to have to tell three of her loyal detectives about the situation with Peter Gibson, but she couldn't let them hear about it through a grapevine that was no doubt already buzzing with the news.

After she ran through what they knew so far on the current cases, Sam handed out assignments and sent the others on their way. "Detectives Cruz, Gonzales and Arnold," she said. "A minute of your time, please?"

They stopped and waited until the others left the room.

"Shut the door," Sam said.

They exchanged nervous glances.

"What's up, LT?" Cruz asked.

"Yesterday I received word that Peter Gibson's attorney has requested a hearing to determine whether the evidence collected at Gibson's apartment was fruit of the poisonous tree because you went in without a warrant."

As she expected, they erupted in protest.

Sam held up her hands to stop them. "I know exactly how it went down, and I would've done it the same way. We had every reason to believe he was involved."

"Except at that time we only had suspicion," Gonzo said. "Not solid proof."

"Yes." Sam was not at all surprised that he was the first to figure out what Gibson's attorney was using to force the hearing. "I want to be clear on this—no matter what happens, I don't blame you, and I don't want you to blame yourselves. We were all operating on adrenaline and high emotion that day. I appreciate how fast you all worked to find him and bring him in."

"It sounds like we worked *too* fast," Cruz mumbled, clearly undone by the news.

"Maybe so, but let's wait to see what the judge has to say before we jump to any conclusions. In the meantime, we have two vics who need our full attention right now, so let's keep our focus where it needs to be."

With muttered agreements, they headed for the door, shoulders stooped and heads down. Sam hated to see them like that. "Detective Gonzales, one more minute, please?"

After Cruz and Arnold stepped out, Sam took another long look at Gonzo's face, concerned by the unusual pallor. "Are you feeling better today?"

"Yeah. Sorry about yesterday. Something came up that I had to deal with."

"And everything's all right now?"

He hesitated. "It will be. I hope."

"Anything I can do?"

Once again he hesitated, and she realized he was tormented over something. "Gonzo, what is it? What's going on?" She really, *really* hoped he wasn't going to say that things weren't going well with Christina. Sam truly did not want to hear the details of their romance. She already had her hands full enough with Cruz's romantic troubles.

Gonzo looked so tortured that Sam experienced a pang of fear. "Sit." She gestured to a chair and took the one next to him. "Talk."

He dropped into the chair and released a deep sigh. "It seems that I have a son."

She stared at him. "*Whoa.*"

"That's what I said too." He filled her in on what he knew as well as the steps he was taking to confirm paternity and file for custody. "I hope it's okay that Christina set me up with Nick's lawyer friend Andy. He specializes in family law. I know I should have called you first."

"Of course it's okay," Sam said. "That's exactly what you should've done. What do we know about the mother and her boyfriend?"

"Nothing about him, except he looks like a biker dude. Tattoos everywhere. Leather, the works. Doesn't make him a criminal, but I caught a bad vibe from him."

"If I'm you, my first order of business is to get a last name on him and run them both to see if they have priors."

"Except I'm not supposed to use department resources for personal matters."

"Of course your superior officer never made this suggestion and you never told her you planned to use department resources for personal matters."

"Of course." A hint of a smile graced his face. "I won't let this affect my work. Don't worry."

"Never crossed my mind that you would. Let me know what I can do to help."

"Thanks. I'd appreciate you keeping this between us for now. Until I know for sure he's mine…"

"I understand."

He got up, seeming somewhat relieved to have shared his burden. "Thanks, LT."

"Any time."

"This thing with Gibson…if he gets sprung, it's on me. I should've known better—"

"Don't," Sam said. She had expected nothing less from him as the most senior detective on the scene that night at Gibson's apartment. "Don't take this on. There were three of you there, and I knew what you were going there to do. Even my dad and Malone were aware of it. Any of us could've stopped you just as easily as you could have stopped it. We can't rewrite history. We can only go forward from here."

"How are you staying so calm about this?"

"Compartmentalization. You oughta try it."

"I suppose that's as good a plan as any. I still can't believe everything that's happened this weekend."

"Hang in there, and let me know what I can do to help you."

"Thanks."

ON THE WAY to reinterview JoAnn Smithson, Sam called Nick. "So color me crazy," she said when he answered. "But I had what might be my most brilliant idea ever this morning."

He snickered. "Can't wait to hear this one."

"You won't be laughing when you hear my idea. You'll be basking in my brilliance."

In the passenger seat, Freddie made barfing noises. Sam shot him a glare.

"I'm breathless with anticipation," Nick said.

"Good. I like you that way. What do you say we hire someone to make all this wedding crap go away?"

"Hire someone? To plan *our* wedding?"

"Yes, exactly. They can figure out the where, the what, the how. We'll do the who and the clothes and the personal stuff."

"I don't know, Sam. How do we turn something that important and personal over to a total stranger?"

"How about we turn over the most important day of our lives to a trained professional who can tell us exactly what to do so we can just show up and get married without all the stress and aggravation of trying to plan it ourselves?"

"When you put it that way…do you know any of these people who magically make weddings happen?"

"No, but I'm sure you do."

"I can assure you that I don't. You'll recall that this is my first rodeo."

"Oh, come on. With that network of yours, someone knows someone who knows someone. Put the word out, and you'll have a dozen people clamoring for the job by the end of the day."

"You aren't seriously suggesting I make use of our newfound notoriety, are you?"

"Maybe I am. For once it might actually benefit us."

"All right. If you're sure you want to go that route, I'll look into it."

"Good. Thank you. I promise this will keep us from losing our minds over the next six weeks."

"Speaking of losing our minds, I just got off the phone with Forrester."

At the reference to the U.S. Attorney, Sam's good mood dissipated. "And?"

"After he chastised me for abusing my office, he let me know that he wasn't inclined to do the police any favors."

"Isn't he a Republican?"

"Gee, how'd you guess?"

"Well, thanks for trying."

"I've got a few other irons in the fire."

"Seriously, Nick, don't set yourself up for trouble over this. He's not worth it."

"Don't worry about me, Samantha."

"I *am* worried about you doing something on my behalf that causes you political trouble. We don't need that on top of everything else."

"I hear ya, babe, but I've got to run. Committee meeting in ten."

"Talk to you later."

"Be careful out there."

"Always am." Sam pulled into the parking lot at the Capitol Cleaning Services' office and cut the engine.

"Good idea on the wedding planner," Freddie said.

"I'm glad you approve. I have another brilliant idea I wanted to run by you."

"And what's that?"

"Have a dinner party for your mother and Elin. Give them a chance to spend time together in a relaxed setting."

"Are you really helping me with this problem when I've caused such a huge problem for you?"

"How do you figure? What problem did you cause for me?"

"Hello? Gibson? I can't *freaking believe* he might get sprung."

"I'll tell you the same thing I told Gonzo—it's not your fault. I was aware of what you were doing, my dad and Malone were aware of it. None of us stopped you."

"We should've waited for the warrant."

"Maybe so, but you had good reason to believe he had bomb-making supplies in there. I can't say I would've waited either."

"Sam, if he gets out—"

She held up her hand to stop him. "*If* he gets out, I'll deal with it then. I don't have to deal with it now."

"I'm sorry," he said, his expression rife with regret and dismay. "I feel so awful about this. I wanted to nail him so badly."

"We all did. So let's talk about this dinner party you're going to have."

She watched him make an attempt to rally past his

worries about Gibson getting sprung. "I thought you didn't approve of her any more than my mother does."

"I don't disapprove of her. I just wonder if she's right for you."

"But you're still offering me advice?"

"You say she is what *you* want. I'm trying to respect that." Sam got out of the car. "Take or leave the dinner idea."

"It's not a *bad* idea."

"Gee, thanks."

"We're in the middle of a case. When do you propose I have this dinner?"

"Today's Monday," Sam said, thinking it out. "Aim for Friday. We should have this wrapped up by then."

He followed her into the office building. "And if we don't?"

"Then I'll still give you the night off."

"And the night before to get ready?"

Sam scowled at him. "The night before too."

"In that case, I accept your idea and the time off."

"How did that just backfire on me?" Sam asked.

Freddie laughed. "I've learned from the best."

In JoAnn Smithson's outer office, Sam and Freddie found the older woman huddled with several colleagues. They were all in tears.

"Oh," Mrs. Smithson said when she saw them. "Detectives! Someone is killing my employees! I don't understand."

"Try to calm down, Mrs. Smithson," Sam said. "We're doing everything we can to find the person who killed them." Leading her away from the other women,

Sam said, "I need a list of all your employees—their names, addresses, immigration status and anything else about them you can tell us that might be relevant."

"I can't give you personal information about my employees."

"Do you want it on your conscience when another of them ends up dead?"

Mrs. Smithson wiped tears from her cheeks. "Of course not."

"Then cooperate with our investigation so we can make sure no one else gets hurt."

"I'll need a few minutes to print the list for you."

"We'll wait."

She scurried off.

"I was thinking," Freddie said, "that we might also want to match up that list to the offices they cleaned and see if there are any patterns."

"That's good thinking. Tell Mrs. Smithson to add that to the info she's getting for us."

"You got it, boss."

Since she had a few minutes to kill, Sam called Lindsey. "What've you got, Doc?"

"Another pregnant victim."

"You don't say."

"Fifteen weeks."

"Jesus. What the hell is going on here?"

"I have no idea," Lindsey said. "But I have full confidence that you'll figure it out."

"What else did you find?"

"Semen from only one man this time. You know, it occurs to me that this guy must be one arrogant SOB."

"Why do you say that?"

"Indulge me for a minute here."

Sam glanced over at the office full of women hard at work on her request. Freddie was overseeing them. "I've got a minute."

"So if I'm a guy who's going to rape and murder women, I think I'd take the time to suit up so I wouldn't leave my calling card behind. My guess is we're looking for someone who never thinks for *one second* that he's ever going to get caught. Like he's above such menial things such as criminal justice."

"It's a good theory," Sam acknowledged. "What I need from you now is confirmation that the DNA from Maria matches guy number two from Regina."

"Running it now. I'll get back to you as soon as I know for sure."

"Great, thanks." Sam ended the call as Freddie rejoined her with the list she'd requested from Mrs. Smithson. "Let's stop at City Hall and figure out who Regina was married to. After we talk to him, we'll start with the immigrants and go from there. For whatever reason, he's targeting them."

"I'm with you, boss."

SAM WAITED IMPATIENTLY for the City Hall clerk to pull Regina's marriage license. "You'd think they'd have all this crap on computers by now," she muttered to Freddie.

"You'd think."

The clerk returned a few minutes later, carrying a binder. "Here we go." She put the book down on the counter and turned it so Sam and Freddie could read the copy of the license.

"Seamus O'Grady," Freddie said as he wrote down the name.

"Call it in. Let's see if he's in the system." While he was on the phone, they returned to the car.

"Got a hit," he said. "A B&E charge from four years ago. He's on probation."

"Finally, a break," Sam said. A call to O'Grady's probation officer yielded his place of business, a restaurant on Massachusetts Avenue. "Let's go."

They double-parked outside the restaurant and showed their badges inside. One of the waitresses pointed to the kitchen where they found Seamus working the grill. Medium height and build, he had red hair and blue eyes.

"Oh, Jesus," he said when they flashed their badges. "What now? I talked to my PO yesterday. Whatever it is, I didn't do it."

"When was the last time you saw Regina?" Sam asked.

"Who?"

"Your ex-wife, asshole."

"Shit, that bitch?" As he spoke, he flipped burgers and sautéed onions. "Been more than a year since I laid eyes on her. Biggest mistake I ever made. All she wanted from me was a green card. Totally played me."

"Why do you say that?"

"Because the second she got it she was out the door. I thought she was home visiting her mother until I got served with divorce papers. Too bad for her that she set off INS alarms when she filed for divorce."

"They rescinded the green card?"

He nodded. "She was able to get a work visa, but that was temporary."

"You never saw her again?"

"Nope. She didn't need me anymore, and I certainly had nothing to say to her."

"How long were you married?"

"About fifteen months all told. Together about ten of them."

"All that time, you had no inkling that she was playing you?" Freddie asked.

"I made the mistake of falling for her." For a moment, he seemed lost in his memories, but then he seemed to remember the hurt. "What's this all about? Is she in some kind of trouble? Wouldn't surprise me."

"She was killed Saturday night," Sam said.

He froze mid-burger-flip. "*Killed*? What happened?"

"She was murdered in her apartment."

"God, I can't believe that."

"Where were you Saturday night?"

His eyes bugged. "You don't think…I hated her for what she did to me, but I'd never *hurt* her."

"Where were you?"

"Right here. Two to midnight."

"You didn't leave at all."

"Not until the end of my shift."

"And someone here can attest to that?"

"Sure, the manager. He's out front."

After confirming Seamus' alibi, Sam and Freddie left the restaurant.

"Another dead end," she said.

GONZO KNOCKED ON the door of the apartment upstairs from Maria's and waited impatiently. He'd told Sam that his personal crisis wouldn't affect his work, but that was proving much easier said than done. His body hummed with tension while he waited to hear something—*anything*—from Andy.

The door opened, and a middle-aged woman greeted him and his badge with a grunt. "This about Maria?" she asked.

"Detective Gonzales, Metro Police. May I have a moment of your time?"

She gave him a good once-over before admitting him into her apartment.

"Do you mind if I ask your name?"

"Debbie Hopkins."

"Have you lived here long?"

"Six years."

"What about Maria?"

"Coupla years, I guess. I didn't know her very well."

"If you could tell me anything you did know about her, that would help."

"She never had much to say but wasn't unfriendly. Just quiet."

"Was she seeing anyone?"

"Not that I ever noticed, but she wasn't around much. She worked a lot."

"Did she work for just the cleaning service?"

"I don't know. It seemed that she worked every night. I heard her shower go on in the mornings because the pipes would clang."

Gonzo's cell phone rang. "Excuse me. I have to take this."

She gestured for him to proceed.

His heart stuttered when he saw Lori's number on the caller ID. "Hello?"

"You had to send fucking *social workers* over here? *Are you fucking kidding me?*"

"Wait a minute—"

"No, *you* wait a minute. I'm sorry I ever called you. You can keep your money and your social workers and your DNA tests. Just stay the fuck away from us."

"I'm not staying away from my son, Lori. I don't care about the money or anything else. I want my kid."

"Then I'll see you in court, because you're not getting anywhere near my son if I have anything to say about it!"

Before he could form an answer to that, the line went dead. His hands shook as he returned the phone to his pocket. He took a moment to collect himself before he turned back to finish the interview. "Sorry about the interruption," he said, forcing a calm tone to his voice when he wanted to shriek with frustration. Withdrawing his card from his pocket, he handed it to Debbie. "If you think of anything else that might be helpful to the investigation, please give me a call."

"You might want to talk to Mrs. Ellison in 4B. I think they were friendly."

"Thank you," Gonzo said, grateful to leave the airless apartment.

Once outside, he sat on the stoop, taking deep breaths of cool fresh air. When he managed to calm down, he reached for his phone again to call Andy.

The moment the lawyer came on the line, Gonzo said, "We've got a problem."

SAM KNOCKED ON the door of Selina Rameriz's apartment. They had turned the non-immigrant portion of the employee list over to McBride and Tyrone. "Miss Rameriz," Sam called when she knocked. "Metro Police. We need to speak to you about Regina and Maria."

"I have nothing to say," came a small voice from inside the apartment. Her English was smooth but accented. Mrs. Smithson had told them Selina was Colombian.

"Miss Rameriz, please open the door. We just want to talk to you. You're not in any trouble."

"Show your badges."

Sam and Freddie held them up to the peephole.

Another minute passed before they heard the sound of locks being disengaged. The door opened to reveal a tiny young woman with dark hair and skin. She wrapped her arms around herself protectively. "What do you want?" Her eyes, which were rimmed with red, darted between them and then past them to the hallway.

"Have you been threatened, Miss Rameriz?" Sam asked.

She shook her head. "Someone is killing the people I work with. I'm frightened."

"Did you know of anyone that either of them was involved with who might've wanted to harm them?"

Again, she shook her head.

"Did you spend time with either of them away from work?"

"No."

"Can you tell us anything about who some of their other friends might've been? Any men they were seeing?"

"No, I'm sorry. I know none of that."

Sam glanced at Freddie.

He handed Selina his card. "If you think of anything that might be helpful to the investigation or if you feel threatened in any way, please call me."

She took the card, shut the door and engaged a series of locks. "The poor girl is terrified," Freddie said once they were outside.

"I can't help but think she knows more than she's saying."

"I agree. If she barely knew them, why did she look like she'd been crying all night?"

"Good point. Let's keep her on our list to talk to again if we don't get anywhere with the others. Maybe if we take her downtown we'll get somewhere with her. Who's next?"

TWELVE

AFTER INTERVIEWING FIVE other Capitol Cleaning Services employees with similar results, Sam and Freddie returned to HQ at the end of their shift. Frustrated by the stonewalling from the women they'd spoken to, Sam gathered the other detectives working the case into the conference room for updates.

"Someone please tell me you have something we can work with," Sam said. "This case is starting to piss me off."

"I found one thing kind of interesting," Jeannie McBride said.

"Where'd you come from?" Sam asked the third-shift detective. "Shouldn't you be sleeping?"

Jeannie flashed a sheepish grin. "Couldn't sleep so I came back to work."

"Hear that boys?" Sam said. "Look at that dedication." Enjoying the dirty looks from the male detectives and a bright smile from Jeannie, Sam waved at her to proceed.

"I dug a little deeper on the financials for Regina and Maria. Both recently wired large sums of money to their families at home. Maria sent seventy-five hundred and Regina five thousand."

Sam released a low whistle. "Where do cleaning

ladies making seventeen bucks an hour get that kind of money?"

"They had something going on the side—drugs, gambling, prostitution," Freddie said. "Something that pays big."

"Would they take a chance like that when they were desperately trying to stay in this country?" Gonzo asked. "They get caught and they're looking at automatic deportation."

"They take the chance if they—and their families— desperately needed the money," Jeannie said.

"And the babies are insurance policies to keep them here if all else fails," Sam said, hearing the click of pieces coming together. "I'd really like to know who fathered Maria's baby."

"Her neighbor, Mrs. Ellison, was friendly with Maria," Gonzo reported. "But she said she never saw her with a man or heard her talk about being involved with one."

"Check her travel status," Sam said to Cruz. "See if she's been back home recently. The father could be someone there. Follow up with the family to see if she had a significant other there who might be the father."

Cruz nodded and made a note of her instructions.

"I'd also like to know from both families where they were told the money came from. They'll be lies, but I want to know how they explained away that kind of money."

Freddie added that to his list.

"Did we get anywhere with matching them up with the offices they cleaned?" Sam asked.

"They both worked in the Hart Building," Detective Arnold reported. "In addition to Lightfeather, Regina cleaned Ackerman's and Cook's offices."

"Ahh, our old friend Senator Cook," Sam said, glancing at Freddie. Thanks to some inflammatory statements the senior senator from Virginia made to Nick about Julian Sinclair, Sam and Freddie had interviewed Cook after the Supreme Court nominee had been murdered. To say that Cook had been less than hospitable would be putting it mildly.

"Maria cleaned Lewis's, Cappuano's, Trent's and Stenhouse's," Arnold continued, casting a nervous glance her way as he mumbled Nick's name.

"Another blast from the past," Sam said. Senate Majority Leader William Stenhouse was a bitter enemy of former Senator Graham O'Connor, John O'Connor's father. Sam had interviewed Stenhouse during the investigation into John O'Connor's murder, and like his colleague Cook, Stenhouse had been indignant and outraged by the implication that he might've had something to do with a murder. "Very interesting. In the interest of full disclosure, Nick mentioned that he knew Maria and that she cleaned his offices."

Her comment was met with muttered acknowledgments. She hated when her two worlds collided this way.

"I want someone on Selina for a day or so," Sam decided. "She was hiding something today when we talked to her. I want to know what it is."

"Tyrone and I will take the first shift on her tonight," Jeannie said.

"Excellent," Sam said. "Have patrol show their photos around at the local shops, markets, restaurants again. Let's find some of their other acquaintances. Get me some threads to pull."

"You got it," Jeannie said.

"I'll see the rest of you in the morning," Sam said.

As THEY FILED out of the conference room, Gonzo gestured for Cruz to follow him down the hallway.

"What's up, man?" Cruz asked when they were alone.

"This thing with Gibson…"

Cruz groaned. "*I can't deal.* We totally screwed up, and if he gets sprung…"

"I hear ya. It's eating me up too."

"I keep going over it and over it in my mind. Why didn't we wait for the warrant?"

"Because we knew we had him, and we wanted to nail that son of a bitch for what he did to Sam."

"Yeah," Cruz said, regretfully. "Wish we had it to do over."

"Well, we don't, but the way I see it, we owe her one."

"No kidding."

"So let's get serious about finding the former tenant at Reese's house. No doubt the people who lived there before Reese know something about her father's shooting. I don't care what we have to do…"

"I'm with you. Whatever it takes."

"Let me think about the next step, and I'll get back with you."

"I'll give it some thought too."

"Good."

"Everything okay with you?" Freddie asked. "You've seemed preoccupied today."

"Yeah," Gonzo said, startled by the question. Despite his best efforts, he was apparently wearing his personal turmoil for everyone to see. "Everything's fine. I'll see you tomorrow."

"Later."

After Cruz walked away, Gonzo reached for his cell phone to call Christina. "Can you break free yet?" he asked when she answered.

"Just about. Why? What's up?"

"Bad day. I need you."

No doubt surprised by his stark admission, Christina said, "I'm here. What can I do?"

"Meet me at my place in an hour?"

"I'll be there."

"Thanks."

"You don't have to thank me. There's nowhere else I'd rather be."

Overwhelmed by the rush of emotion, Gonzo closed his eyes and leaned his head back against the wall. "Same here."

As he ended the call, he took a moment to marvel at the recent changes in his life. He couldn't recall ever saying the words "I need you" to a woman before nor had he imagined rearranging his life for a baby he hadn't even known about three days ago. But the truth was, he did need Christina more than he'd ever needed anyone, and there was nothing he wouldn't do to gain custody of his son.

With that in mind, he made another phone call, to the friend who'd introduced him to Lori.

"Dude," his buddy Mark said when he answered. "Long time, no see."

"Too long. How are you?"

"Hanging in there. You?"

"I've got a little problem I was hoping you could help me with."

"What's up?"

"Remember Lori Phillips?"

"Sure. What about her?"

"You know the baby she had recently?"

"I heard a rumor about that. What about it?"

"She says the kid is mine."

"Holy shit! For real?"

"I saw him yesterday. Looks like me. He's got my chin dimple."

"Wow. I didn't think you guys were all that involved."

"We weren't. Really. But apparently, it doesn't take much."

Mark released a nervous laugh. "So I hear."

"The thing is, I'm not digging the scene where they're living. Do you know anything about that guy Rex she's seeing?"

Mark released a low whistle. "Rex Connolly?"

Bingo. Gonzo made a note of the name. "I don't know his last name."

"Lots of tats? Rough-looking dude?"

"That's the guy. What's his story?"

"I'm not really sure, but Sara said Lori is pretty serious with him." Mark's sister Sara was a close friend of Lori's. "I figured the kid was his."

"So they've been together awhile then?"

"About a year maybe. What about the kid? What're you going to do?"

"I'm considering my options," Gonzo said, purposely evasive. He'd played in a softball league with Mark years ago and considered him a friend, but he didn't want it to get back to Lori that he planned to seek custody. "Do me a favor and don't mention to Sara or Lori that you talked to me?"

"No problem. Let me know if you need anything."

"I will." He had what he needed. "Thanks."

Gonzo ended the call and returned to the detectives' pit just as Sam was leaving her office.

"You're still here?" she asked.

Gonzo glanced at the crowded pit where shift change was still under way. "Would you mind if I borrowed your office for a minute?"

She studied him for a long moment. "Sure. Lock up when you're done."

"Will do. Thanks."

"See you tomorrow."

Gonzo was relieved when she left without asking any questions. He went into her office and shut the door. While he waited for her computer to boot up, he thought about Andy telling him to get anything they could use in court to prove the baby would be better off with him than with his mother. In the meantime, Andy had filed the motion to demand a DNA test.

Gonzo typed in Rex's name and was surprised to find five Rex Connollys in the system. He scanned through the mug shots, half hoping he'd find one he recognized and half hoping he wouldn't. The fifth photo was his guy. As his heart thudded, Gonzo clicked on the link to his rap sheet.

Multiple arrests on drug charges—possession and dealing—a breaking and entering charge that was later dropped and a sealed juvenile record. Feeling sick and riddled with anxiety, Gonzo printed the sheet. As long as he was committing acts that could get him fired, he also ran Lori's name through the system and was shocked to find a recent drug charge on her sheet too. The possession charge had been adjudicated six months prior, and she'd been placed on five years' probation.

"Bull's-eye," he whispered as he printed both records.

As his final act of things that could get him fired, Gonzo faxed the information to Andy's office and stood watch over the fax machine until all seven pages had transmitted. He collected them and turned to leave.

"Working late, Detective?" Lt. Stahl asked.

Gonzo almost jumped out of his skin. "Just finishing some paperwork, Lieutenant."

"You're awfully jumpy."

"Am I?" Gonzo just wanted to get the hell out of there, and there was no one he cared to speak with less than the unpleasant man who used to be his boss. "I wasn't expecting anyone to sneak up on me."

"I didn't sneak up on you," Stahl huffed, his multiple chins jiggling with indignation.

"Is there something I can help you with, Lieutenant?"

"Nope."

"Then I'll be on my way," Gonzo said. Feeling Stahl's beady-eyed stare burning a hole in his back, Gonzo tucked the rap sheets under his arm, grabbed his coat and headed out while the getting was still good. Not until he was in his SUV and headed for home, did he manage to take a deep breath. Right before he pulled up to his building, he called Sam.

"What's up?" she asked.

"Just thought you should know that Stahl was skulking around the pit tonight."

"What was he after?"

"Wouldn't say, but as usual, he was acting weird. Just thought I should mention it."

"Thanks for the heads-up," she muttered. "I wish he would stay in the rat squad where he belongs." Stahl had been transferred to the department's internal affairs division after Sam had been given his old command.

"Wouldn't that be nice?"

"I'm betting he had something to do with this situation with Gibson."

"You really think so?" Gonzo asked.

"Wouldn't put it past him."

"He's freaking evil. Why can't they get rid of him?"

"I'm sure they're trying. Did you get anywhere with your situation?"

"I got what I needed."

"Good."

"Thanks for the help."

"Sure thing."

Gonzo ended the call and rested his head on the steering wheel, forcing himself to breathe through the anxiety that cycled through him. His entire life was spinning out of control, and he felt powerless to stop or control it. A tap on his window interrupted his thoughts. Gonzo looked up to find Christina waiting for him.

He reached for his keys and got out of the car.

She held out her hand to him.

Gonzo linked his fingers with hers, and just like that, his world stopped spinning. He stared at her, dazzled and breathless. "I love you," he whispered.

She gasped. "You...you..."

He realized he was doing this badly. Pocketing his keys, he raised his hands, cupped her face and brushed his lips gently over hers. "I love you."

Tears flooded her blue eyes. "You do?"

Nodding, he kissed her again. "Surprised the hell out of me too."

Christina laughed through her tears and leaned into his embrace as he escorted her into his town house. He had no idea if he'd left the place a mess, but he suspected she wouldn't care.

Inside, she turned to him and gripped his hands.

Looking up at him with a shy smile gracing her gorgeous mouth, she said, "I love you too."

It was exactly what he needed to hear and exactly what he'd never expected to find. Gonzo leaned his forehead against hers.

"What happened today?" she asked.

He eased the coat from her shoulders and let it fall to the floor. "Later," he said, kissing her with more intent. "I'll tell you later."

She looped her arms around his neck and fell into the kiss.

THIRTEEN

IN NEED OF a top-notch wedding planner, Nick went to the one source he could always count on—his adopted mother, Laine O'Connor.

"Senator!" she said when she answered the phone. "What a lovely, *lovely* surprise."

Nick smiled at the effusive greeting. From the first time John brought him home from Harvard freshman year, Laine and her husband, Graham, had made Nick a part of their family. After John's death, they had gone out of their way to let Nick know that nothing would change—he would always be an honorary O'Connor.

"How are you, honey?" she asked.

"I'm good. How about you?"

"Oh, you know," she said with a sigh. "Good days. Bad days."

The pain he heard in her voice made Nick ache for her, for all of them. "I miss him. Sometimes I forget he's gone, and then it all comes rushing back…"

"He'd be so proud of you, Nick. I saw the VCU rally on the news. The people of the Old Dominion love you!"

"I'm not sure what I ever did to deserve such an outpouring."

"You stepped in when they needed you." Her voice caught. "You stepped in when *we* needed you."

"Well now I need *you*," he said, steering the conversation in a lighter direction before his emotions got the better of him. He still found it difficult to talk about his best friend's violent death, and he knew she felt the same.

"What can I do for you?"

"Sam and I are looking for a wedding planner. Someone who knows Washington, knows how to deal with the million details, someone who can make it all go away for us. Do you know anyone?"

"You need Shelby Faircloth."

"Who?"

"Lizbeth's friend from Georgetown," she said, referring to her daughter. "She's the go-to person for Washington weddings."

"You think she'd be interested in taking on ours?"

Laine chortled with laughter. "Are you *serious*? You two are the *it* couple of the decade. She'd *kill* for the chance to put together your wedding."

"I don't want her to kill anyone. I'm trying to get Sam a full day off, and the last thing she needs is another body to contend with." Nick winced, realizing it was too soon to be cavalier about murder, especially with John's mother. "I'm sorry. I shouldn't have said that."

"Don't apologize for making a joke, honey. We could all use a little more levity in our lives these days. Do you want me to get in touch with Shelby for you?"

"That'd be great. Ask her to come by the house at nine."

"Tonight?"

"If she wants the job, tell her she has thirty minutes to convince us to hire her."

"I'll give her the message."

"And save March 26th."

"*This year?*"

"Why does everyone keep saying that? Including the bride?"

Once again, Laine chortled with laughter. "If anyone can make it happen, Nick Cappuano, you can."

"I guess we'll find out. So how's Graham?"

"Oh, honey, some days I wonder if he'll ever be the same. The double-whammy of John's death followed so closely by Julian...I don't know."

"I need to get out to see him."

"He'd enjoy that. Why don't you and Sam come for dinner on Sunday?"

Pulling up his calendar, Nick was already figuring how he could rearrange his schedule to make it to the family's weekly Sunday dinner. He hadn't made it to a single one since the campaign began. "I can do it, but I'm not sure she can. She's caught up in another hot case."

"The business with Henry, I'm sure."

"Yes."

"What could he have been thinking? And poor Annette."

"Do you know her well?"

"We've been friends for years. She has to be beside herself. They're speculating on the news that he's going to resign. Have you heard anything?"

"Nothing definitive, but there've been some rumblings on the Hill."

"Might be for the best—for Annette and the children."

"Maybe so."

"I'm sure you'll be hearing from him, but Terry is due home this week. I think the additional two weeks were what he really needed. It was good of you to hold the job for him."

"I'm looking forward to working with him." Nick had offered the deputy chief of staff job in his office to John's older brother Terry, provided he spend at least thirty days attending in-patient alcohol rehab. On his own, Terry had tacked on two extra weeks, which Nick had taken as a good indication of Terry's determination to stay sober. "Well, I won't keep you. Thanks for the info about the wedding planner."

"Happy to help. Let me know if there's anything else I can do."

"I certainly will. Give Graham my love. I'll be there Sunday."

"We'll see you then."

Nick put down the phone, and reached for the framed picture of him and John that he kept on the credenza. Blond, handsome and utterly charming, John O'Connor had had it all until his twenty-year-old son murdered him in a fit of rage. As Nick stared at the brother of

his heart, he realized John's death had left him without
something else he'd soon need: a best man.

SAM SPENT THE evening online reviewing the websites
of senators whose offices were cleaned by the dead
women. Lightfeather, Ackerman, Stenhouse, Trent,
Lewis, Cook and finally Cappuano. Sam hadn't visited
Nick's site since he took office and was immediately
captivated by the photo of him. "Wow," she said. "Will
you look at that?" Tall, handsome and distinguished,
wearing a dark suit and a serious smile, he projected
an aura of quiet authority that stirred her.

"Whatcha looking at?" Nick asked as he came into
the room.

Embarrassed to be gawking at her fiancé's photo,
Sam spun around in the chair. "You, as a matter of
fact."

His brows knitted with confusion. "What about
me?"

Sam turned back around so he could see the
computer screen. "I *love* that picture."

"Do you? I thought it was kind of dorky."

"Um, no. Definitely not dorky."

"Is that so?"

"No wonder the women of the commonwealth are
filling stadiums to overflowing at your rallies."

"Cut it out," he said, flustered. "What are you doing
on my website anyway?"

"Something my dad said earlier. I stopped to talk
shop with him after work."

"What did he say?"

"That people only kill 'the help' when they know too much."

"What's that got to do with my site?"

"I was just looking at the sites of every senator they worked for—yours more out of curiosity than anything."

"What're you looking for?"

"Not sure yet. Anything that ties the seven of you together."

"Who are the other six?"

Sam rattled off the names.

Nick sat in one of the other chairs in the comfortable study. "Some heavy hitters on that list."

"What do they have in common?"

"Ackerman, Cook, Lightfeather and myself are all Democrats. Stenhouse, Lewis and Trent are Republicans. Ackerman and Stenhouse are party leaders. Cook and Lewis have more than thirty years in the Senate, but Trent is relatively new. The Oregon governor appointed him after Tornquist flamed out in a scandal, and Trace was later elected. He's still in his first full term."

"A few are on the same committees. Any bad history between any of them like there was between Graham and Stenhouse?"

"I could do some digging into that and let you know."

"Keep it on the down low for now. I don't want any of them to know I'm even looking into them at this point."

"You really think it was one of them?" Nick asked, incredulous.

"The thing is, I have no idea. This investigation is going nowhere fast. We have two dead immigrant women, both of them pregnant, working for a company that provides a service to Congress. One of them was romantically involved with a senator, carrying his child and had an uncertain immigration status. And despite Lightfeather's airtight alibi, I can't help but wonder how it's possible he didn't have something to do with her murder. He had so much to lose."

"But you're not focusing on him, are you?"

"Not at the moment. I just feel like I'm missing something—something huge that's staring me right in the face."

He reached for her hand and drew her out of the chair and into his lap. "What you need," he said, massaging the tension from her shoulders, "is some time away from the case, some TLC and some sleep."

"Mmm," Sam said with a sigh. "You're good at that. If things don't work out for you in the Senate, you might find work as a masseuse."

Nick laughed and pressed a kiss to the top of her head. "Remember how you solved Julian's case? How it all came together while you were sleeping?"

"In the hospital with my head throbbing from a concussion and my hairline on fire with forty stitches." They'd both been injured in a car crash that occurred after gang members shot at them. "Maybe you should knock me over the head rather than giving me a massage."

"The point is you need to step back from it to gain some perspective."

His talented fingers drew a moan from her. "So no knock on the head?"

"Nope."

The doorbell rang, drawing Sam back to reality.

"That'll be your wedding planner," he said.

She moaned again. "I really have to do this right now?"

He nudged her off his lap and stood. "Remember, this was *your* big idea."

"I already hate her."

"I already feel sorry for her."

"Awww, I love you too."

Laughing, he nudged her toward the door.

Standing on their doorstep was the tiniest pixie of a woman Sam had ever seen.

The pixie extended her hand. "Shelby Faircloth, at your service," she said. Her Southern accent was deep and charming. Even though she had to be in her early forties, she could've passed for twenty-five.

Sam always felt like an Amazon next to tiny perfect blondes like Shelby and Christina Billings.

"Come in," Nick said. "Can I get you anything? A glass of wine maybe?"

"Oh, I'd love that," Shelby said. "It's been a *really* long day."

While he went to get the wine, Sam took a moment to study Tinker Bell. She wore a pink suit and sky-high pink stiletto heels that reminded Sam of those favored by Assistant U.S. Attorney Charity Miller.

On another woman, the abundance of pink might've looked ridiculous. On Shelby Faircloth, it just worked.

"I can't believe we've never met before," Nick said as he handed Shelby a glass of pinot grigio.

"I don't get out to the farm very often," she said, referring to the O'Connor's Leesburg home. "But I see Lizbeth and Royce socially and occasionally have the pleasure of running into her parents. I know there's nothing I can say to ease your grief, but I was so very saddened by John's death."

"Thank you," Nick said. "It was a terrible loss for all of us."

"I can't imagine." Shelby took another sip of her wine and then put the glass on the table. "Well, you only gave me thirty minutes to convince you to hire me, so I'd better not waste any time. Now if I had my druthers and could do anything I wanted for you two, I'd have the service at St. John's, the Church of the Presidents, with a reception immediately following at the newly renovated Hay-Adams. I can picture you, hand in hand, dashing across H Street with the White House in the background." She sat back in her chair and sighed, caught up in her own vision. "Old Washington, classic, timeless. Just like the two of you."

Sam and Nick exchanged glances. While she wanted to barf at Shelby's description of them, she had to admit she could see the wedding just the way Shelby described it and the vision wasn't totally repulsive.

"What do you think?" Shelby asked.

"I'm intrigued," Nick said. "You can make this classic, timeless wedding happen in six weeks' time?"

"Oh, absolutely. The whole town will be clamoring for a piece of this one."

"And you'd keep all that clamoring far, *far* away from us?" Sam asked.

"As far away as humanly possible. That's what you'd be hiring me to do."

"How much would we be paying you to run interference for us?" Sam asked.

"It doesn't matter," Nick said. "Whatever it takes to make it as stress-free and perfect as possible, I'll pay it."

Sam wondered if he had lost his mind. "Wait a minute—"

He leaned over to kiss the words right off her lips. "We'll fight about that later."

"Aww," Shelby said, "you two are even cuter than you seem on TV."

That earned her a glare from Sam.

"Mentioning our cuteness will not gain you favor with the bride," Nick said with a smile.

Shelby made a poor attempt to curb her grin and stood up. "Duly noted. I don't want to outstay my welcome. Shall I send y'all an estimate along with ideas for flowers and some of the other details I have in mind? In the meantime, you can check out my website for photos from other weddings I've done, testimonials, references, the works."

She and Nick exchanged cards.

"Sounds good," he said. "Thank you."

"Are both the venues you suggested handicapped accessible?" Sam asked.

"Absolutely. I never would've proposed them otherwise."

"Will you mind if I call you Tinker Bell?"

Shelby laughed. "No problem at all. I like to think of myself as a magician of sorts."

"That's exactly what we need right now."

Shelby shook hands with Sam and Nick. "It was so great to meet you both. I promise if you hire me, you'll have a wedding they'll talk about for years to come."

Sam wasn't at all sure how she felt about that.

Nick saw her out and joined Sam on the sofa. "So? What'd you think?"

"I still can't believe you got Tinker Bell to plan our wedding."

Nick cuffed her jaw. "How about St. John's and the Hay?"

"You don't want to get married in a Catholic church?" She'd been surprised to note at John's funeral that Nick had obviously spent a lot of time in church.

"With you not being Catholic, St. John's would be less complicated," he said. "I can't picture you going through the marriage retreat the Catholics would want us to do."

Sam made a face at that. "I bet even the Catholics would make an exception for the dashing Senator Cappuano."

"Maybe, but I'm fine with St. John's. Episcopal is close enough."

"I'm worried about a media circus."

"We can handle that. I'm sure Shelby is an expert at such things."

"I liked what she said about the church and hotel being handicapped accessible. Shows she did her homework."

"I thought the same thing, but we don't have to decide anything right away. We can meet with a couple of other wedding planners before we pick one."

"We have *six weeks*, Nick. How much of that time do you suggest we spend interviewing wedding planners?"

"So we should just go with her?"

"I want to see the estimate first."

"I don't care about what it costs. I don't want you to worry about that."

"You're not paying for this whole thing. We're splitting it."

"I *am* paying for it, and we're not splitting anything."

"Whoa, Caveman Joe! Hold on just a minute!"

"John left me all that money," he said, referring to the two-million-dollar life insurance policy he'd been shocked to learn John had directed his way. "I can't imagine any better use for some of it than buying my best girl a bang-up wedding that'll make her forget she was ever married before."

All the wind puffed out of Sam's sails. "I don't know how you do it."

"Do what?"

"I'm spoiling for a fight and then you go and say something like that and all I want to do is kiss you."

His smug grin should've made her mad, but she just loved him so damned much. "Don't let me stop you."

She leaned in and set out to blow his mind with a kiss he'd never forget.

FOURTEEN

His HEART POUNDING and his lungs burning from exertion, Freddie flopped onto his back and reached for Elin to bring her with him. He wiped a bead of sweat from his brow.

"It's official," he said when he could speak again.

She nudged his nipple with the tip of her finger. "What is?"

"I'm officially addicted to you." He rolled on his side and cupped her breast, watching in fascination as her pierced nipple hardened. "Can't get enough." In truth, having sex with her was becoming a borderline obsession that had him worried—thanks to his mother and Sam who had planted all kinds of doubts in his head. Maybe they were right. When he tried to remember how he used to pass his time before he started spending every night burning up the sheets with Elin he came up totally empty.

"I must be addicted to you too, because I can't get enough either," she said, kissing her way from his chest to his belly.

Freddie sucked in a sharp deep breath when he realized her intent. A minute ago he would've guessed they were done for the night, but his recently satisfied libido roared back to life when she wrapped her talented lips around his shaft.

He clutched the sheet and gave himself over to her. She applied just the right amount of suction and tongue. Then she squeezed his balls and almost sent him into yet another climax. She surprised him when she suddenly straddled him and took him in.

Whereas the last time had been fast and frantic, this time she took it slow, teasing and tormenting him until he was on the verge of begging. He gripped her hips, held her still and surged into her, coming with a roar.

She slumped down on top of him, and he wrapped his arms around her.

All night long, he'd been nervous about broaching the subject of the dinner party. Now that he could feel her starting to inch toward sleep, he couldn't put it off any longer. "I was thinking..."

"About?"

"Getting you and my mom together so you can get to know each other better."

He felt her stiffen in his arms the instant before she shifted off him.

"What?" he asked.

She drew the sheet up and over her. "Let's not do that."

"Why not?"

"Why can't we just be about this?" She gestured to the bed.

"About what? Sex, sex and more sex?"

"What's *wrong* with that? Aren't we having a good

time together? Why does it have to involve other people?"

"Because. She's my mother, and you're my...well, girlfriend. I want you two to get along."

"I'm hardly your girlfriend, Freddie."

"Yes, you are." Once again his heart beat faster, but this time it was due to the odd bolt of fear that traveled through him. "Why would you say that?"

"Um, maybe because ever since we started fucking, we haven't been anywhere or done anything—except fuck, that is. I'd say that makes me your fuck buddy rather than your girlfriend."

Put off by her crude language, he sat up in bed. "That's not true! I took you to Skip's wedding. I offered to take you to dinner—"

She rested a finger over his lips. "We're both doing exactly what we want to be doing. Just don't make it into something it's not."

Disentangling himself from her, he got up and went to find his jeans.

"Where're you going?"

Trying to control his anger, he pulled on his pants and zipped them, not bothering with the button.

"Freddie, come on. Don't go."

"I don't want a fuck buddy," he said, making an effort to keep his tone even. "I want a girlfriend. I want a *real* girlfriend. I want this too." He gestured to the bed. "But that's not all I want. So unless you're up for more than this, I'm done." As he said the words, he had the presence of mind to wonder if he could really do without the sex. He was, after all, addicted.

"You don't mean that."

He swallowed hard. "Yes, I do."

Looking over at her as he tugged on his shirt, he said, "I'm making dinner on Friday night, and I've already invited my mother. If you're interested in a real relationship, come to dinner. If you're not, well, then it's been nice, but it's over."

Her blue eyes flashed with anger. "So you're giving me an ultimatum? Have dinner with your mother or we're done?"

He sat on the bed, reached for her hand and linked his fingers with hers. "It's not about my mother, Elin. It's about me wanting more than a sex-only relationship. Maybe that works for you, but it's just not who I am." As he said the words, Freddie realized this was exactly what his mother and Sam had been trying to tell him.

"They've gotten to you," she said, tuning into his thoughts. "That's what this is really about."

Shaking his head, he leaned in to kiss her. "I care about you. I enjoy being with you, but I need more than this."

"You can't just change the rules midstream. That's hardly fair to me."

"It's terribly unfair. I agree." With one last squeeze, he released her hand and got up to find his boots. "I hope I see you Friday night—any time after seven."

"I won't be there."

He ached with regret, but he had no doubt he was doing the right thing for himself. "That's your choice, but I really hope you'll come. I'd miss you if I never saw you again."

"You'd miss the sex," she muttered.

"I'd miss everything," he said as he donned his coat. With one last long look at her, he left her pouting in bed and walked out of her apartment—maybe for the last time. Every guy he knew would call him ten kinds of crazy for walking away from a woman like her who wanted a sex-only relationship. But Freddie wasn't most guys and he never had been. That much he knew for sure.

How would he live without the sex he'd come to crave? Well, that was another matter altogether.

THE WORDS, ONCE he started, kept coming and coming. For more than an hour, the normally reticent Tommy Gonzales talked to Christina about Peter Gibson, about his role in the search that yielded enough evidence to put the guy away for life, about his memories of the day his friend and colleague had nearly been murdered by her ex-husband, about his great fear that Gibson would be released from jail to come at Sam again, and about how he and Detective Cruz planned to redouble their efforts to find the person who shot Sam's father. He talked about his baby son, who he would name Alejandro, after the baby's grandfather, but would call him Alex. A child growing up in America should have an American name.

Lying next to him in bed, holding his hand between both of hers, Christina listened without interruption.

Finally, he seemed to run out of words. He turned

his head so he could see her, his expression sheepish and adorable. "I'm talking your ear off."

"I don't mind." His earlier profession of love was still settling with her. She wanted to pinch herself to make sure this was really happening. For years, she'd pined after John O'Connor who hadn't even known she was alive—as anything other than a good friend and dedicated employee, that is.

And now this.... Despite the differences in their backgrounds, despite the baby who might be entering his life, despite their busy, unpredictable jobs, she and Tommy had each other, and Christina had never felt more lucky or certain that she had found the one for her.

His beautiful brown eyes were so somber, so serious. Before the call from Lori, Christina had never seen them that way before. "What're you thinking?"

"I have to fight for him, you know?"

"Of course you do."

"I just keep worrying about what I'll do if I win."

She pushed herself up on one elbow. "What do you mean?"

"When I say I know nothing about babies, I mean *nothing*. Maybe he's better off with her."

"You know that's not true." She combed her fingers through his hair. "And just like any new parent, you'll figure out what you need to know when you need to know it."

"But what if I break him or something? Yesterday when she handed him to me...?"

Her lips quivering, Christina nodded.

"That was the first time I've held a baby since my nephew was born, and that was *years ago*."

Trying to suppress the urge to laugh, Christina placed her hands on his face. "Tommy, honey, you won't break him." She brushed a kiss over his lips. "You'll be great with him. I promise."

"What if I never get the chance? She's so pissed about social services showing up at her house."

"You're his father. You have rights, just like she does."

"What if I'm not really his father? Until we get the DNA test results back, I won't know for sure."

Christina touched her finger to the dimple on his chin, following with a kiss. "The proof is in the dimple."

He drew her down so she rested on top of him. "I'm doing the right thing, aren't I?"

The vulnerability she heard in his voice and saw on his face touched her heart. "I wouldn't expect you to do anything else."

Sifting his fingers through her hair, he studied her intently. "I couldn't deal with this without you."

"Yes, you could."

"I'm glad I don't have to."

Christina rested her head on his chest and listened to the strong beat of his heart, thrilled to know he'd given it to her.

His hands traveled from her shoulders to her back to her bottom.

Her entire body tingled with awareness. No one

had ever made her feel the way he did. "Tommy," she whispered.

"Hmm?"

"You really love me?"

His arms tightened around her. "I really do. You really love me?"

"Yes."

"You're the best thing to happen to me in a really long time. Maybe ever…"

Christina sighed. "Me too."

He tilted her chin and kissed her.

She'd been on her way to sleep, but within seconds was wide awake again. "You have to work in the morning."

"I know," he said.

His lips went to work on her neck, raising goose bumps over her entire body. "*Tommy*!"

Laughing, he kept up the mischief until their laughter faded to moans.

For the first morning since she'd given up her diet cola addiction, Sam didn't feel like she was slugging through quicksand. That, she supposed, was progress. At HQ, she arrived to utter chaos in the pit.

"Whoa," she said to the noisy group of detectives gathered outside her office. "*Whoa*!"

All eyes turned to her.

"What the heck is going on?"

"McBride is missing," Freddie said quietly.

A quick look at his face confirmed that what he'd said was true.

As a surge of fear and adrenaline zipped through her, Sam zeroed in on Detective William Tyrone, McBride's partner. "Define missing."

Tyrone swallowed hard. His usual composure had given way to panic, which added to Sam's growing anxiety. "We did like you said—we followed Selina last night. She went to work, came home and that's it. Nothing really happened. So me and Jeannie... I mean, Detective McBride, we parted ways. I told her I'd do the report from home and send it in. When I got home, I had a question I needed to ask her so I tried to call her, but there was no answer."

"Maybe she's asleep?"

He shook his head. "She always takes my calls. Always. Even when she's asleep or with Michael." Sam understood that. She and Cruz had a similar arrangement.

"Did you go to her place?"

Tyrone nodded. "And Michael's. That's when I started to get worried. She goes over there every morning after the nights she's on duty to see him before he leaves for work. She never showed up, and he's been trying to call her too. No way she'd ignore calls from both of us. That's just not her. Something's happened, LT, I know it."

Sam's stomach ached with the sharp pains she hadn't experienced since she quit soda. The others were looking to her for direction. She bit back her own surge of panic, and tried to focus. "Recall second and third shifts. Put out an APB for her and her car.

I want all available department resources directed toward finding her."

As the others scattered to follow her orders, Sam stepped into her office and reached for the phone to let Captain Malone and Chief Farnsworth know what was going on. Both arrived in the pit within minutes.

"What do you know?" Farnsworth asked, his gray eyes flat with concern and stress. Once Sam had updated him, he demanded that Tyrone go through his story once more. By the time he was done, Sam could tell the young detective was coming unraveled.

"Cruz," she said, "take Tyrone to the cafeteria. Get him something to eat."

"I can't eat, LT. I just can't. Give me something to do. Anything."

Sam thought for a moment. "Dump her cell phone. And the boyfriend's."

"He didn't have anything to do with this," Tyrone said emphatically. "He's crazy about her."

"Just do it, Detective."

"Yes, ma'am," he muttered as he walked away.

"What can I do?" Freddie asked.

"Go with Gonzo and Arnold and get over to Columbia Heights. That's where she was last seen. Take pictures of her with you and start a canvas."

"Do you think it's related to our case?" he asked hesitantly.

Sam thought about Maria and Regina and the bloody crime scenes at their homes. Then she thought of Jeannie—beautiful, smart, funny Jeannie. Her stomach ached. "I sure as hell hope not."

"But?"

"Is it coincidental that she might've been snatched after watching one of their friends all night?"

Freddie released an unsteady breath as the possibilities settled on him.

"Go start the canvas, and report in every half hour."

Nodding, he hurried off.

The chief stepped into the office.

"I authorized all department resources be devoted to finding McBride," Sam said. "But I realized I don't have the authority—"

"In a case like this you do. You absolutely do."

"I know I'm supposed to stay calm and take command…" If only her hands would quit shaking.

"Give yourself a minute and then do just that."

"If anything happens to her…"

"Things happen on this job, Lieutenant. You know that as well as anyone."

His words were the splash of cold water she'd needed. "I'll set up a command post in the conference room and keep you informed of every development."

"Malone and I will run the command post. You're more effective on the streets."

"That's where I'd rather be." She reached for a portable radio. "I'll report in as soon as I have anything."

"Lieutenant," Gonzo said from the doorway. "Jeannie's boyfriend is here."

"Show him in."

Gonzo led a tall, black man dressed in a sharp-looking suit into the office. Sam could see how he and the tall, gorgeous Jeannie would make for a striking couple.

"Thanks," she said, dismissing Gonzo. "I'll see you out there shortly."

"Michael Wilkinson," the other man said, extending a hand.

She shook his hand. "Sam Holland. I've heard a lot about you."

"Likewise. Can you tell me what's being done to find Jeannie?" His voice was calm but Sam could hear the hysteria lurking just below the surface.

"We have every member of the department assigned to the search. When did you first realize something was wrong?"

"Just after seven. Whenever she works at night, she always comes by as soon as her shift ends so we can spend some time together before I have to leave for work around nine. We work opposite schedules, so we grab the time when we can. If she's ever detained, she always calls. So when she didn't come and didn't call and wasn't answering her phone, I started to get worried. But I know how things can be with her job, so I didn't think too much of it at first. Then Will showed up. I could tell something was wrong because he seemed kind of freaked-out and that's not like him."

Sam was getting a better understanding of the dynamics between McBride and Tyrone. He did the reports so she could steal an hour with her boyfriend. Knowing McBride, she picked up the slack elsewhere when she could to pay him back for the courtesy.

"Mr. Wilkinson, I have to ask where you were during the night."

His eyes flashed with surprise and then flattened with shock. "You can't be serious."

"I have to ask."

Hands on his hips, frustration radiating from him, he said, "Since Jeannie came back here early yesterday, I worked late, grabbed dinner on the way home and was home by nine. I have an alarm system in my house that I set after I got home if you want to check."

"I appreciate your candor, and I'm sorry I had to ask."

"I love her, Lieutenant," he said softly. "She's *it* for me. I could never harm her. In fact, I was planning to propose this weekend." He withdrew a small box from his suit pocket and showed her the ring.

"It's beautiful," Sam said sincerely. "She'll love it."

"We have to find her," he said. "We have to."

"We will." Sam's mind raced as the possible scenarios ran through her mind like a horror movie. "We'll find her."

FIFTEEN

THEY LOOKED FOR her all day. A few minutes after seven that night, Sam stood on a sidewalk in Columbia Heights and fielded another call from Jeannie's frantic mother. She did what she could to calm and reassure the woman while wishing someone would do the same for her. Just as she had the thought, Nick called.

"Hey," Sam said.

"Any sign of her?"

"Just her car. We found it down by the Capitol Mall an hour ago. Crime scene is on it, but so far nothing that'll help us find her."

"Shit."

"Yeah."

"What can I do for you, babe? I'll do anything, just name it."

"I can't think of another thing we could be doing. Malone called in the FBI an hour ago." Under normal circumstances, Sam would resent federal agents butting into one of her cases, but in *this* case, she'd take all the help she could get.

"How're you holding up?"

The tender tone of his voice brought tears to her eyes. Sam blinked them back. If she gave into them she might never stop. "I've had better days."

"Babe," he said, sounding agonized. "I wish there was something I could do for you."

"It helps to hear your voice," she said. "I've gotta go."

"I'm here if you need me. For anything."

"I know."

"Hang in there, and please be careful."

"I will." She ended the call and gripped the phone for a long time, as if to hold on to him and his strength. Clearing the emotion from her throat, she turned to head back down the block and ran smack into Lt. Stahl—the very last person she wished to see just then.

"Having trouble keeping track of your people, Lieutenant?" he asked. The smirk on his face took her over an edge she'd been hovering at for hours.

"Are you *enjoying* this? *What the hell is wrong with you?* A decorated officer is missing and you have time to needle me? Get your fat ass out of my face, and go *look* for her!"

She left him sputtering in her wake as she stalked off to find Cruz and Gonzo. Half a block later, she happened upon Captain Malone who'd left the command center in Chief Farnsworth's hands an hour earlier to come out and check on their progress.

"Anything?" Malone asked, his face tight with tension and fatigue.

She shook her head. Her stomach continued to ache and the adrenaline that had fueled her all day had begun to give way to bone-deep fatigue. "What else could we be doing? There has to be something."

"We're doing all we can."

She checked her watch. "We need to release some people to go home and sleep."

"You can release them, but they won't go."

"Is it all over the news?"

He nodded.

"We may as well have put out the word that today would be a really good day to commit that crime you've been planning in the District."

"No kidding."

Their radios suddenly crackled with activity. They stopped walking to listen to the dispatcher relay a 911 call that was received about a naked black female found in an alley six blocks from where Sam and Malone were standing. Sam set off running and heard the captain following close behind her.

"Is she alive?" Sam screamed into the radio. Her heartbeat rang through her ears like thunder, making it difficult to hear anything over her own heavy breathing.

"The victim's condition is unknown," the dispatcher replied. "Paramedics are en route."

Detectives Arnold and Gonzales reported in from the scene a moment later that the woman in question was in fact Detective McBride and she was alive but unconscious, badly beaten and bleeding.

The relief nearly caused Sam's knees to buckle, and she faltered for a moment before regaining her stride.

"Thank God," she heard Malone say.

They watched an ambulance come around the corner, practically on two wheels with lights flashing and sirens blaring. Sam and Malone arrived on the scene seconds before the ambulance.

Gonzo had covered her with his coat so Sam couldn't fully assess her injuries, but her pretty face was bruised and battered, almost beyond recognition. Sam suppressed a gasp when she noticed the cut across her throat. "Jesus."

When Cruz and Gonzo looked up at her, their expressions were grim.

They all stood back when the paramedics pushed through the crowd that had gathered in the alley.

"Get these people out of here," Sam said. "I'll stay with her. Call Tyrone, have him update her family."

Cruz and Gonzo cleared the spectators out of the alley. Malone answered a cell phone call and followed them.

Sam crouched down by Jeannie's head as the paramedics worked frantically to stabilize her for transport.

"Do you know her blood type?" one of them asked Sam.

"No, but it'll be in her record." She called dispatch and requested the information as the paramedics transferred her onto a stretcher and covered her. "What've you got?" Sam asked them, fighting to retain her professional composure when she wanted to beat the shit out of something or someone.

The words flew at her in a blur as she chased after the paramedics. "Lost a lot of blood from the cut to her neck—even though it was a surface cut—probable sexual assault, possible fractured wrist, abrasions and contusions."

"Will she make it?" Sam asked, choking on a surge of nausea when she imagined what her friend and colleague had endured.

One of the paramedics looked up at her. "Heart rate is steady, BP is low, but not dangerously so."

She knew he couldn't give her any assurances, but it sounded like Jeannie's condition, while grave, could be worse. Sam gestured to Freddie and Gonzo. "Get crime scene down here and go through every inch of this alley. Start a canvas. Someone saw him dump her here. Get me something."

As they took off, the dispatcher called back with Jeannie's blood type. "AB positive."

Sam conveyed the information to the paramedics as she climbed into the ambulance to ride along with Jeannie, who was still unconscious. Sam was grateful the other woman's body had given her a respite from having the relive the trauma—for now, anyway. The respite didn't last for long, however. Halfway to the hospital Jeannie began to moan.

Sam reached over to place a hand on the other woman's shoulder. "Shh," she said. "You're okay. You'll be okay."

When tears leaked from Jeannie's eyes, Sam wiped them away. "Hurts," Jeannie whispered.

"Can you give her something for the pain?" Sam asked the paramedic.

He nodded and called ahead to the E.R. for instructions.

Jeannie licked her badly swollen lips and winced. "Drugged me. Something pricked my neck."

So that's how they'd gotten to her.

"Just relax." Sam resisted the urge to go into interrogation mode. "We can talk about what happened later, when you feel better."

"I fought him." A sob erupted from her throat. "Hard as I could."

"I know. You did good, Jeannie."

"Never saw him coming. I was going to Michael's." Her eyes flipped up to meet Sam's. "Don't let him see me like this. Please."

"He's out of his mind with worry."

Her tears descended into whimpers that broke Sam's heart. "Keep him away."

"Whatever you want. Just relax and focus on getting better."

"He said…" Her swollen eyes fluttered shut.

"What? What did he say, Jeannie?"

"To tell you to back off or you'll be next."

Sam choked back a gasp as the implication registered. The man they were looking for had grabbed Jeannie, tortured and raped her and sent her back with a message. That was why he'd let her live. She patted Jeannie's shoulder. "We'll get him. For you and Maria and Regina and every other woman this sick bastard has attacked." She had no doubt there were more women who probably hadn't come forward.

"Lieutenant," the paramedic said. "We're just about there."

Sam sat back on the bench so she wouldn't be in

the way as they unloaded the stretcher. She followed them into the Washington Hospital Center Emergency Room where most of the HQ detectives were waiting.

In the instant after Jeannie was whisked into a trauma room Sam was bombarded with questions. She held up her hands to stop them. "She's awake and talking but lost a lot of blood. I know she appreciates you being here, but I need you all to go home and get some sleep so we can hit it hard in the morning. Everyone, please, go home. You did good work today."

After a lot of mumbling and grumbling, most of the detectives left. Cruz, Gonzo, Arnold, Tyrone and Malone remained.

"I thought you were handling the canvas," she said to Cruz and Gonzo.

"Second shift insisted on taking over because they know she's our friend," Cruz said.

Sam nodded. "Okay."

A nurse emerged through the swinging double doors. "Lieutenant Holland? Detective McBride is asking for you."

To Malone, Sam said, "Don't leave. I need to talk to you." She followed the nurse through the corridors to Jeannie's room where a team of doctors worked feverishly on her.

A lump settled in Sam's throat. She had no idea what to say so she reached for Jeannie's hand and just held on while the plastic surgeon stitched the nasty gash on her throat.

"They'll do a rape kit," Jeannie said, her eyes

shining with unshed tears. She looked up at Sam. "Will you stay with me?"

"Of course, but wouldn't you rather have your mother—"

"No!"

"Okay," Sam said, taken aback by her vehemence. "Whatever you want. I need to update the others, but I'll be right back."

Sam returned to the waiting room and signaled to Cruz and Gonzo. "There's nothing more you can do tonight, so go on home. I want everyone well rested for tomorrow."

"Call if you need anything," Gonzo said. "I'll come back."

"Me too," Cruz said.

Sam promised she would and sent them on their way. She turned to Malone and relayed the message the perpetrator had sent.

"Christ." Hands on his hips, he studied her. "I don't suppose you'd allow me to assign a couple of officers to escort you until this is over."

"Get real."

"This guy's good, Sam. He snatched a veteran officer right off the street in broad daylight. Don't tell me it can't happen to you too."

"He won't get to me."

"Um, I hate to remind you of what happened recently with Reese." Clarence Reese had caught Sam off guard by jumping into the backseat of her car and holding her at gunpoint.

MARIE FORCE 193

"That was a fluke. I was off my game. I assure you I'm fully on my game right now."

"You're exhausted and pissed. We all are. I don't need another of my officers snatched by this guy."

"He won't do it again," Sam said.

"You're awfully certain of that."

"He snatched Jeannie to send a message. We're getting too close in the investigation."

"He's been awfully brazen. Leaving DNA all over the place, as if he thinks he's above the law ever catching up to him."

"Lindsey said the same thing. What do you think would happen if I demanded DNA samples from the senators the two dead women worked for?"

Malone uttered a harsh chuckle. "Best of luck with that."

"Based on the profile, I'm starting to think it's one of them—well, one of five. We know it's not Lightfeather, and we know it's not Nick."

"You're seriously asking me for authorization to request DNA samples from five United States senators?"

"Yeah," Sam said as the idea took hold. "I guess I am."

"You'll be the death of me, Holland. The living, breathing death."

For the first time all day, she smiled. "Run it up the pole and get back to me."

"Yeah, I'll get right on that."

"You're the best."

Muttering, he stalked out the door.

Sam turned to Tyrone, the only remaining detective. "You should go home, Will. There's nothing more you can do for her today."

"If it's just the same to you, LT, I'd rather stay."

Sam could see there was no point in arguing with him. "I know you're beating yourself up, but there was nothing you could've done to prevent this."

"I keep telling myself that, but still..."

Michael Wilkinson rushed in, arm in arm with an older woman who had to be Jeannie's mother. The two of them looked like they'd been to hell and back.

"Lieutenant!" Michael cried as Jeannie's mother hugged Tyrone. "Where is she? I want to see her. Will they let us see her?"

"She's banged up pretty badly," Sam said, "but she's awake and alert. She can't have any visitors for the time being." She had no idea how she'd tell him what had happened to Jeannie or that she didn't want to see him.

"Someone should be with her," he said.

"I'm going back now to talk to her about what happened," Sam said. "I'll be out as soon as I know anything." She also needed to talk to Jeannie to find out what she wanted them to know about the attack.

"Tell her we're here and we love her," Mrs. McBride said.

"I will."

When Sam returned to the trauma room, a nurse was explaining the need for an HIV test and preventative drugs as well as the morning-after contraception pill. Jeannie sobbed as she signed the consent form.

"Your mom and Michael are in the waiting room,"

Sam told her. "They said to tell you they love you. I told them the docs said no visitors for now."

"Thank you." Jeannie winced as she wiped tears from her swollen face.

"They really want to see you, Jeannie."

"I can't," she whispered. "I just can't."

A portable X-ray machine was wheeled in to take a film of her wrist.

Sam tried to stay out of the way while remaining close to Jeannie as doctors and nurses filtered in and out over the next half hour. A nurse-practitioner schooled on rape kits and evidence retrieval explained the process to Jeannie, even though the detective had worked many a sexual assault case and was well aware of the procedure.

Sam stood by her shoulder and whispered words of comfort as the nurse took photographs of Jeannie's injuries, including the rope burns on her wrists and ankles. The nurse clipped her fingernails, retrieved hair from Jeannie's head and pubic region, identified and collected semen from her legs and vagina, swabbed her for DNA and conducted a pelvic exam. The entire process took about three hours but Sam never left her side, and Jeannie never stopped crying.

When it was over, Sam felt like she too had been beaten up. She couldn't imagine how Jeannie must feel. An orthopedic doctor appeared next and got to work on setting Jeannie's broken wrist, another agonizing ordeal. A short time later, as they were finally ready to settle her in a room upstairs, Sam noticed that Jeannie had stopped crying.

"Is there anything I can get for you?" Sam asked.

"No. Thank you so much for staying with me. I really appreciate it, but you're probably anxious to get home." Her new eerily calm state was almost harder to deal with than the crying. That, at least, was understandable.

"I don't mind staying with you. They're sending up a rape crisis counselor to check in with you."

"That won't be necessary."

"Jeannie, you need to talk to someone—"

"Please tell them not to send the counselor. I need to sleep, not talk."

"What do you want me to tell your mother and Michael?"

"You can send them up to the room after they get me settled."

"Are you sure you're up for seeing them?"

She nodded. "I want no mention of the rape to them. Do you understand?"

"Of course." Sam hesitated before she said, "You'll have to tell them eventually…"

"It doesn't have to be now."

"Okay. I'll get them and bring them up to your room."

"Then I want you to go home. I'll be all right, and you need to sleep so you can get busy catching the monster who did this to me and Regina and Maria. We need you, Lieutenant."

After hours of tears, Sam couldn't figure out where this calm, collected Jeannie had come from. Sam squeezed the hand that wasn't encased in plaster. "You have me. I'll give it all I've got."

"I have no doubt about that." She looked up at Sam, her normally animated eyes dull and flat. "I'll never forget what you did for me today."

"I just did my job."

"You did much more than that and I won't forget it."

"I wish it could've been more, that we could've found you before…"

Jeannie shook her head. "What's done is done. Let's not rehash it."

"We'll need to get into the details tomorrow. What you remember, where he took you…"

"I understand."

"I'll get your mom and Michael and see you upstairs."

SIXTEEN

NICK RETURNED FROM yet another fundraising dinner and hated coming home to an empty house, especially knowing Sam was at the hospital with Jeannie. He'd been so relieved to get the cryptic text from Sam, indicating McBride had been found injured but alive. Rather than spend the rest of the evening pacing the floor waiting to hear from Sam, he took advantage of the quiet to go through the thirty-eight messages that had collected on his voice mail. Number twenty-four was from Scotty.

"Um, ah, Senator Cappuano, this is Scotty Dunlap." Nick smiled at the way the boy stammered through the message. "Mrs. Littlefield told me it was okay to call you to say I really love the jersey you sent me. That was the nicest thing anyone has done for me in a long time. If you, um, want to call me back, I can get calls until nine." He rattled off the number. "Ok, um, bye."

Nick checked his watch. Twenty minutes to nine. He dialed the number Scotty had given him, asked for the boy and waited while the woman who answered went to find him.

"Hello," Scotty said a few minutes later, sounding breathless.

"Hi there, it's Nick Cappuano."

"Oh. Senator."

"You can call me Nick if you'd like to."

"Really?"

"Sure. I get tired of everyone calling me senator. It's not like that's my name or anything."

Scotty giggled.

"So you liked the jersey?"

"I *loved* it. All the other guys were so jealous."

"Maybe I should get jerseys for them too."

"Nah, let 'em be jealous."

Nick laughed. "So there's this family dinner thing on Sunday. I was wondering if you might want to come along with me."

"To *your* family?"

"My adopted family."

"You're adopted?"

"Well not officially. Their son John was my best friend, and when he took me home when we were in college, his parents made me part of their family."

"What about your own family?"

"I don't have a lot of family."

"Just like me."

"Right."

"You said he *was* your best friend. Isn't he anymore?"

The burst of pain caught Nick off guard. He ought to be used to it by now. "He died a couple of months ago."

"I'm sorry. You must've been really sad."

"Yeah. I still am."

"It took a long time after my grandpa and my mom died before I stopped being sad every day."

Nick cleared the huge lump from his throat. "Is that so? How long did it take?"

"A year or so. Maybe a little longer."

"That must've been hard on you all by yourself."

"It was, but you're not alone, are you?"

"No, buddy. I've got my fiancée and lots of good friends and John's family. They're helping me through it."

"You're lucky."

"I know."

"Mrs. Littlefield told me your fiancée is a police officer."

"She is—a detective, in fact."

"That's *really* cool."

"Cooler than being a senator?"

"Ah...*duh*. Yeah!"

Nick's smile faded as he thought about her desperate search for Jeannie McBride. "Some days it is. Other days it's really stressful. I told her about you, and she's looking forward to meeting you."

"She is?"

Nick laughed. "She sure is. So what do you think? Dinner on Sunday?"

"How would I get there?"

"I have a campaign thing in the morning. Afterward, I'll drive down to Richmond to pick you up. Then we'll head up to the farm."

"They live on a *farm*?"

"A working horse farm."

"That's awesome!"

Nick smiled at Scotty's enthusiasm. "Have you ever ridden a horse?"

"Nope."

"Maybe we can give it a whirl on Sunday?"

"I'd like that."

"I'll be there to get you about noon, okay?"

"What should I wear?"

"Jeans and a nice shirt. Sound good?"

"I can do that."

"Then I'll look forward to seeing you Sunday."

"Me too. I mean I'll look forward to it too. Thank you so much for taking me."

He was so sweet and mature and thankful. "I have a feeling it'll be my pleasure. See you soon."

Nick closed the phone and sat back against the sofa. He'd spend most of the day on the road, but that was okay. He couldn't wait to see Scotty again.

DISMAYED BY JEANNIE'S sudden calm, Sam headed for the waiting room. While she was glad that Jeannie had stopped crying and settled down, the calm was worrisome in light of what the other woman had endured that day. When Sam entered the waiting room, Michael jumped to his feet.

"Lieutenant, how is she? Can we see her yet?"

"They're moving her upstairs, and I'll take you up. But you should know that her face is swollen and bruised."

A nerve in his cheek pulsed with tension, and he looked like he could kill someone. Sam understood.

She'd felt the same way most of the day. Mrs. McBride wept softly as she listened to their exchange.

"I'll take you up now," Sam said.

Detective Tyrone followed along as they took the elevator to the fourth floor. Sam led them to the room number she'd been given and stepped aside to let them go in ahead of her. Michael and Tyrone hung back as Jeannie's mother rushed to her daughter's bedside.

Jeannie hugged her sobbing mother, assured her she was just fine and held the older woman until she got herself together. Tyrone stepped up next, gave his partner a hug and brushed a hand over her hair.

"Scared the shit out of me," he said.

"Sorry."

"You've got nothing to be sorry about. We're going to nail the bastard."

Jeannie nodded. "I know you will. Go on home now and get some sleep. I'll be okay."

"Are you sure?"

Jeannie worked up a smile for him. "Positive."

"I'll be with her," Michael assured Tyrone.

The detective joined Sam in the doorway. "I'll be in early."

"Take some time if you need it," Sam said.

He shook his head. "I want to help."

"I'll see you in the morning then."

Tyrone left, and Sam tuned back into the scene unfolding in Jeannie's room. Michael enveloped Jeannie in a big hug, his broad shoulders shaking as he finally broke down.

"Thought I'd never see you again, baby," he said between sobs.

"I'm here." She ran a hand up and down his back. "I'm right here."

The emotional exchange was almost too much for Sam to handle after the grueling day. Over Michael's shoulder she made eye contact with Jeannie and was startled by the flat expression on the detective's face. Something inside her had broken, and Sam wondered if her friend would ever be the same. She turned to leave the room to give them some privacy but Jeannie called her back.

"You must be anxious to get home to Nick," Jeannie said.

"I can stay as long as you need me."

"I'll be with her," Michael said.

"Go on home, LT," Jeannie said. "I'll be okay."

"I need to talk to you more in-depth in the morning."

Her face set in a resigned expression, Jeannie nodded. "I know."

"I'll see you then."

"Sam?"

Sam turned to her.

"I'm sorry, I should say, Lieutenant…Thank you. For everything."

Sam nodded and left her colleague in the hands of her devoted boyfriend. Trudging out of the hospital, every bone in Sam's body ached and exhaustion clung to her like a wet blanket. Outside, the fresh cold air was like a wake-up call, snapping her out of the fog she'd been in for hours. The suppressed fear, emotion and horror of the long day caught up to her all at once, and her hands began to shake so violently she wondered how she would drive home. Then she remembered her car was somewhere in Columbia Heights, so she called Nick.

"Hey, babe," he said, sounding sleepy. "How is she?"

"As well as can be expected." Sam glanced up at the clear, starry sky as her breath came out in white puffs in the cold air. "I hate to do this because it's so late, but do you think you could come get me? I seem to be stranded at the Washington Hospital Center."

"I'll be there in a few minutes."

"Thanks."

While she waited for him, Sam sent a text message to her entire squad, ordering them to a seven o'clock meeting at HQ. Fifteen minutes later, Nick's black BMW turned into the hospital complex. He pulled up to the curb and opened her door from the inside.

Sam scurried in and released a sigh of pleasure when her aching body made contact with the heated seats. "Oh, that feels good." She leaned over to kiss him and smoothed his mussed hair. "I got you out of bed. Sorry."

"I wasn't sleeping." He shifted the car into drive. "I was hoping you'd come home." They drove in silence for a few minutes before he glanced at her. "She's really okay?"

"She will be," Sam said, even though she harbored significant doubts. "Eventually."

"What happened?"

With her head resting against the seat, she turned so she could see him. "Will you hate me if I just can't go through it again? Not tonight anyway."

"That bad, huh?"

"Yeah."

He rested a hand on her leg.

Sam yearned to cover his hand with hers, but she didn't want him to feel how badly her hands were shaking so she kept them tucked into her coat pockets.

At home, Sam headed straight to the shower and stood under the water for a long time, thinking about what had happened, what might've happened, what needed to happen and the threat Jeannie had brought back with her.

Sam had hoped the shower would take care of the trembling, but it only made it worse. Battling her shaking hands, she pulled on sweats and a long-sleeve T-shirt and joined Nick in bed.

"Are you going skiing or something?" he asked as he put his arms around her and drew her in close to him. Like him, she usually slept in as little as possible.

"Freezing," she muttered, hoping he'd accept her explanation for the trembling.

"Let me warm you up."

Sam clung to him and breathed him in, trying to clear her mind of the horror. She knew she needed to tell him about the threat that had been made against her. She'd been working hard to be more open and honest with him, but with her emotions hovering perilously close to the surface, she was afraid to move let alone speak for fear of losing control.

"Why are you still shaking like a leaf?" he asked many minutes later.

"Dunno."

"Samantha." He kissed the top of her head and then her forehead. "I've got you. It's over. She's okay and so are you. Everyone is safe."

Sam would've been fine. She would've survived the bout of trembling if he hadn't figured out exactly what had caused it. His tender words tore a sob from somewhere deep inside her. As if a dam had broken, tears streamed down her face, wetting her hair and his chest.

He held on tight but didn't say anything. His hand moved up and down her back, offering just the right amount of comfort. Once again it occurred to her that before him, before *them*, she never would've let the emotion out. She would have tamped it down and found a way to power through the nightmare. His steady presence reminded her that she didn't have to do that anymore.

Nick wiped the tears from her face and combed his fingers through her hair.

After a while, Sam noticed the trembling had stopped. She released a deep sigh of relief. The crisis had passed.

"Feel better?" he asked.

Suddenly embarrassed by the outburst, she tried to pull away from him. "Yeah."

"Don't, Sam."

"Don't what?"

"Don't be ashamed of being as human as the rest of us mere mortals."

For whatever reason, that made her laugh. She looked up at him, not even caring that he would see her tear-ravaged face. "You are exactly perfect for me, and I love you."

"Well," he said, clearly caught off guard, "that works out well because you're exactly perfect for me too, and I love you."

She snuggled back into his chest. "We ought to get married or something."

"Or something."

"Did you hear from Tinker Bell today?"

"She sent over her estimate."

"And?"

He rattled off a number that made Sam sit up and gasp.

"You gotta be freaking *kidding* me."

"That's for everything—her, the reception at the Hay, the church, the flowers, the cars, the cake. Everything except dresses and tuxes."

"That's outrageous! We could sponsor a third world nation for a year with that much money!"

"We can always elope—fly to Vegas and be done with the whole thing."

As much as that idea appealed to her, she couldn't deny him the wedding she knew he wanted, even if he'd skip it to spare her. "We're not flying to Vegas." She sounded sulky, even to herself.

"Are you sure?"

She realized this was her last chance to beg off the big white wedding. Once they signed the contract with Tinker Bell, it would be out of her hands. "Yeah, I'm sure."

He arranged her under him and gazed down at her. "I'm not convinced."

Sam studied his handsome face as a new swell of emotion reminded her that there was absolutely nothing she wouldn't do to make him happy. She lifted her arms to encircle his neck. "It's *so* much money."

He bent his head and gave her a sweet kiss. "Don't worry about that. I've got it covered. I have some of my own money too." She knew he meant in addition to what John had left him. "Back in the day, all I did was work. The money tends to add up when you're all work and no play."

"You're *sure* this is how you want to spend it?"

His sexy mouth twisted into a sinful smile. "I'm very sure, but only if it's what you want too."

"I'll allow it on one condition."

"I can't wait to hear this."

"I get to pay for the honeymoon."

"You don't have to—"

Sam tugged his head down and kissed him. "That's my final offer."

He leaned his forehead against hers. "You drive a tough bargain, but okay. I'll allow it."

"You'll *allow it*? *Allow it*?" As Sam started a wrestling match that would no doubt lead to lovemaking, she realized the cloud of sadness and despair had lifted. Since he was the only guy who could've done that for her, she supposed it was the least she could do to give him a day neither of them would ever forget.

SEVENTEEN

FOR A LONG time after Sam finally fell asleep, Nick lay awake watching her. She was always so strong and in control. To see her any other way was disconcerting, even if the breakdown was understandable. The long day of looking for Jeannie, finding her bruised and battered—and God knows what else she'd endured— would make anyone crack under the pressure, even his cool, competent Samantha.

Running his fingers through her long toffee-colored curls, he was glad that she'd let go of it all with him, glad he could be there when she needed him. He wanted to always be there when she needed him. Their wedding couldn't happen soon enough for him. Sam would prefer to run off and elope. He knew that. But Shelby would make sure it was a day they'd remember always, and Nick wanted that for both of them.

His cell phone rang, startling him since his phone wasn't the one that rang in the middle of the night. Nick reached for it, hoping it wouldn't wake Sam. "Hello," he whispered.

"Senator Cappuano? This is Dr. Manchester at Huron Hospital in Cleveland."

Baffled, Nick pulled on gym shorts and left the

room, closing the door behind him. "What can I do for you?"

"I wanted to let you know that your mother was brought into the emergency room tonight. She fell down a flight of stairs."

"Is she…is she okay?" Nick wondered why the doctor had called him. He hadn't seen his mother in more than five years.

"She's suffered a number of bumps, bruises and abrasions but no broken bones. We did a CT scan to rule out a head injury, and that came up clear."

"Okay." Nick swallowed hard. "What can I do?"

"She would like you to come, if that's at all possible."

Nick had no idea what to say as he was revisited by the old familiar twinge of hope. It took him right back to countless occasions during his childhood when his mother promised to come see him and then never showed up.

"Senator?"

"She really wants me to come there?" Nick heard the confused ten-year-old he'd once been in the wistful tone of his voice.

"She said she doesn't have anyone else."

Nick bent his head, took a deep breath and wondered what had become of the guy she'd married the last time he saw her. Before he could wrap his head around all the reasons why it was a bad idea, he said, "I'll be there in the morning. Will you let her know?"

"Yes, of course."

He went downstairs to the kitchen, looking for a

pen. "Is there a number I can call to check on her before I leave?"

The doctor gave him the number for the nurses' station. "I'll see you tomorrow."

"See you then," Nick said. He ended the call and leaned against the counter for a minute before he went into the study to log on to the computer to buy a plane ticket.

When he returned to the bedroom Sam sat up in bed and turned on the bedside lamp. "Who was on the phone?"

He was sorry to have woken her. "No one, babe. Go on back to sleep."

"Didn't sound like no one to me."

Still holding the phone, Nick sat on the bed. "My mother fell down the stairs. She's in the hospital."

"Oh. Wow. And she called you?"

"The doctor did. She told him she didn't have anyone else."

Sam shifted so she was behind him, her arms looped around his shoulders and her chin propped on his head. "What're you going to do?"

"I'm going out there tomorrow."

"I don't even know her name—your mother."

"Nicoletta Bernadino. That was her maiden name, anyway. I have no idea what name she's using these days."

"When was the last time you saw her?"

"Five years ago."

"How about talked to her?"

"Two or three."

"Hmm."

"What?"

"Nothing. Let's go back to sleep." She tried to cajole him into bed.

He turned to her. "What do you want to say?"

"Nothing," she said, but he didn't believe it. He could see the questions in her cool blue eyes.

"Samantha…"

"I'm just, you know, finding the timing interesting."

"How so?"

"You recently came into a lot of money. I hope that's not what this is about."

Nick experienced a pang of worry. It certainly wasn't outside the realm of possibility. His mother's life had been nothing if not a hand-to-mouth existence marked by multiple marriages and an equal number of divorces.

"I'm sorry," Sam said after a long moment of silence. "I shouldn't have said that."

"It's fine." He got back into bed and shut off the light. "It's nothing that hasn't occurred to me too."

"But you're still hopeful that maybe she just wants her son with her when she's in the hospital."

He shrugged. Leave it to Sam to hit the bull's-eye.

Sam shifted so she was on top of him and kissed his chest. "I don't want to see you hurt, Nick. That would hurt me too."

Sighing, he put his arms around her.

"Don't let her hurt you, okay?" she whispered

Easing her down to rest on him, he kissed the top of her head. "I won't." But as he said the words he wondered if, even at thirty-six, he was capable of seeing his mother and not hoping for anything.

SAM DROPPED NICK at Reagan National Airport just after six. He looked so handsome in a black leather jacket and well-worn jeans. In his hazel eyes, Sam saw a hint of anxiety and vulnerability that worried her.

"Call me when you get there," she said, kissing him at the curb.

"I will." He tapped his finger on her nose. "Don't worry about me."

"Too late."

Hugging her, he whispered, "Love you, babe."

"Love you too, Senator."

A flash interrupted the moment.

Sam snarled at the photographer who had taken their picture.

"Where ya headed, Senator?" the photog asked.

Sam noted he was from *The Washington Star*. "None of your business," she said. To Nick, she added, "You'd better go before you witness a murder."

Nick laughed. "Behave yourself. I'll be back tonight."

"I'll be here."

"Be careful today."

Rather than her usual reply, she said, "You too." Filled with trepidation, she watched him go and returned the wave he sent her as he approached the terminal door. She wished she could go with him to protect him from whatever emotional firestorm awaited him in Cleveland.

"What happened with McBride yesterday?" the nosy photographer asked.

Sam had forgotten he was there. "Also none of your business."

"Is it related to the dead immigrants?"

She went around her car to get in. "No comment."

"You're Miss Congeniality today," the photog grumbled.

Sam took great pleasure in flipping him the bird as she drove off, heading for the meeting she'd called at HQ. When she remembered what she needed to tell her detectives about what had happened to their colleague she felt sick.

At seven, she found a somber group gathered in the conference room. Just like breaking news to victims' families, Sam knew that short and to the point was the best course in situations like this. As she geared herself up to begin, Captain Malone and Chief Farnsworth stepped into the back of the room.

Sam nodded to them and returned her focus to the roomful of grim-faced detectives who were looking to her for leadership and answers to questions. They'd get answers for Jeannie and Regina and Maria and every other woman that animal had attacked. Sam had no doubt about that.

"As you all know, Detective Jeannie McBride was abducted in the Eye Street/Foggy Bottom neighborhood sometime between 0700 and 0730 yesterday morning. She was found fourteen hours later in an alley in the Adams Morgan neighborhood. She had been beaten and sexually assaulted."

A gasp went through the room. Detective Tyrone dropped his head into his hands. Freddie placed a comforting hand on his colleague's shoulder.

"She returned with a message from her attacker," Sam continued. "According to Detective McBride, he told her to tell me to back off the case or I'd be next."

She glanced at Malone and Farnsworth, certain they'd be all over her about protection after the meeting.

"I'll be interviewing Detective McBride further about the abduction and attack this morning. It's important to note that she has asked that her boyfriend and family members not be told about the sexual assault until she feels ready to tell them. It goes without saying that no one is to speak to the media or anyone else about the details of Detective McBride's abduction. Except for emergencies, all leave is canceled until we get this guy."

"What can we do, Lieutenant?" Cruz asked, looking fierce and furious.

"Where are we on that cell phone data?"

"I just talked to the phone company," Gonzo replied. "They promised it by ten a.m."

"Let them know that at one minute past ten, I'm going to Forrester," she said. "This is bullshit. We've got two dead women and the cell company is worried about their privacy?" Trying to control her anger, Sam rested her hands on her hips. "Tyrone, check on what the lab found in Jeannie's car and get me a report."

He seemed relieved to have something to do. "Yes, ma'am."

MARIE FORCE   217

"I want all available personnel on Eye Street by 0900. Let's find a security camera or someone who saw the abduction."

"I'll authorize overtime," Farnsworth said.

"Thank you, Chief. Cruz, give Regina's mother a call," Sam said, her mind racing. "Make it a courtesy call, as if you're checking on how she's doing. See what you can find out about Regina's life here, anything she might've told her mother about men or friends or hobbies. Anything you can get."

"Do you want me to call Maria's family too?" Freddie asked.

Knowing how difficult the calls would be for her sensitive partner, she appreciated his offer. "That'd be great. Let me know what you find out." To the others, she said, "One of our own has been drugged, kidnapped, attacked and beaten. Let's show this son of a bitch the full might of the MPD. That's all."

Their faces tense and determined, the detectives left the room to go do what they did best.

"I KNOW WHAT you're going to say," Sam said as soon as she was alone in the conference room with Malone and Farnsworth. "So don't get going on safe houses and taking me off the street or any other nonsense. One of *my* detectives was snatched. There's no way you're taking me off this case."

"All right." Farnsworth's eyes locked on her and his jaw ticked with tension. "Why don't you tell me how you plan to ensure that this guy, who managed to grab a smart, savvy detective off a city street in broad daylight, won't do the same to you."

"Because I'll be watching for him, and she wasn't."

"Now you have eyes in the back of your head too?" Malone asked.

"One of my many gifts."

"This guy is brazen, Lieutenant," Farnsworth said. "He won't think twice about coming after you if he sees you as a threat to his freedom."

"I'll be vigilant."

"You'll also be tailed while on duty."

"No way! That is *not* happening—"

"It's either that or you're off the case," Farnsworth said.

"I don't need a tail! It's a ridiculous waste of resources."

"They're my resources to waste. Take it or leave it."

Fuming, Sam stared him down for a long moment in which he never blinked. The old guy still had a good bit of scary left in him. "Fine. Whatever. Just tell them to stay the hell out of my way."

"You might want to consider offering them hazardous duty pay, Chief," Malone said with a grin aimed at Sam. "Ever since she was forced off the diet soda she's been a bit…grouchy."

She glared at him.

"Before you hit the streets, you need to meet with the press," Farnsworth said.

"This day just gets better and better," Sam said. What she wouldn't give for a diet cola right about then. Maybe she'd have one in defiance of Dr. Harry's orders. Surely just one couldn't hurt anything, right?

"They're clamoring for information about Detective McBride's abduction."

"I'm not telling them anything."

"You don't have to," Farnsworth said. "You just have to go out there and tell them we're closing in on a suspect. Keep them from storming the building for another few hours."

"We're not even close to a suspect. In fact, we've got zilch on this guy." Frustration gripped her. "Where are we with requesting DNA from the senators Maria and Regina worked for?"

"It's a no-go," Farnsworth said. "I went all the way to the mayor on this one, and he said absolutely not— not without probable cause."

"The probable cause is that the dead women worked for these guys, had regular contact with them and we're working with a profile of a killer who thinks he isn't going to get caught, which leads us to believe he's powerful—or at least caught up in his own presumption of power."

"But we don't have anything *specific* tying any of the senators to the crimes," Farnsworth reminded her. "Until we do, no DNA."

"If it turns out to be one of them we'll have wasted a ton of time while he's out raping and killing women."

"You may be right about that, but we're not conducting a witch hunt on Capitol Hill."

"We'll get him with or without the DNA," Sam said.

"I have no doubt about that," the chief said. "Shall we meet the press?"

"If I have to," Sam grumbled as she followed him from the conference room. After a stop to grab her coat in her office, she met him outside the main door of the public safety building where the media had gathered, waiting to take another piece out of her hide. "We meet again," she said.

Questions flew at her.

"Is Detective McBride's abduction related to the dead cleaning ladies?"

"Was she raped too?"

"Is it the same guy?"

"How did he manage to grab a cop off the street in the middle of the day?"

"How close are you to a suspect?"

Sam held up her hands to stop the flurry. She proceeded to tell them what she knew about the abduction, minus the detail about the sexual assault. Of course they couldn't let that go.

"Was she raped?"

"I will not discuss the details of her abduction at any time during this investigation. If Detective McBride chooses to speak publicly about the incident, that'll be her decision. That is all I'll say about it—now or ever."

"Is it the same guy who killed the other women?" Darren Tabor asked.

"We're waiting on the lab to tell us that."

"So he did leave DNA on the detective?"

"No comment."

"What do you mean no comment? Either he left DNA or he didn't. Which is it?"

Sam turned a frosty stare his way. "No. Comment. Need me to spell that for you, Darren?"

"How close are you to a suspect?" another reporter asked.

"Not as close as I'd like to be, but we're following every lead and one of them will be the one that closes this case. He's got a mob of angry cops looking for him, that's for sure."

"Where did Senator Cappuano fly off to so early this morning?" Tabor asked.

"That's it," Sam said. "We're done."

EIGHTEEN

SAM ENTERED JEANNIE'S room a short time later to find her sleeping. Her face was swollen and the bruises had darkened to a deep purple overnight.

Michael was standing in front of the window, staring outside. When Sam came in, he turned to her, his face a study of exhaustion, worry and sadness.

"How is she?" Sam asked.

"They gave her a sedative a couple of hours ago, and she's been sleeping ever since."

"If you want to get something to eat, I'll be here for a while."

Seeming torn, he glanced at the bed and then at Sam.

"You're no good to her if you get sick," Sam said.

"I'm sensing there was more to this attack than anyone is telling me."

Sam worked at keeping her expression neutral. "What matters right now is getting her back on her feet and out of here."

"Would you tell me? If there was more to it than a kidnapping and beating?"

"No."

He took a moment to absorb that. "I guess I can

understand that." Looking at Jeannie, he said, "I hope she knows I love her, and I'd do anything for her."

"I have no doubt that'll make all the difference to her. Go on and get something to eat. I'll sit with her."

"She speaks so highly of you. I can see why."

"Thanks," Sam said, taken aback by the compliment. "That's nice to hear."

"I'll be back. Shortly."

"I'll be here."

Michael leaned over to kiss Jeannie's forehead before he left the room.

Sam stepped up to her bedside.

"Thanks," Jeannie whispered, her eyes still closed. "For not telling him."

"Not my place to tell him anything. That's up to you."

Tears leaked from Jeannie's closed eyes. "I can't imagine telling him. Telling anyone…"

"You don't have to think about that right now." Sam placed a comforting hand over Jeannie's. "Can I do anything for you?"

"I'd love some water."

Sam poured some from the pitcher on the bedside table and held the straw up to Jeannie's cracked lips.

She winced as she took a sip. "Everything hurts today."

"I can only imagine."

"You need to know what happened. That's why you're here."

"That's not the only reason I'm here."

"You need to know. For the case."

"Only if you feel up to talking about it."

Jeannie's face tightened with pain as she tried to sit up.

Pressing the button on the hospital bed took Sam right back to the grim days following her father's shooting and all the hours she'd spent by his bedside. "Is that okay?"

"Yeah," Jeannie said. Grimacing, she reached for a device tied to the bed rail and pressed the big red button. "Pain meds."

"We can do this later if you want."

"I'd rather get it over with."

Sam tried to be subtle when she reached for the notebook in her back pocket. "You said the last thing you remembered was a prick to your neck?"

"Yes. I was about two blocks from Michael's house." She gave Sam the Foggy Bottom address. "There's never anywhere to park near Eye Street, so I usually walk a short distance."

"Do you remember anything about who was on the street with you?"

Jeannie shook her head. "I was in a rush because Michael only has so much time before he has to be at work. I wasn't paying much attention, to be honest. I was thinking about seeing him."

"I can understand that. He seems quite devoted to you."

"He is," she said softly. "Although after this…"

"Jeannie, he loves you. This won't change anything for him."

New tears rolled down the other woman's cheeks.

"I guess we'll see, won't we?" She carefully wiped her sore face and seemed to be summoning the fortitude to continue her story. "The last thing I remember is someone bumping into me from behind and then the needle in my neck. Everything went dark."

"And when you came to? Can you describe where you were?"

Jeannie closed her eyes. "In a room with just a bed. The walls were yellow and there was a small window. They had…he had…my clothes. They were gone and I was tied to the bed. I was shaking so hard, and I remember I had to pee desperately. I started screaming. I screamed until my throat hurt, but no one came for the longest time."

Sam wondered if her abductor had been out moving her car from Foggy Bottom to the Capitol Mall area. "How long do you think you were awake before he returned?"

"An hour. Maybe two. It was really cold in the room, and I was freezing with no clothes. Between that and the fear, I was shaking like a leaf."

Sam had taken a lot of victim statements in the course of her twelve-year career, but this had to be one of the more excruciating. She forced herself to stay focused on Jeannie and getting her through this as quickly as possible. "What happened then?"

"I heard a key in the door."

"Did it sound like a padlock or a deadbolt or something else?"

"A deadbolt. Definitely. He…" She took a deep breath. "He came into the room wearing a ski mask over his face, but I could see his eyes." Shuddering from the memory, Jeannie began to breathe faster. "They were dark and mean. I could see there were some lines at the corners, so I don't think he was young."

"Can you describe his build?"

"Tall. Six feet, maybe a little more. Broad shoulders. Bulky muscles, like he spent a lot of time at the gym."

"How about race?"

"White."

"Did he say anything?"

"No," Jeannie whispered. "He just started taking off his clothes. I was crying and begging him to let me go, but he never said a word as he took off everything but the ski mask."

"Can you describe his body at all? Any scars, tattoos, distinguishing marks?"

"He had a lot of gray in his chest hair and some scratches on his neck, but I can't say I noticed anything else."

"What happened next?"

Blinded by tears, Jeannie used her free hand to wipe them away. "He...he got on the bed." Sobs wracked Jeannie's body.

Sam started to get up, but Jeannie held up her hand to stop her. She took a moment to get herself together. "I asked him why he was doing this. What had I done to him? He just laughed." Sniffing and wiping her face frantically, she focused on a point on the far wall. "And then he...he started to rape me. I screamed for him to stop and he hit me in the face. Twice. I think I blacked out for a short time. When I came to he was…inside me. I tried to fight him off, but I couldn't move because I was tied to the bed. I bit his shoulder, and he hit me again."

"Take a minute," Sam said, her own hands shaking.

"After he was…done…he grabbed my throat and started to squeeze. He got really close to my ear and said, 'Tell your boss to back off on the dead whores, or she'll be next.'"

A shudder rippled through Sam. This case was rattling her in a way that not many did.

"I really think he meant it, Lieutenant. You have to be careful."

"Don't worry about me. Just focus on what you need right now." Sam tapped her pen against the pad. "Did he have any kind of accent or dialect that stood out to you?"

"Not that I noticed."

"What happened after he said that?"

"He raped me again. It just seemed to go on forever. I was crying and screaming the whole time. I thought it would never end. At some point, I lost consciousness again. He might've given me something."

"But you don't remember him giving you a shot?"

She shook her head. "The next thing I knew I was in the ambulance with you."

"How did you break your wrist?"

"I assume it happened when he dumped me in the alley. It wasn't broken yet when we were in that room."

"How about your throat?"

"I don't know when that happened. I assume it was after I was knocked out because I didn't feel it."

Sam reached up to squeeze her detective's arm. "You did great. You gave me a lot to work with."

"I didn't give you much."

"It could be enough to break this case wide-open."

"What if we never get him? How will I ever walk down a street again without worrying about who is behind me?"

"We'll get him," Sam assured her. "The entire department is out looking for him. I wouldn't want to be him right now."

"He won't care that we're all looking for him," Jeannie said.

"Why do you say that?"

"He thinks he's above the law. That's the only reason he'd be so brazen as to grab and assault a cop."

"Lindsey said the same thing." Sam's cell phone chimed. A text from Gonzo reported the cell phone records were being transmitted. She passed the information along to Jeannie.

"Took them long enough," Jeannie said.

"No kidding. I was hoping it would be Nick. He flew out to Cleveland this morning. I need to know he got there okay."

Against all odds, Jeannie chuckled. "Your fear of flying extends to other people's flights too?"

Chagrined but encouraged by Jeannie's lighthearted reply, Sam smiled at her. "Yep."

"What's in Cleveland?"

"His deadbeat mother. She's in the hospital and

somehow didn't have anyone else to call but the son she hasn't seen in five years who recently came into a truckload of money."

Jeannie winced. "Ouch."

"I'm worried this'll go badly for him. After everything with John and Julian…"

"He doesn't need any more right now."

"No," Sam said. "Sorry. I shouldn't be dumping my worries on you."

"Don't be sorry. It's nice to think about something besides my own problems for a minute. And besides, after what we went through together yesterday, I'd like to think that maybe we crossed the threshold from great colleagues to good friends."

Sam leaned over the bed to carefully hug the other woman. "Definitely," she whispered, caught off guard by a rush of emotion. "Call me if you remember anything else or if you need anything at all. Day or night."

"I will. Thanks."

"We'll get you through this, Jeannie. I promise."

As tears swam in her eyes, Jeannie nodded.

"I'll be back later."

"I'll be here—at least until tomorrow the doctor said."

Sam stepped into the hallway and found Michael leaning against the wall.

He straightened when he saw her. "I figured you two needed a few minutes to be cops."

"We did, thanks."

"I want to know what happened to her, but I'm not sure I can hear it, you know?"

"What she needs right now is to know that you're here, you love her and that no matter what happened to her it won't change anything between the two of you."

"It won't."

"Keep telling her that. It's what she needs to hear."

He nodded. "Thanks." Seeming to fortify himself to be strong for Jeannie, he went back into the room.

As Sam watched him go, she didn't envy the long road they had ahead of them as Jeannie recovered from the trauma of her attack. But Sam was more optimistic today than she'd been last night that Jeannie would bounce back.

Eventually.

THE MINUTE THE plane touched down Nick powered up his phone to send Sam a text, knowing how she worried when anyone she loved was in the air. Before he could finish composing his message to her, the phone beeped with an incoming message.

Tell your girlfriend to back off before she gets hurt.

Nick sat up straighter in the seat and fumbled with the phone, looking for the sender's number, which was unavailable. He immediately called Sam.

"Hey," she said. "Did you get there?"

"Babe," he said, filled with relief at the sound of her voice. "I got a text." He relayed the message.

"Damn it," she muttered. "How did he get your number? Unless it's someone you know who would already have it."

"Sam! I don't *give a shit* how he got my number! What are you going to do about the threat he made against you?"

"I've got a tail assigned to me, so don't worry."

"Which means this isn't the first threat." He gritted his teeth. "You'd better start talking, Lieutenant. Right now."

"You've got enough to deal with today with your mom. I'll tell you about it when you get back."

"Samantha, I'm not ending this call until you tell me what the *hell* is going on."

"McBride came back with a message for me. Similar to the one you received."

Nick closed his eyes and leaned his head back against the seat as the plane taxied to the gate. "I never would've come here if I'd known that."

"There's nothing you can do that's not being done. Farnsworth put a tail on me."

"Which I'm sure you objected to."

"It's ridiculous! I don't need two patrolmen following me around like I can't take care of myself."

"Samantha, I swear to God, you're to do exactly what they tell you to do or you'll answer to me."

"Oh boy," she said. "I love when you get all bossy with me like that. It makes me hot."

"I'm not joking!" he said loudly enough that the people sitting near him on the plane turned to look at him. He lowered his voice. "This isn't funny. He's already abducted and done God knows what to one of your detectives. Don't you dare be so cocky as to think he can't get to you too."

"I'm not being cocky, don't worry."

"Don't worry. Right."

"Can I have permission to dump your cell phone? We might be able to trace the source of the text."

"Whatever you have to do."

"Try not to worry. We're taking every precaution."

His mind immediately went to the recent day when he'd been absolutely certain she'd been shot in Clarence Reese's house. In fact, it had been Freddie who'd been shot. Shuddering from the memory, he said, "Not *every* precaution. If I had my way you'd be locked up somewhere until this freak is found."

"I'm okay, Nick. I'll continue to be okay. Focus on your mother and what you're there to do today. I'll be waiting for you when you get home."

"Promise?"

"I promise."

"I'm not even going to tell you to be careful."

"I always am. You know that."

"I'm counting on it."

"Let me know how it goes with your mother."

"I'll call you when I'm back at the airport."

"I'll be waiting."

"Don't let anything happen to my fiancée," he said gruffly. "I love her very much."

"She loves you too. I'll talk to you later."

Nick followed the stream of people off the plane. Once inside the terminal, he called Skip Holland. When Celia put him on the phone, Nick said, "I thought you should know that the guy who grabbed McBride threatened Sam."

Sam would be pissed with him for alerting her father, but Nick had no doubt Skip would make sure the cops were doing everything they could to protect her.

NINETEEN

In the cab to the hospital, Nick tried to brace himself to see his mother, to expect that nothing would have changed since the last time, to accept once again that she would never be the mother he'd yearned for all his life. He hated the way thoughts of her took him right back to that tiny apartment he'd shared with a grandmother made bitter by the unwanted responsibility of raising her son's child. His grandmother used to love to remind him of what a good-for-nothing bitch had given birth to him and then saddled *her* with "the kid."

So many times his mother had called to arrange visits that never materialized. As often as she'd disappointed him, though, he never stopped hoping she'd change, even if she'd rarely given him any reason to hope. He'd worked long and hard to build a life for himself that wasn't based on bitterness and disappointment. Seeing his mother set him back like nothing else ever could. It had happened before and would happen again if he wasn't careful.

This time, he was determined not to let her rip him to shreds. He was a grown man, about to marry the love of his life and inherit a family of in-laws he liked and respected. He had great friends and colleagues, was closer to his father than he'd ever been and he still had John's family, which considered him one of their own. Keeping all those positives in mind, Nick stepped into the elevator.

As he approached her room, the doctor stepped out. "Senator Cappuano?"

"Yes," Nick said, extending a hand. "How is she?"

The doctor shook his hand. "Anxious to see you. I told her you were on your way."

Hearing she was anxious to see him put Nick immediately on guard. To his knowledge, she'd never been anxious to see him in his entire life. At least not that he could recall. Sam's warning echoed through his mind. He'd be wise to keep that guard up.

"When can she go home?" Nick asked.

"We're waiting for the results of several tests. Provided everything checks out, she can leave this afternoon."

"Okay, thank you."

The doctor walked away, and Nick stood outside the door. His stomach was queasy, the way it used to get when he'd sit in his grandmother's window for an entire Saturday waiting for a mother who wasn't coming. Taking a final unsteady breath, he pushed the door open and stepped inside.

"Oh! There he is! Look at him," Nicoletta said to the nurse who was checking her monitors. "My son, the United States *senator*!" She held out her arms. "Come, darling. Give your mother a hug."

Nicoletta had often been compared to Sophia Loren with wavy auburn hair, flawless skin and dazzling smile. However, as Nick approached the bed to hug her, he noticed lines on her face that hadn't been there the last time he saw her.

His mother drew him in tight, and Nick was surrounded by her familiar fragrance. Releasing him from the hug, she framed his face with her hands. "Isn't he so handsome, Roberta? Didn't I tell you?"

"He sure is, and you sure did," the nurse said. "I'll leave you two to visit. Ring the call button if you need anything, Nicoletta."

"Thanks." Turning back to Nick, she said, "Well, look at you. So grown up and *so* handsome. Thank you for coming, sweetheart."

Despite all the warnings he'd given himself before seeing her, Nick glommed on to the compliments and endearment like a starving man who'd just found food. "Um, sure, no problem."

She dropped her hands from his face. "I know how busy you must be. When I heard you'd become a senator, well…I just couldn't believe it!"

"I thought I might hear from you." Nick hated that he sounded like a sad little boy who still sought his mother's approval.

"I had every intention of calling, but one day became two and then three. I didn't want to bother you."

He dropped into the chair next to her bed. "Too bad you didn't call. Maybe you could've come for the swearing-in. The president and first lady were there." Inside, Nick winced at his shameless name-dropping.

"You don't say! I'd love to meet the president. How lucky you are!"

"I've been very lucky lately. I'm not sure if you've heard that I'm engaged."

"I read that in the paper. Congratulations."

"They reported our engagement *out here*?"

"I read the Washington paper on the computer," she said, chagrined. "I was so curious after I heard you'd taken office."

Sam's warnings echoed through his mind, louder than ever. If his mother had read about his engagement, she'd no doubt read about the two-million-dollar life insurance payment too. "Her name is Samantha, but she goes by Sam. She's a homicide detective in Washington."

"And you're happy with her, Nicky?"

The nickname was a shot to the heart. His parents were the only people who'd ever called him that. "I've never been happier in my life."

"I'm glad for you," she said, sounding sincere. "You certainly deserve to be happy."

"I certainly do."

Nicoletta looked down at her hands in her lap and then at him. "I know I have no right to call you here, and it's no thanks to me that you're the kind of man who comes when his mother needs him even if she's never done the same for you."

Nick couldn't deny that, so he said nothing.

"It's just that I've, you know, fallen on some hard times. And now this accident..."

Here it comes, Nick thought. "What happened to Mel?" he asked, referring to the man she'd married the last time Nick saw her—at her third wedding during which she'd refused to introduce him as her son. Nothing like being a walking, talking symbol of someone's youthful indiscretion.

"He's been gone awhile now."

"What do you want from me, Nicoletta?" She'd asked him to call her that at the wedding. Apparently, it was easier for her to introduce him as an old friend than the son she'd never wanted.

Right on cue, fat tears began to roll down her flawless face. "When Mel left, he took everything. I had a job for a while, but I got laid off and now my benefits have run out. I didn't know who else to turn to."

"So you thought this would be a good time to hurl yourself down a flight of stairs?"

Her eyes widened with shock at his cold tone. "Don't be ridiculous! I could've been killed! I tripped over the runner on the stairs." She held up her arms so he could see the bruises she'd sustained on the way down. She turned those potent, tearful eyes on him again. "You'll help me, won't you, Nicky?"

Nick schooled his face into what he hoped was a flat, emotionless expression. "How much do you need?"

GONZO SIFTED THROUGH the phone records the cell company had finally produced, highlighting common numbers that appeared on the lists for both Regina and Maria. There were three, which gave Sam some of those threads she liked to pull. He was about to report in to her when his cell phone rang.

"Tommy, it's Andy," his lawyer said. "I just got off the phone with the child protective services representative who did the home inspection."

"And?"

"Apparently, when she went to the house, the conditions were so poor that she immediately removed the baby from the premises."

Gonzo sat up straighter in his seat. "Where is he?"

"At the moment, in foster care, but here's the good news—a family court judge has agreed to hear our petition for custody. Today."

"On what grounds?" Gonzo asked, his heart and mind racing. "We haven't even gotten her to agree to the DNA test to establish my paternity."

"We don't have to," Andy said, sounding ebullient.

"Okay, you've totally lost me here."

"Tommy," Andy said, "she listed you as the father on the baby's birth certificate!"

All the air left Gonzo's body in one long whoosh. "*Seriously*?"

"Yep. Normally, they send written notice of a hearing, but the judge waived the notice."

"Who is it?" Gonzo asked even though he suspected.

"Morton. Do you know him?"

"I caught his sister's killer two years ago. Got the guy put away for life with no chance of parole."

"Well, that explains it. Unless he says something in court, don't mention that. If he's doing you some sort of favor, we don't need to point it out."

"Don't worry, I won't say a word."

"So while the judge will no doubt order formal

paternity testing, there should be nothing standing in the way of them awarding you temporary custody today. Can you be in court in an hour?"

Gonzo thought about the case they were working and Sam's declaration that all leave was canceled. Surely, this counted as an emergency, right?

"I'll be there," he said.

"Not to be premature, but I hope to be saying, 'Congratulations, Dad,' before the end of this day. See you soon."

Dad. The word struck every emotion he'd ever experienced. Joy warred with fear as he remembered he didn't know a damned thing about taking care of a baby. He'd figure it out, though. If it meant he got to bring his son home, he'd do whatever it took to make it work. Picking up his phone again, Gonzo called Sam.

"Give me something, give me anything," she said when she answered.

Her familiar line made him smile. He brought her up-to-date on what he'd found on the cell records. "I'll run the common numbers now and see what we get."

"Excellent work. Thank you."

"How's McBride?" When he thought about what had happened to his friend and colleague, Gonzo saw red. He wanted to be right in the thick of tracking down the monster who'd attacked her, but today he had something else he had to do.

"A little better. It's gonna be a long road."

"Yeah. Listen, Lieutenant…something's come up, and I wondered if I could take some emergency leave."

The request was met with silence.

In a rush of words, he told her about the call from Andy. "I know this is the worst possible time and you canceled all leave, but if I'm awarded custody I need to be there and the judge needs to see that I'm a fit father and—"

"Gonzo! *Gonzo!* Of course you have to be there. No question."

"But the case—"

"We've got it covered. Go take care of your kid."

"Jeannie—"

"Would tell you the same thing."

"Okay," he said, releasing a deep breath he hadn't realized he was holding. "Sam…"

"Yeah?"

"What the hell do I do with a baby? My parents are in Arizona for the winter, my sisters are hours from here. *What the hell do I do?*"

Laughing, she said, "I'll call my sisters. They'll set you up with everything you need. Leave it to them."

"I can't ask that of you—or them."

"You didn't ask. I offered them up, and trust me, they love to butt into other people's business. They'll have you fixed up in no time."

"Wow, thanks. I mean that. Really."

"I'm not doing it for you. I'm doing it for the poor kid."

Gonzo laughed. "And for that he will be eternally grateful."

"What's his name, Tommy?" she asked softly.

"It's going to be Alejandro, after my father. But we'll call him Alex."

"That's a beautiful name."

After a long pause he said, "You really think I can do this?"

"Absolutely. I have no doubt that you'll be great. Let me know how you make out in court. I'll call my sisters and give them your number."

"Thank you so much—for that and the flexibility."

"Go take care of your family. Keep me posted."

His family. The whole thing blew his mind. "I will." He ended the call with her and called Christina to bring her up to speed. "Can you come to court? I'm totally freaking out over here."

"*I can't*," she said in a protracted wail. "Nick got called away on a family emergency today, and I'm scrambling to shift all his appointments and meetings to tomorrow. The office is insane, and I'm *still* waiting for my deputy to show up after his stint in rehab. I can't believe I'll miss it!"

Gonzo couldn't believe he had to get through it without her by his side. "I wish you could be there."

"I do too," she said with a whimper. "I'll be *dying* over here waiting to hear something."

"I'll call you as soon as I can."

"I love you, Tommy. I'm so happy for you."

The words were still so new that they caught him by surprise. "I love you too. Thank you for all the support. I couldn't have gotten through this without you."

"That's nice of you to say, but getting custody might turn out to be the easy part," she said with a laugh.

"No kidding. I'll call you."

"Good luck!"

As soon as Sam ended the call with Gonzo, her dad's number beeped in. "Hey, Skippy, what's up?" She pictured him in the kitchen wearing the headset that allowed him to use the telephone.

"Just checking on my daughter who's been threatened once again."

"How do you know about that?" Neither Malone nor Farnsworth would've wanted to worry him, which left… "Nick. Ugh, I'll shoot him."

"He's worried, Sam, and rightfully so. If this guy could grab McBride the way he did, what's to stop him—"

"I hear you. Farnsworth put a tail on me. They're right here." She glanced at the two young officers, who waved at her. When she scowled at them, they had the good sense to look elsewhere. Coupla probies, right out of the academy, no doubt, but at least they were armed.

"If I hear you dodged them or did anything other than exactly what your superior officers tell you to do, you'll answer to me. Am I clear?"

"You did get the memo that I'm thirty-four now and don't have to do what you tell me anymore, didn't you?"

"You'll do what I tell you for as long as I draw a breath on this earth, missy."

Sam laughed. "Did you really just call me 'missy'? I haven't heard that one since middle school."

"You drove me to it with your insolence."

"I apologize for my insolence, and I promise to do what I'm told. Happy now?"

"I'll be happy when you catch this bastard."

"So will I," Sam said with a sigh. "Believe me."

"Come see me if I can help."

"Freddie and I will be by later to run a few things past you."

"I'll be here."

"Counting on it."

"Right back atcha. Be careful."

GONZO SAT IN the courtroom wishing he'd had time to go home and change. In a room full of suits, he felt woefully underdressed in the jeans and pullover sweater he'd worn to work. Even though the room was warm, he kept his black leather jacket on because it made him feel more dressed up. He had, however, unzipped the jacket so the gold shield clipped to his belt was visible. That had to count for something, right?

Looking harried, Andy rushed into the courtroom and joined Gonzo in the gallery's front row. Lori and Rex walked in a minute later and the glare she directed his way was sharp enough to cut glass. After noting that Rex had dressed up for court by removing his bandana, Gonzo looked away from them. She wasn't his problem. No, the baby who arrived in the arms of a woman wearing a suit had Gonzo's full attention. Under the woman's arm was a manila file folder. A yellow diaper bag hung from her shoulder.

Lori cried out when she saw the baby, and Rex held her back as she dissolved into tears.

Gonzo rubbed his sweaty palms on his jeans.

A few minutes later the judge entered the chambers and court was called to order. Feeling like he was watching a movie rather than a scene from his own life, Gonzo observed the proceedings with an odd sense of detachment. Surely all this talk about competency and best interests of the child and other legalese was making sense to someone because a lot of it was lost on him. The judge thoroughly quizzed the social worker about the condition of Lori's home as well as her criminal record and Rex's.

Lori's attorney stood up. "Your honor, may I please address the court?"

"No. Sit down."

Andy surged to his feet. "Your honor, Andrew Simone, representing Detective Thomas Gonzales, the child's father."

"Detective, please approach the bench." The judge gave no indication they had ever met before.

Andy nodded at him to go ahead and followed him to the front of the courtroom.

"Is it my understanding," the judge said, "that you had no knowledge of the child until this past weekend?"

"Yes, Your Honor."

The judge glanced at Lori, who was quietly weeping as Rex kept an arm around her.

"And you believe you could provide a loving home for the child?"

"I do, Your Honor."

"Do you have a crib, car seat and other necessary equipment?"

"It's being procured for me as we speak by two experienced mothers. One of them will deliver the car seat here momentarily."

"Have you ever cared for an infant before?"

Gonzo swallowed hard. "No, Your Honor. But I'm a fast learner, and I have friends who can show me what I need to know. My parents will come too. There's nothing I wouldn't do to ensure he has a safe, clean, comfortable home."

The judge cast a distasteful look at Lori. "And will you see fit to give him a name?"

"Yes, Your Honor. His name would be Alejandro, after my father. Alex for short."

The judge seemed satisfied with his answer. "I'm granting temporary custody to Detective Gonzales. Miss Avery," he said, referring to the social worker. "Please conduct weekly visits with Detective Gonzales and report to the court. We'll reconvene in thirty days to determine how the arrangement is working out."

As the judge's words registered, Gonzo couldn't believe this was actually happening. Any moment now, he was going to wake up and discover he'd dreamed the whole thing.

Lori's attorney once again stood up. "Your Honor, if I may, will his mother be permitted to see the baby?"

"Two hours a week, supervised," the judge said. "Work out a schedule that suits Detective Gonzales and Miss Avery."

"You can't do this!" Lori screamed. "He's *my* baby! You're only giving him to his father because he's a cop!"

The judge's eyes narrowed with displeasure. "Unless you'd care to spend a few nights in the city jail, I'd suggest you contain your outbursts in my courtroom. Do you understand me?"

Through her sobs, Lori managed a nod.

"I'm giving him to his father because your home is a pigsty and frequented by criminals."

Rex pulled her back down to her seat.

"Two hours a week. Take it or leave it." The judge banged his gavel. "Next case."

Just like that, it was over, and Miss Avery was handing him his son. The baby's big eyes, so wide and trusting, gazed up at him, his lips forming that adorable pucker that Gonzo remembered from the other time he'd seen him. He held the tiny body against him, struck by just how small he was. Had he been that tiny the other day? Or did the baby seem smaller because it was now up to Gonzo to keep him safe? The enormity of the moment came down on him all at once.

Oh my God, he thought. *How in the world am I going to do this?*

TWENTY

"What'd you get from the mothers?" she asked Freddie by phone once she'd gotten her team started on the canvas in the Foggy Bottom neighborhood where Jeannie was abducted.

"Not much, unfortunately. Neither of the women talked to their mothers about anything other than their families, their work and their immigration status when they called home."

"Damn it," Sam said. "How did they explain the money?"

"Regina's mother said she had been saving up her pay from the cleaning company—or at least that's what Regina told her."

"No way a seventeen-dollar-an-hour cleaning lady has an extra five grand laying around—not living in this city. What did Maria's mother say about the money?"

"She said she didn't know where it came from and didn't think to ask because everyone is rich in the U.S., or so she seems to think. So what's next?"

"Gonzo was running the phone numbers that appeared on both Regina's and Maria's phones. Did you get that report?"

"Not yet. The computer geeks are backed up. They promised it by the end of the day."

Sam wanted to shout with frustration. *Didn't these people realize she was running a homicide investigation?* "I wish to hell Farnsworth would let me test the senators for DNA."

"That'll never happen," Freddie said. "Not without probable cause."

"Then let's get it."

"Define 'get it.'"

"Time to do some digging into senatorial closets."

"Do I have to?"

"Yes, you have to. Let's go run this one by Skip. Maybe he can help us figure out a way to do this without ending up unemployed afterward."

"That'd be preferred. I'll meet you there."

"Anything yet on Nick's phone?"

"Not yet."

"You put a rush on it?"

"Sure did."

Sam sighed. More delays. "Alright, I'll see you at Skip's."

On the way to her father's house, she debated whether to call Nick. She wanted so badly to know how things were going in Cleveland—and to give him a piece of her mind for calling her father about the threat. But every time she imagined Nick's mother wanting nothing from him but his money, she ached for him. How she hoped she was wrong about that, but her gut was telling her to be worried. In the end, she decided not to call him. She'd wait to hear about it when he got home, even if the waiting was killing her.

Ignoring the patrol car that followed her, she parked on Ninth Street and took the ramp to her father's house. With a quick knock she entered the living room to find Skip and Celia sitting in front of the TV.

"What did I tell you about knocking?" Celia asked without removing her eyes from the screen.

"I'll do better next time," Sam said. "What's going on?"

"Senator Lightfeather is resigning from the Senate," Skip said.

"Oh man," Sam said.

"...and so I've decided," Lightfeather was saying, "that I need to spend as much time as I can with my family, to repair the damage I have caused." Next to him, his wife stood with a tight-lipped frown. The dais sported a Washington Hilton logo, so at least he hadn't left the building where Sam had told him to stay. "As such, today I announce my resignation from the United States Senate. I have treasured every moment of the years I spent representing the people of the great state of Arizona. I thank the citizens for the faith they had in me, and I will work for the rest of my life to once again be worthy of that faith. I ask that you respect my family's need for privacy at this difficult time."

The moment he stepped off the stage, the network's anchor and political analyst began speculating about Lightfeather's association with two Capitol Cleaning Services employees who'd been murdered. "A well-placed police source tells Capitol News that Regina

Argueta de Castro was expecting Lightfeather's baby," the analyst said.

Sam let out a shriek. "*How the hell do they know that*? *Goddamn it*!" She reached for her phone and called HQ. "It's Lieutenant Holland. Put me through to the chief immediately." When told he was in a meeting, she said, "Interrupt it."

The chief came on the line a minute later. "Lieutenant."

"Sorry to interrupt your meeting, but we have a leak." She told him what she'd heard the reporter say. "I will guarantee you none of my people breathed a word of that to the media, so I want to know who this 'well-placed' source is."

"So do I."

"You might want to start with Stahl."

"He may have it in for you personally, but he'd never squeal to the press."

"And you're *sure* of that?"

"Not as sure as I'd like to be. Have you seen Detective McBride today?"

"Yes. She's hanging in there."

"I wanted to see her or send her something, but I wasn't sure if I should go there…"

It was so unlike him to be uncertain. "In this case, it might be best to send some flowers. A visit from the chief might be more than she can handle."

"Then that's what I'll do. Keep me posted on the investigation."

"Find that mole," Sam said.

"On it."

Returning the phone to her coat pocket, Sam turned to her father and stepmother.

"How's Jeannie?" Celia asked, her pretty face etched with worry.

"As well as can be expected."

"Did he…?"

They knew she couldn't give them details and would never ask her to. Her silence spoke for her.

"Oh, God," Celia said. "I was so hoping…"

"Me too."

"What's the status of the investigation?" Skip asked, his voice gruff. Sam had no doubt he was deeply affected by what had happened to McBride. Even as a disabled retiree, he was still one of them. Sam made sure of that, as did Farnsworth, Malone and Skip's many other friends within the department.

"Stalled," Sam said, falling onto the sofa. "I'm convinced we're probably looking for a senator or someone equally powerful, but Farnsworth won't let me request DNA without probable cause."

"So you're going to get it," Skip said.

"That's the plan."

"You gotta be *really* careful."

"That much I know. How do you suggest I approach it?"

Before he could answer, Sam's cell phone rang again. She didn't recognize the 202 number, but took the call anyway.

"Holland."

"Darren Tabor."

Sam suppressed a groan. "I'm *busy*, Darren."

"I saw Detective Gonzales coming out of the courthouse with a baby in his arms. I didn't think he had kids, so I'm smelling a story."

While Sam was thrilled for Gonzo, who'd apparently prevailed in court, the fact that Darren knew about it wasn't good news. "Don't go there, Darren. Please. I'm asking you to do this for me as a personal favor."

"That'll mean you owe me one."

Sam grimaced. "What do you want?"

"Tell me there's a connection between McBride's abduction and the dead cleaning ladies."

"There's a connection, but I can't say more than that right now."

"And when you can?"

"I'll keep you in mind."

"Excellent."

"And you'll forget about the thing with Gonzales?"

"What thing?"

Sam released a sigh of relief. "Thanks. While I have you, maybe you could do me another favor."

"That'd put you pretty deep in the hole to me," he said, but she could hear the laughter in his voice.

"It'd be worth owing you if you can find out where the leak about the father of Regina's baby came from."

"Is it true? It's Lightfeather's?"

"Maybe, maybe not. Either way, I'd like to know how the media got that tidbit."

"I'll do some sniffing around. See what I can find out."

"Keep it down low that you're doing it for me."

"Lieutenant, I am nothing if not the *soul* of discretion."

"Sure you are," she said, chuckling. "Let me know what you hear."

"Maybe you should program my number into your phone so you'll have it when you need me in the future."

"Hanging up now."

"Where did Nick go today?" Darren asked.

Sam slapped the phone closed.

"If I didn't know better," Skip said, "I might think you enjoy sparring with that boy."

"He's not as bad as some of them."

"He was tough on you after Johnson."

Sam shuddered at the reminder of the child who had died in a shoot-out she'd ordered at a crack house. "He gave us a heads-up when the *Reporter* was getting ready to trash me," she reminded her father.

"That's true," Skip said.

Sam hated remembering that the entire city knew about her near-abortion—the one she'd planned to have in college before she miscarried. An employee of the women's clinic that had treated her had decided to cash in on Sam's newfound notoriety. But they'd taken care of her and ensured she'd be tied up in a legal web for many years to come.

"So you want to talk about how to get those guys in high places to talk?" Skip asked.

Anxious to think of anything other than the long-ago nightmare that she believed had led to her current fertility issues, Sam nodded. "Yeah. Tell me what you'd do."

SAM AND FREDDIE took over the dining room at Nick's place, using laptops to search the internet for every detail they could find about the lives of the five senators who'd had regular contact with Regina and Maria. The daylong canvas in Foggy Bottom had yielded two security cameras that had caught only shadowy images and not a single witness who reported seeing the abduction. They'd also gotten nothing helpful from a thorough investigation of the alley where Jeannie had been dumped. Sam was about to tear her hair out in frustration.

"Get this," Freddie said, his eyes dancing over the screen. "Trent was in a car accident his senior year of high school."

"Fatalities?"

"Two—both girls. He was driving, and his pants were unzipped when the cops cut him out of the car."

"Drunk?"

"High. They found marijuana in the car."

"Whoa. How'd the press never get ahold of this?"

"They did." He spun the laptop around so she could see the video Freddie had found of Trent's interview on Oprah in which he'd taken full credit for what he called a "youthful mistake." The Montana voters had bought his story and sent him to Washington ten years earlier, as an appointee to finish out the term of a senator who was forced to resign after a scandal. He'd won the seat on his own in the last election.

"Once again, the little woman stands staunchly by her husband's side while he admits to being a scumbag," Sam said of the Oprah video that featured Trent and his wife.

"You've got a real beef with that, huh?"

"I just don't get these women who think so little of themselves that they blindly stand by these guys."

"What would you do if the press found out about something stupid that Nick had done as a kid? You wouldn't stand by him if it turned into a media circus?"

"Nick doesn't do stupid things."

"Everyone does stupid things at some point in their lives."

"Nick never did." Sam chewed on her pen as she wondered once again how things were going with his mother. "He had an odd upbringing. Not a lot of time for foolishness." She was quite certain, in fact, that he'd been so focused on hockey and school and his goal of going to Harvard on an academic scholarship that he never had time for youthful stupidity.

"Why do you have that worried look on your face?"

"Do I?"

Freddie nodded.

Sam told him about where Nick was and who he was dealing with as well as her worries that his mother might be after his money.

"Damn," Freddie said. "I can't imagine having a mother like that."

"Speaking of mothers, is the dinner party on?"

"I don't know if I should do it. With the case and McBride..."

"You need to get this issue resolved once and for

all. You can't be caught in the middle between your mother and Elin the way you are now."

"We'll see what Friday brings. I asked them both to save the night, but I'm not sure Elin will show. She wasn't too happy about the idea. If she does come, I might take them out to eat rather than cooking. I figure if we're in public, they can't claw each other's eyes out."

"True." Turning back to the case, she tapped a pen against the table as she mulled over the thoughts swirling around in her mind.

"What're you thinking?"

"Something Jeannie said today keeps nagging at me."

"What's that?"

"The message he told her to give me—'Tell your boss to back off on the dead whores, or she'll be next.'"

"What about it?"

"He called them whores."

"So?"

"So nothing in our investigation has led to any kind of promiscuity. Even though both were pregnant and Regina was involved with Lightfeather, we haven't found a single other man linked to either of them."

"Figure of speech?"

"Could be," Sam said. "But I keep going back to the money they were sending home. Where would they get that? You said drugs, gambling or prostitution. Remember?"

"Yeah, so you think they were hooking on the side?"

"Gonzo spoke to Maria's neighbor who said her

routine was exactly the same seven days a week. She came home from work and took a shower. The woman upstairs heard the pipes clanging every morning."

"Okay…"

"JoAnn Smithson told us they work five nights a week, Monday through Friday nights. So what was Maria doing the other two nights?"

"Good question."

"One to ask her friend Selina. We can follow up with Lightfeather again about Regina's weekend schedule. In the meantime, let's finish the research on the senators. I'd love to find some skeletons in the closets of Stenhouse or Cook."

"If they've got 'em, we'll find 'em."

BY ELEVEN, SAM and Freddie had read every word they could find about their five senators, but hadn't found any other bombshells. "I guess we'll start with Trent in the morning," she said.

"Sounds like a plan. Should I meet you there?"

"Let's go to HQ first to see if third shift got anywhere tonight. I also want to know if we've got DNA results from Maria. Will you check to see if there's a report on Nick's cell yet?"

"Logging in right now." He scrolled through his emails. "Not yet."

"What the hell is taking so long? Everything on this case is taking forever!"

"A couple of dead cleaning ladies certainly don't inspire the same sense of urgency as a dead senator or Supreme Court nominee. That's for sure."

"They're just as urgent to me."

"Which is why you're a rare and special woman, Lieutenant."

She made a face at him even though she was amused, as always, by his sucking up.

At the sound of the front door opening and closing, Freddie gathered up his laptop and shoved it into his backpack. "I'll see you at HQ in the a.m."

Filled with anxiety, Sam followed Freddie into the living room where Nick was hanging his coat in the closet. One look at his handsome, exhausted face and Sam could tell it hadn't been a good day.

Freddie said a quick hello to Nick and showed himself out.

Sam went to Nick and slipped her arms around him, snuggling into his chest. At first he was rigid, but then his arms encircled her and the starch left his spine.

"You were right," he said after a long period of silence.

Sam closed her eyes tight, aching from the hurt she heard in his voice. "I'm sorry." While she wanted to know how much the day trip had cost him, she didn't ask because it would embarrass him.

"I should've known," he said in a bitter tone that was so unlike him. "People like her don't change."

Sam looked up at him and raised her hands to frame his face. "We don't need her. *You* don't need her."

He nodded in agreement.

"It's her loss, Nick. She'll never know the wonderful, kind, loving, generous man that I know, because she's too selfish to be bothered."

With his hands on her hips, he held her close to him. "I couldn't wait to get home to you. All day, I stayed focused on that, and it got me through. *You* got me through."

"I felt so helpless, wanting to do something for you," she said, hugging him again.

"You did, babe. By being here waiting for me, you helped." He bent to kiss her. "I've had enough of this day. Let's go to bed."

TWENTY-ONE

GONZO STOOD OVER the crib and watched his son sleep. In the course of one amazing evening, he'd learned how to feed, change and bathe him, how to properly hold him, how to console him and he'd been told that at this young age, smiles usually mean gas. Sam's sisters, Angela and Tracy, had spent hours turning his empty second bedroom into a fully outfitted nursery and teaching him everything he needed to know to care for little Alex.

Now the rise and fall of his tiny chest held Gonzo mesmerized. He had his hands thrown over his head, and when Gonzo touched one of them it squeezed shut around his finger in a surprisingly tight grip. Gonzo's heart contracted just as tightly. Ever since Ms. Avery placed the baby in his arms, Gonzo's every emotion had hovered close to the surface.

Christina came up behind him and slipped her arms around his waist. "You should sleep when he sleeps," she whispered. "He'll be awake and hungry in a few hours."

"I'm afraid to leave him. What if he stops breathing or something?"

"He won't," she said. "I promise."

Gonzo gazed at the baby for another minute before

he extricated his finger from Alex's grip and let Christina lead him from the room.

Even though his bedroom was right across the hall, Gonzo still checked to make sure the baby monitor Tracy had set up was working properly. He turned to find Christina watching him, amusement dancing in her eyes.

"Are all new parents this much of a mess?" he asked as he tugged the T-shirt over his head.

"Probably, but most of them have nine months to prepare for it. You've only had a few days."

"What do you think about Angela offering to watch him for me while I'm at work?"

"It sounds ideal to me. She's someone you trust who certainly knows what she's doing."

He sat next to her on the bed and reached for her hand. "I can't believe how it all worked out. A week ago, I didn't even know he existed. And now…"

Christina leaned her head on his shoulder. "Now you can't imagine your life without him."

"Yes. Exactly." He squeezed her hand, appreciating that she seemed to understand how he was feeling. "I have to find a way to tell my parents about this—soon."

"I'm sure they'll be very excited for you and on the first plane back from Arizona."

"I hope they won't be disappointed about how it happened. Not my finest hour."

"But look what it got you—an adorable son."

"True."

"They might be upset at first by how it happened,

but once they see him and that dimpled chin of his, they'll fall in love too."

"I hope you're right."

"Come on." She tugged his hand to urge him into bed. "You need to sleep."

"Shouldn't I check on him one more time?"

She laughed. "He's fine, Tommy."

Reluctantly, he let her draw him into bed. If she hadn't been there, he probably would've stood watch by the crib all night long. After she shut off the light, he reached for her. When she was settled in her usual spot with her head on his chest, her arm across his belly and her leg intertwined with his, he exhaled a long deep breath. So this was what it felt like to have a family of his own, he thought. A woman who'd become indispensible to him and a baby he'd fallen for at first sight.

It hadn't happened the conventional way his mother probably would've preferred, but somehow it had happened.

"What're you thinking about?" she asked.

"That I like this—having you here with me and him sleeping in the next room."

"You sound surprised."

"I guess I am a little. I never saw my life turning out this way."

"And what way is it turning out?"

"Settled."

"Is that bad?"

He heard vulnerability in her question and wanted to reassure her. Kissing the top of her head, he said,

"It's good—very, very good. I know it's a lot for you to take on, Christina. You didn't sign on for a guy with a baby…"

"I signed on for you, and Alex comes with the package now. I get that, Tommy, so please don't worry about me." She rested her fingers on his lips. "Shut it all off for a while and get some sleep. You're going to need it."

He tried to close down his whirling mind because he knew she was right. The baby would be up before the night was out, and he needed to sleep while he could. For a long time after she drifted off, he stared into the darkness. When he was sure she was asleep, he extricated himself from her embrace, got up, tugged on a pair of boxers and went across the hall—just to make sure his son was still breathing.

SAM WOKE UP to find Nick studying the ceiling. She shifted to her side and rested her hand on his chest. "Did you sleep?"

"Some."

Which meant not much. "Want to talk about it?"

"Nope." He surprised her when he abruptly got up and headed for the shower.

"Hmm," Sam said to the empty room. Not sure how to play this one, she lay there for a few minutes mulling over her options. Then she got up and went into the bathroom. She opened the shower door. "Want some company?"

"Sure."

The one-word answers were driving her nuts, but

she kept her mouth shut and got busy washing her hair. Usually, he liked to do that for her, but today he didn't offer, and she didn't ask. In the aftermath of Julian Sinclair's murder, she'd learned to give him space to let him deal with things his own way. But Sam worried about him bouncing back from yet another setback when he was still grieving his lost friends.

"I wonder how Gonzo is making out with the baby," Sam said, deciding that he'd prefer to talk about anything other than the elephant in the room.

"He got custody?" Nick asked.

At least he was up to three words. That was progress. "Yes." Sam filled him in on what had happened the day before.

"Wow. That's amazing. Good for him."

"Tough timing right in the middle of the case."

"I can imagine."

Under normal circumstances, Sam might try to talk to him about the odd feelings pinging around inside of her since hearing that Gonzo won custody of the son he hadn't even known he had until a few days ago. Here she was, desperately wanting a baby she probably couldn't have, and one had landed in her friend's arms. While she was genuinely happy for Gonzo, she couldn't help being a little jealous too. But with Nick nursing his own hurts, she didn't think this was the time to mention hers.

They went through the motions of getting dressed and eating breakfast, and still Nick remained quiet and withdrawn.

Sam put her cereal bowl in the dishwasher and

turned to study him. He seemed to be absorbed in the *Washington Post*, but she wondered if he was really reading or using the newspaper to avoid talking to her. She went to him and rested her hands on his shoulders, bending to press a kiss to his smooth cheek. "May I say something?"

Reluctantly—or so it seemed to her—he nodded.

"I get that you're used to dealing with this stuff on your own because you didn't have anyone else to share it with, but now you do. You don't have to go through this or anything else by yourself anymore."

He reached up to take her hand and brought it to his lips. "I appreciate that you want to help, babe, and as soon as I figure out what I need, you'll be the first to know, okay?"

"Fair enough. I can't stand to see you suffering in silence, Nick."

He shifted the chair and brought her down to sit on his lap, wrapping his strong arms around her. They sat there for a long time, until Sam pulled back to caress his face and kiss him. "I love you. I wish I had time to go to Cleveland and tell her what I think of her."

That drew a short laugh from him. "She wouldn't know what hit her."

"Might be just what she needs."

"No doubt, but it won't change anything. It is what it is."

"Will you be okay today?"

He nodded. "I've got another long day and dinner with Richard and Judson at the Old Ebbitt after work," he said, referring to the Virginia Democratic Party leadership.

Recalling that John O'Connor had spent his last night alive doing the exact same thing, Sam shuddered.

"What?"

"That was how John spent his last night."

"Yeah."

The sadness she saw on his face made her sorry she'd mentioned it, especially right now when he had something else making him sad.

"Life goes on," he said. "Even when we think it won't."

The statement reminded her of the aftermath of the ectopic pregnancy during her marriage to Peter that had nearly taken her life and her sanity. "I'm here if you need me today." She got up from his lap. "Don't hesitate to call. I'm never too busy for you."

"You're being extra careful, right?"

"I'm being tailed." She frowned as she checked her watch. "In fact, my posse should be arriving any second." As if on cue, the doorbell rang. Sam forced a smile. "Right on time."

He stood up to hug her. "I know you hate it, but remember, it's temporary. The faster you find this guy, the faster you lose the tail."

"I know, I know. I just wonder if they'd insist on a tail if he'd threatened a male cop."

"They probably would."

"*Right…*"

"I haven't forgotten that I offered to do some digging

on the senators Maria and Regina cleaned for. I'll do that today."

"Thanks. While you're at it, see if Christina gave your cell number to anyone new this week."

"Be careful today, Sam."

"I always am." She cradled his face in her hands and left him with one last kiss. "Hang in there, Senator."

"I always do."

"TELL ME YOU have *something*," Sam said to Lindsey McNamara.

"Just stuff you already suspected—the DNA from Maria matched guy number two from Regina, and he's not in the system. Regina's fetus was definitely Lightfeather's."

"Okay," Sam said. "I needed the confirmation even though we already knew, so thanks for that. How soon until you can confirm that guy number two grabbed Jeannie?"

"I'm running her rape kit now." Lindsey's green eyes went soft with compassion. "How is she?"

"Not good," Sam said. "Not that all rapes aren't vicious, but this one was particularly so. Probably because she's a cop."

Dismayed, Lindsey shook her head. "Unbelievable. Let me know if I can do anything else to help catch this asshole."

"You got it, Doc. Thanks."

Malone came in as Lindsey was leaving.

"What's up?" Sam asked him.

"No luck from our end figuring out who your mole is."

"You talked to Stahl?"

"Denied it vehemently and was 'offended' you suggested it could be him."

"Whatever."

"They've set a date for Peter's hearing."

Sam braced herself. "When?"

"Tomorrow."

"I can't believe they're really going through with this."

"Neither can I or anyone else around here, but you need to prepare yourself, Sam."

"How do I prepare myself to have the ex-husband who tried to kill me and my fiancé back on the streets?"

"If he screwed up once, he'll do it again, and next time we'll nail him."

"Will that be before or after he kills me—or Nick?" Remembering that day—the huge explosion, being propelled through the air into the bushes outside Nick's former home in Virginia, the smells, the blood on his face, the shattered glass, the ringing in her ears… A shudder rippled through her.

"We'll be watching him, Lieutenant. Count on that."

"Well, since my life—and Nick's—probably depends on it, I'll count on you to make sure we have eyes and ears on him." She glanced up at him. "You really think he'll get sprung."

He gave a short nod. "Unfortunately."

"Sometimes our justice system really sucks."

"Yes, it does, but it's the only one we have. We'll get him next time, Sam. I promise."

"I just hope I'm alive to see it."

Malone winced. "I'm sorry about all of this. I feel like we failed you so profoundly."

Sam shook her head. "No, you didn't. I was as responsible as anyone for what happened that night. I should've known better."

"Will you attend the hearing tomorrow?"

Sam thought about that for a minute. "No, I don't think I will. Why should I give him the satisfaction of thinking he's that important to me? You'll be there, right?"

Malone nodded. "You bet I will."

"Just make sure he comes out with a big fat restraining order keeping him as far away from me, Nick and my family as we can get him. I want every member of my family named in the order."

"That much I can do," he said on his way out.

Just the thought of Peter back on the streets was enough to make her sick, so Sam took a moment to clear her mind and refocus.

Freddie came in a few minutes later.

"Grand Central Station around here this morning," Sam said.

"What's the matter with you? You're pale as a ghost."

"Peter's hearing is tomorrow."

"Crap."

"Yeah," she said, shaking it off. Time to get back to work. She refused to give that asshole one more ounce of her energy. She'd already given him far too much. "What's up?"

"Someone here to see you, boss."

"Who is it?"

"Patricia Donaldson," he whispered.

Sam's eyes widened. She was the mother of John O'Connor's son—the son who had murdered his father and several other people. "What does she want?"

"To talk to you. That's all she would say."

"Ugh," Sam said. "Like I need this today. While I'm with her, get me the names and addresses of the numbers that showed up on both Regina's and Maria's phones. Also, tell Archie he has thirty minutes to get me the dump on Lightfeather's phone and Nick's," she said, referring to Lt. Archelotta, who ran the IT squad. "I don't care what he has to do."

"I was just going to tell you—the phone company wants a subpoena for Nick's phone."

"Tell them to *call him*. He'll authorize it, for Christ's sake."

Freddie scowled at her use of the Lord's name. "Should I show Patricia in?"

Sam moaned. "If you must…"

A well-dressed blonde came through the door a minute later, looking nervous and out of place. "Thank you so much for seeing me, Lieutenant."

"Of course. Please, have a seat."

She perched on the chair on the other side of Sam's desk. "I understand you were the detective in charge of John's case."

"I was, yes."

"I wanted to thank you for moving so quickly to get justice for him, even if I wish justice had led in a direction other than my son."

"Ms. Donaldson…"

She fiddled with a tissue she produced from her purse. "It's just, I wondered…you're absolutely certain that it was my Thomas who killed his father?"

Oh God, Sam thought. *God, God, God.*

"They were always so close, and I'm having trouble imagining that my son could've done these horrible things he's accused of. I figured you'd tell me the truth. I don't know who to believe anymore."

"I'm absolutely certain it was Thomas," Sam said. "I'm sorry if that's not what you want to hear, but the evidence is irrefutable. In addition to the evidence, he confessed in front of me as well as Senators O'Connor and Cappuano. I'm afraid the case against him is solid."

Her eyes filled with tears. "He must've had some sort of breakdown and didn't know what he was doing. The boy I raised would never hurt anyone, let alone his father or those other people he didn't even know." Two of his father's ex-lovers and the husband of one of them had been among Thomas's victims.

"I'm sure his attorney will take that under consideration," Sam said, desperately wanting to end this excruciating interview. "Hearing that his father had been unfaithful to you did something to him."

"They're considering an insanity plea, as you must already know."

"I've heard that."

"I'm sorry to have taken up your time. I was just looking for some answers."

"I wish I could've been more helpful." As she said the words, another thought occurred to Sam. "I know someone you could talk to who might understand what you're going through."

Patricia's eyes brightened with hope. "Who?"

"Laine O'Connor."

Patricia's hope was quickly replaced by despair. "She won't want to talk to me. They think I ruined John's life by getting pregnant. I'm sure they blame me for his death too."

"They don't," Sam assured her. "If anything, they blame themselves for forcing John to live a double life. I've come to know them quite well in the last few months, and I'm fairly confident Laine would welcome the chance to make amends with you." At least Sam hoped so. She was dallying in areas she probably had no business butting into. The bad blood between the O'Connors and Patricia went back decades. "Would you like me to call her for you?"

"If you're sure she won't mind," Patricia said.

"I'm sure she won't."

TWENTY-TWO

"That was a good thing you did back there," Freddie said when they were in the car.

"Huh?"

"Hooking Patricia up with Laine—two grieving mothers, two women who loved John O'Connor. It was a good thing."

"I hope so," Sam said. "I'm half expecting a 'what the hell were you thinking' phone call from Nick."

"Nah." Freddie bit into one of the three cream donuts he'd bought from the roach coach outside HQ. "He'll approve. In fact, I hate to say it, LT, but you're becoming sensitive in your old age. Being in love has softened you."

"Screw you."

He chortled with laughter and then downed a second donut.

Sam's mouth watered at the smell of sugar and cream. "If you're done stuffing your face, tell me what we know about Bradford Tillinghast."

"He's a lobbyist with the firm Tillinghast-Young. They represent oil company interests to Congress."

"And what was his number doing on the cell phone records for both our dead cleaning ladies?"

"A very good question indeed."

Sam smiled. "I have a feeling this interview is gonna make my day." Sensitive. Whatever. She loved nothing more than watching smug, powerful people— or people who *thought* they were powerful—come unglued when they became the subject of a murder investigation.

"What about our plan to talk to Senator Trent first thing?" Freddie asked.

"We'll get to him. Eventually. Gonna be a long-ass day."

At the well-appointed K Street offices of Tillinghast-Young, Sam and Freddie were told that Mr. Tillinghast was in a meeting and couldn't be disturbed.

"I love that answer," Sam said to Freddie. "Don't you love that answer?"

"It's one of my favorites," he said.

The pretty receptionist's eyes darted between them, and Sam noticed the slight tremble of a manicured hand.

Sam leaned on the reception desk and brought her face in close to the other woman's. "Here's the deal—go tell Mr. Tillinghast that two homicide detectives from the MPD are here to see him. Tell him we can either do this here in the comfort of his office, or we can arrest him and do it downtown where the interrogation rooms are not nearly as comfortable. Got me?"

The receptionist scurried down a long hallway as if her pants were on fire.

"Mean and scary," Freddie said.

"Sensitive, my ass."

"Is your ass sensitive? Hmm, I wouldn't have thought that."

Sam glowered at him. "You'd better shut up before you find out how sensitive my fist is."

"Yes, ma'am," he said, but she caught the smirk he directed her way.

"You're in a good mood for a guy who is isn't getting any."

The smirk was replaced by a frown. "I'll be back in the saddle after tomorrow night."

"You're certain she's going to show, huh?"

"Of course she will. She's into more than just the sex."

"Sure about that?"

"Yes," he said, but he didn't sound sure. "She'll show."

"Hmm, hope so."

"Do you? Do you really hope so?"

Before Sam could reply, the receptionist returned and gestured for them to follow her.

"This is the kind of cooperation that goes a long way toward earning the favor of the MPD," Sam said to Freddie who rolled his eyes at her.

Bradford Tillinghast was exactly what Sam expected him to be: tall, blond, built like a former college football player and dressed in a navy pinstripe suit that had been cut just for him. The luxurious office completed the picture of an all-American success story.

"What can I do for y'all?" he asked in a drawl that sounded like Texas.

"You can tell us how you know Regina Argueta de Castro and Maria Espanosa."

For a brief instant his eyes widened before his expression became impassive. But Sam caught the flash of fear.

"Who?"

"Don't screw with us, Mr. Tillinghast. We've got your number on both their cell phones. So unless you'd like to move this interview downtown, you have five seconds to tell me how you know them."

She watched his Adam's apple bob up and down.

"I'd like to speak to my lawyer."

"Great," Sam said. "Have him meet you at MPD Headquarters." She nodded to Freddie who pulled out his handcuffs.

"Wait." Tillinghast glanced warily at the coworkers who were pretending to not watch the goings-on behind his glass-walled office. "Are the handcuffs really necessary?"

"We don't transport anyone uncuffed. Department policy."

As he ran a trembling hand through his well-coifed hair, Sam caught the glint of a wedding ring.

"What's it going to be?" she asked. "Here or there?"

He took a deep breath and released it. Hands on hips, he fixated on the wall displaying his trophies and framed awards. Life had been good to Bradford Tillinghast. Until today.

"I paid them for sex," he said in a rush of words. "I didn't know their last names or anything else about them. And I only met with each of them twice."

Buzzing from the first big break in the case, Sam said, "Where did you meet for these encounters?"

"The Ambassador," he said, naming a four-star hotel in the heart of downtown Washington.

"How did you make contact with them?"

Hesitating, he shifted his gaze to the window. "I'd really like to speak to my lawyer now."

Apparently, he was far more concerned about giving up the information on how he found Regina and Maria than he was about being paraded through his office in handcuffs. Interesting. She gestured for Freddie to cuff him.

Freddie slapped the cuffs on Tillinghast's wrists and read him the Miranda warning. Tillinghast kept his head down as they walked him past his shocked colleagues.

Sam tried not to be judgmental, but she figured the walk of shame was the least of what a married guy deserved for paying for sex four times—or so he said—with other women. She wondered how long it would take for official Washington to be set abuzz by Tillinghast's arrest.

Just as she had the thought, her cell phone rang. A quick glance at the LCD showed Nick's number. She hoped he wasn't annoyed at her for asking Laine to see Patricia.

"Hey," she said.

"Did you really just arrest Brad Tillinghast?"

"Christ have mercy. That didn't take long. How did you hear?"

"Trevor saw it on Twitter," he said, referring to his communications director.

"Fabulous." Tillinghast's coworkers hadn't wasted any time spreading the word.

"You are one *ballsy* chick, Holland. What'd he do?"

"Stonewalling. That's all I can say right now."

"The news has set the Hill on fire."

"Wait 'til you hear the rest of the story."

"I'll look forward to that."

"So, um, you might be hearing from Laine today."

"Already did."

"Is she pissed? The idea was out of my mouth before I took the time to consider—"

"She thinks it's a great idea, babe. As she said, if she'd done it years ago, maybe her son would still be alive."

"Oh, well, I'm glad she's not mad. I just figured, you know, they both loved John. Maybe they could help each other."

"You did good, Samantha."

Shrugging off the praise, she said, "How are you?"

"I'm okay."

Sam stood on the K Street sidewalk and watched Freddie load Tillinghast into the back of her car. "Really? Or are you just saying that?"

"It usually takes a week or two to bounce back from seeing her." He released a bitter-sounding chuckle. "You'd think I would've learned by now not to get my hopes up."

Sam closed her eyes. The pain she heard in his voice

was unbearable. "I don't want you to see her anymore. At some point you have to say enough already."

"I think maybe I've reached that point this time."

"Good," she said. "Well, not good, but you know what I mean."

"Yes, babe, I know what you mean."

"We have each other now. We don't need people who bring us down." She thought of Peter being released from jail—possibly tomorrow—and knew she needed to tell him. "I hate to pile on, but I heard Peter's hearing is tomorrow. Malone made it sound like there's almost no way he won't get sprung."

"Goddamn it," Nick muttered. "I know I've said this before, but you've just gotta be fucking kidding me. He tried to *kill* us!"

"I know, babe. Believe me, I know." She hated to hear him so upset on top of what he was already dealing with. "We'll be on him like white on rice. He won't be stupid enough to pull another stunt like the bombs."

"You hope."

"I hate to say it, but I've got to go."

"You're not trying to dodge the tail, are you?"

The thought had occurred to her—more than once—but she'd never admit that to him. "I've been on my best behavior."

That drew a short laugh from him. "That'll be the day. Talk to you later. Be careful out there."

"Always." As Sam ended the call and got into the car, she experienced a pang of fear about what he might do to keep Peter in jail.

"THIS IS SENATOR Nick Cappuano for Mr. Forrester."

"One moment please, Senator."

Even though Nick knew this phone call was not a good idea from a personal *or* political standpoint, there was no way he could sit idly by and not make one last effort to keep that scumbag Gibson in jail where he belonged.

"Senator," Forrester said in his nasally New York accent. "What can I do for you or do I already know?"

"You can tell me you're doing everything in your power to keep that bastard Gibson in jail."

The U.S. Attorney cleared his throat. "As I mentioned the last time we spoke on this subject, I don't have the evidence to retain Mr. Gibson."

"That's bullshit, and you know it."

"Senator, this conversation is so far outside the realm of appropriate that it may be of interest to the Senate Ethics Committee."

"Go ahead and report me. But if I were you, I'd be far more concerned about releasing a murderer who will no doubt come after my future wife again."

"I'll remind you that Mr. Gibson was only charged with *attempted* murder. Your future wife and her team failed to follow procedure, Senator, and that's the only reason we're having this conversation. If they can get me something else that ties Gibson to the items found in his apartment, I'll certainly entertain new charges. Until then, we have nothing to talk about."

"If something happens to her, Forrester, I hope you'll be able to live with it."

"My conscience, Senator, is crystal clear. Your

fiancée and her team had Gibson by the short hairs. All they had to do was wait for the warrant. They chose not to do that, and there's not a damned thing I can do about it now."

"You could find a way to delay his release to give them time to gather more evidence."

"If there was more evidence to be gotten, I'd have it by now. You know that as well as I do."

"There has to be something you can do—"

"I have to get back to work, and I'm sure you do too. Have a good day, Senator."

Before Nick could reply, the line went dead. Furious, he threw his BlackBerry across the room and watched with satisfaction as it hit the wall and shattered into pieces.

Christina stepped into the office, surveyed the remnants of the phone and then turned to him. "Everything all right in here, Senator?"

"No." He reached for his suit coat and headed for the door. "Everything is *not* all right."

Nick stalked out of his office in the Hart Building and hustled through the underground tunnels that led into the Capitol building. In one of the hallways a network news reporter was interviewing one of his colleagues. He waited until they were finished and then flagged down the reporter and cameraman. "I have a statement I'd like to make."

Since Nick rarely gave interviews despite frequent requests, the reporter's eyes lit up with anticipation.

When the cameraman was in place, Nick tried not to think about the political fallout that might occur in the aftermath of his statement. "As many of you know, Peter Gibson, the ex-husband of my fiancée, Lieutenant Sam Holland, affixed bombs to her car and mine in December. When the device attached to her car detonated, we were both injured. Later that night, believing Gibson had dangerous bomb-making materials in his apartment, officers entered the dwelling prior to obtaining a search warrant. Once inside they discovered items that could've leveled his building as well as several others nearby. Even though a partial fingerprint ties Gibson to the bomb that was attached to my car, the charges against Gibson may be dropped tomorrow because the officers entered his apartment without a warrant. U.S. Attorney Forrester tells me there's nothing he can do to stop this from occurring. This time tomorrow, Peter Gibson may once again be free to resume his bomb-making activities. I thought it was important that the citizens of the District were aware of this so they can be vigilant. That's all I have to say."

The stunned reporter and cameraman stared at him.

Nick turned away from them and found Christina and his communications director, Trevor Donnolly, also staring at him.

"*You called Forrester about this?*" Christina's voice was an octave higher than usual.

"You're goddamned right I did. Gibson tried to *murder* us. You really think he ought to be let out of jail?"

"I just, um…Wow."

"Forget it," Nick said, needing to get out of there.

"I'm going to the gym. Tell Richard and Judson I can't meet them tonight. I'll see you tomorrow." He left his overcoat and belongings in the office and exited through the south entrance to the Capitol. On the way out, several other reporters tried to stop him, but he waved them off. He had nothing left to say.

TWENTY-THREE

WHEN SAM AND Freddie entered the interrogation room, Bradford Tillinghast sat up straighter in his chair. His attorney, an older man with snow-white hair, sat next to him.

"May I please make a phone call?" Tillinghast asked.

"Eventually," Sam said.

"I need to talk to my wife. Before she hears about this from someone else."

Judging by how quickly Nick had heard, Sam guessed that ship had already sailed, but she wasn't about to tell Tillinghast that. Funny how he was thinking of his wife *now*.

"May we have your permission to record this interview?" she asked.

The lawyer acquiesced. "What about the phone call?" he asked.

"Later."

Tillinghast released a tortured sigh, as it seemed to settle in on him that his wife would probably hear about his arrest from someone other than him.

"I'd like to know how you made contact with Regina and Maria," Sam said.

"I don't wish to disclose that information," Tillinghast said, his face suddenly red and flushed.

Sam cast a glance at the lawyer, who'd no doubt provided the line, and then back at Tillinghast. "Will you disclose the details of the various encounters with the women?"

His eyes darted to the lawyer, who nodded.

A bead of sweat ran down Tillinghast's face. "I, um… I met Maria first. We…I ah…have 'appetites' that my wife finds offensive." He'd no sooner swiped away one drop of sweat when another appeared.

"And what about Maria? Did she find your 'appetites' offensive?"

"If she did, she never said so to me."

"How much did you pay her to satisfy your perversions?"

His eyes flashed with outrage. "I'm not perverted! I just like certain things…"

"How much?"

"Two thousand."

"And that bought you how much time to satisfy your 'appetites'?"

"Four hours," he mumbled.

"So you saw her twice?"

He nodded.

"I'd like the dates of these encounters."

Tillinghast looked again to his lawyer.

"Do you know the dates?" the lawyer asked him.

"Not off the top of my head."

"Where would they be?" Sam asked.

"On my calendar at work."

How stupid could he be? Sam wondered. "Which is where?"

"In my top desk drawer."

Sam looked to Freddie, who nodded with understanding. He briefly left the room to find someone to go get the calendar and returned a minute later with a consent to search form that Tillinghast signed, granting them permission to retrieve the calendar and place it into evidence.

"Did you contact them outside of the organization they worked for?"

He looked down at his hands.

"Mr. Tillinghast?"

"I offered them twice what the service paid—in cash—to meet with me the second time."

"That's how you came to have their cell numbers."

"Yes."

Sam wondered if their "freelancing" was a motive for murder. "Where were you last Friday and Saturday?"

"At a family wedding in Long Island. My wife and children can attest to that as well as scores of other family members who were there and saw me."

"Is there any chance you got Maria pregnant?" Sam asked.

At that, Tillinghast's face went from red and flushed to chalky white. "*Pregnant*?" he squeaked.

"You heard me."

"No. There's no chance."

"And you know that how?"

"Because I used condoms."

"Provided by you or her?"

The question seemed to catch him off guard. "Her," he said. "She insisted."

Sam trained a steely stare on him, waiting for the realization to set in.

"Oh my God," he said softly, so softly she wondered if the recording would capture it. "Are you saying...?"

"I'm saying she was pregnant at the time of her death."

"And you think it was *mine*?"

"I have no idea who the father is." Sam wondered if even Maria knew, but this hunk of successful all-American manhood would no doubt have made an attractive candidate to a woman looking to anchor her place in America. "Would you be willing to submit to a DNA test?"

Frantic, Tillinghast turned to his lawyer, his expression beseeching.

"If my client's DNA matches that of Maria's fetus, what would he be charged with?"

"Nothing—unless it also matches the DNA of the man who raped and murdered her."

"I did not murder her!" Tillinghast cried. "I saw her twice. We had sex, I paid her and I left. I never saw her again! I wasn't even in town when she was killed!"

"If that's the case, I'd think you would welcome a DNA test."

After a charged moment of silence, the lawyer said, "We'll submit."

"Detective Cruz, please ask Dr. McNamara to join us." After Freddie left the room, Sam said, "How soon after your liaisons with Maria did you meet up with Regina?"

"A couple of weeks."

"Why the switch to a different woman?"

"Maria refused to see me again after the second time."

"Why was that?"

"Do we really have to get into the details?"

"Yeah, we really do."

Sighing, he tightened his crossed hands until his knuckles went white. "She said I was too rough."

"But Regina didn't mind that?"

"After the second time, she wouldn't see me either."

"You're a prince among men, Mr. Tillinghast."

"Look, I can't help—"

"Save it. Were there any others?"

"Just one."

"Her name?"

"I don't know her last name."

"What was her first name?"

"Selina."

Sam suppressed a gasp. "When was the last time you saw her?"

"Last night," he muttered.

Hearing that lovely buzz of pieces falling together, Sam said, "I'm going to need to know how you initially found these women."

"I'm not willing to tell you that." His earlier bravado had been replaced by what looked like fear to Sam.

"What were you told would happen to you if you ended up in this situation?"

"I'm not willing to tell you that."

"Until you're willing, you'll be our guest in the city jail."

He launched out of his chair. "You can't do that! I didn't kill those women. I have an alibi!"

"You have information pertaining to a homicide investigation that you are not willing to divulge. That makes you an accessory to murder."

Tillinghast appealed to his lawyer. "*Do something*!"

"Tell him," Sam said to the lawyer. "There's nothing you can do."

"There's nothing I can do," the lawyer said, tugging his client's arm to get him to sit back down.

Tillinghast slumped in his chair. His robust complexion had gone pale and pasty under the fluorescent lights at HQ.

Sam smiled. "See? Told you."

Freddie returned with Lindsey McNamara.

"He's all yours, Doc." Sam called Detective Arnold from the pit. "When Dr. McNamara is done with Mr. Tillinghast, take him to central booking. Cruz, you're with me."

"Where're we going, Lieutenant?"

"To pick up our old friend Selina Rameriz. Our new friend Tillinghast hooked up with her last night."

"No way."

"Yep." Because she was concerned that the word was out about Tillinghast's arrest, Sam used her radio to order patrol officers to Selina's apartment as quickly as possible. In her car, Sam flipped on the lights and siren and made quick work of getting to Columbia Heights.

Two department cruisers were parked outside Selina's building. Sam was filled with anxiety as she wondered whether she'd find a witness or a victim waiting for her. A quick look at Freddie's tense face told her he was worried about the same thing.

Sam was relieved when she saw Selina emerge from the building, escorted by two patrol officers. The young woman was crying and resisting their attempts to escort her to the street, but she was alive. Taking a good look around at the crowd gathered on the street to watch the proceedings, Sam had no doubt that if they hadn't gotten to her when they did, their killer would have. After they talked to her downtown, Sam planned to arrange a safe house for her until they caught this guy.

Despite Tillinghast having had contact with both dead women, Sam believed him when he said he didn't kill them. Besides, his eyes were blue, and Jeannie had described her attacker's eyes as dark and mean looking. The proof would be in the DNA and in the alibi, which she asked Freddie to confirm with Tillinghast's wife.

"Why are you arresting me?" Selina cried. "I haven't done anything!"

Sam stepped up to the handcuffed woman. "Solicitation and prostitution. Ringing any bells, Ms. Rameriz?"

"I don't know what you're talking about," Selina said even as her face drained of color.

"You know exactly what I'm talking about." She gestured to Freddie. "Let's get her downtown."

"Please," Selina said as tears cascaded down her face. "Please don't do this. I needed the money. I was desperate."

"If you cooperate with our investigation into the murders of your colleagues, I might be willing to talk to the assistant U.S. attorney about immunity for you."

"What do I have to do?" she asked, her expression wary.

"Let's talk about it downtown."

AT HQ, SAM was met by the usual pack of reporters. The questions flew at her.

"Lieutenant, what do you think of the senator's statement to the media?"

"Did you put him up to calling Forrester about Gibson?"

"Why did you arrest Brad Tillinghast?"

Sam pushed past them and directed Freddie to take Selina to interrogation. She headed for her office where Captain Malone greeted her.

"What has Nick done?" she asked.

"He went to Forrester and the media about Gibson. Made quite a statement."

"Shit," Sam muttered. "He shouldn't have done that."

"It seems to have touched a chord in the city. We've been bombarded with calls."

"Fabulous," Sam said, wondering what Nick had been thinking.

"They've been calling Forrester too," Malone continued, "and he is *not* pleased."

"It won't stop them from releasing Gibson, and Nick has probably created a boatload of political trouble for himself." This was exactly the type of thing she'd been concerned about when the Virginia Democrats first approached him about finishing out the last year of John O'Connor's term—her crap landing on his crap and causing him deep shit.

"That's on him, Sam. You certainly didn't ask him to call Forrester for you." Malone hesitated. "Did you?"

"No! You know I hate that good old boy network bullshit that goes on in this town." Frustrated, Sam released the clip that held her long hair and let it fall past her shoulders. "He had a run-in with his deadbeat mother yesterday. He's not in a good place today. I don't know why he'd make that kind of statement. He has to know the media will jump all over both of us."

"Maybe it'll help."

"I guess we'll see," Sam said even though she doubted it would do anything more than cause him a great deal of political heartburn. It would probably also please Peter to see Nick so spun up over his release, but Sam refused to care about what Peter thought of anything.

Before she joined Freddie in the interrogation room, she tried to call Nick, but his phone went right to voicemail. She wondered if he'd shut it off to dodge the deluge of calls from the media or to avoid the call he knew would be coming from her.

When Sam entered the interrogation room, Selina startled and wiped the tears from her face—a pointless gesture, since they kept right on coming.

"Are you going to report me to INS?" she asked. Her English was slightly accented but fluent nonetheless.

"That depends on whether or not you cooperate with our investigation."

"What do you want to know?" Her eyes darted between Sam and Freddie.

"May I have your permission to record this interview?" Sam asked.

Selina stared at the recorder for a long moment before she nodded.

"Tell us how you came to be involved in providing sex for money," Sam said.

"You have to understand, if I hadn't been desperate, I never, *ever* would've gotten involved in something like this."

"We're not here to pass judgment, Ms. Rameriz," Sam said. "We're trying to figure out who killed your coworkers. How did you become involved?"

"It was on a break at work," she said softly. "I mentioned that my mother needed an operation and we didn't have the money. Regina said she might be able to help me."

Questions cycled through Sam's mind, but she stayed quiet and gave Selina the chance to collect her thoughts.

"Regina said she knew someone who helped girls like us who needed fast money."

"Who was this person she referred to?"

"I don't know," Selina said. "Regina gave me a phone number and told me to call if I was interested. She said I could make thousands of dollars in a single night."

"Did you know what you'd have to do when you made that call?"

Selina shook her head. "I was led to believe that we provided escorts—literally—to men who needed dates for events. I thought that's all it was. Apparently, if another of their girls refers you, she gets a bonus. I found that out later."

"What kind of information did they want from you before they took you on?"

"I had to send a photo, a health screening, background. That kind of stuff."

Sam couldn't believe the health screening hadn't been a giveaway for what the men were really after. "How did you find out it was more than dates to parties?"

"The first time I called, the woman I talked to was really nice. She said a man had requested a date for a black-tie gala and was willing to pay for a beautiful woman. All I had to do, she said, was dress formally and meet the man at the event."

"Which was held where?"

"At the Reagan Building downtown. I was told to enter the building on the 14th Street side and to wait for him inside security."

"And this was when?"

"January 18."

"Did your contact give you the name of the man you were meeting?"

She shook her head. "I was told he'd know to look for me. A short time after I arrived, he came through security and walked right over to me."

"What did he look like?"

"Older, balding, overweight." A shudder rippled through Selina's petite frame.

"He never gave you his name?"

"He said his name was John and asked me not to speak to anyone we met other than to exchange greetings."

Sam wanted to laugh at the absurdity of the guy using the name John. "So you went to the event?"

"We made a brief appearance, said hello to a few people, but it was obvious he didn't want to be there. I couldn't understand why he'd gone to so much trouble and expense to hire me if he didn't want to go to the party. For what it's worth, I think he was someone important—people were very...solicitous toward him." She took a drink of the glass of water Freddie had gotten for her.

"How long were you at the party?"

"Less than an hour."

"What happened when you left there?"

Sam noted Selina's hands were trembling so badly that the water in the glass threatened to spill over. "He had a car waiting, and he said he'd take me home except once we were inside, the car headed away from the address I had given him. I asked him where we were going, but he wouldn't answer me. While we were in the car, he started touching me." Her voice had gotten so soft it was almost a whisper.

"What did you do?"

"I asked him to stop. I said that wasn't what I'd agreed to, but he just laughed. He said he loved it when girls played hard to get. We were in the car for a while before it stopped at a hotel outside the city. I wasn't sure where we were. That's when I started to get really scared. I couldn't believe Regina had done this to me." She took another drink of water. "He told me if I didn't want to get hurt, I'd be very quiet and do exactly what I was told. Then he dismissed the driver and all but dragged me into the hotel."

"Did he check into the hotel?"

She shook her head. "He already had a room key."

"Did you have to go through a lobby or were the rooms outside?"

"Outside."

He'd chosen the place with that in mind, Sam thought, so no one would see him dragging an unwilling woman into a room.

"What happened once you were inside the room?"

Selina looked at Freddie and then beseechingly at Sam.

"Detective Cruz," Sam said. "Would you mind giving me a few minutes alone with Ms. Rameriz?"

"Not at all," Freddie said.

On her pad Sam wrote: Get the info on the Jan. 18 event @ Reagan. Video. Witnesses that put her there with bald guy.

He nodded, got up and left the room.

"What happened at the hotel, Selina?"

"He…he ordered me to take off my clothes. I begged him not to touch me. I told him he could have his money back, that I'd never tell anyone if he'd let me go. He laughed at me, and when I bolted for the door he dragged me back and slapped me so hard I saw stars. After that I was kind of out of it, but I was aware of him undressing me and touching me." Her voice caught on a sob. "I kept pleading with him to stop, but he wouldn't. He said he'd paid for sex and that he wasn't leaving until he'd gotten what he'd paid for." By now she was crying so hard she could hardly speak.

Sam gave her a couple of minutes to regain her composure. "Did you have sex with him, Selina?"

She nodded. "He hurt me. I was screaming and crying, so he put his hand over my mouth. I couldn't breathe. I think I blacked out for a time. When I came to…He was…I was facedown on the bed and he was… Oh God, *the pain*. I've never felt pain like that."

Sam reached across the table for her hand. "He raped you, Selina. He raped and sodomized you. No matter what he paid for, the moment you said no, it became a rape."

"I was so stupid," she said between sobs. "How could I have been so naive? Of course that's what he wanted. No one pays thousands of dollars for a date to a party."

"How long were you in the room with him?"

"All night," she whispered. "It went on and on. I was in and out of consciousness. Every time I came to, he was on top of me, inside me. I thought it would never end." She wiped away tears. "Finally, I woke up and he was gone."

"You never saw him again?"

She shook her head. "I took the longest shower and

got dressed before I ran out of there and hailed a cab to take me home."

"You have no idea where you were? You didn't notice any landmarks or anything that stood out to you?"

"No. Wherever it was, I'd never been there before. I was so anxious to get out of there that I didn't pay much attention to anything but finding a cab."

"Do you still have the dress you wore that night?"

Selina glanced up at her, startled. "It's in the back of my closet in a suitcase with the other things I wore that night."

Sam wanted to jump up and down with glee. "What compelled you to keep it?"

"I remembered that intern who slept with the president...No one believed her until she produced the dress. I figured I should keep it just in case I ever had a chance to punish him for what he did to me."

"That was very good thinking. May we have your permission to retrieve it?"

"Yes, of course." Selina folded her hands on the table, but Sam noticed they were still trembling.

Sam got up and went to the door to find someone to get the suitcase from Selina's apartment. "Take it to the lab right away," she said to the officer after Selina signed a consent to search form. Returning to the table, she encouraged Selina to continue her story.

"The next day, three thousand dollars was deposited to my checking account. It was enough for a down payment on the surgery my mother needed."

"Did you seek out medical attention?" Sam asked, knowing the answer before she asked the question.

She shook her head. "I don't have insurance, and I wired all the money to my family."

"Were you injured enough to need medical attention?"

"Probably. Everything...down there...hurt. I had bruises all over. I could barely move for days. I had to call in sick to the cleaning company for the first time since I worked there."

"What did you say to Regina the next time you saw her?"

"I asked her how she could've led me to believe it was just a date. She seemed shocked that I didn't know what 'date' meant when thousands of dollars were involved. She apologized profusely and said that what had happened to me had never happened to her. I think she reported the guy."

"To whom?"

"To the people who run the service."

"And who is that?"

"I don't know. I was just given a number to call to arrange the initial date."

"Do you still have that number?"

"It changes all the time."

"How do you get word of the change?"

"I receive a text message from an unavailable number."

"How did you end up going on another 'date'?"

Selina's shoulders sagged. "I needed more money. My mother's surgery cost forty thousand dollars."

"I find it hard to believe that you were able to bring yourself to do this again after what happened the first time."

"I was terrified. But I was far more terrified of the cancer killing my mother before she could have a surgery that doctors said would save her life."

"You were able to um...perform, despite being terrified?"

Selina looked down at the table and then back up at Sam. "The fear seemed to...you know...turn them on. I've since learned that fear is a fetish."

Sam fought back a shudder. Just when she thought she'd heard everything on this job... "How many other guys were there?"

"Eighteen," Selina said, chagrined. "As of last night, I have the money I need. I'm all done."

So Brad Tillinghast had been the last, Sam thought. "Walking away is an option?"

Selina seemed taken aback by the question. "What do you mean?"

"The people who run this...operation. They allow women to say 'no more'?"

"Of course they do. Why wouldn't they?"

"I'm wondering if Regina and Maria tried to quit."

Selina's eyes went wide. "They were *killed* because they wanted to quit?"

"It's a possibility."

Selina's hand landed on her chest over her heart. "Oh my God."

"Did you tell anyone you were done after last night?"

"Not yet."

That may have saved her life, Sam thought. "What were you told about confidentiality?"

"Just that it was imperative I never speak of these liaisons with anyone. Not that I would have anyway." She pinched her lips as if to hold back a sob. "I was so ashamed. If my parents had any idea where the money was coming from…"

"Where do they think you're getting it?"

"I told them I'd met a lovely man who was well-off, and he gave me the money."

"They believed that?"

Selina nodded. "She's very ill."

"There was no other way for your family to raise the money?"

"We tried everything, even selling the family home in Santa Elena, but we couldn't find a buyer, and she was just getting sicker. We needed money, and we needed it fast."

"I need the details of every encounter you had. Names, ages, description, where the liaisons took place, what kind of sex you had with them and anything distinctive about them you remember."

Selina stared at her, eyes agog. "You can't be serious."

"I'm dead serious. If you want me to catch this guy before he makes you his next victim, you'll tell me everything you know about these men and the outfit that connected you to them."

"But I told you! I don't know anything about the business other than the most recent phone number."

"Then we'll start with that."

"What if I refuse to cooperate?"

"Then I'll release you."

Selina brightened at that possibility.

"I hope you've got your affairs in order since you probably won't have long to live once you walk out of here."

"You're just trying to scare me into cooperating."

"You should be scared. This guy has already brutally raped and murdered two of your 'colleagues' as well as kidnapping and raping one of my detectives. If you think you'll be spared after spending a couple of hours with me, you're more naive than I thought."

"But you could protect me! You could assign officers to watch me!"

"Why should I do that when you won't help me?"

"I've told you everything I know!"

"No, you haven't, and until you do, I'm afraid there's nothing I can do to help you." Sam hoped and prayed the bluff would work. No way would she let Selina walk out of HQ—with or without an escort—but Selina didn't know that.

"I don't know their names. They have numbers. That's all I'm given. Most of them give me a name to call them when we're together, but I know they're not their real names."

"I'll take whatever you can give me—including the most recent phone number."

Selina stared at the wall for a long moment, no doubt weighing her options and finding all of them less than appealing.

"What's it going to be?" Sam asked.

After another long stretch of silence, Selina looked at Sam. "Could I have some paper and a pen?"

TWENTY-FOUR

"Tonight, I'm buying you a hooker," Sam announced to Freddie as she met him in front of the murder board that he'd updated while she was with Selina.

He wondered if she had finally lost her mind. "I'm not that desperate. Yet."

Sam laughed and waved a piece of paper in front of his face. "The phone number Selina uses to get in contact with the call girl ring."

"Let me guess—I'm going to call that number and arrange a date."

"You got it. Archie is setting us up with a secure line. The goal is to stay on the line long enough to get a trace. You're going to have a long list of fetishes that need to be satisfied."

An awful thought occurred to him. "I'm not expected to actually have sex with this woman, am I?"

"Now, Freddie, would I do that to you?"

"I'm not entirely sure."

She made a face at him. "All you have to do is arrange the meeting and keep the appointment. We'll take care of the rest. I figure if we can nab another of the women, we can start to narrow in on the johns. They'll lead us to the organization."

"Or so you hope."

"So I hope."

"What about your crooked senator angle?"

"I'm still almost certain that one or more of them is involved. Think about it—they had access to all three of these women. All of the women were financially insecure, their long-term immigration status was in question and they had people depending on them at home. Someone recruited them knowing they'd be easy marks. That someone is going to turn out to be one of Nick's colleagues. Mark my words. If we can't go at them directly, we'll get them through the women."

"Have you spoken to Nick? Since he gave the statement?"

"He's not answering his phone."

Her phone chimed with a new text. "Maybe that's him now." She glanced at the screen, which said, *Back off bitch or you're dead.* "Not him," she said, showing the text to Freddie.

"How would they have gotten your number?"

"That's a very good question."

"Want me to have Archie put a trace on it?"

"You can try, but I'll bet my last dollar it'll be another throwaway phone."

"Maybe we'll get a ping on a cell tower."

"Worth a shot. I also want to arrange for computer renderings of some of the johns. Can you get Officer Jackson in here ASAP to do that? I like his work."

"Yep."

"While you're doing that, I'm going to talk to Tillinghast again. Hopefully, I can get him to tell me if there's a code or anything he has to give when he calls in to request a 'date.'"

"Good luck with that."

"Your evening plans depend on my success."

Freddie watched her go, not sure whether he should wish for or against her getting the information from Tillinghast. Maybe if his mother heard he was arranging for an evening with a call girl, Elin would start to look more appealing to her. As he laughed at the outrageous thought, his cell rang. Freddie took the call from Gonzo.

"Hey, man, what's up?" In the background Freddie heard crying. "Is that a baby?" What the hell?

"That'd be my son, Alex," Gonzo said.

"*Your son*? What're you talking about?"

"I'm talking about the son I never knew I had until last weekend."

"And now he's *living* with you?"

"For the time being. I'm hoping it'll be permanent."

"Wow. I don't know what to say."

"Congratulations works."

"Of course. Yes. Congratulations! No wonder you've been on leave."

"Believe me, this is the only thing that could've kept me away after what happened to McBride. I'll be back on Monday. I just needed a couple of days to get him settled before I came back to work. But the reason I'm calling is I spent the morning on the phone trying to get some more info on who owns Reese's house."

"Did you get anywhere?"

"I got a name. Not sure if it's the right name, but it's a start. Can you run it for me? I don't have my laptop."

"Absolutely."

"Gerald Price."

As Freddie typed the name into the system, his heart raced with hope and anticipation. Could this be the guy they'd been looking for since a bullet rendered Skip Holland a quadriplegic two years ago? "Okay, here we go." Freddie scanned the screen that detailed Price's extensive criminal history. "Fifty-six years old, long list of priors. He's doing time in Jessup," Freddie said, referring to the state prison in Maryland. "Mostly drug stuff."

"How long has he been in?"

"Fourteen months, six to go, which puts him on the streets at the time of the shooting."

"Damn it," Gonzo said. "I can't get up there right now."

"Neither can I. Sam has me arranging dates with hookers."

"What?"

"You heard me."

"Wow, I picked the wrong week to become a dad."

"I couldn't agree more. You'd be much better at this than I am."

Gonzo snorted with laughter. "Not sure if I should take that as an insult or a compliment."

"Both probably."

"As soon as we close this one, what do you say about a field trip to Jessup?"

"I'm in."

"Tell Sam I called to check in, but let's keep Price between us until we know more."

"Agreed. Did you hear that Gibson's hearing is tomorrow? Malone told Sam there's almost no way he won't get sprung."

"God, we fucked that up, didn't we?"

"Big time."

"I can't even think about it without wanting to rip someone's head off."

"I hear ya. I feel the same way."

"Maybe we can make it right if this thing with Price leads somewhere."

"God, I'd love to solve Skip's case—for her as much as him."

"Me too. Good luck with the hookers. I'll see you Monday."

"Congratulations on the baby, Gonzo. Seriously."

"Thanks, man."

AT THE CITY jail, Sam asked the officer at the desk to put Tillinghast in a room for her.

"Right away, Lieutenant."

When Sam was ushered in a few minutes later, she encountered an entirely different Bradford Tillinghast than the K Street star he'd been a few hours ago. This one wore a jumpsuit rather than a hand-sewn business suit. His expensive gold watch and wedding ring were gone. In prison orange, he looked like any other average white guy.

"They fucking strip-searched me! They treated me like a fucking criminal!"

"Accessory to murder is a felony, Mr. Tillinghast."

"I had nothing to do with those murders, and you know it."

"You have information that could lead to an arrest. Are you still unwilling to share that information?"

His jaw shifted from side to side. "Yes."

"What did they threaten you with? Did they say they'd harm your wife and children if you ever got caught?"

Eyes widening, he gasped.

"That's it, isn't it?"

"I can't let them hurt my family. I can't take that chance."

"I'll put them in protective custody." Sam would do that with or without his cooperation. As long as he was here, his family was in danger. "Tell me who they are, Brad. I can't help you if you don't help me."

He shook his head. "I won't risk it."

"You had to know what you were risking the first time you made a call to this service."

"I had no idea," he said, before he seemed to catch himself. The unguarded moment passed as quickly as it had come.

"When you order up a woman, how does it work? Can you tell me that much?"

He hesitated for a minute and then got up to pace the room. "Will you take care of my family? I tried to reach my wife, but she won't take my calls. I need to know they're safe."

"I'll take care of your family."

"I have two girls, five and seven. I can't let anything happen to them."

"I'll do everything I can, but the longer I'm in here with you, the more danger they're in. News of your arrest is all over town. No doubt the very people you're worried about know full well where you are right now."

He ran his fingers roughly through his blond hair. "God, *what was I thinking*? I never should've—"

Sam slapped her hand on the table. "Brad! Tell me what I need to know so I can go take care of your family!"

He startled and stared at her for an instant before he started to talk. "When I call, I punch in my number—18262. They have a database of men and their interests that matches them to compatible women. I punch in the date I wish to meet the woman and the zip code where I want the meeting to take place. They do everything else."

"So you never talk to a person?"

He shook his head.

"Do you know who's behind the operation?"

"I've heard rumors."

"And these people are powerful?"

"Extremely."

"How did you first hear about the service?"

"From a colleague. He swore it was totally safe and completely anonymous. Safe and anonymous, my ass."

"How do you pay?"

"I have a separate credit card just for this."

"Do you know the number?"

Sighing deeply, he rattled it off.

Sam headed for the door. "Keep talking and I might see fit to drop the charges."

"Lieutenant."

She turned back.

"You need to be very careful. If the rumors are true, this touches the very highest level of the federal government. Do you understand what I'm telling you?"

Sam's heart began to pound. "By highest levels are we talking legislative, executive or judicial?"

"All of the above." He turned his back on her. "That's all I'm saying until you can prove to me that my family is safe."

"I'll be back."

SAM RETURNED TO the detectives' pit, tore the page out of her notebook that contained Brad Tillinghast's credit card number and handed it to Freddie. "He uses this card to pay for the call girls. Do a run and see what you can find. Before that, though, send the U.S. Marshals to Tillinghast's home in Potomac. I want his wife and daughters put into protective custody immediately."

"Got it. Gonzo called to check in. He said he'll be back on Monday."

"Okay, good." She checked her watch. Almost six o'clock and no word from Nick.

"Um, so you knew about Gonzo's baby?"

"He told me when he requested the emergency leave."

"Why didn't you tell me?"

"Not my news to tell. I've got to make a phone call, and then I'm going back to talk to Lightfeather again."

"What about?"

"Something Tillinghast just said. I'm wondering if this call girl ring is one of Washington's worst-kept secrets." She'd love to know if Nick had ever heard rumblings about it—if only he'd answer his damned phone.

"So Tillinghast was a little more forthcoming this time around?"

"The strip search and jumpsuit seemed to have changed his attitude a bit."

"They tend to have that effect."

"Let me know what the card shows." Sam went into her office and closed the door to call Gonzo. "Hey," she said when he answered. "How's it going?"

"I'm getting the hang of it, slowly but surely. Cruz told you I called?"

"Yeah, thanks for checking in. Listen, I need a favor." She pinched the bridge of her nose, hoping to hold back a headache she felt forming. "Is Christina there by any chance?"

"Yeah, why?"

"I can't reach Nick, and I'm starting to get a little worried. It's not like him to be out of touch for hours. And after his 'performance' this afternoon, I'm doubly concerned."

"Let me get her for you."

Christina came on the line a minute later. "Hi, Sam."

"Hi there." Sam paced the office, hating that she'd had to call his chief of staff like a clingy, nagging girlfriend. "So, um, Gonzo told you I'm trying to reach Nick?"

"His phone is broken." She told Sam about the incident in the office. "After that, he stalked out and went to find the reporter. I guess you know the rest."

Sam sighed. "I can't believe he went off in front of a camera like that."

"Or that he called Forrester. He'll be lucky if the Senate Ethics Committee doesn't take issue with that."

"Damn it. What was he thinking?"

"I guess he was thinking about the guy who tried to kill you both being released from jail."

"Do you have any idea where he might be?"

"He said he was going to the gym. I bet he ran into some friends there, played some basketball and probably went out for a few beers. He might even be home by now."

They'd never bothered to install a landline on Ninth Street since they both had cell phones, so Sam couldn't call him. She could, however, call her stepmother and ask her to go check to see if he was home. "Thanks for the info, Christina. I appreciate it."

"I hope he's okay. He was really spun up today."

"I'm sure he's fine. I'll talk to you later." She ended that call and found Celia on speed dial. After explaining what was going on, she asked Celia to run up the street to see if Nick was at home.

"I'm going right now, honey. Did you see him on TV earlier? I've never seen him looking so furious."

"I didn't see it. I heard about it, though." The

headache between her eyes was taking hold despite her efforts to will it away.

"The house is dark, and he's not answering the door."

"He must not be home yet. I'll be there after a while. Thanks for checking, Celia."

"You're worried, Sam. I can hear it in your voice."

"It's not like him to be out of touch all day."

"How did things go with his mother yesterday?"

"About like I expected. She wanted his money, not him."

Celia sighed. "Poor guy. Between that and Peter possibly getting out of jail..."

"Yeah. No good."

"Let me know if you need anything tonight, honey. I'll be here."

And that, Sam realized, brought comfort. "I will. Thanks."

TWENTY-FIVE

As SHE WAS ending the call with Celia, Lt. Archelotta knocked on her door.

"Hey, Archie. You got the secure phone?" Sam glanced at the tall, handsome, dark-haired officer and tried to forget that she'd once seen him naked. They'd had a brief fling after her split with Peter, and like she did every time she ran into him, she wondered if he imagined her naked whenever he saw her.

He handed the phone to her. "Let me know when you're ready to make the call, and we'll set up the trace."

"Can we do it now?"

"Sure." He reached for his own phone and called down to his department. "Lt. Holland is ready to make the call. Everything in place?" He paused and nodded. "Good. Standby." To Sam, he said, "You're good to go. The best we can do is attempt to intercept the pings on the cell tower to narrow it down to a neighborhood."

"I'll take whatever you can get." Since Tillinghast had told her the system was automated, Sam made the call herself, typing in Brad's access code. "Good evening, sir," the recording stated. "Thank you for your call. Please enter the date for which you require services." Sam punched in today's date. "Please enter your zip code." Sam entered the code for downtown. "Thank you. Your date will meet you at 9 p.m. at The Ambassador Hotel, room 482. Your key will be waiting for you at the front desk. Shall I charge the credit card on file? If yes, press the pound key. If you wish to enter a different card number, press the star key." Sam pressed pound. "Do you require any special services this evening? If so, please press pound for our menu."

Sam glanced at Archie, who was watching her with a barely disguised gleam in his eye. "This is so gross," she said.

"Never arranged for a call girl before, Lieutenant?"

She rolled her eyes at him and pressed pound, bracing herself for the menu.

"For domination, please press one. For restraint, please press two. For animals, please press three."

"Oh my God," Sam whispered. "I'm going to be ill."

Archie snickered.

"For anal intercourse, please press four. For auto-erotic asphyxiation, please press five. For whips, chains and S and M, please press six."

Sam decided she'd heard more than enough and pressed the number one.

"Thank you for your selection. Your date will be prepared to fulfill your every fantasy. Please call again soon. Goodbye."

Sam closed the phone and glanced at Archie. "I need a shower."

He laughed and took the phone from her. "Who's the lucky john?"

"Cruz. He can barely contain his excitement."

"What've you got planned for him?"

"Just some domination. I figured animals might be too much for him."

Grimacing, he said, "Ugh. Disgusting."

"Totally."

"I'll go see what we were able to get from the cell towers."

"Thanks."

"Hey, Sam, this thing with Gibson…sucks."

"It is what it is. I'll deal with it."

"I hope you know every cop in this city will be keeping tabs on him. He wouldn't dare step out of line again."

"Yes, he probably will, and when we nail him next time, we'll do it right."

"You bet we will."

"Appreciate the support."

"I haven't had a chance to say congrats on the engagement, either. Seems like you got a good guy there."

She smiled. "Thanks, I like him."

"You deserve to be happy after all you've been through."

Sam remembered that in a weak moment she'd told him about the miscarriages she'd suffered while married to Peter. "Thanks."

"I'll get back to you with what we got from the call." He left with a wave, and Sam watched him go. He was the only fellow cop she'd ever dated, and no one they worked with had ever known they were together. She was relieved that they were now able to be good colleagues without the "we used to sleep together" baggage.

Sam grabbed the portable radio off her desk and her coat. In the pit, she found Freddie on the phone. When he hung up, she said, "Nine o'clock at the Ambassador. Tell all of second shift I want them on backup."

"What'd you order for me, or do I not want to know?"

"Probably better if you don't know. How's Selina making out with Jackson?"

"Slow going. He's having trouble getting her to focus."

"When you have a picture, text me. Nick knows everyone in this town. He might be able to ID the guy."

"Have you heard from him?"

"Not yet. I'm off to see Lightfeather. See you around eight-thirty in The Ambassador lobby."

"I'll be there."

"Call me if anything comes up between now and then."

"Sam?"

She turned back.

"Are you going to court tomorrow? For Peter's hearing?"

"Hell no."

"Why not?"

"I won't give him the satisfaction of thinking that I care enough to waste part of my day on him." She would've told Nick the same thing if he'd consulted her before he lost his mind on TV.

"I've been worried about how you'll deal with this."

"He tried to run my life for four long years. I'm not giving him one more minute."

"It might help Nick to hear you say that."

"You're probably right. I'll tell him if I can find him."

"If you need help with that, you know where I am. Otherwise, see you in a couple of hours."

On the way to see Lightfeather, she thought about what Freddie had said. She wished she knew where Nick was just then. If she knew, she'd go find him as soon as she finished with Henry. Hopefully, Nick would be home by then.

Sam's cell phone rang, and hoping it was him, she put the phone on speaker. "Holland."

"Sam, it's Shelby Faircloth. Have I caught you at a bad time?"

"Tinker Bell," she said, "it's always a bad time in my world. That's why I need you."

Shelby's girlish giggle made Sam smile. "I'm at your service. I received a phone call today from Vera Wang."

"The *actual* Vera Wang?"

"The one and only. She saw some photos of you wearing her at the White House and asked about the possibility of doing your dress."

Sam had to suppress her own urge to giggle like a girl. "Vera Wang—*the Vera Wang*—wants to do *my* dress?"

"You heard me. I thought you might approve, so she's sending several options for you via overnight express. Could I bring them by after work tomorrow?"

"Sure, but I'm in the middle of a murder investigation. I can't promise to be there by a certain time."

"That's all right. I'll start with a fitting for your sisters and the girls for their dresses, and we'll work up to the main event once you break free. Is seven-thirty okay?"

"I'll make sure they're there, and I'll get there as soon as I can."

"You might also want to make sure the groom has other plans."

"Ohhh, good thought."

"See you then."

After indulging in a most un-cop-like squeal, Sam called her sisters to share the news. Angela and Tracy, after some major squealing of their own, agreed to meet Shelby at Nick's place. Tracy promised to bring her daughters Brooke and Abby, who were Sam's junior bridesmaids. She couldn't wait to tell Nick that she'd actually managed to handle some wedding business during the long workday.

ON THE HOTEL'S seventh floor, she found the same two police officers guarding Lightfeather's door. "Anything going on?" she asked.

"They've been fighting," one of them said.

"Been going at it all day," the other said. "How much longer do you think we'll need to be here?"

"Hopefully, not much longer." Sam knocked on the door.

"Thank God," the younger of the two officers muttered.

Annette Lightfeather answered the door, grimacing once again at the sight of Sam and her badge. "What now?"

"May I please speak to your husband?"

Annette stepped aside to admit Sam. A suitcase sat inside the door.

"Going somewhere?" Sam asked.

"Home to my children."

"Lieutenant," Henry said. "What can I do for you?"

He looked like he hadn't slept in days. Wearing a polo shirt and wrinkled khaki pants, his eyes were rimmed with red, and he seemed to have given up on shaving.

As Sam crossed the room to him, she heard Annette's suitcase roll over the tile foyer. The hotel room door opened and snapped closed behind her.

"Well," Henry said. "I guess that's that."

"Sir?"

"She asked for a divorce."

"I'm sorry."

"No job, no wife and probably no kids either, since she vowed to fight me for custody. Best part is I have no one but myself to blame."

Since Sam had no idea what to say to that, she sat down in the same chair she'd occupied the last time they met. "I'm afraid I have some news that's going to add to your dismay." She watched him brace himself for further disaster. "Regina was involved in a call girl ring."

His mouth fell open and then closed. "That can't be true."

Sam had learned to stay quiet at times like this. People needed to reach their own conclusions in their own time. Saying it a second time didn't help it go down any easier.

"You're sure?" he asked softly.

"Yes."

Henry got up and went over to the window. Hands in his pockets, his shoulders were hunched. "This entire week, as my life unraveled around me, do you know what has kept me sane?" He turned to face her. "Knowing that she loved me. She *loved me*."

"She needed money. That doesn't mean she didn't love you."

He picked up a glass and rolled it between his hands. Suddenly, he whipped his arm back and sent the glass hurling across the room. It smashed on contact with the wall. Sam wondered if Nick had looked as fierce when he threw his phone across his office.

"I gave up *everything* for her, and she was screwing other guys the same time she was screwing me?"

Sam held her tongue and gave him a chance to absorb the blow.

Another thought seemed to occur to him. "The baby..."

"Was yours. The DNA confirmed that."

His eyes, which had been fixed on a spot on the wall, shifted to her. "Why are you telling me this?"

"I believe there's a major, high-level prostitution organization ring at work in the city, and everyone knows about it but those of us in law enforcement."

Returning to the sofa, he sat. "I don't know about it."

"You've never heard rumors, innuendo, talk, *anything*?"

"I'm known on the Hill—or I *was* known—as a family man. My colleagues would hardly discuss hookers around me."

"We believe Regina, Maria and their colleague Selina Rameriz were recruited into the organization by one of your colleagues."

Lightfeather stared at her. "One of my *Senate* colleagues?"

Sam nodded. "Someone whose office is in the Hart Building. All three of the women worked there."

"A lot of people work in the Hart Building. Some of the senior staff wield as much power behind the scenes as the senators themselves."

"We'll be investigating everyone who works in that building, but I'd bet my badge it's not going to be a staffer. Anything you can tell me would help us to find the person who murdered Regina."

"After hearing she was sleeping around, I'm supposed to still care about who killed her?"

"The sooner we find the killer, the sooner we'll release you from this hotel room. Maybe then you can attempt to put your life back together."

Lightfeather ran his fingers through his hair. "Talk to Bob Cook," he said, referring to the senior senator from Virginia. "Nothing happens on the Hill that he doesn't know about."

"What about Trent?" Sam asked.

"Other than the car accident in high school, he's squeaky clean. As far as I know anyway." He released a short laugh. "A week ago, people would've said the same about me."

Sam stood up. "I appreciate your candor, Senator."

"I'm not a senator anymore."

"I still appreciate your candor. Let me know if you think of anything else that might help our investigation."

TWENTY-SIX

FREDDIE CALLED AS Sam was heading home. "Tilling-hast's wife is refusing protective custody."

"Oh for Christ's sake. Have the marshals call me so I can talk to her."

"On it."

Sam closed her phone and waited for the callback. When it came, she said, "Put her on."

"Here she is, Lieutenant."

"I know what you're going to say, but—"

"Shut up and listen to me," Sam said in her best cop growl. "The man we're protecting you and your daughters from has viciously raped and murdered two women as well as kidnapping and raping one of my officers. Now, I want you to pack your bags and *get into the goddamned car with the marshals*. Do I make myself clear?"

"Yes," she said, sounding more subdued now. "Fine. What about my low-life husband?"

"He's probably safer in jail than he'd be with you."

"No question about that."

"Cooperate with the marshals so we can keep you and your girls safe. No screwing around."

"For how long?"

"As long as it takes. Don't tell anyone where you've gone."

"Anywhere is better than here. Media trucks are lining my street."

"Then get the hell out of there."

When Sam parked on Ninth Street a short time later, she was distressed to see their place still dark and Nick's car nowhere in sight. "*Where is he*?" For a brief, horrifying moment, she wondered if the sicko she was hunting down had nabbed him to get at her. "No," she whispered, refusing to entertain the possibility. He was out with his friends, and he knew she was busy with the case so he wasn't worried about getting home.

Since she had ninety minutes until she was due to meet Freddie and the others at The Ambassador, she took her radio and went inside, hoping Nick would come home before she had to leave again. In the kitchen, she contemplated making something to eat, but her stomach turned at the idea of food. As the possibility of something untoward happening to Nick took hold, Sam paced the living room. "Maybe I should be out there looking for him," she said to herself. But where to even begin? She didn't even know what gym he frequented.

Just as she was about to call Freddie to see if he thought they should be looking for Nick, the doorbell rang. Sam ran for the door, threw it open and was relieved to find Nick and his doctor friend Harry on the stoop. After the thorough examination she'd recently withstood at Harry's hands, it was all Sam could do to make eye contact.

"I understand this belongs to you," Harry said. His sinfully handsome face became even more so when he smiled.

Nick stepped into the light, and Sam gasped at the bruise under his right eye. "What happened? Did you get into a fight?" She was so damned glad to see him that she didn't even care if he'd been fighting.

"Nothing so dramatic, babe," he said, a slight slur infecting his words. "An elbow to the face on the basketball court."

Sam stepped aside so Harry could escort Nick to the sofa. Once there, Nick put his head back against the cushions and closed his eyes. His white dress shirt was dirty and his loosened tie was crooked. She'd never seen him even slightly buzzed, so drunk and disheveled was unexpected, to say the least.

"I joined them after happy hour," Harry whispered to Sam. "Never did manage to catch up."

"Did anyone see him like this?" Sam asked, wondering what kind of media coverage he was in for the next day in addition to losing his cool on TV.

"Only his close friends. We take care of our own, Lieutenant."

Since Nick seemed to be asleep, Sam said, "He's had a rough couple of days."

"He mentioned that he saw his mother yesterday, but we sort of suspected since that's the only time he really hits the bottle."

"So this has happened before?"

"Couple of times over the years. After her last wedding, he was drunk for a week. We found out later that she refused to introduce him as her son because she didn't want the new husband to think she was lying about her age. You probably already know this latest encounter cost him twenty-five grand. Now that she knows he has money, no doubt she'll be back for more."

"What a bitch." Sam had suspected he'd given his mother money, but not that much. "I'd like two minutes alone with her to tell her what a piece of shit she is."

"You and everyone else who loves him. He told me once, years ago in a weak moment, that the scent of her perfume undoes him. I think he said it's Chanel No. 5 or some knockoff version. Every time he catches a whiff of that stuff he goes into a tailspin. He said when he was little, he use to be able to smell her for days after she visited until his grandmother forced him to take a bath."

Sam's heart broke in half for the little boy who'd craved his mother's love and attention—and never got either. "Will he be okay?"

"Usually takes him a week or two to shake it off, but with your ex-husband about to get sprung, might take longer this time. He's taking that really hard too."

Listening to his friend, Sam realized she still had a lot to learn about the man she loved. "Thanks for bringing him home, Harry."

"No problem." He headed for the door. "You and I are overdue for a little chat."

"We are?"

"Don't play dumb with me, Lieutenant."

Sam smiled, remembering how much she'd enjoyed

his wit the first time they met—over an exam table in his office.

"How's the soda famine going?" he asked.

"I'm cranky as hell but my stomach is better."

"Shocking! Maybe it was that gallon of diet cola you were drinking every day that was giving you crippling stomach pain. What an incredible coincidence!"

"Do they teach sarcasm in medical school?"

"I come by that naturally. What about the other thing we talked about?"

Sam's smile faded, and her heart raced.

"Given it any thought?"

Sam gave him a withering look. "What do you think?"

"And?"

"I'm late...I think." She hadn't been able to even ponder the possibility that had been hovering in her subconscious, let alone say it out loud.

Harry's eyebrows came together in an expression that took him from carefree friend to concerned doctor in an instant. "Define late."

"A week. Maybe two. I don't really keep track because my periods are so erratic, but I probably should've had one." She cleared her throat. "By now."

"I told you if you had all your parts that it was possible..."

Sam gripped his arm. "I can't be pregnant, Harry. *I just can't.*"

Laughing, he eased her into a chair and squatted down in front of her. "Of course you can."

Sam shook her head. "I can't go through that again.

I can't lose another one." She'd rather stare down the barrel of a loaded shotgun than go through that hell again.

"I'll tell you what—I'm off tomorrow, so come into the office on Monday. We'll do a quick test and see what's what, okay?"

"It's not okay." No other subject had the ability to render her so powerless against the overwhelming array of emotions.

He reached for her hands and held on tight. "It will be. I promise. If you are…" He seemed to know better than to use the "p" word just then. "I have a friend who's an amazing OB/GYN who I'll refer you to." Flashing a sheepish grin, he added, "Well, to be honest, I've been seeing her for a while now, but I haven't told the guys yet. Keep my secret?"

"If you keep mine. Until we know for sure…Nick has had enough with his mother and everything."

"My lips are sealed. Let me see your phone."

"What the hell for?"

"Hand it over."

Confused, she drew it out of her pocket, put it into his outstretched hand and watched him program his number into her address book. "If anything comes up, anything at all, call me. Night or day."

"That's nice of you. Thanks."

He stood and helped her up, giving her a quick hug and a kiss on the cheek. "Take good care of my buddy," he said, looking over at Nick.

"Always."

"And try not to worry, Sam. Everything will be okay."

"I hope you're right."

He flashed that charming dimpled smile that made him so adorable. "I was right about the soda, wasn't I?"

"Oh *brother*. Am I ever going to hear the end of that?"

"Not in this lifetime. Sleep tight."

After she showed Harry out, she turned to study her fiancé. The idea of him being in so much pain that he'd felt the need to drink excessively was shocking to her. The Nick she knew and loved was *always* in control. Except, it seemed, when his loser mother turned his world upside down. She couldn't add to that right now by sharing the possibility that she *might* be pregnant—might being the operative word. Resting her back against the closed front door, Sam reached for her phone to call Freddie.

"What's up, boss?"

"Something's come up, and I can't be there tonight. Can you all handle it on your own? You know the drill—arrest the girl for solicitation and prostitution. Offer her a deal if she'll give up what she knows about the operation. Cue Malone in too." She should've done that herself but hadn't gotten to it.

"We can handle it. I just heard from Archie that the trace came up empty. The signals were all blocked."

"Son of a bitch. Another dead end."

"The text to your phone came from a throwaway, as we suspected. We're trying to track it down."

"We can't catch a break on this one."

"I know. Is everything okay? Did you find Nick?"

"I found him, but I can't leave him right now." She had no doubt that he'd never leave her in the same condition. Nothing, not even her all-consuming job, was more important to her than he was. If ever there'd been a time to prove that, it was now. "I'll tell you about it tomorrow. Call me after it goes down?"

"You got it."

"Go in with backup, and be careful."

"We will."

Sam closed the phone, stashed it in her pocket, sent the two officers who were tailing her home for the evening and went to sit with Nick.

"WHAT TIME IS it?" Nick mumbled.

Sam put aside her laptop and turned to him. "Almost nine."

"How'd I get here?"

"You don't remember? Harry brought you home."

"Oh, yeah. Right." He ran his hand over his face and winced when he came into contact with the bruise under his eye. "Andy's elbow. Did you know he's been helping Gonzo with the baby?"

"I'd heard that."

"Sorry you had to see me like this. Won't happen again."

Sam reached out to caress his face. "Don't apologize. You needed to blow off some steam, and I'm glad your friends were there to help you do it."

"I blew off some steam on TV earlier too."

"So I heard."

"Are you pissed?"

She shook her head. "I've never had anyone to defend me against Peter. I used to have to deal with him and his games all on my own. So it's rather nice to have someone in my corner."

He reached for the hand on his face and brought it to his lips. "I'll always be in your corner, babe. You don't have to deal with anything alone anymore."

"Neither do you." She rested her head on his shoulder.

"Seeing her screws me up. Always has. You'd think after all these years I'd be better equipped to deal with it, but I never have gotten the hang of it."

"I wish there was something I could do for you."

"You're doing it. Just by being here. I want to take a shower. I must smell like the inside of a whiskey bottle."

"I could use one too. Come on, I'll go with you."

They walked up the stairs together. In the bathroom, she helped him out of his clothes and into the shower before she followed him. He reached for her, brought her in tight against him and held her while the warm water beat down on them.

"This goes a long way toward fixing what ails me," he said, sighing with what sounded like contentment.

"Good." Sam closed her eyes and held on to him, thankful that she'd chosen to stay home with him rather than go back to work. After a while, she reached for his bottle of shampoo and washed his hair. When she was done, he returned the favor.

He filled his hands with liquid soap and ran them reverently over her.

Sam watched him, wondering what he was thinking.

"I gave her twenty-five thousand," he said.

"Harry told me."

He looked at her, his beautiful eyes filled with pain. "Are you horrified?"

Sam combed the wet hair off his forehead. "Of course not. You did what you felt you needed to."

"She'll probably be back for more when that's gone."

"Probably." Sam turned off the water and reached for their towels. "But we'll be ready for her next time."

A hint of a smile graced his face. "Will we?"

"Next time," she said, kissing him, "she'll deal with me."

He chuckled. "I almost feel sorry for her."

Sam secured a towel around his waist and then wrapped another around herself. "Don't bother feeling sorry for her. She isn't worth your time. Neither is Peter, for that matter."

"That's different."

"It's really not, Nick. We can't give these people power over us. The minute we do, they win."

"So I'm not supposed to be concerned about what he might do to you once he's out of jail?"

"We'll take every possible precaution, but there's no need for us to give him the satisfaction of knowing that we care in the least about him."

"If that's how you feel, you have to be pissed about what I did today."

"I'm concerned about political fallout for you, but

I'm not mad at you for doing it. From now on, though, how about we deny him the satisfaction?"

"Won't that infuriate him?"

"He's already infuriated. Nothing we do or don't do will change that. We don't care, remember?"

"I'll care if he comes at my wife. I'll definitely care about that."

Sam rested her hands on his chest. "She's very capable of taking care of herself. You need to keep that in mind."

He put his arms around her. "As capable as she is, even she didn't think he'd strap bombs to our cars."

"She knows better now. She'll be looking for the first chance to nail his ass—but she'll *never* let him know that."

"You're sure this is the best way to handle it?"

"Making a lot of noise hasn't gotten us anywhere, has it? They're still going to let him out."

"So we just say nothing and let it happen?"

"We don't have any choice. How about we let our happiness be our revenge? He wants what he can never have again. Sooner or later, he'll figure that out."

"I'm still worried about him trying to hurt you."

"And I'm worried about him trying to hurt *you*. In his mind, you're the only thing standing in the way of what he wants. I'm sure he's forgotten all about the year we were divorced before you and I got back together. To him, you're the root of all evil, so you'll need to be careful too."

"Hopefully, his stint in jail will have scared him straight and he'll leave us alone."

"Hopefully."

"You don't think so, though, do you?"

"Who knows? I guess we'll find out soon enough." She glanced up at him. "Can we please change the subject?"

"Absolutely."

Following him into the bedroom, Sam told him about the call from Shelby and the appointment for the following evening. "You'll have to make yourself scarce so you don't see the dress."

"I never pictured you as the superstitious type," he said.

"I'm not usually. But I've got one failed marriage behind me. I'm not inviting any bad mojo into this one."

He sat on the bed and reached out a hand to her. "This one won't be anything like the first one."

Taking his hand, Sam sat next to him. "No, it won't, but you're still not seeing the dress until March 26." She leaned over to kiss him. "Nice try, though."

Hooking an arm around her, he anchored her for another kiss. "Did you get to eat?"

"Wasn't hungry. You?"

"I had some pizza with the guys." He nuzzled her neck, nibbled on her earlobe and tugged on her towel. "Wanna go to bed?"

"In a little bit. I'm waiting to hear from Freddie. We've got something going down tonight."

Nick raised his head to meet her eyes. "Shouldn't you be there?"

She shrugged. "I let them deal with it."

"Samantha…"

"What? It's no big deal. I chose to stay here with you."

His face softened, and he stole another kiss. "Thank you."

"It's nothing you wouldn't have done for me."

Hugging her, he said, "I love you. I don't think I've told you that today."

"Don't start slacking off before we're even married," she said with a teasing grin.

"No chance of that," he said, bringing his lips down on hers for a kiss that sucked every other thought right out of her head.

HEARING THAT SHE had stayed home to take care of him set off a powerful swell of emotion inside Nick. No one had ever loved him the way she did, and her love went a long way toward soothing the hurt he'd carried with him for as long as he could remember.

He wished he had the words to tell her what she meant to him. If he lived forever, he'd probably never find the perfect words.

Cupping her breast, he teased her nipple with his tongue and teeth.

Sam gasped and pushed at him.

"What?" he asked, surprised. She usually loved that.

"Nothing," she said, but the almost panicked look in her eyes caught his immediate attention.

"What, honey? What's the matter?" He watched, shocked, as she blinked back tears. There was only one issue that could be guaranteed to bring his fearless, gutsy cop to tears every time. "Samantha?"

She looked up at him with those eyes that saw right through him. "I can't be," she said as tears rolled down her cheeks. "I just can't."

"Sweetheart, you're scaring me. What're you talking about?"

She crossed her arms over her breasts. "The only time they're that sensitive…"

The realization hit him all at once, and all the air whooshed from his lungs. "Sam…"

"I don't know! Don't look at me like that! They told me I can't…" She broke down into tears and hiccuping sobs. "They said I couldn't have any more. They told me that. I believed them!"

Overwhelmed with joy and excitement and trepidation, Nick put his arms around her. "How long have you known?" he asked after several quiet minutes.

"I *don't* know. Not for sure. I've just noticed some… signs. And just now, when you did that…"

"This?" He kissed his way from her neck to her breast and twirled his tongue around her nipple before sucking hard on it.

She cried out, her fingers gripping his hair. "*Nick…*"

"Hmmm?"

"I can't do it. I can't."

"Oh, honey, sure you can. I have no doubt." He kissed a path from oversensitive breasts to belly. Just the *possibility* that she could be carrying his child had him blinking back his own tears.

"I can't be terrified for nine months. How will I work or do anything but be afraid?"

He rested his face on her belly and wrapped his arms around her. Looking up at her, he said, "You'll just do what you always do and let the rest take care of itself."

"What if I am…and then…what if…"

"If the worst happens, we'll deal with it together and we'll try again. We'll never stop trying until we get it right."

"I'm so scared. I've noticed a few signs, but I've been afraid to even consider the possibility. The other times, my breasts… They were so sensitive. That's the only time they've ever been like that. It's almost like confirmation…"

He kissed his way back up her body, from her belly to her lips. "We need to get you in to see Harry."

"Monday." Raising her hands to his face, she brought him down for a soft, sweet kiss that shattered his remaining defenses. She owned him. There was nothing he wouldn't do for her, nothing he wouldn't give her, nothing he wouldn't do to protect her, even if she didn't want his protection. And now, maybe, a baby too…

"Samantha," he whispered against her lips as he entered her, "I love you so much."

"Mmm, me too." She wrapped her arms and legs around him, holding him tight against her, and gazed up at him with eyes still shiny with tears but also full of love—for him.

Before she returned to his life, he'd had no idea

MARIE FORCE 341

what he'd been missing. Now she was so much a part of him that he couldn't imagine a life without her at the center of it. Knowing what she liked, he wanted to pick up the pace, but held back, afraid to do anything to hurt her or the baby.

"Nick…"

"What, babe?"

"Faster."

"We have to be careful, just in case."

"It's okay." She slid her hands down his back. "Really."

Gripping her hips to hold her still, he pumped into her, giving her what she wanted. His heart raced from exertion and emotion until he thought it would burst from his chest.

As Sam cried out, he felt her nails score his back, which sent him surging into her one last time in a release that seemed ripped from his very soul. Afterward, he fought to catch his breath as her hands soothed his back.

"I can't believe I scratched you," she said, laughing.

He rested carefully on top of her, his lips pressed to her neck. "I don't care."

"Good thing you're required to wear a shirt to work."

"I've given them enough to talk about for a while."

Her fingers combed through his hair, a loving gesture of hers that never failed to stir him. She had given him exactly what he'd needed most, and he hadn't known he needed it. She just knew.

"Will you do something for me?" she asked.

"Anything. Name it."

"I have to give this case my full attention until we close it. Can we not talk about the *other thing* until after that? If I let myself get all nutty about it, I won't be able to focus on anything else. I've become an expert at compartmentalizing this stuff so I can function at work."

"Of course. I understand."

She rested her head on his chest and released a deep, contented sigh. "You always do."

He tightened his hold on her and kissed her forehead. "I try."

Bon Jovi interrupted the peaceful moment when "Livin' on a Prayer" sounded through the room.

"I need to get that," she said. "It's probably Freddie."

Nick rolled to his side and reached for her phone on the bedside table, handing it to her.

As she took the call, she linked her fingers with his, letting him know she was still right there with him.

Touched by the gesture, he shifted to his side so he could see her.

"How'd it go?" she asked.

Nick watched her process what Freddie was telling her.

"What?" she said, laughing. "They asked for your preferences. I figured you'd *love* a dominatrix. Was I wrong?"

Nick chuckled, imagining Freddie's indignation.

"She wouldn't give you *anything* on the organization?" Sam paused, listening. "We'll let her cool her heels in jail for the night since we've still got her on solicitation and prostitution. Maybe she'll be more forthcoming in the morning. Good work, thanks."

"Do I even want to know?" Nick asked when she'd ended the call.

"Have you ever heard any references to a high-level call girl ring in the city? We're talking *highest* level."

"I've heard rumors over the years, but nothing concrete."

"What kind of rumors?"

"Just that it exists but no specifics."

She shot him a coy look. "Were you ever tempted to dial up a girl?"

He cringed. "*No.*"

Sam laughed at his indignation. "That's right—you didn't have to. According to your buddy Harry, you were the ultimate chick magnet."

Rolling his eyes, he said, "Whatever."

"You never talk about them, you know."

"Who? My friends?"

"The women."

"What women? You're the only one who's ever mattered. You know that."

"So you were a monk for the six years between when we first met and when we got back together?"

"Absolutely. I sat at home and thought about you."

She poked his ribs. "You're so full of crap." Looking over at him, she said, "I was really hoping you'd have the lowdown on the call girls."

"I'm sorry to disappoint you, but I can't believe you thought I'd know about that. I should probably be insulted."

"You never heard *anyone* talk about it? I thought guys loved to share the dirty details."

"Guys talk about a lot of things, but they don't talk about hookers, especially not in this town where the word 'hooker' has the power to end careers."

"I guess I'll have to talk to Cook tomorrow. I was hoping to avoid that after our last friendly encounter."

"What the hell does Cook have to do with it?" Nick asked, his eyes widening. He'd had his own run-ins with the senior senator from Virginia.

"Tillinghast said if anyone would have the skinny, Cook would. He said Cook knows everything that happens on the Hill."

Nick reached for his phone.

Sam yawned. "Who're you calling?"

"Someone who knows even more than Cook does about what happens on the Hill."

TWENTY-SEVEN

"YOU'RE SURE THEY won't care if we show up there this late?" Sam asked as they approached the Leesburg home of Nick's adopted parents, retired Senator Graham O'Connor and his wife Laine.

"I'm positive. They're night owls."

"This sure is a nicer ride than mine," she said of Nick's BMW, which she was driving for the first time.

"I should hope so."

She made a face at him. "You're such a snob."

"Only about cars—and hookers. Only the best will do."

"Very funny."

"Connect the dots for me. What does the call girl ring have to do with your case?"

"Regina and Maria were involved as well as another woman from the Capitol Cleaning Services, Selina Rameriz. There could be more, but we've confirmed those three so far."

"Wow," Nick said, "I can't picture Maria as a call girl. She was so quiet and unassuming."

"It was all about the money. They sent every dime home." Sam pulled into the O'Connors' driveway. "Our theory is they knew they might not have much time here, so they had to make it any way they could before they were sent home. In Selina's case, she needed the money for her mother's surgery." Sam's phone chimed to indicate a message. "Check that for me, will you?" She handed the phone to Nick.

"Why are you guys drawing pictures of Jack Bartholomew?"

"Who's that?"

"Chief of staff to the vice president."

Sam released a low whistle. "When Tillinghast said the top levels of government, he wasn't kidding."

"Are you saying *Bartholomew* has something to do with the call girl ring?"

"At the very least, he's a customer. He attacked and raped Selina Rameriz."

"You've got the wrong guy, Sam. There's no way he has anything to do with this."

"Not according to Selina. She worked with the computer artist all afternoon."

Nick sat back in the seat. "I can't believe it. This could rock the entire administration."

Her mind racing, she brought the car to a stop in front of the garage. "How well do you know Bartholomew?"

"Not all that well, but I've seen a lot more of him since I took office. The vice president is leading the president's new accountability and transparency effort, and Bartholomew is the VP's point man. He's been in a number of meetings I've attended over the last few weeks."

"If Selina's account is true, he's one sick bastard."

"You think he could be killing these women to shut them up?"

"He fits the profile. All along we've said it's going to be someone who thinks he's above being caught. He's left DNA all over the place, so if it is him, we've got him nailed."

"What're you going to do?"

Sam thought about it for a moment before she opened her phone and called Freddie. "Jack Bartholomew," she said, "chief of staff to Gooding."

"Whoa. How do you know?"

"Nick recognizes him. Do a run on him, and get me an address."

"We're going to talk to him at home?"

"We're going to *arrest* him at home."

"Holy shit," Nick said.

Sometimes Sam really loved this job. "I don't care who he is, if he's running a prostitution ring in my city and murdering women to gain their silence, I'm taking him down."

"Right there with you, boss."

"Put someone on Bartholomew for tonight until we can get subpoenas for his DNA and phone records. I don't want him killing someone else in the meantime. Meet me at HQ at six-thirty. We'll go together."

"Got it."

"Is Selina still working with Jackson to ID some of the other johns?"

"He's giving it another hour. They're both running out of steam. I've got a house set up for her as soon as they're done."

"After that, go home. We've got another long one ahead of us tomorrow, and you've got a very important evening to prepare for."

"Thanks for reminding me," he mumbled.

"See you in the morning." To Nick she said, "Let's see what your buddy Graham knows."

GRAHAM AND LAINE ushered them into the family room of their comfortable farmhouse where a blazing fire cast an amber glow over the cozy room.

Sam was surprised to see Terry O'Connor jump up from the sofa. "Senator," he said, adding almost begrudgingly, "Lieutenant."

The two men shook hands.

"You look great, Terry," Nick said.

Dressed in sweats and a Georgetown T-shirt, Terry appeared to have lost at least twenty pounds since Sam last saw him, and his eyes seemed clearer than she'd ever seen them—not that he looked at her. Ever since she'd interrogated him as a suspect in his brother's murder, things had been tense between them. But he was going to be Nick's deputy chief of staff, so Sam decided to at least make an effort to be cordial. "You really do look terrific," she said.

"Thanks," Terry said with only the slightest of glances her way. He ran his fingers through his prematurely gray hair almost as if he needed something to do with his hands.

"What brings you out our way this time of night?" Graham asked.

"Sam's working on a case I thought you might be able to help her with," Nick said.

"Whatever I can do—anytime," Graham said, gesturing for them to sit on the love seat.

"I appreciate that," Sam said. "Tell me what you know about high-end call girls in Washington."

Laine gasped, and Terry snickered.

"Well, I ah…" Graham said, sputtering.

"I'm probably better versed on that subject than my dear old dad," Terry said, looking chagrined.

Laine cast a disparaging glance at her eldest child. "Honestly, Terry."

"I'm not proud of the way I used to live, Mother, but the truth is, I've met my share of call girls."

Sam handed him a slip of paper. "Have you ever seen this phone number before?"

"No, but that doesn't mean anything. If it's the same outfit I think it is, the number changes all the time."

"How do customers keep up?"

"Text messages."

"Do you have any idea who runs the organization?"

"Not specifically, but there're always rumors and speculation."

"Humor me."

"I've heard Gooding's name," he said, referring to the vice president. "And Daniels."

"The *speaker of the House*?" Nick said, incredulous.

A burst of adrenaline had Sam's heart pumping hard.

"I've also heard Cook's name in the mix," Graham said.

The other three stared at him.

"You gotta be kidding me," Nick said.

Graham shrugged. "I always chalked it up to rumors started by the Republicans."

"If what you're telling me is true," Sam said, "the Republicans are squeaky-clean compared to the Democrats."

"That's just what we want to hear," Graham said, glancing at Nick. "This could be a freaking nightmare for us."

Sam got a kick out of the way Graham always stuck to the present tense when speaking about politics, as if he still had an oar in the race. She supposed he did with his protégé Nick now holding the office that had once been his.

"I just can't believe Bob Cook would be involved with call girls," Laine said. "Millie will kill him."

"I believe it," Graham said. "He's a money-hungry pig."

"Graham!" Laine said, shocked. "He's our good friend. How can you say such a thing?"

"Because it's true, Mother," Terry said. "With the tight reins the Senate puts on members' outside income, it wouldn't surprise me at all that Cook had something like this going on the side."

"Something that could ruin his career and his marriage?" Laine asked.

"Millie enjoys the lifestyle he provides," Graham said. "And just because he's running the ring, doesn't mean he's sleeping with the employees."

"*Right*," Terry said, dripping with sarcasm. "As if he could resist that kind of temptation."

"This is so shocking," Laine said.

"I know I don't have to tell you that it's vital to my investigation that none of you repeat a word of this to anyone," Sam said.

"Of course we wouldn't, honey," Laine said. "We'd never do that to a member of our family."

Nick smiled at Laine who reached over to squeeze his hand.

"Well, you've given me a lot to think about," Sam said.

"Be careful, Sam," Terry said, surprising her. "If this is true, there's nothing they won't do to protect their cash cow *and* their reputations."

"They've already resorted to murder," she reminded him.

"Which is why they'd think nothing of gunning for a cop. What else do they have to lose?"

"I appreciate the warning, but I can take care of myself."

"I hear that a lot," Nick said, grinning. "She thinks she's bulletproof."

They spent another half hour talking about wedding plans and catching up on O'Connor family news.

As Sam and Nick got up to leave, Terry stood to shake hands with Nick.

"You ready to start on Monday?" Nick asked.

"I'll be there." Terry hesitated, as if there was something else he wanted to say. "I just want you to know... Thinking about the opportunity you've given me got me through rehab. It gave me something to look forward to. I haven't had that in a long time." His DUI weeks before he'd been due to declare his candidacy for his father's office had derailed his promising political career, clearing the way for his younger brother John to run for an office he'd never wanted. Terry's spiral had continued unabated ever since—until recently.

"I'm looking forward to having you on my team," Nick said. "In fact, I know Christina would love for you to take over the campaign, especially now that she and Tommy have a baby to contend with."

"She's having a *baby*?"

"No," Nick said, laughing, bringing Terry up to speed on how Gonzo came to have a son.

"That's amazing," Laine said. "He had no idea about the child?"

"None at all," Sam said.

"We're going to stay at the cabin tonight," Nick said. "Give us a call if you think of anything else that might help the investigation."

"We will," Graham said as he and Laine walked them out.

"You'll be here for dinner on Sunday, right?" Laine asked.

"Wouldn't miss it," Nick said, kissing her cheek. "I hope it's okay that I invited a friend. Don't worry, though, he won't eat much. He's only twelve."

Laine chuckled. "You know you can invite anyone you want. Any friend of yours is a friend of ours." She hugged him and kissed his cheek. "When I see you on Sunday, you can tell me what has you looking so troubled, young man."

"Yes, ma'am," he muttered, clearly taken aback by her insight.

Laine turned to Sam. "I want to thank you for putting Patricia in touch with me. We had a lovely visit, and we both felt better afterward."

"I'm glad to hear that. I wasn't sure I was doing the right thing."

Laine reached out to squeeze Sam's arm. "It was the exact right thing, and I appreciate it."

"It was nothing," Sam mumbled.

"We'll see you on Sunday," Graham said, hugging them both.

Sam couldn't stop yawning on the short ride to the cabin John had left to Nick.

"Aren't you glad now that I made you pack a bag?" Nick asked from the passenger seat.

"Yes, dear."

"You ought to get used to saying that. I plan to be right most of the time."

She rolled her eyes at him. "Whatever." Reaching for her cell phone, she pressed speed dial number four.

"Sleeping," Malone answered, his voice gravelly.

"I need you," Sam said.

"Are you going to take years off my life again?"

"Well, if requesting subpoenas for personal cell records and DNA for the vice president, his chief of staff, the speaker of the House of Representatives and the senior senator from Virginia doesn't give you heartburn, I'm not sure what will."

Malone uttered a tortured moan. "You're screwing with me again, Holland."

"I wish I was."

"Speak."

Sam told him what she knew.

"Because Rameriz identified him, we can justify asking for Bartholomew's records and DNA, but not the rest," Malone said. "We're not going after the vice president, the speaker and a senior senator without more than rumors. Bring Bartholomew in. Maybe you can get him to roll on the others if you make it seem like he'd be going down alone."

"I guess I'll take what I can get. Wait until after seven to request the subpoena. I don't want to tip him off."

"Is there anything else I can do for you, Lieutenant?"

"We took a suitcase to the lab today. Inside are the clothes Selina Rameriz was wearing when Jack Bartholomew raped her. I need you to put a rush on that report."

"Consider it done."

"That's it for now, Captain. Sleep tight."

"The death of me, Holland. The living, breathing death."

Laughing, Sam ended the call. As they were pulling up to the cabin, her phone chimed with a new text. *You don't do what you're told. Time to teach you a lesson.* Sam swallowed hard and slapped the phone closed.

"What?" Nick asked.

"Nothing." Following him into the cabin, Sam was suddenly glad that no one, other than the O'Connors, knew where they were just then.

Nick flipped on a light, illuminating a comfortable living room filled with John O'Connor's belongings. "I probably need to get around to packing up John's stuff for his parents."

"When you're ready. There's no rush."

He picked up a picture of John with his young niece and nephew. "He sure did love those kids." After studying the photo for a moment, he returned it to the shelf and held out a hand to her. "Let's go to bed."

Curling up to him a short time later, Sam thought about the first night she'd spent at the cabin, in the midst of the O'Connor investigation.

With his arm around her, he brushed his lips over her forehead. "What are you thinking about?"

"The first night we spent here."

"In separate bedrooms."

"That was back when I was trying to do the right thing by resisting you."

"Which of course was the exact wrong thing."

Sam laughed and pressed her lips to his chest and breathed in his endlessly appealing scent. "Very wrong."

"You still think that even though you got suspended for hooking up with me in the middle of the investigation?"

"I've learned it's not wise to resist that which is meant to be."

"That's very profound, Samantha."

"And very true."

"Very true indeed." His arms tightened around her, and Sam drifted into sleep. What seemed like minutes later, her ringing cell phone woke her up. A glance at the digital clock on the bedside table told her it was just after three. Clearing her throat, Sam reached for the phone.

"Holland."

"Oh, Sam!" Celia sounded frantic. "Thank God I reached you."

Sam sat straight up in bed. "Is it Dad?"

"There's a fire at your place! You need to get out of there!"

"Celia, we're in Leesburg. What do you mean there's a fire?"

Now Nick was also awake and sitting up.

"Thank goodness you're not there." Sam heard Celia telling her father they weren't home. "Your place up the street," Celia said. "The fire engines woke us up."

"Oh my God." To Nick, Sam said, "The place on Ninth is on fire."

"Shit," he said, leaping from the bed and pulling on jeans as Sam did the same.

"We're on our way," Sam told Celia. As she recalled the text threat from earlier, her stomach took a nosedive.

Minutes later, they left the cabin with Nick driving as fast as he dared.

"This is my fault," Sam said after several tense minutes of silence.

"How do you figure?"

"I got a text earlier. They said because I didn't back off the investigation like they told me to it was time to teach me a lesson."

He took his eyes off the road long enough to look over at her. "Why didn't you say anything?"

"After the day you'd had, I didn't want you to worry."

"If we'd been in the house, Sam, we could've been killed!"

"I realize that."

"Who're you calling?"

"Malone. He needs to know about this."

"But I didn't?" He shook his head. "Just when I think we're really getting somewhere you go back to keeping things from me."

After Sam had reported in to her superior officers, she turned to Nick. "I was going to tell you in the morning—after you got a good night's sleep."

"It's a good thing I was sleeping in Leesburg and not on Ninth Street."

"I'm sorry about the house," she said.

He smacked the heel of his hand on the wheel, startling her. "I don't *give a shit about the house, Sam*! It's insured. Anything in there can be replaced. That's not what you need to be apologizing about!"

"I'm trying." After years of living with passive-aggressive Peter, Sam had become a pro at keeping things from her significant other. "I can't completely change who I am overnight. I'm doing the best I can."

"You need to do better."

"Pardon me for thinking you'd had enough for one day."

"You should've told me."

Sam bit back a retort that would've escalated the disagreement to a full-blown argument, and they passed the rest of the ride in tense silence.

EMERGENCY VEHICLES BARRICADED the entire block around their home. Nick grabbed the first spot he could find on the next block and took off running with Sam right behind him.

She flashed her badge to one of the firefighters. "Lieutenant Holland, MPD. This is my place. What've you got?"

"You got lucky, LT. Someone called it in, and we got here before it got past the front room. You'll have some smoke and water damage on the first floor as well as a broken window and front door, but that's about it."

"How'd it start?" Nick asked.

Looking from Nick to Sam and then back to Nick, the young firefighter's eyes bugged. "Oh, Senator. Um, ah, let me grab my captain."

"It doesn't look too bad," Sam said, staring at the house where smoke billowed from the broken window.

Keeping his eyes fixed on the house, Nick said nothing.

"Senator, Lieutenant, I'm Captain Grayson. Our investigator will be here shortly. Looks like something went through the window and ignited the carpet inside, but I'll let the fire marshal give you the official findings."

"So the window was broken from the outside?" Sam asked.

"That's how it appears to us. You're welcome to take a look."

They followed him through the maze of police and firefighters and curious neighbors who were braving the cold to watch the proceedings. The exploding flash of a camera blinded Nick.

"Goddamn it," he muttered. No doubt the vultures were loving this new story on top of his rant earlier in the day.

The stench of smoke and puddles of water greeted them inside the house where the floors, walls and ceiling closest to the front were damaged. He watched Sam zero in on the window as well as the smashed, fire-blackened glass on the floor.

"Some of the glass is too thick to be window glass," she said. "Looks like some kind of bottle."

"My guess," the captain said, "is there will be traces of gas or some sort of accelerant in the bottle glass." He turned to Sam. "Any idea who might've tossed a Molotov cocktail through your window?"

"I'm in the midst of a hot case, and I've been receiving threatening texts."

"I've gotten one too," Nick said.

"When was the most recent one?" the captain asked.

"A couple of hours ago. It implied that it might be time to 'teach me a lesson.'"

"Well, this certainly does make a statement," a new voice said.

Sam and Nick turned to find Chief Farnsworth in the doorway.

"Are you both all right?" he asked.

"Yes, sir," Sam said. "We weren't here."

"What's this about threats?" he asked, giving Sam a stern-faced stare.

"I've reported them," she said, clearing her throat. "Most of them. Sir."

"Where's your detail?"

"I sent them home for the night because I was staying in."

"And yet you weren't here when a fire broke out in your home." Stepping further into the room, the chief bent to take a closer look at the glass on the floor. "I haven't been a detective in years, Lieutenant, but if you weren't here when the fire started then I have to deduce that you went somewhere." He glanced up at Sam. "Without the detail your superior officers assigned to you until you close your current case. Is that possible?"

Apparently sensing trouble brewing, Captain Grayson headed for the door. "I'll wait outside for the inspector."

"I didn't plan to go anywhere," Sam said to the chief. "But Nick thought Senator O'Connor might be able to help with the case, so we went to Leesburg. Since we were there, we stayed at Nick's place rather than drive all the way back to the city. Turned out to be a good thing we weren't here."

"That's true, and I do appreciate your after-hours

dedication. However, if you go *anywhere* again without your detail—until I say otherwise—I'll have your badge. Am I clear?"

"Yes." She cleared her throat again. "Sir."

"You'll need to vacate the premises until the inspector finishes his work. I assume you'll be at your father's place?"

"Yes, sir."

"I'll have your detail meet you there in the morning."

"Thank you, sir."

As they followed the chief out of the house, Sam grimaced, and Nick choked back a laugh. After what she'd kept from him earlier, he'd rather enjoyed watching the chief take her to task—not that he'd ever admit that to her.

Leaving the fire scene to the experts, Farnsworth escorted Sam and Nick to Skip's house. He and Celia were waiting in the living room.

"Everyone all right?" Skip asked.

"We're fine." Sam bent to kiss her father's forehead. "The damage to the house isn't too bad."

"That true, Joe?" Skip asked his old friend the chief.

"That's how it looked to me."

"Celia wouldn't let me out to see for myself," Skip said, glaring at his wife.

"It's too cold out," she said. "Not good for your lungs."

Skip rolled his eyes at her.

"I'm going home," Farnsworth said. To Sam, he added, "I'll see you in the morning—with your detail."

"Yes, sir."

"Good to see you newlyweds."

"You too, Joe," Skip said. "Thanks for coming."

"Anytime."

Sam turned on her father after the chief left. "*You called him*? What the hell for?"

"If someone's throwing fire through my daughter's window when she's in the middle of a case, then he needs to know."

"Thanks to you I got a major chewing out for being out without my detail."

"Good," Skip said. "You had no business leaving without them."

Watching the exchange, Nick suspected that Sam had never given her detail a thought before they left for Leesburg. Neither of them had.

"What were you doing in Leesburg?" Celia asked.

"We went to see Senator O'Connor for background on the case," Sam said. "We decided to stay at the cabin."

"Thank goodness for that," Celia said.

"Anything else you want to tell me?" Skip's sharp eyes zeroed in on his daughter.

"The case is getting hot," Sam said. "We've uncovered a call girl ring operating at the highest levels of the government. We're arresting the vice president's chief of staff in the morning."

"You don't say," Skip said. "What'd he do?"

"We know he raped one woman, and we suspect he may be one of the organizers of the ring. If that turns out to be true, it certainly gives us a motive for murder."

"I wonder what he'd be more interested in protecting," Skip said. "The ring or his reputation."

"A very good question," Sam said. "One I hope to have answered by this time tomorrow."

"Sounds like you two kids could use a place to sleep for a few hours," Skip said. "Your old room is available."

"Thanks," Nick said.

"I'll get you some towels," Celia said, hustling up the stairs.

Sam consulted her watch. "I've got about two hours."

"Go shut your eyes while you can," Skip said. "Sounds like tomorrow is going to be one hell of a day."

TWENTY-EIGHT

EVEN THOUGH SHE badly needed the sleep, Sam lay awake in her old bedroom staring at the ceiling, thinking over every aspect of the case. This one had felt disjointed from the very beginning, with an early suspect in Lightfeather who'd ended up having an airtight alibi. Since then, they hadn't had so much as a person of interest. Judging by the lengths the perp (or perps) had gone to by making personal attacks on two cops, however, it was clear someone was watching their every move.

"Why aren't you sleeping?" Nick asked.

Sam turned to him. "Why aren't you?"

"Someone threw fire in my window after threatening my fiancée. Stuff like that tends to make me a bit...anxious."

"Are you still mad at me?"

"Yes," he said, but she could tell by his tone that the true mad had passed.

She sighed. "I didn't think you needed any more bad news."

He looked over at her. "Don't keep things from me, Sam. Please don't."

"Even when it might be what's best for you?"

Reaching for her hand, he laced his fingers through

hers. "What's best for me is knowing what's going on with you. Even the hard-to-hear stuff."

"I'm trying really hard to be more forthcoming with you. I meant what I said earlier about not being able to change who I am overnight."

"I'd never want to change who you are. I just want you to change this one little annoying habit…"

"*Annoying*?"

"Very. But luckily for you—and for me—you're also annoyingly cute, distractingly sexy, and perfectly imperfect."

Sam smiled. "Perfectly imperfect. I like that." Rolling to her side, she kissed his chest and then his lips. "Try to get some sleep."

"Where're you going?"

"Sleep isn't happening, so I'm going to get an early start."

"With your detail."

"Yes, dear."

"I do so love the way you say that."

Sam laughed as she pulled on jeans and a sweater. "Before this day is over, I may have to arrest the freaking speaker of the House—or better yet, the vice president. Not your typical day at the office."

"Are any of your days at the office typical?"

Sam pretended to think about that for a minute. "Um, no, but I wouldn't have it any other way." She leaned over the bed to kiss him one last time.

He gripped a handful of her hair. "Be careful out there."

"Always."

"More so than usual today."

"I promise." She kissed him again. "Gotta go."

NICK WENT TO survey the damage at the house, hoping he could get in to get clothes for work. The crime scene tape had been removed, and all that remained was the charred exterior and broken front door. A lone police officer stood watch outside.

"Am I allowed in?" Nick asked the officer.

"Yes, sir, Senator. The fire inspector has cleared the scene. They asked me to keep an eye on things because the door was broken and because of the threat the lieutenant received."

"Thanks for that." A few of their favorite reporters would no doubt love to gain access to their house if given an easy opportunity.

"Looks like quite a mess you've got there, Senator."

Nick turned to find a man he'd seen around the neighborhood. He was young with dark blond hair that could use a cut and a friendly, engaging smile.

"Craig Lowry," he said, extending his hand.

"Nick Cappuano. Nice to meet you."

"Likewise. What happened?"

"Molotov cocktail, or so I'm told."

"You gotta hate when that happens."

Nick laughed. "This kind of thing happens far too often in our lives."

"So I've read. Not sure if it would help, but I'm a contractor. I'd be happy to squeeze you in."

"That'd be great. Are you sure you have time?"

Craig shot him a sly grin. "Landing this job will put me on the map. I think I can make some time."

Amused, Nick said, "Let me show you what needs to be done."

Craig followed him inside and marveled—as most visitors did—at the size of the double town house. As they inspected the damage and discussed the work that needed to be done, Craig whipped out his measuring tape and made notes in a pad he pulled from his pocket.

"Is this related to one of your fiancée's cases?"

"Unfortunately, yes."

"I've seen her around. Her dad is the one that's paralyzed, right?"

"Yes." Nick contemplated the damaged doorway. "Let me run something by you…"

"Sure."

"How hard would it be to install a ramp? I've been thinking that Sam will want to have her father over at some point."

"Shouldn't be too difficult. A buddy of mine works in the city's permitting office. I could run it by him for you, but I'm sure it won't be a problem when I tell him about her dad."

"Would he be doing a special favor because, you know, of who we are?" Such things still made Nick uncomfortable, and he knew how Sam felt about special favors too. In this case, however, she'd probably make an exception.

"Maybe a little. But Skip Holland is a hero in this city. They'd do anything for him." Craig gestured to the door. "The whole frame and stoop will need to be replaced anyway, so it's the perfect time to demo the stairs and do the ramp."

"Absolutely." Nick shook his hand. "Do it. As soon as possible."

"Pending building inspection approval, I can have the stairs mostly out by the end of the day. You'll have to use the back door for a while."

"That's no problem."

"Do you need to wait for the insurance company?"

Nick shook his head. "Just do it. I'll pay whatever. I'd like to forget this ever happened."

"You got it, Senator. I'm on it."

SAM INDULGED IN a rare cup of coffee to give her a badly needed jolt after the nearly sleepless night. She logged into her email, looking for a report on Selina's clothes from the lab. "Crap," she said. "Nothing yet. That's all right, Jack." She called up the computer rendering of Jack Bartholomew. "I've got you on a victim ID. We'll do a lineup, and then we'll have you nailed. But I have a feeling Selina is just the tip of the iceberg."

"Talking to yourself, Lieutenant?"

Sam looked up to find Lieutenant Stahl standing in the doorway. "What do you want?"

"Heard you had some excitement at your place last night."

"How'd you hear that? Were you there?"

His eyes narrowed at the insinuation. "You'd love that wouldn't you?"

"To have you out of my life forever? Sure, throw a cocktail through my window. By all means."

"I'd never give you the satisfaction."

"I'll get it some other way. Eventually."

"Doesn't look like you're going to get it with Gibson."

"I'll get him too. Assholes like the two of you always end up where they belong."

Stahl's rotund face turned the unhealthy shade of purple that so often colored his conversations with Sam. "You can have the last word. I've already gotten what I want today."

What the hell did that mean? "Good for you. Unlike those of you in the rat squad, I have real work to do, so if you don't mind…"

"Have a great day, Lieutenant." He left her with a creepy smile that made her crave a shower.

"Dick," she whispered. She'd suspected he'd had something to do with Peter's pending release. Now she was all but sure of it. Once she had a minute to call her own, she'd look into what role her nemesis had played. Until then, she had a murdering rapist to catch. With that in mind, she printed out photos of the vice president, the speaker of the house, Senator Robert Cook and three other members of Congress who were not involved in the investigation. To ensure that her photo array held up in court, six was the magic number. She took the photos with her to the safe house where Freddie had stashed Selina.

On her way out, she ran into Freddie. "You're here early."

"Couldn't sleep."

Sam knew the feeling.

"I'm glad I caught you," he said. "Crime scene found something in Regina's stuff that you'll want to see." He produced a plastic bag with a Valentine card opened to the inside. In it, Regina had written the message in Spanish.

Freddie translated for her, "My darling Henry, how did I ever get so lucky to find you? I love you so much and I can't wait to meet our baby. Forever yours, Regina."

Sam thought of how despondent Henry had been upon hearing of Regina's involvement in the call girl ring. She was oddly relieved to know that Henry's entire life hadn't blown up in his face just so Regina might be able to stay in the country after her baby was born.

"What do you want me to do with it?" Freddie asked.

"Take it to him."

"Keep it as evidence?"

Sam shook her head. "I'm going to talk to Selina again. I'll catch up to you after."

"Sounds good."

At 5:20 in the morning, the city's streets were all but deserted, but Sam still kept a close eye on the rearview mirror to make sure she wasn't being followed by anyone other than the two officers in the unmarked sedan behind her—as if that wasn't a dead giveaway to anyone who might be watching her.

Outside the house, two officers stood watch. Even though she knew them, Sam still showed them her badge and gave them a moment to thoroughly study it, as they were required to do.

"Go ahead, Lieutenant."

"Thanks."

Sam found Selina on the sofa in the living room, curled up under a blanket nursing a cup of tea.

"You couldn't sleep either?" Selina asked.

"Someone tossed a Molotov cocktail through the window at my house last night. Do you know what that is?"

Eyes wide with fear, Selina nodded. "Was anyone hurt?"

Sam took a seat across from her. "Fortunately, my fiancé and I weren't home at the time."

"That's good."

"Do you know why I told you that?"

Selina shook her head.

"Because I want you to know that these people aren't above throwing fire into the home of a high-ranking police officer and a United States senator. Did I mention my fiancé is a senator?"

Selina swallowed hard and shook her head again.

Sam placed the six photos she'd brought on the coffee table. "Have you ever provided sexual services for any of these men?"

A tear rolled down Selina's cheek. Judging by the raw redness of her eyes, it wasn't the first she'd shed during that long night. "Him," she said, pointing to the speaker. A shudder rippled through her petite frame. "And him." Grimacing, she gestured to Cook.

"What about him?"

"No. I haven't had sex with the vice president of the United States."

"Well," Sam said. "That's a relief. The speaker of the House of Representatives and the senior senator from Virginia will be enough for one morning."

Selina gasped. "*Oh, my God!* I didn't know! *I didn't know who they were!*"

"I know that, Selina, and they knew it too. In fact, that's exactly why they recruited immigrant women." Sam heard the click of the final pieces fitting into place. "It was *because* you wouldn't recognize them. They were counting on that. Even though some of you worked on Capitol Hill, you probably didn't pay much attention to politics."

"What's going to happen to me?"

"I need you to testify."

"I can't do that! I can't have my family find out how I really got the money. I could never live with the shame of that."

"Could you live with another woman being murdered or raped because you didn't help me stop these bastards?"

Tears streamed down the young woman's face. "How can this be happening? I just wanted to save my mother...I didn't know what else to do."

"I can help you, Selina, but I need to know I can count on your testimony before I arrest Bartholomew." Sam paused to let her words sink in before she went for the jugular. "You'll have to pick him out of a lineup of men and then testify against him in court. You'll have to recount—in detail—what he did to you."

Hand to mouth to muffle her sobs, Selina shook her head.

"If you refuse to testify, Selina, my case against Bartholomew will hinge on whether he left any DNA on your clothing the night of the attack. And even if he did, the assistant U.S. attorney may refuse to prosecute without your testimony. That means he goes free to do this to someone else. He continues to get away with victimizing women while holding a lofty government job."

Selina's muffled sobs echoed through the silent room.

"I need you, Selina. Regina and Maria need you."

"*Regina can go to the devil*! This is all her fault."

"Maybe so, but she helped you find a way to pay for your mother's surgery. And trust me when I tell you that no one deserves what was done to her. No one."

Sam sat very still and let Selina think it through as the other woman continued to weep bitterly.

"I went to college, you know? In Belize. I got a degree in business, and I came here hoping to make something of myself." She swiped at her face with the sleeve of her shirt. "But when I got here, it was so bad. No one would hire me because I wasn't a citizen or because they had someone better. I was lucky to get the job with the cleaning company."

"I'm sure you worked very hard," Sam said, trying to be patient.

"I worked until my hands ached and my fingers were blistered and sore. I worked overtime and weekends, but it wasn't enough. If only my mother hadn't gotten sick. None of this would be happening."

"My father was shot two years ago," Sam said. "He was a police officer doing a routine traffic stop and was shot by the driver. He's paralyzed and in a wheelchair. We still don't know who did it, and sometimes when I think that whoever shot him is out there going on with his or her life while he's stuck in that chair…" Sam's throat tightened with emotion. "I understand that you'd do anything you could for your mother. I get that."

"Even something illegal?"

"Whatever you had to do."

"Will I be charged?"

"I'll talk to the assistant U.S. attorney about immunity for you as soon as I leave here. But first I need to know if I can count on you to testify. That'll be her first question."

"How do I go into a public court and tell people what that animal did to me? How do I do that?"

"We'll get someone to help you through every step of the process. We have rape counselors specially trained to assist victims and prepare them for court. I'll get you all the help and support I have at my disposal."

"And how will you keep me alive long enough to testify?"

"Our entire case hinges on you. We'll take good care of you. You have my word on that."

After another endless stretch of silence, Sam leaned forward, elbows on knees. "Will you help me, Selina? Shall I go arrest Jack Bartholomew so he can pay for what he did to you and probably other women too?"

"Will the others come forward so your case doesn't hinge only on me?"

"We can hope for that, but in the meantime, it all comes down to you."

"If I testify, do you promise it won't be for nothing? He's a powerful man. I don't want to see him go free."

"I'll do everything in my power to make sure he gets what's coming to him." She thought of Peter being released from prison and remembered that even her powers had limits. "But I won't make you a promise I may not be able to keep. We'll do our very best. That's all I can do."

"Will you arrest the other men too? The speaker and the senator?"

"I don't know that yet, but we'll be pursuing charges against anyone who was involved with running the organization, anyone who provided the services and anyone who sought them out. If that includes the speaker and the senator, so be it."

Selina sat very still as she thought it over.

Sam's heart beat hard and fast. This was it. The whole thing hung on one tiny woman who was in way, *way* over her head.

"Since I need you to keep me alive as much as you need me to testify, I guess we both need each other."

"Yes, we do."

"Okay," Selina said, seeming resigned now to her fate. "I'll do it."

Sam reached over and clutched the other woman's hand. "Thank you."

SAM FELT LIKE she'd expended a day's worth of energy on the half hour she'd spent with Selina. But she'd gotten what she needed, and that's what mattered. Before going to HQ to meet Freddie, she headed for the Washington Hospital Center. Even thought it was still early, she hoped to find Jeannie McBride awake.

Michael was coming out of Jeannie's room as Sam approached the door.

"How is she?" Sam asked.

"Seems a little better today. They're going to release her later on."

"That's good."

He shrugged.

"Are you okay?"

"She refuses to talk to me about what happened. I'm trying not to push her, but it's just…it's hard. Not knowing…"

Sam rested a hand on his arm. "Try not to push. She'll tell you if and when she feels able to. Until then, you just have to be patient and supportive. That's what she needs from you right now."

"I know."

"Hang in there. It's only been a few days."

He nodded. "You're right. It's all about her and what she needs."

"Did she talk to the counselor?"

Shaking his head, he said, "Sent her away. Said she didn't need it."

Sam hated to hear that. "I hope she'll consider it at some point. You might want to, as well. Can't hurt anything."

"I'll think about it. She's awake if you want to go in. I'll give you a few minutes."

"Thanks." Sam pushed open the door to find Jeannie sitting up in bed. "Hey there. How're you feeling?"

"A little better. Did you see Michael?"

"In the hallway. He seems like a really nice guy, Jeannie."

"He is," she said, sighing. "He wants me to tell him what happened…"

"There's no rush. You don't have to talk about it until you feel ready."

"What if I never feel ready?"

"Well, you may have to testify…"

Jeannie shook her head, as if the very idea of it was too overwhelming to imagine.

"You're sure you won't consider talking to the counselor?"

"I'm sure. At least the HIV test came back negative—for now. I have to be tested again in three months."

"That's a huge relief."

"It's something. Right about now, I'll take it."

"I hate to ask you this, but do you feel up to looking at a few photos?"

Jeannie cast a wary glance at Sam. "Of what?"

"Possible suspects."

Jeannie gripped the blanket so tightly her knuckles turned white. "Do I have to?"

"I could really use your help. We have a pretty good case for rape against one of them, but I can't pin the murders on him. At least not yet."

"I only saw his eyes…"

"Then that's what I'll show you. Okay?"

Gritting her teeth, Jeannie nodded.

Sam took a moment to fold the six sheets of paper so just the eyes of the men were showing. And then she lined them up on the bed next to each other. "Take your time." She watched Jeannie force herself to look at the first one. And then her eyes darted across the array.

"No. None of them."

"You're sure?"

"I'll never forget those eyes. Ever."

"I appreciate you taking a look. I know it was hard for you."

"I know you'll need my help and my testimony. I just have to find a way to tell Michael first."

Sam reached for the other woman's hand. "May I offer a suggestion?"

Jeannie nodded. "Of course."

"It seems to me that worrying about telling him is causing you grief that you hardly need on top of everything else. Maybe if you just tell him and get it over with, you'll have one less thing to worry about."

"That's not a *bad* suggestion."

Sam smiled at her. "Gee, thanks."

Jeannie thought about it for a moment. "I'm going to tell him and get it over with. Then I'll let him tell my mother. I *really* couldn't deal with that."

"It always helps to have a plan. Just remember he loves you—all he's thinking about is you and what you need."

Jeannie bit her lip and nodded. "He's been amazing."

She blinked back tears. "He's hardly left my side since it happened."

"Where will you go when they release you?"

"His house has a security system, so I guess I'll go there even though it's in the same neighborhood where it…happened."

"The security system is a good idea—especially until we catch this guy." Sam checked her watch. "I'm sorry, but I have to run. We're arresting the chief of staff to the vice president this morning."

"Wow! Wish I could be there for that."

The spark of interest she saw in Jeannie's soft brown eyes reassured Sam. "You'll be back with us before you know it. Until then, focus on recovering from your injuries and anything that makes you feel better."

"I'll feel better when you find the guy who did this to me—and the others."

"I'll find him, and I'll make him pay."

"I'm counting on that."

Sam hugged her detective. "I'll check in with you tomorrow."

"Thanks. If you see Michael out there, will you tell him I need to talk to him?"

"Sure." Sam left the room and found Michael in the waiting room at the end of the long hallway. "I think she might be ready to talk…"

He jumped to his feet. "Really?"

"I have to warn you…I've heard a lot of hideous crap in twelve years on this job, but what happened to her…it's bad. You need to prepare yourself."

A tick of tension pulsed in his tightly clenched jaw. "I appreciate the warning."

"If either of you need me for anything, she has my number."

"Thanks for everything."

"No problem."

TWENTY-NINE

SAM'S NEXT ORDER of business was a phone call to the U.S. Attorney's office as she drove back to HQ to meet Freddie.

"What've you got, Lieutenant?" asked Assistant U.S. Attorney Faith Miller.

Sam laid out her case against Jack Bartholomew. "I'll need a warrant for his DNA, which will hopefully be a match for DNA that may or may not be on the clothes Selina was wearing the night of the attack. But even without the DNA, she's willing to do a lineup and she'll testify. I'm hoping other victims will come forward after we arrest him. We've got him on rape and soliciting a prostitute."

Faith was silent for a long time. "Did she seek medical attention?"

Sam had been expecting that question. "She couldn't afford it. She sent all the money she made home to her family, but she took several days off of work after it happened. I can get the owner of the cleaning company to testify to that."

"She didn't tell anyone what had happened?"

"No."

Faith went silent again.

"Come on, Faith, you're killing me here! You know we've got enough."

"I don't want to see another case fall apart before we get to trial."

"That's a dig on Gibson, right?"

"Forrester isn't happy with how that case fell apart. He's warned us to be more careful in the future that all our ducks are in a row before we move forward."

"So where does that leave me with Bartholomew?"

"Call me when you hear from the lab. Until then, hold off."

"You gotta be kidding me—"

"Sam, I'm not budging on this. You're talking about the top aide to the vice president of the United States. I want an airtight case before you go near him."

"Fine. You want airtight, I'll get you airtight."

"Excellent. I'll be here when you're ready."

Sam ended the call and let out a growl of frustration. Opening the phone, she called the chief. His administrative assistant put her right through.

"Good morning, Lieutenant."

"I need your help with the lab." She explained the urgency of the situation to the chief. "Can you lean on them for me?"

"I'll do what I can."

"He's the key. I have a feeling if I can get him in here and lean hard on him I can get him to roll on the others. He won't want to go down alone. All I need to know from the lab right now is that there's male DNA on the clothes. We can test it against a sample from him after we have him in custody."

"I'll make the call. Where's your detail?"

Sam glanced in her rearview mirror. "Right up my ass where they belong."

"That sounds rather…uncomfortable."

"You said it."

Snorting with laughter, the chief hung up.

Now all she could do was wait—and hope the killer didn't strike again while they were waiting on the lab.

NICK AND CHRISTINA were in a meeting with other key campaign staff going over the next week's schedule when one of the administrative assistants interrupted them.

"I'm sorry to disturb you, Senator, but Judson Knott is here with Mitchell Sanborn."

Startled, Nick glanced at Christina.

Looking equally surprised, she shrugged.

"Send them in," Nick said. To the others in the room, he added, "Would you please excuse us for a moment?"

The staffers collected their belongings and passed Knott and Sanborn on their way out.

"Gentlemen." Nick shook hands with both men and invited them to sit across from him and Christina. "This is a nice surprise." The last time Nick had seen Sanborn, chairman of the Democratic National Committee, he'd mentioned the party's potential interest in Nick making a run for the White House in four years. Nick still had trouble believing he'd actually been part of that conversation. "What can I do for you?"

"We've been hearing some disturbing rumblings on the Hill," Sanborn said in his deep Kentuckian accent. The former governor of the Bluegrass state had sandy brown hair shot through with silver and intense dark eyes. "Things that have us quite...worried."

Pretending to be baffled, Nick glanced at Judson, the chair of the Virginia Democratic Committee. "What kind of rumblings?" he asked.

Sanborn's eyes narrowed. "That your girlfriend—"

"Fiancée," Nick said.

"My apologies," Sanborn said. "Your *fiancée* is investigating members of our own party for consorting with call girls. I don't have to tell you what that kind of scandal would do to the party, especially with the midterm elections just a few short months away."

Nick decided the best way to play this was the dumb way. "I'm afraid you gentlemen have me at a disadvantage. This is the first I'm hearing of it." In hindsight, he realized he should've expected this visit. If they'd had any idea who exactly Sam was targeting, they'd be too busy having apoplexies to be bothering him.

"Senator, I'd like to think we're all one big happy family in the Democratic Party," Sanborn said with a charming smiling lighting up his handsome face. "Wouldn't you?"

"I suppose."

"And a family takes care of one another, am I right?"

Not my family, Nick wanted to say but didn't. "Mitchell, why don't you save us all a lot of time and trouble and tell me what is you want from me?"

"Let's talk first about what I want *for* you, Senator, shall we? I believe you'll recall our last conversation in which I mentioned the very high aspirations the party has for you as our brightest new star."

Starting to get a feel for where this was heading, Nick said, "You'll recall that I told you I wasn't ready to have that particular conversation."

"Indeed. However, I'd like to think that when you *are* ready, your party will be standing by, willing to lend you the support and encouragement you would need."

"In exchange for what?"

Sanborn's face once again lost its amiable expression. "Tell your fiancée to back off."

"Wait a minute," Knott said, practically levitating out of his chair. "You never said you were going to say that to him!" To Nick, Knott added, "I didn't condone this. He asked me to come with him to see you, but he never said he planned to do that!"

Nick put up a hand. "Easy does it, Judson. Let me make this real simple for all of us."

"That'd be preferred," Sanborn said.

"Get out of my office."

Sanborn sputtered, and his face turned very red. "You can't...I won't..."

Nick stood up to his full six-foot-four-inch height. "Get. The. Hell. Out. *Now*."

Sanborn stood up slowly, smoothing his hands over his suit. "You're making yourself a powerful enemy, young man."

"That's *senator* to you, and by the time I'm through

telling the party leadership what you came in here asking me to do, you won't have much power left, so enjoy it while it lasts."

"Judson," Sanborn said. "Let's go."

"You go on ahead. I'm not going anywhere with you."

Sanborn turned on his heel and stalked out of the room.

"There goes my chance to be president," Nick muttered with a chuckle intended to defuse the tension in the room.

"I'm so sorry, Senator," Judson said. "I had no idea…"

Nick rested a hand on the older man's shoulder. "Don't worry about it." Judson and the rest of the Virginia Democratic Party had been nothing but supportive of Nick and his staff since John O'Connor's sudden death turned their lives upside down.

"If he had told me what he planned to do," Judson said, "I would've told him it was a waste of time."

"What did he tell you he wanted with me?"

"To talk about the campaign and check in with you."

"Well, he checked in."

"And checked out," Christina said.

"They must be really scared," Nick said as another thought occurred to him. He drew his new BlackBerry from his pocket. "Would you mind giving me a minute?"

"Of course, Senator," Judson said. He and Christina quietly left the room, closing the door behind them.

The moment he was alone, Nick dialed Sam's number. "Hey, babe."

"Hey."

"What's wrong?"

"How can you tell something is wrong with one word?"

"Because I know you."

"The AUSA won't let me go after Bartholomew until we have more than Selina's testimony. I'm waiting on the freaking lab, and it's taking them *all* goddamned day! Tell me things are going better over there."

"They were going well until a few minutes ago." He told her about Sanborn's visit and how infuriated the party chairman had been by Nick's refusal to interfere with the investigation.

"And you just handed me a new suspect."

"That's what I was thinking too."

"Have I mentioned lately that I love you?"

He smiled. "I'll take it whenever I can get it."

"I'm sorry you were put in that position."

"It's certainly not your fault."

"I told you so," she said.

"What did you tell me?"

"That my shit was going to bang up against your shit and cause you trouble."

"I *love* when your shit bangs up against my shit."

"That's so gross. I'm trying to be serious here."

"And I'm trying to say that I don't *care* if your shit bangs up against my shit. I'm doing the best possible job I can for the people of Virginia. If Election Day comes and they're not happy with me, so be it. I refuse to let this job take over my entire life."

"You're very evolved. How did you get so evolved?"

"Thanks to you and the murders of two of my good friends, I've figured out what really matters in life, and I absolutely refuse to let people like Sanborn think I'm for sale."

"I'm seriously turned on right now."

Nick laughed. "For all the good that does me."

"Luckily for you, it'll keep until I see you."

"Mmm, can't wait."

"Thanks for the new lead and for standing up to Sanborn. For what it's worth, I'm proud of you."

"It's worth a lot," he said. "It's worth everything."

"I'll see you when I see you."

For a moment, he debated telling her about the ramp at the house but then decided he'd rather it be a surprise. "Be careful with my fiancée. I love her more than life itself."

"Nick…You make me all fluttery. No one has *ever* made me fluttery. How do you do that?"

Ridiculously pleased, he smiled. "What can I say? It's magic. Take care, babe."

WHILE SHE WAITED for the results from the lab, Sam did a run on Mitchell Sanborn. As his photo popped up on the screen, her skin tingled with goose bumps. Those eyes… Remembering Jeannie's description of her attacker's eyes, Sam sat riveted, staring at the screen. She read through his impressive biography, which detailed his Ivy League education and meteoric rise through the ranks of the Democratic Party. But she kept returning to that photo and those eyes…

She printed it—along with five other random men—and grabbed her radio. "Cruz!"

He popped up in his cubicle, a dollop of cream clinging to his bottom lip. "Right here, boss."

"Let's go."

Grabbing his trench coat, Freddie scrambled after her. "Where to?"

"First to see Jeannie and then, hopefully, to start arresting evil bastards."

"Oh, I *love* when we get to arrest evil bastards!"

"Will you please finish that donut so I don't have to smell it?"

"Want some?"

"Yes, but my ass is growing at such an alarming rate that my wedding dress will have to be sewn by a tentmaker rather than Vera Wang. Keep it away from me."

"Your ass is not that big. Not that I've looked or anything…"

Sam shot him her most withering look.

He swallowed the last bite of donut. "Is Vera Wang really making your dress? Even I've heard of her."

"Apparently so. That reminds me…" Reaching for her phone, she texted Shelby and her sisters, moving the evening's appointment to her father's house since hers was fire damaged at the moment.

"Everything okay with Nick? I assume he eventually showed up last night."

"Yeah. He's kind of a mess after seeing his deadbeat

mother this week. She shook him down for twenty-five grand."

Freddie released a low whistle. "Poor guy. He's had enough lately."

"I couldn't agree more. What about you? All ready for tonight?"

His mood changed in an instant. "I guess."

"Any word from Elin?"

Dejected, he shook his head. "Not since I told her to show up tonight or else."

"Are you regretting the ultimatum?"

"Kind of. I like her. I don't want it to be over."

"You don't think she's going to show?"

"No."

"Maybe you're not giving her enough credit."

He shrugged. "Why should she have to put up with the cold shoulder from my mother? She can have any guy she wants."

"Seems to me she wants you."

"I guess we'll see, won't we?"

Over the top of her car, Sam said, "There're a lot of women out there, Freddie. If things don't work out with this one, there are plenty of other fish in the sea."

"Took me twenty-nine years to reel this one in. I'm not ready to throw her back yet."

Inside the car, Sam started it and gave it a minute to warm up. Her cell phone rang, and she took the call from Captain Malone.

"Tell me you've got news from the lab," Sam said.

"We'll get to that. But first I wanted to let you know that Peter Gibson was just released from custody."

Sam had known it was coming but hearing confirmation sent her stomach into a tailspin. Resting a hand over her churning belly, she said, "Okay."

"I'm sorry, Sam."

"Not your fault." A knot of fear settled in her throat, threatening her legendary composure. "What've you heard from the lab?"

"Semen was found on the clothing."

"Thank you, Jesus."

"You're to tread lightly with Bartholomew until we know the DNA is his."

"We know it's his."

"We know that a call girl told us it was. Until the *lab* tells us, you're to consider him a person of interest not a suspect. That's right from Farnsworth and Forrester."

"Semantics," she said, scoffing. "Did you get me the warrant for his DNA?"

"Signed, sealed and delivered."

"Cruz and I are heading out now. I need to see McBride for a moment, and then we'll track down Mr. Bartholomew."

"What're you up to with McBride?"

"Not sure yet. Could be something, could be nothing."

"Let me know if it's something."

"I will."

"Where's your tail?"

Realizing she had once again forgotten all about the two police officers following her, she glanced in the mirror. "Right where they belong."

"Excellent. Keep me posted."

Closing the phone and dropping it into her pocket, she took a moment to absorb the news that Peter Gibson was once again walking the streets. Sam gripped the wheel but didn't put the car into drive.

"Gibson?" Freddie asked.

She nodded.

He let out a curse that was so wildly out of character for him that Sam couldn't help but laugh.

"He'll screw up again, and when he does, we'll be ready," Freddie vowed.

"I have no doubt."

"I'm sorry, Sam."

"Not your fault. We all screwed this up, and now we have to live with it. The best thing we can do now is to get justice for our current victims. They're counting on us."

"I admire the way you're rolling with it."

"What choice do I have?"

"None I suppose."

"I had a somewhat major revelation while talking to Selina Rameriz this morning," Sam said to Freddie as they pulled out of the HQ lot.

"And that was?"

"The reason they recruited immigrant women for the call girl ring—so they wouldn't recognize the schmucks paying for their services. Sure, they might recognize the president and vice president, but how many Americans can pick out the speaker of the House let alone one of the senators from Virginia?"

"Well, everyone in America would know Nick."

"Luckily, he has no need for call girls," Sam said dryly.

"Cook is a pretty big name in American politics."

"People new to the country wouldn't recognize it."

"True."

"So it's rather brilliant of them to recruit beautiful young immigrant women who'd have no idea who they were servicing," Sam said.

"And who wouldn't raise much suspicion if they suddenly turned up dead."

"The person who killed them certainly wasn't counting on a senator being in love with one of them."

"He also wasn't counting on us," Freddie said. "They probably thought the MPD wouldn't care much about a couple of dead cleaning ladies."

"They thought wrong."

"You bet your ass they did."

"Such language, Lieutenant," he said, frowning.

Sam gave him the finger.

"I'm offended."

"You'll survive."

"What're we seeing McBride about?"

"I have a picture I want to show her. Just a hunch."

"Your hunches are usually spot-on."

"If this one is, we've got our killer."

THIRTY

JUDGING BY JEANNIE'S visceral and almost violent reaction to one of the six photos Sam showed her, they'd found their man.

As she pushed the picture away, Jeannie began to sob.

Michael, whose haggard face and red eyes told the story of how he'd taken the news about the rape, crawled right into the bed with her and wrapped his arms around her.

"Who is he?" Jeannie whispered.

Sam folded the photo and jammed it into her coat pocket. "Mitchell Sanborn, chairman of the Democratic National Committee."

"Oh God, it'll be all over the news."

"Yes."

"Will you arrest him right away?"

"I'm going for him as soon as I leave here." Sam hesitated but only for a second before she reached for Jeannie's hand. "If there's anyone who should hear about what happened from you, the time to tell them is now."

"My mother," Jeannie said, turning frantic eyes on Michael. "My family."

"It's okay, honey," Michael said. "I called your mom. She's bringing your sister over. I'll talk to them."

"It's not enough that this had to happen, but now it'll be blasted all over the news too," Jeannie said as her tears turned to anger.

"We'll get you through this," Sam said, gripping the other woman's hand. "I had an idea, and it might not seem to make any sense…"

"What idea?" Jeannie asked.

"Remember when *The Reporter* was getting ready to publish the story about my near-abortion years ago?"

Jeannie nodded.

"Nick encouraged me to get ahead of the story—to tell it my way before they could tell the incorrect version."

"You're not suggesting I actually talk to the media…"

"I'm saying you might want to consider talking to *one* reporter, and tell him you're all right, you survived, you're on the mend. Show him—and the rest of the world—that this guy didn't ruin you."

"I'm still not sure he didn't."

"People don't need to know that."

"If I did this, wouldn't it hurt the case?"

"Only if you gave away things that only you and he would know. I'm suggesting a very high-level interview that puts the story in your words but doesn't jeopardize the case. You know what you can say and what you can't."

Jeannie glanced at Michael. "What do you think?"

"It's entirely up to you, of course, but I agree with Sam that it's worth considering."

"I can't imagine telling a stranger…" Her voice faded to a whisper, and her eyes filled with new tears.

"Exposing your personal pain to strangers is difficult," Sam said. "But Nick was right in my case. Once we put out the statement, the lies *The Reporter* printed lost some of their power over me. I don't think I would've gotten through that episode as well as I did if I hadn't gotten the chance to tell the story my way."

"Do you know someone? A reporter I could talk to?"

"I have just the guy. He'll do right by you. Darren Tabor from the *Star*. He did the joint interview with Nick and me."

"I loved that interview. He did a beautiful job."

"It was okay," Sam said begrudgingly. Talking to reporters about her personal life would never sit well with her, but she'd done it for Nick and his campaign.

"Would you be there with me?" Jeannie asked Michael.

"Always. For as long as you need me, I'm right here."

Jeannie sent him a small but grateful smile and tightened her hold on his hand. "Okay," she said. "I'll do it."

"I'll make the call and have Darren meet you at Michael's house later this afternoon. That way you'll have time to get home and settled first."

"Thank you, Sam. I feel better just knowing who did this and that you're going to get him."

"I'm going to nail his ass to the wall," Sam vowed. "For you and the others."

"I'm counting on that."

GONZO AWOKE AND sat up quickly, his heart racing. Alex had been crying relentlessly for hours. Finally, the baby had worn himself out and drifted into restless sleep a little over an hour ago. Gonzo and Christina had fallen into bed to sleep while they could. Through the baby monitor Gonzo could hear the little coos the baby made in his sleep, and was reassured. Sam's sisters had told him the panic receded eventually. He certainly hoped so. Living in a perpetual state of terror was draining, to say the least.

Gonzo glanced over at Christina. He wanted so badly to kiss her, but he hated to disturb her after she'd been up most of the night helping with the baby. He shifted onto his side, put an arm around her and drew her in closer to him. As much as he loved having the baby in his life, he missed the uninterrupted time with her.

She murmured in her sleep, and he kissed the top of her head, breathing in the sweet fragrance of her hair.

"Tommy," she whispered.

"Hmm?"

"Why aren't you sleeping?"

"I woke up and couldn't hear him. I got worried."

"He's fine. You're fine. We're all fine."

"Are we?"

She looked up at him, smiling. "Of course we are."

"I love you so much, Christina. I spent my whole life trying to avoid this kind of committed relationship. Now that I have it, I can't imagine why I was so eager to avoid it. And I'm not just saying that because you're helping me with the baby."

"I know." She caressed his face. "I love you too. I can't believe how fast everything happened and how content I feel."

He curled his hand around her neck and pressed his lips to hers. Sinking into the kiss, Gonzo's heart beat harder as he understood with a clarity he'd never experienced quite so vividly before that she was *it* for him—the one he'd been waiting for without even knowing he'd been waiting.

Shifting on top of her, he reveled in the feel of her soft skin.

Her hands moved on his back, soothing and arousing. She raised her hips in invitation, and he entered her in one swift stroke. No other woman had ever affected him the way she did. When they were first together, he'd expected to grow tired of her the way he had all the others. But the more time he spent with her, the more he wanted her. He was beginning to realize he would never get enough. That was certainly unprecedented.

Resting on his elbows, he brushed the hair back from her face and touched his lips to hers. "So beautiful. Such a lady."

"Not always," she said with a coy grin. Her hands cruised down his back to grip his ass, tearing a groan from deep inside him.

She triggered something primal in him, something possessive and altogether new as he made fierce love to her.

Afterward, he rested carefully on top of her, worried as always about how much bigger than her he was. Her fingers sifted through his hair as she ran her foot up and down his leg.

Gonzo breathed her in, wanting her again, wanting her forever. "Marry me," he said. The words were out of his mouth before he had a second to consider the implications.

She gasped. "Tommy..."

"I'm sorry. I didn't mean to just blurt that out. I don't have a ring, and a classy woman like you deserves a romantic proposal..." At the sight of her tears and the sound of her laughter, he stopped. "What?"

"If you don't stop talking you'll ruin the most romantic moment of my life."

She staggered him. "Yeah?"

Nodding, she reached for him and brought him down for a kiss that made his head spin.

"Let me try this again...Christina Billings, I love you. Will you please marry me?"

"Yes," she said, laughing through her tears. "Yes, I'll marry you, Tommy Gonzales."

"I'll get you a ring. As soon as I can."

"I don't need one." She hugged him tight against her. "I have everything I need right here."

Alex chose that moment to let out a lusty wail.

"And then some," Christina whispered, smiling as she kissed him.

SAM AND FREDDIE sat in the car outside the headquarters of the Democratic National Committee on South Capitol Street.

"How's this gonna go?" Freddie asked.

"We're going in there and arresting Sanborn for Jeannie's kidnapping and rape. Once we get him to HQ, we'll hammer him on the rest."

"What about Bartholomew?"

"He's next."

"Isn't that Sanborn over there?" Freddie pointed to where two men were having a heated discussion.

"It is! And that's Daniels with him," she said, referring to the speaker of the house. "He was third on my list. Gee, wonder what they're fighting about."

"How about we go see?"

They emerged from the car, and with Sam's detail following them, made their way toward the two men who never saw them coming until they were nearly upon them.

Sanborn looked up, saw Sam and blanched. Then he took off running. Daniels bolted in the other direction. "Get him," she called to Freddie as she took off after Sanborn. "One of you go with him," she said to her two-officer detail. To the cop who followed her she said, "Stay out of this and leave it to me."

"Yes, ma'am."

Sanborn ran down South Capitol Street, darting in and around pedestrians. Sam's legs and lungs burned with exertion, but when she thought about what this monster had done to Jeannie, a new burst of adrenaline brought her within an arm's length of her prey. Worried about him managing to slip through her fingers, she sprung at him from behind and took him down hard on the pavement. The impact briefly knocked the wind out of both of them. As she struggled to cuff him, he fought her off, and his elbow caught her hard in the abdomen.

"Let me go, you fucking bitch. You have no idea who you're screwing with."

The shot to her gut had left her seeing stars and fighting for every breath. "I know exactly who I'm screwing with—and your days of raping and murdering women are over."

"You've got the wrong guy, and I'll have your job for this."

"We'll let the DNA tell the story."

That seemed to shut him up. Choking back a surge of nausea, she pressed her knee to his back and managed to get the cuffs on him. She left him lying facedown on the sidewalk and stood to call for backup. A sharp pain in her belly had her bending in half, hands on knees as she tried to breathe through it the way she used to do before she gave up the soda that had caused crippling stomachaches. This pain, however, felt different...

"Are you okay, Lieutenant?" her detail officer asked.

"Fine. Just need a minute."

"That was an awesome tackle."

"Thanks." A second, sharper pain ripped through her when she tried to stand up. Son of a bitch...When she tried to stand up straight another pain ripped through her.

"You don't look too good, Lieutenant."

"I'm okay," Sam managed to say.

Within minutes the street was swarming with MPD

officers and cars. Sam ordered that Sanborn be taken to HQ and held in an interrogation room until she arrived.

"I think Lieutenant Holland needs medical attention," the young detail officer said.

Sam looked daggers at him. "I do *not*. I told you I'm fine."

"You don't look fine."

Sam stalked off in the direction of where they'd parked, hoping Freddie had managed to grab Daniels. She was aware of the young officer scurrying after her, but all her focus remained on breathing her way through the pains that continued to come fast and furious.

Of course she recognized the pains for what they were. After all, she'd been through this three times before. This time, though… This time… If she allowed herself to acknowledge what was happening, she'd never be able to finish the job on behalf of Regina, Maria and Jeannie. So she kept breathing, kept walking, kept functioning when inside her heart was shattering.

Outside the DNC building, Freddie jogged up to her. "Did you get him?"

"Yep. You?"

"In custody and on the way to HQ."

"Let's go pick up Bartholomew."

"Are you okay?" he asked, following her to the car.

"Fine."

"Then why are you pale as a ghost, sweating and breathing funny?"

"Took an elbow to the gut. Hurt."

"Maybe we should hit the E.R."

She dug out her phone to update Malone. "The only place we're hitting is the vice president's office and then HQ to nail these bastards."

"With you, boss."

SAM AND FREDDIE had to surrender their firearms to get through security at the Eisenhower Executive Office Building, located adjacent to the White House. Being without her weapon always made her twitchy, but when added to the growing discomfort in her abdomen, she was downright anxious.

They were escorted to the vice president's suite where they were told that Mr. Bartholomew was in a meeting.

Sam and Freddie exchanged glances.

She leaned on the reception desk to bring her face down close to the nervous-looking man. "Go get him," she said in her lowest, most sinister tone.

The young man scooted back from his desk and disappeared into the office.

Another sharp pain stole Sam's breath.

"Sam…"

"It's nothing."

"It's not nothing."

"Um," the receptionist said when he returned, "right this way."

Sam and Freddie followed him to a large office that was filled with pictures and political memorabilia—yet another shrine to a long, successful career.

Bartholomew stood as they entered the room. He

was tall, heavy and bald. Sam tried to imagine poor Selina Rameriz trying to fight him off. She'd never stood a chance.

"What can I do for you?"

"Jack Bartholomew?" Freddie asked.

"Yes."

Freddie flashed his badge. "We need you to accompany us to MPD Headquarters for a conversation about Selina Rameriz."

"*Who?*"

"The call girl you raped and sodomized?" Sam said. "Remember her?"

Bartholomew blanched. "I did no such thing! I don't know what you're talking about!"

"You know *exactly* what I'm talking about."

"You've got the wrong guy!"

Sam had to laugh at how they all said that. "If that's the case, then you won't mind coming with us, giving us a sample of your DNA and clearing this whole thing up. Will you?"

At that, a bead of sweat appeared on his forehead.

Sam nodded to her partner.

Freddie approached the other man and recited the Miranda warning.

"This is an outrage!" Bartholomew said as he resisted Freddie's attempts to cuff him.

"What's going on in here?" another voice asked from the doorway.

Sam turned to find the vice president himself watching the proceedings.

"Mr. Bartholomew is a person of interest in an aggravated sexual assault case," Sam said.

Gooding's mouth fell open for a second before he quickly recovered his composure.

"Mr. Vice President," Bartholomew said. "You have to believe me. I swear to God. I didn't do this."

"You shouldn't swear to God," Freddie said. "You'll go to hell."

Gooding studied his aide, but his expression remained unreadable. Handsome with snow-white hair and piercing blue eyes, Gooding was taller than he appeared on TV.

"Bill," Bartholomew said, pleading as Freddie directed him to the door. "Help me. Please."

As Freddie took Bartholomew out, Sam hung back. "If I may say so, sir, you don't seem as shocked as I'd expect you to be after seeing your top aide arrested for aggravated sexual assault."

Gooding finally blinked. "Of course I'm shocked. I've known Jack Bartholomew for twenty-five years."

"And never had any reason to believe he was capable of attacking women?"

"Absolutely not," he said, but Sam noted that his words lacked the conviction she'd expect from someone who'd just watched a close colleague be arrested. "Is this going to be on the news?"

"That the vice president's chief of staff is a person of interest in a rape? That he and other high-level government officials ran and patronized a call girl ring that was Washington's best-kept secret? I'd guess it'll probably make the news."

At that, Gooding finally looked a bit concerned. "I have things…I need to do."

Sam gestured for him to go on ahead. The moment she was alone, she grasped the back of a chair and held on through another sharp pain. As soon as she was able to she left Bartholomew's office and ducked into the first ladies' room she found in the vast office building.

Inside the stall, her hands shook as she unzipped her jeans. "Oh my God," she whispered at the sight of blood—a lot of blood. "No, no, *no…*" She pulled herself together enough to purchase a couple of pads from the vending machine on the wall. Her hands shook as she tried to clean herself up and deal with the pads.

Sweating and nauseous, she closed her eyes and gave herself a moment—just one moment to absorb the shock and pain. Her ringing phone ended the moment. Fumbling with the phone, she flipped it open and then dropped it on the floor. It skidded out of her reach. She managed to button her jeans and leave the stall to retrieve her phone.

"Yeah?" she said, breathing through the cramps.

"Sam?" Freddie said. "I've been waiting down here for twenty minutes. What the hell is taking so long?"

Twenty minutes? "Sorry."

"Did Gooding hassle you?"

"What? No."

"Then what's taking so long?"

"Nothing. I'm coming."

"You okay?"

"Yeah." Sam ended the call and scrolled through

her contacts, looking for the number Harry had programmed into her phone. She wanted to call Nick. She *needed* to call Nick. But she had to close the case before she could allow herself to fall apart. If she heard his voice, she'd fall apart.

"This is Sam Holland," she said when Harry answered.

"Hey, Sam. What's up?"

"I'm sorry to bother you on your day off, but I, um…I think I might be miscarrying."

"Oh, no. What's going on?"

"I took a hard hit to the belly, and the cramps started almost right away. Now I'm bleeding too."

"Is it more than a regular period?"

Swallowing the hard lump of emotion that had formed in her throat, she said, "Yeah."

"Can you get yourself to an E.R.? I could meet you."

"I'm about two hours from closing a big case. I'm just wondering…" Her eyes burned with tears. "If I went to the E.R. right now, they wouldn't be able to stop it or anything, would they?"

"How far apart are the cramps?"

"Every minute or so."

Harry sighed. "That coupled with the bleeding…I doubt it could be stopped. I'm sorry, Sam."

"S'okay. Not like I haven't been down this road before."

"I know you might not be able to see it as such right now, but this is actually very good news."

"How in the hell is this good news?"

"It proves you *can* get pregnant."

"That's not good news if it's going to end like this every time."

"It may not. You took a hard hit. The follicle was probably not fully attached to the uterine wall yet, so it didn't take much to dislodge it."

"This is the shit that happens in my job. I take hard hits. You can't exactly wrap me in foam for nine months and expect me to do my job."

"Wanna bet?"

"Listen—"

"Call me when you get home, and I'll bring Maggie over to take a look at you."

"Is she the girlfriend?"

"Yep. She's slipping me a note right now that says until she can see you, if you feel faint or nauseous, the pain becomes sharp and/or constant, or the bleeding becomes profuse get to an E.R. right away. Otherwise, it should be like a bad period with cramps and bleeding. Okay?"

"Yeah."

"I'm sorry this is happening to you again."

"So am I. Thanks for the help."

"Anytime."

She closed the phone and put it in her coat pocket, determined to close this case before she had her fourth miscarriage.

THIRTY-ONE

SAM TURNED THE keys over to Freddie.

"You're sure you're okay, boss?"

"Just drive."

"I sent Bartholomew with patrol. He'll be waiting for us in interrogation. I also called Faith Miller and asked her to meet us there."

"Good. Thanks."

"What did the vice president say?"

Sam put her head back against the seat and fought off the array of emotions storming around inside of her. So much to absorb and no time to do it. "He was concerned about the media catching wind of his chief of staff's arrest."

"Always a politician." Freddie navigated the car through rush hour traffic. "So what's the plan for when we go at them?"

"We'll let them stew for a bit and then tell each one that the others rolled on him."

Freddie nodded. "I like it. None of them will want to go down alone."

"That's the idea."

After a long moment of silence, he took his eyes off the road to look over at her. "I get that you don't want to tell me what's wrong, but I can see you're upset. You have to be thinking about Peter…"

"Yeah." Sam watched the blur of lights and buildings. When tears threatened, she quickly closed her eyes and fought them off. Once she started, she might never stop. "Hard to believe he's out there somewhere."

"He won't be for long."

"I hope you're right." When they arrived at HQ, she went straight to her office where she downed three of the pain pills she kept in her top drawer for emergencies. This certainly counted. "Let's get this sewed up," she said when she rejoined Freddie in the pit. "You've got somewhere to be."

"I'm here 'til we're done. My plans will keep."

Captain Malone and Chief Farnsworth joined them.

"Lieutenant," the chief said. "You've got some high-profile guests taking up space in my interrogation rooms."

"Yes, sir."

Farnsworth tipped his head as he studied her. "What's wrong with you?"

"Nothing." To Malone she said, "Did you get DNA samples?"

"On their way to the lab as we speak."

"Good."

Assistant U.S. Attorney Faith Miller entered the pit. "What've you got?" she asked Sam. The Miller triplets were three of the most stunning women Sam had ever met. They had soft brown hair that each sister wore in a different style, green eyes and figures more often seen on supermodels than lawyers.

"Sanborn is the kingpin," Sam said. "McBride identified him as her attacker. I believe the DNA will also show him to be responsible for the murders of Regina Argueta de Castro and Maria Espanosa. I want to use Daniels and Bartholomew to set up Sanborn. Immunity for both of them on the call girl ring, but if the DNA on Selina Rameriz's clothes matches Bartholomew's, I'll charge him with aggravated sexual assault. Selina worked with Jackson on a composite sketch that's a perfect match for Bartholomew. I can also get her employer to testify that she was out of work for several days after the attack and that she'd never missed a day of work before then. I can get her coworkers to testify to the bruises on her face and arms."

"We've also got several people who attended the gala at the Reagan Building who will testify that they saw Bartholomew with Selina that night," Freddie said. "And we've got videotape showing them there together."

Faith nodded. "With the DNA, that's enough to charge him."

"The lab is rushing the results through," Farnsworth said.

"Glad something can get them to rush," Sam muttered.

"What've you got on Daniels?" Faith asked.

"Involvement in the call girl ring as well as solicitation and prostitution. If I can offer him immunity, I might be able to get him to tell me what he knows. From what I know about him, losing his political career will be significant punishment."

Faith nodded in agreement. "Do it." She zeroed in on Sam. "Are you feeling all right?"

"Cramps," Sam whispered so the men wouldn't hear.

"Ouch."

Gesturing to Freddie, Sam headed toward the interrogation rooms. "Let's talk to Daniels first." On the way, she stopped to remove several photos from her murder board.

When they entered the room, the speaker of the House of Representatives leaped to his feet. "I don't know why I'm here. What did I do?"

"Mr. Speaker, I need to remind you that you have the right to remain silent." Sam reviewed the Miranda warning and received his permission to record the interview. Freddie remained by the door. "Do you understand your rights in this matter?"

"I haven't done anything! I don't know what 'matter' you're referring to!"

"If you didn't do anything, why'd you bolt when you saw us coming earlier?" Sam asked.

"Because Sanborn did. I didn't know what was going on."

"Pardon me if I find that hard to believe." Sam put Selina Rameriz's photo down on the table.

Daniels, who was short and stocky with dark hair and the starting of jowls, went perfectly still as he stared at the picture.

"Know her, Mr. Speaker?"

"I've never seen her before in my life."

"Would you be willing to take a polygraph to confirm that?"

Daniels tore his eyes off the photo and began to pace. "You don't understand..."

Sam pulled a chair out from the table and lowered herself gingerly. "What don't I understand?"

"It was one time."

Sam laughed. "Sure it was. If I ask Ms. Rameriz, will she corroborate your story?"

"Maybe it was twice, but the point is, it wasn't any big deal."

"It's against the law," Sam reminded him. "Especially when you start killing the women to keep them quiet."

Daniels stopped pacing and turned to her. "*Killing*? I've never killed anyone! Give me a polygraph on that."

Sam shrugged. "Funny, that's not what Sanborn said. He claims the whole thing was your idea."

Daniel's complexion got very red. "That son of a bitch. He's lying! If anyone was pulling the strings, it was him!"

Sam leaned forward, elbows on the table. "I want to know what you know about the call girl ring, and I want it now. If the information you give me is credible, I may speak to the AUSA about immunity for you."

"I'd have to testify against the others?"

"Yes." Sam watched him absorb the fact that his political career was probably over.

His face twisted into an ugly snarl. "How can you do this to people in your future husband's own party?"

Sam laughed. "You think I care about that? You think *he* cares about that? We both want justice for the two women who were murdered by one of you. *That's* what we care about."

"He won't have much of a career if he doesn't learn how to manage his woman," Daniels said.

Sam treated him to her most intimidating cop stare. "Keep up that crap and the deal's off the table." She glanced at her watch. "You've got one minute. Do we have a deal?"

"I want to talk to my lawyer."

Ignoring the cramps seizing her midsection, Sam stood. "Then no deal. I need the information, and I need it now. Your choice."

As he stood with his hands on his hips pondering his limited options, Sam watched the starch go out of his spine. "It was all Sanborn's idea."

"What was?"

"A service… For us, by us. Our jobs are stressful, and we needed a way to let off steam and relax. We figured if we had control then we could determine who was allowed to patronize it and keep it secret. We could choose the women…"

"Immigrants who wouldn't recognize most of you."

Daniels sighed and dropped into a chair. "Yes."

"How long has the organization been in business?"

"Twelve years."

Sam couldn't believe they'd never caught wind of

it in all that time. "So why did Regina and Maria have to die?"

"I honestly don't know. I had nothing to do with that. I swear to God."

"But you know who did."

"I have my suspicions."

"Is that what you were arguing with Sanborn about?"

"I wanted him to tell me what he knew about it and why there were cops sniffing around the Hill. I also wanted to know what he knew about the police officer who was kidnapped."

"What did he say?"

"He told me it was none of my business and that I needed to keep my mouth shut and stay out of it."

"How did it work? The service?"

"We hired a woman. She works out of her home and manages the administrative aspects."

"Who else besides yourself and Sanborn are behind the organization?"

"Bartholomew and Cook." Sam couldn't wait to arrest that bastard Cook. "We wouldn't even be here right now if Cook hadn't gotten greedy and pushed us to open the service up to anyone who called. We told him it was a mistake. The more people who knew..."

"What's Gooding's involvement?" she asked, referring to the vice president.

"Nothing that I know of, but he and Bartholomew are tight. I wouldn't be surprised if he knows the ring exists, but I don't think he's ever been a patron."

"You don't know for sure."

"No. The only person who knows all the who, what, when, where and how is the woman who runs the organization."

Sam pushed a pad and pen across the table. "Her name and address."

"She's an innocent party—a wife and mother just trying to make a living."

"Running a call girl ring for pampered politicians? Hardly innocent."

Daniels put down the pen. "Tell me you'll protect her, or I'm not giving you her name."

"Give me her name or our deal is off."

"I gave you what you asked for!"

"I told you the deal was only good if you were entirely forthcoming."

Daniels glared at her.

Sam glared back.

He grabbed the pen and wrote the name and address and shoved the pad back at her.

"That wasn't so hard, now was it?" Sam eased herself up. "Sit tight. I'll be back."

"When? I need to get out of here before my wife hears about this."

"It's probably safe to assume she already knows," Sam said.

Moaning, he dropped his head to folded arms.

Malone was waiting for her and Freddie outside the interrogation room.

"Anything from the lab yet?" Sam asked.

He shook his head. "They said it would be tomorrow at the earliest."

"Goddamn it."

"Lieutenant," Freddie said, frowning at her language.

"It occurred to me that your suspects don't know how long it takes to get DNA results," Malone said. He handed her two sheets of official-looking paper.

Sam studied them and smirked. "Traffic tribunal, huh?"

"Put them in this." He produced a manila folder. "That makes it *very* official. They know it's their DNA, so why wait for the lab to confirm it when they can do it for us?"

"I like the way you think, Captain."

"I still have a few working brain cells after riding the desk all these years."

"This is just what I needed to nail those bastards."

"What's the plan?"

"Bartholomew first and then Sanborn. Depending on how it goes with Bartholomew, I might need you to have someone bring Selina over here for a lineup of fat, balding middle-aged guys. Her ID will put a bow on top of the aggravated sexual assault charge. Can you set that up if I can't get him to roll?"

"Absolutely. Let's wrap this up, people."

If only she didn't feel so shitty, Sam would be salivating in anticipation of toppling two powerful scumbags from their lofty pedestals.

"You sure you're all right, Holland?" Malone asked.

"Girl trouble," she said, knowing he'd drop it once he heard that.

He cleared his throat. "Um, very well then. Carry on."

"I UNDERSTAND YOU'VE been running a call girl ring in Washington for twelve years," Sam said without preamble. She'd witnessed Freddie reading Bartholomew his rights earlier, so she didn't repeat the Miranda warning.

Bartholomew attempted to surge to his feet, but with his girth, the surge was more like a lumber. "Who the hell told you that?"

"Doesn't matter. Is it true?"

"It most certainly is not. I had nothing to do with any call girls. I work for the vice president of the United States. Why would I jeopardize my position, my career, my *reputation* to dally with call girls?"

"That's a very good question. Isn't it, Detective Cruz?"

"Indeed," Freddie said. "Personally, I think it's all about money—and the sex, of course."

"I've never had sex with a call girl," Bartholomew huffed. "I don't need to pay for it."

Sam took a long measuring look at the unattractive man. "If you say so." She produced the folder she'd kept behind her back. "You're sure you've never met Selina Rameriz?"

He eyed the folder warily. "Positive."

"Then how do you explain the fact that you were seen with her at a gala on January 18 at the Ronald

Reagan Building?" She turned to Freddie. "Detective Cruz, do you have several witnesses prepared to testify that Mr. Bartholomew accompanied Ms. Rameriz to the gala?"

"I do," Freddie said. "We've also obtained the security videotape from the Reagan Building where you're seen with her at the event."

Sam directed her gaze from Freddie back to Bartholomew. "Still certain you've never met her?"

"So I hired her to go to a party with me. That doesn't make me a rapist."

Sam withdrew one of the traffic tribunal forms. "No, but your semen on her clothes sure does."

Watching his face drain of color was among one of the more satisfying moments in Sam's career.

"That can't be right," he stammered.

"The beautiful thing about DNA is that, unlike people, it never lies."

His round face was suddenly shiny with sweat. "Okay so maybe I had sex with her. That also doesn't make me a rapist."

"Detective Cruz, when we talked to Ms. Rameriz, did she leave you with the impression that the sex she'd had with Mr. Bartholomew was in any way consensual?"

"No, ma'am."

"And is the owner of the Capitol Cleaning Services company willing to testify that the only time Ms. Rameriz has ever missed work in more than two years was on the nineteenth, twentieth and twenty-first of January?"

"Yes, ma'am."

"And will Ms. Rameriz's coworkers testify that when she returned to work on the twenty-second, her face and arms were still bruised from what was obviously a vicious assault?"

"They will."

Sam returned her attention to Bartholomew. "That, along with the identification Ms. Rameriz will soon make as well as her very compelling and very *believable* story, gives you a rather significant problem, Mr. Bartholomew."

"I'd like to see my lawyer."

"We can arrange for that. Once your lawyer is here, however, I won't be able to offer you any sort of deal on the prostitution charges—money laundering, racketeering, solicitation of prostitution." She'd let the Feds look into the money trail after she'd nailed them on the more serious counts. "When you add those charges to the aggravated sexual assault charges, you're looking at spending the rest of your life in prison."

"What sort of deal?"

"Plead guilty to the sexual assault charge, sparing Ms. Rameriz from having to testify against you, and tell me everything you know about Sanborn's involvement in the call girl ring."

"In exchange for what?"

"Immunity on all the prostitution-related charges."

"And leniency on the assault charge?"

"No way. You'll do the full ride on that one."

"How long do I have to think about it?"

She glanced at her watch. "Two minutes."

His eyes almost popped out of his fat face. "*Two minutes?*"

"One minute, forty-five seconds…"

Bartholomew ran a hand over his mouth and began to pace the small room.

"One minute, fifteen seconds…" Watching him, Sam tried to focus on the time and not on the cramps still rolling through her belly. Was it hot in there or was it her? "What's it going to be, Mr. Bartholomew? Do we have a deal?"

He stopped and turned to her, his expression grim, as if it had just registered with him that life as he knew it—pampered, privileged, successful—was over. "Yes," he said. "We have a deal."

"Tell me something—why did Sanborn kill Regina and Maria?"

"I have no idea."

"None at all?"

"I had nothing to do with what happened to those girls," he said emphatically.

Hands on hips, Sam waited for him to say more.

He rubbed the back of his neck. "They were supposed to take care of birth control. They weren't supposed to get pregnant. It was stipulated in the contract they signed."

"At least now we know why," Sam said on her way out.

Freddie followed Sam from the room. "That was awesome," he said. "Totally *awesome*."

"Suck up."

"The way you got him to cop to the rape *and* to roll on Sanborn. I aspire to be that smooth."

"Why thank you. Even though you're totally sucking up, I do appreciate the sentiment behind the sucking."

He rubbed his belly. "All this nailing of scumbags is making me hungry."

"What *doesn't* make you hungry?" she shot over her shoulder as she pushed open the door to the room where Sanborn cooled his heels.

"Finally," he muttered. "I demand to know what this is all about. I'm a busy man with important people, including the president of the United States, depending on me."

"You're busy, we're busy," Sam said, taking note of healing scratches on his neck, "so let's cut to the chase. Your friends Daniels and Bartholomew claim you're the mastermind behind the prostitution ring."

His mouth fell open. "They wouldn't dare."

"The threat of long prison sentences does funny things to people, Mr. Sanborn. Shockingly, your friends were more concerned with saving their own skins than they were with saving yours." Sam paused to let that sink in. "Doesn't matter, though." She produced the file folder. "DNA links you to the rapes and murders of Regina Argueta de Castro and Maria Espanosa as well as the kidnapping and rape of Detective Jeannie McBride."

His face set into a mulish expression, he said, "I want my lawyer."

When Sam thought about what this man had done to Jeannie, it took every ounce of self-control she possessed to resist plowing her fist into his sanctimonious face. "Great. Just let me know who I should call for you."

"That's it?"

"Yeah," Sam said. "That's it."

"You don't have any questions for me?"

"Nope. Bartholomew and Daniels connected all the dots for me. I'm good."

He seemed to understand all of a sudden that she wasn't going to deal. "But wait—I need to get out of here. We've got a major fundraiser tomorrow evening. I have to be there!"

This is for you, Jeannie, Sam thought, as she leaned forward, hands on the table. "Mr. Sanborn, I hate to be the bearer of bad news, but you're not going anywhere for a long, *long* time."

Leaving him to ponder his fate, Sam gestured for Freddie to follow her out of the room.

"You don't hate to be the bearer of bad news all the time," Freddie said with a droll smile.

"Some bad news is actually good news."

Faith Miller stepped out of the observation room. "Get a hold of his lawyer and take him to central booking. You can also book Daniels and Bartholomew."

"I'll take care of that," Malone said. "I'll make sure every I is dotted."

"I'll see what I can do to get Daniels arraigned and released," Faith said. "The other two will be staying awhile."

"I've got two more to pick up," Sam said.

"Go get 'em," Malone said.

THIRTY-TWO

"YOU CAN HEAD home," Sam said to Freddie as she went to retrieve her coat. "I'll take care of sewing this up."

"I want to be there when you arrest Cook."

"I'll tell you all about it tomorrow."

"But—"

"Freddie, you have plans. *Important* plans. Go."

"What about the reports?"

He usually handled them because of her dyslexia. "I'll take care of them this time. All I need is for you to call Regina's and Maria's parents and let them know we got the guy who killed their daughters. Then you're done."

"But—"

"No buts. I promised you a night off, so get to it."

"I don't feel right about leaving before we're finished."

"We *are* finished. I'm going to arrest Cook and Cheri, the call girl ring's administrative assistant. I'll send them back with patrol to be booked, and then I'm going home too. I'll do the paperwork in the morning."

"All right," he said, frowning. "If you insist."

"I insist." She rested a hand on his arm. "I hope it all goes your way tonight. I really do."

"Thanks. I hope so too. I'll be here in the morning to help with the reports."

"Sleep in. I'll see you at ten." She left him in his cubicle and headed out to the parking lot, her detail in tow. "I'm going to have you transport two people back to HQ for me, and then you're released from babysitting duty. Case closed."

"Yes, ma'am, Lieutenant."

Sam studied the two eager young faces. "Thanks," she said begrudgingly. "For keeping an eye on me the last few days."

"Our pleasure," one of them said with a cheeky grin. Sam smiled. Apparently, she still could turn a head or two. It was small solace in the midst of the physical and emotional pain of losing another baby.

On the way to Capitol Hill, Nick called. Sam saw his number on the caller ID and decided to wait to take his call until after she'd arrested Cook. He was better off not knowing what was happening until it was over and done with. She didn't want anyone questioning him later about what he knew and when he knew it. Her phone dinged to indicate a voicemail message from him, which she would retrieve later. At the moment, it took all she had to focus on the task at hand while enduring the regular waves of pain cycling through her gut.

The police cruiser following her slid into the next parking space in a lot adjacent to the Hart Office Building. Sam noticed that the space reserved for Nick was empty. Hit with a blast of nerves over the grim news she'd have to share with him when she saw him later, she wondered if he had a campaign event that evening. She hoped not. She wanted to go home and feel his strong arms around her.

A black Cadillac Coup de Ville occupied the spot next to Nick's, which was reserved for the senior senator from Virginia.

Sam made her way to Cook's office, which was twice the size of that occupied by his junior counterpart. Having been there before, she knew the layout and strolled straight past Cook's startled receptionist on her way to the senator's vast corner office. She barged past numerous staffers and straight into Cook's inner sanctum. He was in a meeting with three other men and two women.

"What's the meaning of this?" he said, startling when he realized who'd come to call.

"Senator Robert Cook, you're under arrest for solicitation of prostitution, running a prostitution ring and racketeering. I'm sure that once we dig a little deeper, we'll be adding money laundering and other charges to the list."

"You can't come in here and accuse me of these egregious charges without an ounce of proof to back up your claims."

"Oh, I've got proof." She stepped around his massive desk to cuff him. "You have the right to remain silent." He struggled against the cuffs as she recited the Miranda warning. The other people in the room watched the proceedings in stunned silence.

"What proof do you have?"

"Your good friends Daniels and Bartholomew are

fully prepared to testify against you, as is one of the women you paid for sex."

"*What about them?*" he cried. "Daniels and Bartholomew—and Sanborn? They're in it up to their necks too!"

"Daniels and Bartholomew have agreed to testify against you and Sanborn."

"*In exchange for what?*"

"Immunity on the prostitution charges."

"And I don't get the same courtesy?"

Sam thought of the way he'd threatened Nick during the Sinclair investigation. It gave her tremendous pleasure to say, "Sorry, but I don't need you. I've already got enough to put Sanborn away for life."

"You fucking bitch," he said, seething. "*You motherfucking whore.*"

"You've got some nerve calling me a whore, Senator. Or should I call you *Mr.* Cook? Convicted felons can't serve in the United States Senate, can they?" She turned to her audience of shocked staffers. "Anyone know the answer to that? Been a while since high school social studies for me."

"You're enjoying this," Cook said through gritted teeth.

Sam leaned in close to him. "You bet your ass I am." She marched him out of the Hart Building, past startled congressional staffers and one thrilled news photographer, and stowed him in the backseat of the patrol car. "Follow me," she said to the two officers, who appeared as stunned as the staffers when they recognized their passenger. "When we get to Seventh

Street, one of you stay with him and the other come with me."

"Yes, ma'am."

Back in her car, Sam absorbed a particularly painful cramp before she started the engine and headed for Cheri Anderson's house, a few blocks from Sam's and far too close for comfort to the apartment Peter Gibson had rented after their divorce. The thought of running into him only added to the sick feeling in her belly.

Sensing Cook glaring at her from the car, Sam climbed the steps and rang the doorbell. The patrol officer hung back at the foot of the stairs.

The door swung open. An attractive woman in her early forties took in Sam's badge as well as the officer standing on the sidewalk and released a deep sigh. "Come in. I've been expecting you."

Sam gestured for the other officer to wait outside and followed the woman into a comfortable home. Dressed in khakis and a Catholic University T-shirt, Cheri Anderson looked like a typical suburban mom. That the Catholic U grad was running a prostitution ring out of her home would've struck Sam as almost comical if it wasn't for what had happened to Regina, Maria and Jeannie as a result of the criminal activity.

"When I heard on the news that Daniels, Bartholomew and Sanborn had been arrested, I figured it was only a matter of time before they blamed the whole thing on me and sent you here."

"For what it's worth, Daniels didn't give up your name easily. I tied it to his immunity deal."

Blue eyes flashed with rage. "So he gets immunity, and I go down for the whole thing?"

"I want Sanborn. He's the one who murdered two women and kidnapped and raped a police officer."

"He's an evil son of a bitch. I've always known that. When I heard Regina and Maria had been murdered…I knew it was him. He was so furious when I told him they were pregnant. They were no longer any use to him, and he feared they'd be tempted to venture into blackmail since their immigration status was so tenuous. When I heard they were dead…"

"You knew it was him."

"Yes." She glanced up at Sam, eyes bright with tears. "To be honest, I've been worried about my own safety. Two days ago, I bought a gun." She gestured to the artwork decorating her refrigerator. "Having a gun in a house where my children live terrifies me, but I couldn't let him get me too."

"How did they recruit you?"

"I worked for Sanborn at the DNC for a couple of years before I had my son. My husband and I, we had a plan—he'd work and I'd stay home with the kids. Then he got laid off just before my son was born. I'd already resigned from the DNC, so we were in a bad place financially. Sanborn must've heard about that from one of my former colleagues. He called me, asked if I'd be interested in a business opportunity, and of course I snapped it up, even though I was mortified when I realized what I'd be doing." She shrugged. "We needed the money."

"What did you tell your husband?"

"That the DNC had asked me to do some work for them from home."

"And he never questioned that?"

She shook her head. "I handle all the household money. He has no idea…"

"This might be a good time to tell him."

Nodding, Cheri wiped away tears and reached for a CD case on the counter. "Clients, employees, finances, records—the entire business. I signed a very restrictive confidentiality agreement when I started with them, but I assume that's null and void now that they're all in jail."

Sam took the CD from her. "How many careers and marriages will this ruin?"

"Scores." Folding her arms in a protective stance, Cheri said, "What will happen to me?"

"Are you willing to testify against the four principals?"

"To stay out of jail? You bet."

"Let me talk to the U.S. Attorney and see what I can do."

"Are you going to arrest me?"

Sam slipped the CD that cemented her case into her coat pocket. "Not right now. I may be back, though."

Cheri's gaze locked on a photo of her children. "I'll be here."

SAM SENT HER detail to HQ and called Captain Malone to let him know that Senator Cook was on his way. She told him of her decision to hold off on arresting Cheri Anderson for the time being—and why.

"Good call. By the way, DNA came back on Maria's baby—a match for Tillinghast."

"You can let him know that when you spring him and let his family out of protective custody."

"Will do. What else can I do to help you clean up the details? I know you're not feeling well and you probably want to get home."

"You can have Selina Rameriz's detail notify her that we've arrested the four principals, and tell her the information she gave me was critical to closing the case."

"Will do."

"Let her know I'll check in with her in the next few days about the next steps."

"Got it. Good work, Lieutenant—as always."

"Glad to put this one behind me. I'll be in tomorrow to go through the CD Anderson gave me so we can get busy ruining the lives of some other high-ranking scumbags."

His laughter sparked hers. "A lot of times this job truly sucks, but other times, it truly doesn't."

"Eloquently put, Captain."

"Go home and put your feet up. I'll see you in the morning."

"Thanks for handling Cook."

"My pleasure."

Sam hung up with him and called Jeannie McBride's cell number. Michael answered.

"This is Lieutenant Holland. How's Jeannie?"

"Settled in at my place and sleeping. The trip home seemed to wear her out."

"Do me a favor when she wakes up, and tell her we got the bastard."

"Oh God, that's such a relief," he said, sounding jubilant. "She'll be so glad to hear that."

"Tell her I'll be by to check on her in the next day or two."

"I will. Thank you so much for everything you've done for us."

"No problem." Before she stashed the phone in her coat pocket, Sam sent a text to Shelby and her sisters to postpone the dress plans. She couldn't deal with that tonight. Leaning against her car, she took a moment in the fading daylight to breathe in the cold February air and absorb the satisfaction of another case successfully closed.

"Fancy meeting you here."

Shocked out of her reverie, she spun around to find Peter Gibson giving her the once-over. Before he'd affixed crude bombs to her car and Nick's, Sam had never thought to be afraid of her ex-husband. Antagonistic? Absolutely. But afraid? Never. However, when she remembered the bomb-making materials, the photos of her on the job and the newspaper articles about her they'd found in his apartment...Seeing him now, released from jail on a technicality, Sam experienced true terror for the first time since Clarence Reese carjacked her and held her hostage.

"What do you want?" she asked, trying not to think about the way she'd nailed him in the interrogation room and goaded him about her satisfying sex life with Nick.

"From *you*? Not a damned thing. You gave me everything I needed when you let your officers knock down my door without a warrant. Thanks for that, by the way. I can't tell you how much I appreciated it."

"You're required to stay a thousand feet from me and everyone in my family," Sam reminded him. Since their acrimonious divorce Sam had been hard-pressed to remember what she'd ever seen in him. His sandy-colored hair was now mostly silver, and the face she'd once found handsome was filled with bitterness.

"This is *my* neighborhood," he said. "Maybe I need a restraining order to keep *you* away from *me*."

"Enjoy your freedom. I predict it won't last. In fact, we've got a pool going at HQ as to how long it'll take you to fuck up again."

His expression one of mock horror, he said, "Who picked today? I hope it wasn't you. I'd hate to hand you any easy victories."

"What's that supposed to mean?" she asked, her heart hammering.

"Figure it out. Good to see you, Sam. Hope you're taking good care of your senator. He didn't look too hot the last time I saw him. You have a nice night now."

Nick. Oh God, Nick. Leaving her car, she took off running because it was faster than driving this time of day. In the background, she heard Peter laughing. If he'd done something to Nick, she'd kill him with her own hands. Pulling her phone from her pocket as she ran, her hands shook as she pressed No. 1 on her speed dial. The call went straight to voicemail. "Oh my God. *Please...*"

Ignoring the increasingly sharp pain in her abdomen, Sam ran as fast as she could. Odd dots of light danced before her eyes just as the sign for Ninth Street appeared in the distance. "Please, please, *please*."

She rounded the corner and stumbled as she took in the pile of rubble that used to be their front stairs. "Oh," she whispered. The entire front of the house was in shambles. "No…" Instinctively, she reached for her radio and called for backup, relieved to see no sign of Nick's car on the street. Her eyes fixed on the wreckage outside their home, Sam inched forward, certain she had to be seeing things. Would Peter really be so stupid as to plant another bomb—on the *same day* he'd been released from prison?

Taking a quick look around, she didn't see any of the shattered glass that had marked the area surrounding the bombing the last time. What the hell was going on? And most important of all, where was Nick?

BATTLING HIS WAY through rush hour traffic, Nick was riveted by the news on the radio about the arrests of Senator Cook, Speaker Daniels, Mitch Sanborn and Jack Bartholomew. Washington's political machine was on fire, and Nick was enjoying every minute of it. Even though his party had taken a hard hit, he had no patience for people who took advantage of power- ful positions and the public's trust.

He'd been forced to shut off his phone, which had been ringing incessantly for hours as the news ripped through the city. He needed to talk to Sam before he discussed the situation with other members of his party or with the reporters who were clamoring for a statement from the senator whose fiancée had arrested some of the heaviest hitters in town.

All at once it occurred to him that if Cook was forced to resign—and Nick couldn't see how the older man would be able to hold on to his office after helping to run a prostitution ring for twelve years—then Nick would become the senior senator from Virginia, just fifty days after he took office. The thought made Nick's head spin, as it had since the day he'd found John O'Connor dead in his apartment.

Pulling on to Ninth Street, his heart skipped a beat at the sight of flashing lights and emergency vehicles lined up outside his house—again. Sam… Peter… *"No,"* he whispered as he bolted from the car. *"Samantha*!" He'd closed half the distance before he saw her talking to another cop, her hands dancing in the air as she gestured to the ruined front stairs. Right in that moment, he realized she hadn't gotten his message about using the back door, and she'd thought Peter had struck again.

They'd probably laugh about this. Someday…

"Samantha!"

She looked up, and the expression of sheer relief on her face reminded him once again that she loved him more than anyone ever had. Since she seemed frozen in place, he ran to her and swept her up. Right there, in front of no fewer than ten other police officers, the gorgeous cop who despised public displays of affection kissed him square on the lips.

"There you are," she whispered, clinging to him.

FATAL CONSEQUENCES

"Here I am."

"I was so scared. Peter...he said..."

A jolt of shock zipped through Nick. "You *saw* him? *Already*?"

She nodded. "He made it sound like he'd done something to you. He...I was so scared. I couldn't find you."

Nick tightened his hold on her, surprised to feel dampness on her cheeks. "I'm fine, babe. I asked the contractor to put in a ramp so we can have your dad over. He got called away before he could finish. It was supposed to be a surprise. I'm sorry you were scared."

She drew back from him, eyes wide with surprise and emotion. "You're putting in a ramp?"

"I thought he'd like to see our place."

Hugging him again, she said, "Love you so much."

"Love you too, babe."

"Not feeling so good," she said, her eyes closing. "Need to talk to you."

He scooped her up and carried her home.

EPILOGUE

Nick stood at the white split rail fence with Graham O'Connor and watched Graham's daughter Lizbeth lead Scotty around the training ring on a gentle mare. The handsome boy's grin stretched from ear to ear as he adapted to the horse's cadence.

"He's a natural," Graham said. "What an adorable kid."

"He had us laughing all the way from Richmond." They had needed the laughter after the loss they were still struggling to absorb. "I'm totally smitten."

"What're you going to do about that?" Graham asked.

Nick returned Scotty's wave and his big smile. "Haven't decided yet."

"Sure, you have," Graham said. "You've decided you'll do *something.*"

"I suppose I will—when the time is right." He kept his eyes on Scotty, riveted by the boy's laughter. "I once knew a kid like him who was lost and lonely until a boisterous family took him into their home and their hearts and changed his life forever."

Graham cleared his throat and rested a hand on Nick's shoulder, squeezing lightly. "And now you want to do the same for another lost and lonely kid."

That he and Sam might be able to have children of their own after all was still settling with him. He watched the boy who rode the horse with such unbridled and infectious joy, and thought again about the many ways he could improve Scotty's circumstances. "There's something about him."

"I know that feeling," Graham said. "There once was a lost and lonely eighteen-year-old who came to spend a weekend in my home and touched me in exactly the same way."

Nick turned to the man who'd been a father to him in every possible way except biology. "I wondered if I could ask a favor."

"Anything, anytime. You know that."

"Would you be my best man?"

Graham's eyes filled, and for a moment he seemed too shocked to speak. "I'd be honored," he said gruffly, "to stand in my late son's place beside the man I love like a son."

Nick hugged him, grateful that he understood exactly why Nick had asked him. "Thank you."

Sam walked up to them. "Sorry to interrupt."

"Hey, babe." Nick held out a hand to her, pleased to see some color returning to her cheeks.

"There's the woman who's been single-handedly cleaning house in Washington," Graham said, his smile matching the teasing tone. "What's the tally now? Speaker, senator, VP's chief of staff, DNC chair, EPA administrator, deputy secretary of defense, too many lobbyists to count…"

"The divorce attorneys are sending me engraved

thank-you notes," Sam said with a cheeky grin of her own.

Graham barked out a ringing laugh.

"It's a tough job, but someone's gotta do it," she added. "I still can't believe all the other women who came forward claiming Bartholomew and Sanborn had attacked them too. I doubt either of them will ever see the light of day again."

"You think you know people," Graham said, his expression turning pensive. "It's so shocking."

"I imagine it must be. I was sent out to tell you your presence is requested in the kitchen to carve the turkey."

"Ah, duty calls. Give me about fifteen minutes, and then round up the troops."

"We will," Nick said. As Graham walked away, Nick slipped an arm around Sam and returned his attention to Scotty. "He's having a ball."

"He's such a sweetheart."

"I'm glad you think so." He kissed her forehead. "How're you feeling?"

"Still tired and a little achy, but better than yesterday." They'd spent most of the day before curled up to each other, absorbing the loss and sharing the grief. It hadn't exactly been the day off they'd dreamed about.

"Did you talk to Freddie again?"

"Not since this morning. He called to let me know all the reports are done and filed."

"It was good of him to go in and take care of that for you yesterday."

"After Elin didn't show Friday night, he all but begged me for something to do."

"Poor guy."

"He'll recover. In time."

Nick framed her face with his hands and brushed a soft kiss over her lips. "Will you?"

"In time."

Nick held her close for several minutes before he signaled Lizbeth and Scotty to let them know it was dinnertime.

After Lizbeth helped him off the horse, Scotty darted out of the corral and caught up to Sam and Nick, who kept one arm tight around the love of his life.

"That was the coolest thing—*ever*," Scotty said, his eyes dancing with excitement and his cheeks rosy from the cool air. "Can I ride some more after dinner?"

"I don't see why not." Nick held out his free hand to the boy.

"You looked good out there, buddy," Sam said.

"Thanks, Sam. Will you show me your gun and cuffs after dinner?"

She laughed, and Nick felt his heart settle and lighten. She was going to be okay. *They* were going to be okay.

"It's a date," she said.

* * * * *